For Love of the Duke

HEART OF A DUKE SERIES

CHRISTI CALDWELL

SPENCER
HILL
PRESS

Excerpts from a variety of William Wordsworth's poems appear in this work
including: *The White Doe of Rylstone* written 1807 – 1808 and first published in
1815; "Ode: Intimations of Immortality from Recollection of Early Childhood" in
Poems, in Two Volumes first published in 1807; "Home at Grasmere" in *The Recluse
Part First* first published in 1814; *Lines written a few miles above Tintern Abbey* first
published in 1798; *A Poet! He Hath Put His Heart to School* published in 1842; "The
Wanderer" in *The Excursion* portion of The Recluse first published in 1814.

Please visit www.christicaldwellauthor.com

First Edition: October 2014
Christi Caldwell

For Love of the Duke: a novel / by Christi Caldwell—1st ed.
ISBN: 978-1-63392-103-0
Library of Congress Cataloging-in-Publication Data available upon request

Summary: After the tragic death of his wife, Jasper, the 8th Duke of Bainbridge,
buried himself away in the dark cold walls of his home, Castle Blackwood. When
he's coaxed out of his self-imposed exile to attend the amusements of the Frost
Fair, his life is irrevocably changed by his fateful meeting with Lady Katherine
Adamson.

 With her tight brown ringlets and silly white-ruffled gowns, Lady Katherine
Adamson has found her dance card empty for two Seasons. After her father's
passing, Katherine learned about the unreliability of men, and is determined to
depend on no one, except herself. Until she meets Jasper . . .

Published in the United States by Spencer Hill Press.
This is a Spencer Hill Press Contemporary Romance.
Spencer Hill Contemporary is an imprint of Spencer Hill Press.
For more information on our titles, visit www.spencerhillpress.com

Distributed by Midpoint Trade Books
www.midpointtrade.com

Cover design by: Kim Killion Designs
Interior layout by: Scribe Inc.

Printed in Canada

Heart of a Duke Series

TREMENDOUS THANKS TO MY HUSBAND

Who allowed me to disappear for nearly three straight weeks all to tell this story.

TO JILL

Thank you for catching everything that needed catching in this story! You have a brilliant set of eyes!

AND TO MY READERS

Thank you, even as thank you seems so very inadequate.

Contents

Part 2

Part I

Winter 1814

Suffering is permanent, obscure, and dark. And has the nature of infinity.

—William Wordsworth,
The White Doe of Rylestone

Chapter 1

$\mathscr{L}$ady Katherine Adamson discovered very early on
that all bad ideas began with her twin sister.

Far too many erroneously assumed that because Katherine was a whole six minutes and seventeen seconds younger than her sister, she must aspire to the model of ladylike decorum and beauty as evinced by her twin.

Only Katherine, however, seemed to realize Anne had proven a rather poor influence over the years.

She sighed. And yet, for all the years of bad decisions, she continued to follow along with her sister's madcap schemes. After all, that is what you did when you were a sister, a twin sister, no less.

"It is not here, Anne," Katherine said gently. Her breath stirred a puff of white, cold winter air.

Her sister spun around so fast the bonnet atop her golden crop of curls tipped over her brow. She shoved it back and glared at Katherine. "Of course it is here. I have it on good authority the gypsy woman passed along the pendant to a vendor who would be at the fair upon the Thames River." She looked pointedly at Katherine. "Surely she spoke of the Frost Fair. Now we merely need to find the vendor, and . . ." She prattled on, and continued tugging Katherine along.

Katherine fell into step beside her sister. For the better part of a fortnight, she'd tried to convince Anne of the foolishness in hunting around for the small heart pendant their sister Aldora had once worn around her neck. The pendant had been fashioned as a kind of talisman by Aldora and her four friends. They'd sworn the trinket would lead them to the heart of a duke. In the end, all the ladies had found love. Only one had landed a duke. Which in itself should disprove the validity of the claim, and yet . . .

"Ah, it is there, I know it," Anne exclaimed, drawing to an abrupt stop. She stared victoriously out at the bustling Frost Fair upon the frozen Thames River.

Katherine stumbled against her side. "Of course it is," she said dryly.

Her sister either failed to hear or failed to care about the sarcastic twist to those four words. She spun to face Katherine, her hands clasped close to her emerald-green cloak. "I feel it is here. And as soon as we find the merchant, who will sell us the pendant, then I . . . er, we can claim the heart of a duke."

Katherine's lips twitched with wry mirth. "Does the pendant stipulate as to the qualities of the duke? Must he be handsome? Or can he be a doddering, old letch?"

Anne wrinkled her nose. "Whyever would any young lady desire a doddering, old letch?"

"Why, indeed? So then, it is the heart that is more important? Or the ducal title?"

Anne angled her head, and again the bonnet pitched lower over her eyes. She nibbled at her lower lip, and then said, "Why, I rather think they are of equal importance."

Katherine took a deep breath and forced herself to count to ten before speaking. "Anne, there is not an overabundance of eligible young dukes in the market for a wife."

Her sister held up a finger encased in the white kidskin glove. "Ahh, but we do not need an overabundance of dukes, Katherine. We merely require two."

"But—"

Anne planted her arms akimbo. "If it is all the same to you, then you can marry the old, doddering letch. I, well, I shall have the heart of a handsome, young, affable duke. Now, come." She reached for Katherine's hand.

But Katherine withdrew, and took a hasty step backward. She eyed the frozen expanse of the Thames, filled with tents and carts and skaters, it seemed entirely safe. And yet . . .

"Never tell me you are still afraid of the water," Anne said with a touch of impatience in her voice. She stomped her boot in apparent frustration.

Katherine swallowed, not caring to admit to the shameful weakness. And yet, for all the great logic and reason she prided herself upon, she'd never been able to overcome the gripping terror of the day she'd fallen into the river of her father's Hertfordshire cottage. She'd been nearly seven years old, and the horror of that moment, the water filling her throat, burning her lungs, stinging her eyes, still gripped her.

It had been the last time she'd entered the water.

"Katherine?" Her sister prodded.

Katherine drew in a steadying breath. "Go ahead without me. I'll wait here."

The loud squealing laughter of ladies blended with the rumbling chuckles of their gentlemen; the sounds of merriment upon the ice filtered around them.

Her sister frowned. "You know I cannot attend the Frost Fair without you." She glanced around. "We are unchaperoned."

Yes, that had been the second foolish part to her sister's madcap scheme to hunt down a gypsy's bauble. Anne had a remarkable ability to lose her, and subsequently *their*, chaperone.

Katherine could not, however, bring herself to take the necessary steps to move onto the frozen patch of ice. She wet her lips. "I can't do it," she whispered.

Anne passed a searching gaze over Katherine's face. The annoyance seemed to seep from her sister's pretty blue eyes to be replaced by a momentary contriteness. "They passed an elephant across just yesterday," she said on a rush.

Katherine shook her head. Even the custom of leading an elephant from one end of the river to the Blackfriars Bridge did little to alleviate her fears. What if the enormous creature merely was fortunate enough to miss the single thin patch? What if . . . ?

"Please," Anne said, her eyes imploring.

Ever the romantic, bold-spirited of the sisters, Anne had always managed to drag Katherine along on whatever flights of fancy she was set on. Because if Katherine was being truthful with even just herself, she yearned to be so lighthearted and adventurous.

And because it was nearly Christmastide, and the cool, crisp winter air infused her with holiday excitement, Katherine took a tentative step onto the ice. Her breath caught and held in her chest . . .

And nothing happened.

She released the pent up breath, and took another step. Then another. Each step more freeing than the next.

Anne laughed. She took Katherine's hand and raised it to her chest. "See, Katherine, why there is nothing to be afraid of!" She paused, forcing Katherine to a halt and peruse the barbers', butchers', and bakers' tents along the frozen waterway.

There had to be very nearly thirty tents, perhaps more. Ever the optimist, however, Anne looked over at Katherine with a wide grin. "Come along then. We'll never find the pendant standing here."

They weaved their way in between the couples skating upon the ice, onward toward the boisterous vendors loudly peddling their wares.

"Would ye ladies care for an ale?" a young merchant called out to them. He held out two tankards of ale, a wide-gap toothed grin on his pockmarked face.

"No, thank you," Katherine murmured automatically.

Her sister shot her a reproachful look. "You are so very rude, Katherine."

Katherine blinked. "I am not rude."

"Well pompous, then." Anne gestured to the young man in his frayed trousers, who stood at the entrance of his vibrant crimson tent. "That young man is merely trying to earn his livelihood, and you'd condescend to him."

"I am not condescending to him." A defensive note threaded Katherine's words.

"Just because he isn't as neatly put together as the other vendors."

The young man seemed to hear Anne's not so discreetly spoken words, for he cocked his head, and his smile dipped into a frown.

Katherine reached into her reticule and withdrew several coins. "Here, sir. Two ales, please," she said, with a glare for Anne. She most certainly had not been condescending the young man, and she most certainly was not rude or pompous. She merely recognized the folly of two unchaperoned young ladies purchasing spirits of any sort, in the very public event.

The peddler's smile reappeared and he proceeded to hand them each a tankard.

"'Ere ye are, m'ladies."

Katherine handed the coins off to the man, and accepted her ale. As she cautiously picked her way over the ice, trailing after her excited sister's much more hurried movements, she sipped her ale. She grimaced at the bitter taste of the brew upon her tongue, but then tried another. And another. And by the fourth, it really wasn't all that bitter, but rather a tad sweet, and a good deal too delicious.

Anne paused alongside a purple tent lined with black stripes. "I will speak to this vendor." She hesitated, chewing at her lower lip.

Oh, dear. Katherine recognized her sister's distracted movement.

"We shall never manage to speak to all the merchants before dark falls."

The first bells of warning rang in Katherine's head.

"It would be much wiser if . . ."

The ringing grew louder.

"We speak to different peddlers."

Katherine took another sip, and frowned as she realized her tankard was empty.

"Katherine?"

Her head shot up, as she pondered her sister. What had Anne said? Katherine knew there had been a bad idea there, but the warmth that filled her from the ale had also warmed her resolve and stolen her ability to think with the clarity she usually prided herself upon. "Er, yes, fabulous idea," she said, instead.

Anne's eyes widened, and then her smile grew. "Lovely!" She stuck her finger toward a nearby sapphire-blue tent. "Off you go, then."

Without waiting to see if Katherine followed her succinct instructions, Anne turned around and slipped inside the purple tent lined with black stripes.

Katherine alternated her stare between the tent her sister had disappeared into and the sapphire-blue tent. She sighed. Yes, all bad ideas began with her sister. Dear, fanciful Anne, she'd somehow retained all traces of innocence. At nineteen, Anne still possessed girlish hopes and silly dreams. She'd somehow remained untouched by their father's sins . . . sins that had left their family destitute and forced their eldest sister, Aldora, to sacrifice herself at the marital altar to save their family. Granted, Aldora had ultimately found love. But that was neither here nor there . . . men were fickle, unreliable, inconstant creatures not to be trusted. Unfortunately, her romantic of a sister was only drawn by the drivel written about on the pages of her gothic novels.

A snowflake fell and settled upon her nose. Katherine looked up into the thick gray-white winter sky at the sea of flakes that danced a path down onto the frozen river.

Except, just then, with the warmth of the ale and the crisp cleanliness of the holiday air, an uncharacteristic lightness filled her spirit.

Suddenly, the ice, which she'd earlier feared, seemed like a very magical gift.

Katherine made her way back to the vendor who'd sold them the tankard of ale. She returned the empty glass over and waved off his offer for a second.

She turned to leave . . . and walked into a solid, unyielding wall.

Whoosh. All the air left her lungs, and she teetered unsteadily upon her feet. The jolting movement displaced the bonnet atop her head. Her breath fanned little wisps of white into the cool air as she righted herself. When she regained control of her breath she blinked several times, and looked up at the gentleman who'd plowed into her.

A towering, broad bear of a man, he paused to glare down his slightly crooked Roman nose at her. His black, disdainful look dared her to speak.

So she did. Katherine tossed her head back. "Pardon me."

The pompous prig jerked his attention forward and without so much as a murmured apology, continued on his way. The gentleman at his right, a lean, lithe fellow offered her a sheepish smile. His eyes expressed the other man's apology.

Katherine gave a curt nod and turned on her heel, determined not to let the foul fiend spoil the lovely day that portended the coming of Christmas.

Mindful of the fact that she and Anne flouted propriety by being out unchaperoned, Katherine tugged her hideous brown-velvet bonnet down more around her eyes. She adjusted her green muslin cloak closer and peeked about.

But those passing by moved with an excited step, lords and ladies giggling and chuckling as they slipped upon the ice and righted themselves before tumbling onto the sleek surface. Merchants barking out the contents contained within their vibrant-hued tents drew the attention of would be buyers. Katherine realized in that moment, no one noticed the actions of two unchaperoned young ladies. Everyone was too engrossed in the spirit of the fair.

The practical and rational of the twins, Katherine felt herself hopelessly lost in the beauty of the day . . . and she set out to explore. She made her way down the long row of tents, past the pretty sapphire-blue one she'd been instructed by Anne to explore. Ever onward to the end of the row, to where a gray tent rested on the fringe of the activity. Katherine was drawn to it, appreciating the somberness of the lone thrown together shop.

She paused beside it, and peered inside. "Hullo?"

Silence met her greeting.

She frowned, and made to turn back toward the activity upon the river.

"Hello, moi lady."

Katherine spun back around. She squinted in an attempt to adjust to the dimness of the cold, lonely, little tent. "Hullo," she said again. She rubbed her hands together to rub warmth back into her fingers and looked around. Suddenly feeling very foolish for indulging her sister's flight of fancy, Katherine made to leave.

"Is there something oi might 'elp you find, moi lady? A gift for someone, perhaps?"

Katherine shook her head. "No. I'm afraid not."

The gaunt old woman with straggly white hair came closer. "Wot is that, moi lady?"

Compassion filled Katherine at the sight of the poor woman whose tattered brown skirts and thin shawl would offer little protection by way of the elements. Katherine reached into her reticule and fished around for some coins but something in the woman's eyes stayed her movements; something that indicated that even though impoverished, this woman would welcome no charity. "Er, yes. I mean, there is something you might be able to help me find. I'm searching for a gift for my sister."

The woman's small brown eyes searched Katherine's face. She nodded and moved to one of the tables littered with her wares. She held up a pink satin ribbon. "Perhaps some ribbon for the lady?"

Katherine shook her head, and advanced deeper into the store. Anne had no shortage of ribbons.

The woman moved to the next table, filled with bright baubles and trinkets. "Then a kerchief for the lady?" She held up a floral piece of fabric embroidered with red, pink, and purple roses.

Katherine reached for the fabric. The old woman passed it into her hands.

Katherine glanced down at the handkerchief, passing it back and forth between her fingers, her gaze locked on the fuchsia rose expertly stitched upon the cloth. She remembered back to the day she'd learned of Father's betrayal. Mother had been seated on the wrought iron bench within her gardens, weeping bitter, angry tears. She'd caught sight of Katherine and quickly dashed back those tears. *"I've let the gardener go. A silly expense, don't you think, Katherine?"*

"Moi lady?"

The fabric fluttered from her fingers, back onto the table. Katherine gave her head a clearing shake, a bid to dispel the pained musings of the past. "Er, no, no floral items." Since that day in the gardens, Katherine had come to detest the cheerful blooms, the reminder of Father's failings. That day had taught Katherine the perils of love.

The peddler's brow furrowed, and she seemed unaware of Katherine's inner tumult. Her beady eyes went wide in her wrinkled face. She reached into the front pocket of her jacket and withdrew a gold chain. "Perhaps a golden heart, then?"

Katherine looked at the pendant, and her heart paused at the implausibility of it all. She reached for it wordlessly, and studied the golden bauble, turning it over in her fingers. "It is perfect," she said, quietly.

The peddler grunted, and held her hand out.

Katherine blinked, looking down at her open palm. "Oh," she said, and reached into the front of her reticule and withdrew several coins.

The woman's eyes widened at the small fortune Katherine bestowed.

"It is a fine piece, indeed," Katherine murmured. There had been a time when Katherine had lain awake in bed, gripped by fear of her family's dire financial straits. If she could prevent another woman from feeling those sentiments, even for just a bit, then a sovereign was a very, very small price to pay for the pendant.

"There is a story behind that heart, moi lady."

Katherine slipped the heart into her reticule. "I'm certain there is," she said. "Thank you very much." And before the peddler could finish, Katherine stepped outside. Over the years she'd listened rather patiently to her sister's fanciful musings about love; she'd not have to hear the foolish words of a stranger, too.

A blast of cool wind slapped at her skin. Katherine gasped as the frigid breeze sucked the air from her lungs. Her reticule fell from her fingers and skidded along the frozen surface.

"Drat," she muttered, and hurried after it. Katherine took a step, when the flat sole of her kid leather boot slipped on the snowflakes coating the frozen river. She threw her arms wide to balance herself as she slid away from the lone little tent, past her reticule, ever farther.

Craaaaaack.

She swallowed hard. Her heart hung suspended in her breast, and then the ice opened up.

Chapter 2

*T*here was not much Jasper Waincourt, 8th Duke of Bainbridge, detested more than the Christmastide season. His mouth tightened as he scanned the merry frolickers skating upon the river and others moving in and out of the cluttered tents filled with unnecessary fripperies.

There was not much more he detested than Christmastide . . . however, the inane amusements enjoyed by the *ton* were certainly very close.

The Marquess of Guilford stuck his elbow into Jasper's side. "Must you look so severe? You'll scare a small child with that icy, ducal stare of yours."

Jasper continued walking. "I do not see any small children," he said in clipped tones that would have sent most grown men scurrying.

Having known one another since their early years at Eton, Jasper noticed the Marquess of Guilford was the only individual of his acquaintance who seemed undaunted by his presence. "Very well, then. You frightened that young woman off."

Jasper thought of the tart-mouthed, fiery-eyed miss who'd stumbled into him.

"She was not scared." The plain young woman with her brown ringlets didn't take him as one to scare easily—more the fool was she. The nameless creature should have sensed the peril in merely crossing in front of him.

Guilford chuckled and slapped Jasper on the back hard. "Come, Bainbridge. It is nearly Christmas, a time of merriment and joy." He gave Jasper a long look. "You cannot be miserable forever."

Except Jasper hadn't been miserable forever. He'd been miserable for three, very nearly four, years. He clenched and unclenched his hands into fists at his side, as he absently studied the rustic enjoyment being had by the lords and ladies upon the ice.

Laughter carried on the crisp winter wind and surrounded Jasper, mocking him, taunting him for having once been happy, and as lighthearted as the fools at the fair.

"Bainbridge," Guilford said quietly, all traces of amusement gone from his tone.

Jasper shrugged his shoulders. "It is fine," he bit out.

Another round of laughter in the distance punctuated his words, a jeering testament to his lie.

He felt Guilford's stare on him, and stiffened under the scrutiny. Then, Guilford said, "It will serve you well to escape that bleak, dark castle you call home."

The bleak, dark castle as Guilford referred to it was, in fact, Castle Blackwood, Jasper's ducal seat, a Norman castle. Significant portions of the original medieval structure remained, including five towers. Imposing, dark, and menacing, it rather suited Jasper's foul mood.

He balled his hands into fists. Then, it hadn't always been that way. At one time there'd been laughter and joy and cheer within the castle walls.

"Bainbridge? Are you all right?"

Jasper shook his head. "Foolish taking part in such inane amusements," he said, his tone harsh and guttural.

Guilford's patent grin was back in place. He slapped Jasper on the back once again. "Perhaps. But it is Christmastide and the *time* for inane amusements."

Jasper grunted and fell reluctantly into step beside Guilford. He kept his hard-stare trained forward, not sparing so much as a sideways glance at the brightly colored tents and the eager young ladies moving between them to purchase their fripperies.

"Egad, man, must you scowl so?"

"Yes," Jasper bit out.

His friend rubbed his gloved hands together, as though trying to infuse warmth into the frozen digits. *Served the blighter right for forcing him back into this very public setting.*

"Ah, just a moment." Guilford stopped beside a tent. He pulled several coins out of his pocket and approached an old man. Passing the coins to the vendor, Guilford accepted two tankards of ale.

"I don't want ale," Jasper snapped, when his friend pushed the glass into his hand.

"Drink it. If for no other reason than it will warm you."

"I'm not cold."

Guilford snorted. "You're always cold. A frigid, icy man, and you've been that way as long as I've known you."

Yes, Jasper hadn't ever been the laughing, carefree boy. Born to a loveless marriage between two unfaithful parents, Jasper had scoffed at the empty sentiment called love—until he'd met Lady Lydia Wilkes. A smiling, bright-eyed debutante, she'd captivated him, melted his chilled heart.

A muscle in the corner of his eye twitched. And how had he repaid that great gift she'd shown him? By killing her. Oh,

God, the muscles in his stomach tightened. The pain of her loss, a pain he'd thought he'd finally buried with her cold, dead body, mocked him for daring to think he'd ever be rid of the pain.

He shook his head. He'd not be melancholy. Lydia was—dead. Dead. Forever gone. He lashed himself with the reminder of it. His lips twisted. As though he could ever truly forget.

Jasper raised the ale to his lips, and downed it in one long, slow, steady swallow. The brew did little to thaw the cold ice that now moved through his veins. From over the rim of his glass, he spied the too-plain young lady who'd walked into him. With her nondescript brown hair and brown eyes, she was a foil to Lydia's golden-blonde ringlets and pale porcelain skin. There was nothing at all captivating about the fiery-eyed vixen who'd glared at him.

"She is rather lovely," Guilford murmured at his elbow.

Jasper gave his head a curt shake. "Hardly the type of creature to ever be considered a true beauty."

"Goodness, you are in an even blacker mood than usual," his friend chided.

Jasper handed his tankard off to the vendor and continued walking.

Guilford hurried his step to match his stride. "Perhaps we might inspect the peddlers' goods?"

To what end? Jasper had no family. Born the only child to the late Duke and Duchess of Bainbridge, the nearest relative was a distant gentleman on his great-great-great grandfather's side, who resided in Northumberland. Jasper couldn't be more different than Guilford, who had a mother, three sisters, and one brother. He motioned to the tents. "I'll remain here and," his lip pulled back, "enjoy the festivities while you see to the fripperies inside the tent."

Guilford opened his mouth, and then closed it. He shook his head, dislodging his top hat. He readjusted it back into place. "I'll be just a moment." With that he hurried ahead to a canary-yellow tent.

Jasper fought back a yawn of tedium, and continued to survey the tableau with disinterest. Ladies clinging to their suitors' arms as they skated upon the thick surface of the frozen river, peddlers barking their wares at the passing nobles. The strangers' echoing words, empty and meaningless.

His gaze caught sight of the young lady who'd stumbled into him mere moments ago. She hurried outside of a gray tent removed from the bustling activity throughout the fair. A gust of wind tugged free her bonnet, and released several of her brown ringlets into the cool winter wind. They whipped about her face, and with her high cheeks and an almost cat-like slant to her eyes, she had the look of a kind of ice princess. He frowned, thinking of her frigid stare. Yes, ice princess was an apt moniker for the young lady.

With the serious set to her face, she was vastly different than the young ladies he remembered from three years ago. Something slipped from her fingers and slid along the ice. Tired of studying the nameless creature, Jasper glanced over to the tent Guilford had disappeared into.

A blood-curdling scream rent the still winter air. The ungodly cry sent the kestrels noisily into flight; and goose-flesh dotted Jasper's skin. With an intuitiveness born of a man who'd witnessed and experienced horrific things in life, Jasper immediately sought the nameless ice princess.

Time stood still for an infinitesimal moment that seemed to stretch to eternity, and then with a curse, Jasper sprinted down the river toward the gaping hole in the ice. He cursed the slippery surface that slowed his pace, and then tossing aside his cloak, skidded toward the desperate arms flailing through the surface.

Jasper slid forward upon his stomach, arms extended. "Take my hand," he barked, as the woman's head broke through the water.

She sucked in deep, panicky, gasped breaths. Unholy terror lit her eyes; the kind of eyes that had stared into the face of death and knew death would inevitably prevail.

Jasper cursed. "Listen to me," he snapped.

Her brown eyes locked on his. Her bonnet hung sopping down the side of her tangled mat of brown curls. "Help," she rasped, and then her skirts tugged her downward.

Jasper's stomach lurched, and with another curse he inched ever closer. The thin ice cracked under his weight. He made one desperate grab and connected with her hand, tugging her up to the surface.

"Listen to me," he ordered, his tone harsh and hard. "Do not fight me. Allow me to pull you up."

Something in either his words or tone penetrated her fear, calming her, for the panic dimmed in her eyes, and she nodded.

Jasper pulled her soaking wet form, tugging her up, up, up, and then her slim frame broke the surface of the shattered ice.

Short of breath from his exertions, Jasper registered the ice's protest to their efforts, and he found a last surge of energy to edge back, back, ever farther with the young lady and her heavy skirts held close to his chest.

Jasper edged them over to the hard, solid land, and collapsed with the young woman's lifeless body draped over his. He dimly registered the steady crack, and then splash as the wide ice surface fell beneath the Thames River. He sucked in great big, heaving gasps for air and registered the lady's absolute stillness.

His chest tightened as he turned her over; his eyes quickly scanned the pale white of her cheeks, and he searched for breath.

With a curse he thumped her on the back.

By God he'd not been dragged to this infernal affair to pull a woman from the water.

Another thump.

Only to watch her die amidst the mindless amusements.

A harder thump.

Not another woman.

Even harder.

Not again.

Water surged from her lips, gurgling and bubbling, and he turned her onto her side as she choked and gasped for the sweet taste of breath.

Jasper collapsed hard against the earth, and lay back, staring up at the fat white snowflakes as they fell from the sky. He closed his eyes a moment, and then rolled to his side to study the quiet stranger.

She lay with her knees pulled close to her trim waist, her arms folded across her chest. Tremors wracked her lithe body. Jasper cursed.

Christ, at this rate the young lady would have survived her plunge under the water's surface only to die of a chill.

He searched around for his cloak, and found it on the opposite side of the gaping hole left from the missing slab of ice.

Then in a great show of irony, at that very moment, his black cloak slid into the surface of the water. With a sigh, he shrugged out of his somewhat damp coat and tossed it atop the lady. "Here," he said.

His jacket, too large for her diminutive frame, hung upon her, making her appear even smaller. She burrowed deep into the folds.

"Th-thank y-you," she said, between teeth that chattered.

He waved his hand.

"I-I c-can't ever repay you."

He raked a gaze over her. "Madam, you have nothing I want, nor anything I need."

She appeared to flinch and Jasper wasn't certain if it was his bluntly spoken words or the cold ravaging her frame.

Something stirred inside him, something he'd thought dead—emotion. Guilt dug at him. Jasper cursed. He didn't want to feel guilt for his treatment of the lady. He didn't want to feel anything where she was concerned. Hell, he didn't want to feel anything where *anyone* was concerned.

Jasper shoved himself to his feet. "Here, now," he said gruffly, and held a hand out to her. She eyed it a moment, and then placed her fingers in his.

A charge like the kind one received when walking in stock-inged feet across a carpet surged through him. He dropped her hand as if burned.

"Where is your chaperone?"

She shook her head. "I-I've not b-brought one."

With another curse, he scanned the area.

"D-do y-you a-always c-curse in fr-front of l-ladies?" she shot at him.

Ah, the ice princess was back. He found he preferred the snapping, spitting catlike vixen to the nearly drowned, destitute creature he'd pulled from the river. "Ladies do not run around London without a chaperone."

Her brown brows knitted into a single line. Her eyes slid away from his.

Jasper followed her glance to a point beyond his shoulder. "Bloody h—" He snapped his lips closed, remembering her earlier charge. A crowd of observers stood at the central portion of the river eyeing the cracked ice, and Jasper, and . . . and . . .

The ice princess.

He stood, and staring down at her was struck by how frail and helpless she appeared under that icy veneer. Something shifted inside him again. Jasper shook his head, dispelling all hint of emotion. He was now a man who operated under stiff logic and reason.

Fact. The woman had nearly drowned.

Fact. He might be a heartless bastard, but he couldn't have *let* her drown.

Fact. She was a shivering mass of slim, graceful limbs.

Fact. He needed to return her home immediately or she'd perish from cold.

His jaw tightened. And he'd not caused a great scene and risked his own miserable life to save her from the frigid waters only to die of a chill.

Jasper scooped her up.

"Wh-what a-are y-you d-doing?" she squeaked. It didn't fail to escape his notice the manner in which she buried herself close against him, like a kitten seeking warmth from its master.

He stiffened at the feel of her nubile body pressed to his. In spite of the cold, her skin against his heated him.

Jasper tamped down the irrational yearnings. He'd been without a woman for more than three years. His body's reaction was a physical one, nothing more than that.

"I am returning you home," he forced out between tight lips.

The sooner he could be rid of the creature, the better off he'd be.

Chapter 3

$\mathcal{K}$atherine's body ached as though jagged icicles had pierced every portion of her skin. A chill filled her inside and out until she wondered if she'd freeze from the cold. Her disjointed thoughts, still murky from her near drowning, dulled logical thinking.

He'd saved her. This great, hulking, frowning bear of a man. The same stranger who'd nearly bowled her over and raked his gaze condescendingly over her person had risked his life to pluck her from the frozen river.

His flinty glare, the dark expression on the harsh planes of his face, suggested he regretted the decision.

"I am returning you home," he said again. His voice emerged a kind of growl that would give most small children night terrors.

Katherine burrowed deeper into the damp folds of his too-large, black jacket.

For a moment she wondered at what life had done to turn him into such a miserable, odious creature. Because certainly no person could be so deliberately callous . . . so deliberately unfeeling, without reason.

"Has the ice dulled your wits?" he snapped.

She gave her head a clearing shake. "I-I c-can't l-leave."

There was the matter of her sister, Anne. Katherine's eyes slid closed as she imagined their mother's fury. They would be fortunate to live to see the eve of Christmas. But then, considering her fall into the Thames, she was fortunate to have lived even the day.

He gathered her close against his oaken-hard chest. For a moment the events of the day melted away; her and Anne's clandestine efforts to find a silly pendant, the chilling terror of the ice cracking, her submersion under the frozen water . . . the certainty of death. This stranger's arms filled her with a soothing sense of calm she'd never before known from another person. He strode toward the pavement, handling her as easily as if she were a porcelain doll. Katherine closed her eyes a moment and selfishly stole of that warmth provided by his body.

They passed a throng of on-lookers and Katherine blinked, remembering . . .

"My sister!" she blurted. She could not leave Anne to find her own way home.

"How old is your sister?" he rumbled.

"Nineteen."

"Then she can certainly find her way," he said, not breaking his stride.

Katherine gasped at his ungentlemanly reaction. "Y-you a-are a m-monster," she stammered.

Since she'd first stumbled into the gentleman, the unyielding expression gave way to a smile; it was a dark, hard rendering devoid of all merriment and it chilled her like the frozen River Thames. "Yes. Yes, I am."

He stopped beside a black lacquer carriage with a golden crest emblazoned upon the door. A lion reared upon its legs, a blade clenched between its vicious teeth.

The sight of it gave her pause, and she shoved against him. He *was* a monster.

A servant attired in crimson-red livery with gold epaulets pulled the door open.

The monster tossed her unceremoniously inside the carriage. Katherine landed amidst the thick, upholstered red velvet seats. She crawled into the corner of the conveyance, and huddled into the folds of his jacket.

"R-release m-me. I-I need t-to f-find m-my sister."

He climbed inside, and the enormous space shrunk, filled instead with his overwhelming presence.

The door closed behind him and he settled into the seat as though he were King George himself. He folded his arms across his chest and stared at the point above her forehead. "Where is your residence?"

She glanced at the back of the carriage, until she realized he was in fact directing his question her way. He refused to meet her eyes, as though she were some kind of Medusa . . . her lips flattened into a hard line. Well, with his unbending countenance and hard coldness, he'd been turned to stone long before her. "I demand . . ."

He leveled her with a hard glare, and her breath caught.

Perhaps he possessed the potent stare of Medusa.

She wet her lips.

Katherine provided the address of her residence.

He barked the directions of her Mayfair townhouse, and then the carriage lurched forward.

Katherine gulped as the carriage wheels rolled along. They picked up in speed, and her heart's rhythm increased until her pulse pounded loudly in her ears. Her sister was alone . . . and yet, she trusted Anne would take the very same hackney that had been paid to wait for them back, without difficulty. After all, Anne was the mastermind of all the great schemes and scrapes they found themselves in.

The budding panic blended with the terror that had consumed her that day, only exacerbated by the foul stranger's presence, and she reached for the carriage handle.

He settled his large, hand over hers.

Katherine jumped.

"I suggest, unless you merely want to trade death by drowning for death by the wheels of a carriage, that you release the handle, madam."

His flat, emotionless tone conveyed boredom. Why, he might as well have been commenting on the weather or offering her tea.

Katherine snatched her hand back, feeling burned by his touch. "You are a m-monster," she repeated.

He tugged free his wet gloves and beat them against one another. Drops of water sprayed the carriage walls. "Your charge grows unoriginal and tedious, madam."

And in that moment it occurred to Katherine just how ungrateful she must seem. The towering stranger might be a foul-tempered fiend, but he'd saved her. Her lips twisted. Whether he'd wanted to or not.

"Forgive me, I've not yet thanked you." She took a breath. "So thank you. For saving me. From drowning," she finished lamely.

His shoulder lifted in a slight shrug. "I'd hardly ruin the amusements of the day by watching you drown beneath the surface of the Thames."

She expected she should feel outraged, shocked, appalled by those callously delivered words . . . and yet, something in his tone gave her pause. It was as though he sought to elicit an outraged response from her. Instead of outrage, Katherine was filled with her first stirrings of intrigue, wondering what had happened to turn his black heart so vile.

Katherine did not rise to his clear attempt at bating her. "My name is Lady Katherine Adamson." Pause. "I imagine I should know the name of my rescuer."

He said nothing for a while, and Katherine suspected he had no intention of answering her. She sighed and reached for the curtained window.

"Jasper Waincourt, 8th Duke of Bainbridge."

Her eyes widened. "You are a duke," she blurted.

He arched a single, frosty black brow at her. "You'd be wise not to make designs upon my title, madam. I'd not wed you if you were the last creature in the kingdom."

She blinked. Oh, the dastard. Katherine jabbed a finger at him. "And you, well I wouldn't wed you if you were the last creature in the world, and the king decreed it to spare my life."

His lips twitched. But then the firm line was back in place, so that she suspected she'd imagined the slight expression of mirth. "It is good we are of like opinions, then, madam. We are here," he said.

She angled her head. And then the carriage rocked to a halt.

The sudden, unexpectedness of the stop propelled Katherine forward, and she landed in an ignominious heap atop the duke's chest.

It was as though she'd slammed into a stone wall. All the breath left her. She looked up at him through her lids, and found him coolly unaffected by the weight of her figure upon his person.

He yawned.

Yawned!

The lout had the audacity to yawn, as though he found the whole of this day—boring.

He set her back into her seat and rapped on the door.

The carriage door opened.

She glared. She felt frozen through. She didn't think her teeth would ever cease chattering. And she knew she should really be more grateful considering he'd risked his life and limb to pull her from the river, but he was . . . was . . . *bloody miserable.*

And Katherine didn't curse.

Not when she'd found out Father had left them destitute.

Not when the creditors had come to claim every last one of her books.

Not when they'd been forced from their cottage in Hertfordshire Estate while Mother had looked on, weeping piteous little tears.

She jabbed her finger across at him. "You sir . . ."

"Your Grace," he corrected.

"Are a miserable monster." Katherine leaned across the carriage and jabbed her trembling cold finger in his chest. "Which I know is redundant . . . and I'm not. Redundant. Ever. But you are foul. And odious. And if you didn't want to risk your life and limb to save me, then you shouldn't have." Katherine fell back against the cushions, her chest heaving from her near brush with death. The driver stuck his head into the carriage. "Not that I'm displeased with being saved," Katherine clarified. "Because I, unlike some odious, miserable beings, enjoy being alive."

The servant gulped and ducked his head out of the carriage.

The duke's black brows dipped, and his eyes narrowed into deep impenetrable slits. If Katherine hadn't had a brush with death a short while ago, she expected his expression would have terrified her a good deal more. As it was, she was cold, hungry, and too tired to fear a duke with a black scowl. His rudeness had exhausted her patience.

"Are you finished, madam?" The words contained a satiny edge as smooth as the side of a blade.

She swallowed, and tugged his jacket free. "Here," she said. "I'd not care to impose any more on your hospi . . ." A squeak escaped her. "Wha-what are you doing?" she stammered as he tossed the thoroughly rumpled garment back over her shoulders and picked her up. "Your Grace . . ." He leapt from the carriage, holding her as though she weighed no more than a mere babe.

A vein pulsed in the corner of his eye. He stopped and glanced at the row of stucco townhouses.

The servant cleared his throat and gestured to the modest white front townhouse she now called home.

The duke strode onward, up the steps, and rapped on the door.

"Y-you m-may p-put me down, Your Grace."

He rapped again.

"I said . . ."

"I am not deaf, madam." He raised his hand to knock again when the butler opened it suddenly.

Ollie's small blue eyes went wide in his ancient, heavily wrinkled face. "Lady Katherine," he boomed.

The servant, fast approaching his seventieth year, insisted on retaining his post. "Ollie," Katherine murmured.

The duke's frown deepened. "May I enter?" Mocking condescension underlined that question.

Oh the ba . . . *lout*, she silently amended.

Ollie blinked. "Enter?" His high-pitched voice thundered. "Er, yes, right, right," he stepped aside and motioned the duke forward.

His Grace swept through the front doors as though he were in fact the owner of the modest townhouse.

Katherine looked up and swallowed at the sight of her mother descending the long staircase in a flurry of burgundy skirts. "Ollie, whatever is . . . ?" Mother's words ended on a gasp. "Whatever has happened?" she asked, her tone well-modulated, perfectly ladylike to match her sedate, unhurried pace.

Katherine sighed. Mother had always been a stickler for the rules of decorum. A lady must never run.

Not even if one's daughter should appear in a stranger's arms, thoroughly bedraggled, rumpled, and near death.

"Your daughter took herself off to the Frost Fair, unchaperoned, and was rewarded for her efforts by nearly drowning in the Thames."

Well, that was a rather methodical, emotionless recount of her day by the duke. Accurate, but unappreciated.

"Mother . . ." Katherine began.

Mother glared her into silence.

Katherine burrowed closer to the duke, accepting support in the unlikeliest of places.

He glanced down the bridge of his hawklike nose at her. Katherine's breath caught, and for the first time, she truly noticed him. Several inches well beyond six feet, his broad chest and arms were thickly chorded with powerful muscles, so very different than the gentlemen of the haute *ton*. Not one to be considered handsome by conventional standards, the angular planes of his face would be considered too harsh, his narrow lips too hard, his . . .

He quirked a brow.

Katherine felt the first real warmth that day and it came in the form of the mortified heat that stained her cheeks. "Er, well . . ."

"Might we know the name of the gentleman who so gallantly rescued my daughter?"

His mouth tightened, and for the slightest moment Katherine thought he might ignore her mother's request, turn on his heel, and leave.

"Jasper Waincourt, 8th Duke of Bainbridge." That was all.

No bow. No polite discourse. Just five words, one number, and a cold, unfeeling tone.

He seemed to realize in that moment that he still held her in his arms. His body froze, and it was as though he'd turned to granite. He glanced around, as if searching for someone to relieve him of his burden.

Katherine frowned. It didn't matter that he appeared desperately eager to be rid of her. She should want him gone posthaste from her foyer.

She should.

She *did*.

As if a cue had been delivered, the tall footman came rushing forward to relieve the duke of his burden.

The duke hesitated, turning his black glower on the handsome footman, Thomas, and then he turned Katherine over to the servant.

"Your Grace, allow me to extend an invitation to din—"

"No."

Her mother blinked several times. However, as the Countess of Wakefield and not easily cowed, even by a powerful peer, Mother was undeterred. "Surely you must allow us the courtesy of—"

"Madam, the only thing you might do for me is to keep a more watchful eye upon your daughter." He sketched a brief bow. "Good day," he said curtly and without another word, turned on his heel, and made his way to the front door.

Ollie had the good sense to pull the door open, and the duke continued forward, his stride unbroken.

The door closed behind him with a firm click.

Mother's brown eyes widened, giving her the appearance of an owl. "Well," she said on a huff. It was certainly not every day the Countess of Wakefield was left speechless.

Katherine stared at the door where Jasper Waincourt, the 8th Duke of Bainbridge, just exited.

Well, indeed.

Chapter 4

$\mathscr{A}$ sharp rap sounded on Jasper's office door. He didn't pick up his head from the ledger atop the surface of his desk. "Enter," he barked.

The door opened. "Your Grace, the Marquess of Guilford has asked to see you."

"I'm not receiving callers." Jasper dipped his pen into the ink and marked several columns.

"I explained you were not receiving callers."

"But I explained that I'm not merely a caller, but rather a friend," Guilford drawled from the doorway.

Jasper dipped his pen and made another mark. He scanned the first three columns, and then tossed his pen aside. "What is it?" he asked, impatiently. He waved off the butler, and the older servant bowed and hurried out.

Guilford strolled into the room. He stopped beside the sideboard filled with crystal decanters. He studied several bottles and then picked up the bottle of brandy. He poured himself a glass. With the patience better reserved for one of the cloth, he strolled over to Jasper's desk, and sat in the lone chair, directly across from him.

"Really, Bainbridge," he said, after he'd taken several sips. "You ask 'what is it' as though you didn't create quite the stir with your heroic rescue of a mysterious young lady from the Thames River."

A growl worked its way up Jasper's throat, and he reached for his pen. He dipped it angrily into the inkwell, and completed the next row of tabulations. The last thing he desired was to become gossiped about by the bloody *ton*. He'd imagined after three years as the Mad Duke, Society had forgotten about the Duke of Bainbridge and his now dead wife, Lady Lydia.

Dead.

Dead.

Dead and buried. Cold in the grave.

Jasper lashed at himself with the reminder of it. He accepted the stark remembrance of Lydia's smiling visage, and then replayed her face contorting with the pain of being torn apart by their unborn child.

The pen snapped in his hand. Ink smeared across his previously immaculate page. Jasper tossed the pen aside. "I don't hear a question there," he snapped. He appreciated Guilford, but many times he wanted to send his only friend to the devil. This happened to be one of those times.

Guilford folded an ankle across his knee. "Imagine my shock to find you gone." He waved his hand. "Oh, I'd briefly considered perhaps you'd gone to help yourself to another tankard of ale, but then thought you'd never do anything even remotely emotional as to indulge in too much drink." Suddenly, Guilford leaned forward. "Therefore you can imagine my absolute shock to discover you'd gone and done something so very public as to risk your life to save an unknown woman."

The woman, Lady Katherine Adamson, slipped into his mind. With her snapping eyes, the tart edge to her words . . . his initial opinion of the young lady held true—she was no great beauty. And yet, there had been something very intriguing about this woman who'd not been at all cowed by his presence. Jasper refused to rise to his friend's baiting.

Instead, he sat back in his chair, and folded his arms across his chest.

All the air seemed to leave Guilford. "Blast and damn, does nothing I say or do manage to get a rise out of you?"

Jasper scowled. "Is that what your intentions are? To get a rise out of me?" It would take a good deal more than his friend's ineffectual attempts to bait him to rouse any emotion in him. Again, the ice princess, Lady Katherine, slipped into his mind.

And you, well I wouldn't wed you if you were the last creature in the world, and the king decreed it to spare my life. Yes, Lady Katherine Adamson was no grand beauty; brown hair, brown eyes, and the faintest dusting of freckles along her cheekbones. And yet . . . her slender frame, well over a foot shorter than his own six-foot-five-inch figure, had possessed remarkable curves that had layered very nicely against his body. With her body atremble from the cold, and her teeth chattering uncontrollably, he'd imagined her near death experience would have dulled her spirit. Instead, her snappish tone had put him in mind of a hissing and spitting cat cornered in the street.

Guilford continued to sit there in silence, seeming to study Jasper over the rim of his partially emptied glass of brandy. He took another sip. "Who was she?"

"Who was who?" Jasper replied, and tugged open the front drawer of his desk. He withdrew a new pen, and touched his fingertip to the point.

His friend gritted his teeth loud enough for the sound to reach Jasper's ears. "Don't be an ass."

Jasper kept his gaze trained on the ledger in front of him. He turned the page, and dipped his pen in ink. "Lady Katherine Adamson."

Silence.

"Ahh."

Jasper's jaw clenched. He counted to ten, making a desperate bid not to feed that 'Ahh.' And failed. "And?" he barked. "Do you know the lady?" Jasper didn't know why it should matter if Guilford knew the spirited creature. It didn't, he assured himself. It didn't matter who the hell she was.

Guilford uncrossed his leg, a grin on his lips. "There is an elder sister." His brow wrinkled. "I believe Lady Aldora. She's been recently wed to Lord Michael Knightly."

Lord Michael Knightly. The second brother to the Marquess of St. James, purported to be as rich as Croesus, and ruthless in matters of business.

Jasper had heard of the man; knew there was some scandal or another attached to his name, but it went back years ago, to a time when bits of information such as that might have interested Jasper. No longer.

Furthermore, Jasper didn't give a damn about Lady Aldora.

His friend must have followed the unspoken direction of his thoughts, for he continued.

"It is my understanding that Lady Katherine has a twin sister. A lovely creature, far more beautiful than the lady you fished from the river. They made their Come Out this year. Both remain unwed."

And you, well I wouldn't wed you if you were the last creature in the world, and the king decreed it to spare my life.

His lips twitched in remembrance of her spirited outburst.

"I say, did you just smile, Bainbridge?"

Jasper growled. "No."

Guilford downed the remaining contents of his glass and then leaned over, placing it with a loud *thunk* upon Jasper's mahogany desk. The usual easy smile worn by his affable friend now gone, replaced by a somber set to his mouth in a show of pity that was neither wanted nor appreciated. Jasper had seen that look those three years ago. He gripped the arms of his chair hard enough that his nails bit into the wood and left marks upon the surface.

"She would not want you to live like this, Bainbridge."

His grip tightened.

Guilford seemed unaware of the volatile emotion thrumming through Jasper, for if he was, he'd surely have known to cease his barrage.

Instead, he continued. "Lydia loved you. She would want you to be happy."

Jasper looked at a point over Guilford's shoulder, flexing his jaw. "You dare presume to know what Lydia would want?" Not a soul had known another so well as Jasper had known his wife. From her smile to her gentle spirit, he knew her better than he knew the lines that covered his palm.

Guilford shifted forward in his seat; the aged leather cracked in protest. "Then you tell me, Bainbridge, you who knew her better than any other. Would Lydia be so cold and cruel as to want to see you live your life as this hard, unforgiving, empty man you've become?"

"Go to hell," Jasper snapped.

His friend inclined his head. "I believe your response shall suffice as an answer." Guilford climbed to his feet, and fished around the front of his pocket. He extracted a small book, no larger than the span of his palm and dropped it onto Jasper's desk. "Consider it a bit of an early Christmastide present," he murmured.

Jasper dropped his gaze.

Byron's *Childe Harold's Pilgrimage*.

"It is the story of a world-weary man looking for meaning in his life," Guilford went on.

"I don't—"

"Read poetry. I know. But you used to, and I thought perhaps as it is Christmastide, and a time of hope and new beginnings, that you might find a renewed love for the written word." Guilford opened his mouth as if he wished to say more. Instead, he sketched a short bow. "Good day, Bainbridge. I shall see you tomorrow."

"You needn't come by," Jasper barked when his friend grasped the handle of the door.

"I know. But that is what friends do." He paused. "Oh, and Bainbridge?" He reached into the front pocket of his jacket once more and fished something out. He tossed the item across the room. It landed with a solid thump atop Jasper's desk, coming a hairsbreadth away from his ledgers. "I managed to retrieve Lady Katherine's reticule. I thought you might return the item to your lady."

"She's not—"

Guilford took his leave. He closed the door behind him with a soft click.

"My lady," Jasper finished into the silence. He momentarily eyed the small pale-green reticule, reached for it, and then caught himself. With a curse, he shoved it aside and instead picked up Byron's recent work. He turned it over in his hands. At one time, Jasper had read and appreciated all the works of the romantic poets. When he'd courted Lydia, he'd read to her sonnets that bespoke of love and beauty. Her death had shown him that sonnets were nothing more than fanciful words, not even worth the ink they were written in.

Yet, Guilford somehow believed the remnants of the man Jasper had been still dwelled somewhere inside him. When all the servants had fled in fear of the Mad Duke after Lydia's death, Guilford had been unwavering in his steadfastness; the one constant in Jasper's life, when all friends had gone.

And how did Jasper repay that devotion? With curt words and icy dismissals.

Jasper tossed the book down and stood so quickly his chair scraped along the hardwood floor. He proceeded to pace. Guilford dared to drag him away from Castle Blackwood and thrust him back into the joy and merriment enjoyed by mindless members of Society. His gaze skittered off to Lady Katherine's reticule, and he cursed.

Why couldn't Guilford have just left Jasper to wallow in the misery of his own making in the country? There, Jasper was not made to think of anything beyond the loss of Lydia. His staff, a deferential lot, knew to judiciously avoid Jasper's path. Yet, in the span of a day, he'd been forced to take part in the Christmastide festivities upon the Thames River, and he'd not enjoyed any hint of a reminder of the time of year when Lydia had died amidst a pool of her own blood.

He punished himself by dragging the memory of her into focus, except . . .

He blinked.

And you, well I wouldn't wed you if you were the last creature in the world, and the king decreed it to spare my life.

And yet, the fiery vixen whom he'd pulled from the river flashed to his mind.

Jasper raked a hand through his hair. In that moment, he loathed Guilford for dragging him off to that infernal fair, and he loathed himself for allowing Guilford to drag him off, because then he would remain blissfully ignorant of the snapping Lady Katherine, who'd infiltrated his thoughts and robbed him of Lydia's image just then.

His jaw set in a hard angle. If his friend believed Jasper had returned to London to rejoin the living and take part in any of the winter festivities, he was to be disappointed. Outside of his own solitary presence, Jasper had little intention of intermingling with any members of Society.

He picked up the book of poetry at the edge of his desk, and fanned the pages. His friend thought to give him poetry of the romantics. Either Guilford was a lackwit, or foolishly unaware that the last book Jasper would ever pick up was the drivel romantic poets spit upon the written page. There had been a time when he had enjoyed the words of Blake and Byron immensely. Not any longer. Not since life had taught him the perils of love.

He tossed the gift aside. Since that night, he still allowed himself to read, but his interests had changed a good deal. A hard smile formed on his lips. And certainly the last thing he'd care to read were books of romance and love.

Jasper strode over to the table filled with crystal decanters. He pulled the stopper out of one and splashed several fingerfuls into a glass. If he was to remain in London, he had little intention of resuming his previous way of living.

The sooner Guilford realized that, the better off they all would be.

Chapter 5

"*O*h, my goodness, Katherine, will you not speak of it?"

Katherine sat at the window seat that overlooked the back gardens. Her sister knelt at her side, her eyes fairly pleading for details Katherine did not want to give.

She hugged her arms around her waist as the remembered terror of that day came flooding back. "There is nothing to speak of, Anne."

Her sister sat back in a flounce of skirts. "Hmph," she muttered. "You nearly drowned."

"Because I was at that silly fair."

"For which I'm ever so sorry," Anne continued. "If you'd only stayed with me while I shopped . . ."

Katherine glared her into silence.

Her normally loquacious sister had sense enough to let that thought go unfinished.

Katherine returned her attention to the grounds below, and thought of the moment when her water-logged skirts had tugged her downward. And then he'd appeared. A kind of angel rescuer—more of a dark angel, but an angel nonetheless. The Duke of Bainbridge may be an unsmiling, boorish lout, but he had saved her, and for that he would forever have her gratitude.

A smile played about her lips. Whether he wanted it or not. She suspected the last thing the dark, cold duke would ever care for was warm expressions of gratefulness.

"Will you at least speak of the duke?" Anne pressed.

"No," Katherine said automatically. She studied the snow-flakes as they swirled past the windowpane. She'd not speak of him. She'd resolved to remember him for his rescue but, beyond that, to bury thoughts of his harsh coldness.

"Mother said—"

"Anne," she warned.

"Mother said a scandal surrounds him." She leaned close, and braced her hands upon the edge of the window seat. "She says they called him the Mad Duke for several years, and then Society ceased talking of him. Said he disappeared to the ruins of his castle."

Katherine fisted the fabric of her skirts. She told herself she'd not feed her sister's salacious appetite for gossip. She told herself to not ask. The Duke of Bainbridge's business was his own. And yet . . .

"What happened to him?" The words tumbled from her lips.

From the clear pane of glass she detected her sister's slight shrug. "Some say he murdered his wife."

Katherine gasped. "Anne," she chided. "Do not speak so." She thought of the veneer of icy hardness that clung to him, the apathy in his pale-green eyes. Such a man was surely capable of violence, and yet, that same man had risked his own life to save hers. Those were not the actions of a gentleman capable of murder.

Anne rose amidst a flutter of pale-pink skirts. She, however, appeared to have identified Katherine as a captivated audience. "That is all that is known," she said, sounding like a child who'd just been told they are not to receive any plum pudding for Christmas dessert. She settled her hands upon her hips. "How can a man have been said to have murdered his wife, and no one knows any details of the night?"

"That is enough, Anne." She'd not condone such gossip.

"Hmph, very well, then. You are a bore today, Katherine, and I merely sought to provide you company."

"You can join me on my outing to the bookshop."

An inelegant snort escaped her sister. "Don't be foolish." She glanced out the window. "You'd brave snow to go—"

"I'd hardly call it snow. It is merely a few flakes."

"To find some dull books about . . . ?"

"They aren't dull."

"Poetry." Anne continued as though she hadn't spoken. "You should at least read the words of love and—"

"Enough, Anne," Katherine said on a sigh.

She gave a flounce of her golden ringlets. "Well, I for one would far rather see to my pianoforte."

For all of Katherine's lack of ladylike abilities, Anne seemed to excel in every endeavor, particularly her ability to play and sing. And Mother was quite indiscriminate in the frequency in which she pointed out the differences to Katherine.

Katherine flung her legs over the side of the window seat and her brown muslin skirts settled noisily about her ankles. "Poetry is the fruit of the soul."

Her sister snorted. "Not the poems you read."

Katherine closed her lips tight. No, her interests didn't lie with the romantics. As a child, studying with their governesses, upon Father's betrayal, and Aldora's frantic search for a wealthy, titled husband, all foolish dreams had been quashed.

"Are you certain you'd not care to join m—?"

"Quite certain," Anne said with a decisive nod. She paused, and the usual cheerful, carefree glimmer in her sister's sky-blue eyes turned uncharacteristically serious. She took Katherine's hands. "That day, I . . ." she shook her head, dislodging a single golden curl across her forehead. "I saw the crowd of onlookers and I knew. I . . ."

Katherine gave her hands a squeeze.

"I really am just so glad you were uninjured. I would be . . ."

Katherine nodded. "I know, Anne," she said quietly. "I should be lost without you as well."

Her sister kissed her cheek, and hurried from the room.

Katherine stared after her. They always had possessed an eerie ability to know just what the other was thinking, an ability to finish one another's sentences, even. It had grated on Mother's nerves to no end. She grinned in remembrance of the good fun they'd had as children tormenting their poor mother.

Her smile slipped as she considered the great disappointment she'd been to Mother since she'd made her Come Out last Season. Where Anne had a bevy of suitors, who'd come in all ranks and titles, Katherine had nary a one. Mother had held out hope that Anne could make an advantageous match with an available duke or marquess, whereas for Katherine, well, she'd held out hope that Katherine would make a match with anyone.

With her drab brown curls and brown eyes, she held no illusions of her appearance. She would never be the kind of beauty who would inspire any grand passion in any gentleman.

You'd be wise not to make designs upon my title, madam. I'd not wed you if you were the last creature in the kingdom.

Katherine shook her head. As though she'd ever deign to wed such a foul, odious creature. She remembered back to her sister's words about the Mad Duke and hated the blasted tug at her heart. It was hard to imagine the cold, unfeeling duke to have ever been capable of any emotion beyond icy derision, and yet, the Duke of Bainbridge must have truly loved his wife to have removed himself from Society.

She hated this desire to know more about him, and of the pain he carried. He was nothing to her. She would carry on and never see the Duke of . . .

Katherine swallowed as, for the first time in the two days since she'd fallen into the Thames River, she thought of her forgotten reticule.

The pendant!

Not that she believed in the foolishness of such a talisman, per se, but the bauble had been worn by her sister, and her sisters' friends, and they had believed it had brought them love . . . and Katherine had gone and lost it at the Frost Fair.

She shook her head. Anne didn't know of Katherine's find from the old peddler, and she could never find out.

The door opened, and she bit the inside of her cheek as her mother sailed through the entrance. "Anne said you are intending to go to the bookshop." Her tone suggested that Katherine's intended trip was as forbidden as a trip to visit the prisoners at Newgate.

She nodded. "I was just—"

"You are to take a footman."

"Of course," Katherine murmured.

Mother frowned. "I'd hardly say 'of course' is the appropriate response considering your scandalous outing at the Frost Fair."

Katherine bit the inside of her cheek to keep from pointing out that it had been her sister's madcap scheme. Ultimately, Katherine had gone along with those plans . . . and

Katherine wouldn't betray her sister's confidence—even to spare herself from Mother's haranguing.

"Is there anything else you'd like to speak with me about before I attend my shopping?"

Mother's frown darkened at Katherine's insolent attempt to end the conversation.

"I wanted to speak to you about Mr. Ekstrom."

A pit formed in Katherine's stomach. "There's really nothing to speak of, Mother," she murmured, hoping her words would be enough to end the conversation, knowing she was never that fortunate where her mother's tirades were concerned.

"I've grand hopes of the match Anne can make," Mother began, her meaning clear. Katherine had little hope of a truly advantageous union. Unlike Anne. "I do not know why you are being so difficult. If you wed him, then we'll not have to worry about Mr. Ekstrom hovering in the wings."

Katherine closed her eyes and counted to ten. When she opened them, she still felt no better and counted another ten. "Mother," she began calmly. "There is Benedict." Her brother, though young, would one day assume responsibility of the earldom. "He is the heir, there is no need to worry after the properties passing to the next in line."

"Bah." Her mother slashed the air with her hand. "Have you not learned how very easily one's circumstances can change? Think of the reassurance we might have if you were to wed Bertrand."

Reassurance.

So that is what Mother would have her wed for: a secondary protection against the possibility of losing their family's properties.

"Aldora and Michael would not let anything befall us." Her sister Aldora had wed for love but had been also fortunate enough to marry a wealthy gentleman—quite wealthy.

"If something were to happen to Benedict, you'd have us rely upon your sister and her husband's charity?"

Katherine flinched; her gaze fell to the floor. She'd rather not rely upon anyone's charity, and yet, how easily her mother spoke of bartering her happiness on the possibility of what-ifs. She'd not sacrifice Anne's future. No, with her beauty and talents Anne would strike an impressive match all on her own.

Unlike Katherine, who would rely upon the familial connection to her third cousin Bertrand, who stood just several inches taller than her five-foot frame, and possessed a paunch waist and padded chest.

"I can't, Mother." Perhaps if their circumstances were dire, then Katherine would consider sacrificing her happiness and future to a distant cousin with a love for kippers and boiled eggs.

Her mother glared at her. "You would be selfish in this regard?"

Katherine met her mother's glare directly. "I'd ask that we have this discussion after the holiday." Because then there was the hope that even Mother would be overcome by the Christmastide spirit and mayhap find generosity in her heart not to ask this great thing of Katherine. For if she did, Katherine would ultimately be forced to refuse the request.

"If you'll excuse me," Katherine murmured. Before her mother could protest she fled out the door. She wound her way through the house with a lively step, determined to place distance between her and Mother. When the countess dug her talons into something, she very rarely relinquished her hold.

She reached the foyer, and the butler, Ollie, greeted her with a twinkle in his glassy hazel-eyed stare. "I've taken the liberty of having the carriage readied for your shopping expedition, Lady Katherine."

Katherine smiled up at the tall, lean servant. "Thank you, Ollie."

He inclined his head, and held out her cloak.

Katherine fastened the garment at the collar, and reached for the green velvet–trimmed bonnet.

With the exception of the housekeeper, Isabel, Ollie had been in their family's employ longer than any other member of the staff. When they'd been forced to release the other members of the household, Ollie and Isabel had remained on.

They were as dear to Katherine as members of the family.

"Might I be so bold as to suggest you take your leave immediately, Lady Katherine?"

She grinned. His meaning was clear, as well. The countess was surely close, and it would be wise to hurry off, if Katherine truly desired her trip to the bookshop.

"You mustn't tell her where I've gone off to," she said quietly. It would have been one thing if Katherine had been planning an excursion to purchase ribbons or fabrics, but visiting an out of way bookshop on Old Bond Street was quite another.

"Why, I'm sure the countess will not mind in the slightest your trip to the modiste."

"The . . ." He gave her a small wink and her eyes widened. "Oh, ah, yes, the modiste. Very well, then."

Ollie pulled the door open and Katherine stepped outside into the swirl of snowflakes. She closed her eyes a moment and embraced the sweet silence that came from a winter snow, the rattle of carriage wheels muted by the blanket of flakes that covered the pavement.

Katherine opened her eyes and all but sprinted down the steps, into the waiting carriage. She gave a murmured thanks to the driver and settled back into the seat. The carriage lurched forward.

With the privacy of her own company, she considered her mother's request, a request that was coming more and more frequent, and bore the strong traces of a stern command. She'd have Katherine wed Bertrand.

She folded her hands into the fabric of her taffeta skirts, wrinkling the fabric.

You'd be wise not to make designs upon my title, madam. I'd not wed you if you were the last creature in the kingdom.

The duke's taunting words continued to dance along the edges of her musings.

With his thickly muscled, broad chest and towering height, a man such as the duke would have no need for a padded chest, or a padded anything for that matter. Nor would he bear the stench of rotten fish and boiled eggs. Rather, he'd borne the faintest hint of mint and honey upon his breath. She stared out the window at the passing scenery. So very odd to think that one so hard and cruel should smell of anything so delicately sweet as honey.

The carriage rattled along the streets of London until it stopped in front of Fedgewick's Bookshop. The driver pulled the door open, and helped hand Katherine down.

She waved off the footman who jumped from the top of the box. "I'll just be a short while."

He hesitated.

"Rest assured, there is no dangerously thin ice inside the bookshop," she said dryly.

The young man's lips twitched at the corners in what she suspected was amusement, and with a bow, he then climbed back into his seat.

Katherine glanced, first left down Old Bond Street, and then right. It would seem all of London had been scared away by a few snowflakes. She raised her gloved hand to the sky and caught a fat, fluffy flake between her fingers. As long as she could remember she'd loved the purity of the winter season, the hope represented at Christmastide.

Energized by the winter weather, Katherine moved with a bounce in her step up to the door of the shop. She pressed the handle and entered.

A tinny little bell jingled, to alert the shopkeeper of someone's presence. The man hurried over, a wide smile on his face.

"Hello, my lady. I have some new selections for you." The portly, middle-aged shopkeeper pushed his wire-rimmed spectacles back upon his nose.

"Do you?" Katherine said, with a smile. Her gaze caught upon someone at the opposite end of the small shop. "I . . ." The tall figure shifted. "I . . ." There could be no mistaking that bear of a man.

As though feeling her gaze upon him, his broad shoulders stiffened, the muscles straining the fabric of his midnight-black jacket.

The Duke of Bainbridge turned. He raked his cold stare over her person from the top of her head to the tips of her toes.

Bloody hell.

Chapter 6

B loody hell.

    Of all the blasted, rotten luck. He should venture out amongst the living, only to see *her*, once again?!

Jasper glared over at Lady Katherine Adamson. Surely there was no coincidence in her arrival at the bookshop, and yet, how would she have discovered his whereabouts that morning? Perhaps a disloyal servant? He'd sack the lot of them.

"Lady Katherine Adamson," he hissed.

He expected the underlining fury that threaded those three words would have sent her fleeing. Instead, her back went up, and she tipped her chin up a notch. She glared right back at him.

"Your Grace." It didn't escape his notice that she failed to curtsy. She stood there, eyes blazing, with a recalcitrant tilt to her head.

The bookkeeper looked back and forth between them, and cleared his throat. "Er, uh . . . if you'll e-excuse m-me," he stammered.

At least the small, round shopkeeper had the sense to flee.

Jasper returned his attention to the volume of Wordsworth's latest work, in his hands. The hard wood of the floors cracked and groaned in protest, indicating that Lady Katherine had at last moved from her place at the front of the shop.

He stared absently at the title, all the while considering the diminutive vixen. He'd not allowed himself to think of her in two days, had not wanted to think about her, and certainly didn't understand why she continued to traipse through his miserable thoughts. The only rational, coherent, plausible reason he came to was the fact that she, unlike everyone else, seemed wholly unfazed by his presence.

It defied logic and reason and . . .

"You read Wordsworth?"

Jasper's body stiffened, and his fingers tightened around the volume. With a growl, he set it back upon the shelf.

He looked down at her. Her head was tilted at a funny little angle, her brown, unblinking eyes wide in her face.

"Do you not mind your own affairs, my lady?"

Lady Katherine ignored his question. She reached past him, and plucked the copy of Wordsworth's poems from the shelf. Her brown eyes scanned the title. She opened it and fanned through several pages, pausing, and . . .

"What are you doing?" he bit out.

"Reading," she replied, not taking her eyes off the page.

He blinked. The young ladies he'd remembered of the haute *ton* did not issue insolent, one-word utterances.

She snapped the leather volume closed with a decisive snap, and held it to her chest.

Jasper counted to ten. He didn't want to ask. He didn't want to feed the mischievous glimmer in her brown eyes. "What are you doing now?" But the damned words tumbled from his lips.

"I'm purchasing this book, Your Grace."

Jasper's eyes did a quick inventory of the shelf. The lone, solitary copy of *The Excursion* tightly gripped in the lady's fingers. He gritted his teeth. "Madam, you've taken my copy."

She held a finger up. "*You* put the copy back upon the shelf, and *I* am purchasing it."

"Young ladies are supposed to read the drivel spouted off by Byron."

She snorted. "Is that so, Your Grace? My, you are very well-versed in the proper behaviors of young ladies."

His eyes narrowed. What manner of lady ventured out on a snowy day, once again unchaperoned, entered a bookshop, and proceeded to steal the single copy of Wordsworth's latest works from a duke, no less?

He took a step toward her. She remained fixed to her spot. The book clutched to her chest hinted at her nervousness.

Which drew Jasper's attention downward, to the ever so small gap in her emerald-green cloak that revealed generously plump breasts. He froze, transfixed. Not even when he'd rescued Lady Katherine Adamson had he noted the feel of her against him. He'd been so bloody cold, and livid. Now, in the dimly lit bookshop, he fought to tear his gaze away.

"Your Grace?"

Jasper jerked his attention back to her face. She scratched her quizzical brow.

He gave his head a hard shake, and took another step toward her until they were a hairsbreadth apart, until she was forced to either step away or tilt her head back to meet his furious stare.

Jasper should have expected that a spirited woman like Lady Katherine would toss back her head, and meet his gaze squarely.

"I do not know what manner of games you play, madam. I do not appreciate your dogging my steps. I'll not be trapped into marriage."

Katherine's eyes widened, as she met the pitiless Duke of Bainbridge's flinty stare. The condescending pull of his lips, the hard glint in his pale-green eyes perfectly suited a formidable duke used to having his every wish obeyed.

The absurdity of his charge, she expected, should have outraged her. She dug around in search of the proper indignation and yet . . . "You believe I would want to wed you?" she blurted. She giggled. "You believe I would want to trap *you*?" she repeated. His claim was all too preposterous. "Surely you jest?"

The firm, square line of his jaw hardened; the faint cleft at the center pulsed ever so slightly, as testament to his agitation.

It also confirmed how very serious he was.

Laughter burst from Katherine's chest. The book tumbled from her fingers, and she pressed her fingers over her mouth to stifle her mirth. "I-I'm s-sorry. F-forgive me," she managed between laughter. She desperately tried to rein in her outburst, but then she caught sight of the duke's ever-narrowing gaze, and her laughter redoubled. Katherine dashed a hand across her eyes, to wipe away the traces of tears that had seeped from the corners of her eyes. "Your Grace," she began. "I will forever be indebted to you for your rescue at the Frost Fair, however, I would not have you. Ever."

She meant those words to reassure him that she had no designs upon his title. His deepening scowl, however, seemed to indicate that her words were having the opposite effect.

Katherine stooped down, and retrieved the copy of Wordsworth's poems.

"You think my charge so very hard to believe," he said, his voice harsh with some unknown emotion. "You've failed to make a match after your first Season," he pointed out, as though Katherine needed a reminder from the Mad Duke.

Fury moved with a life-force through her veins. Oh, the insolence of the man. How could the gossips possibly be correct about his late wife? This coarse, hateful creature was not, nor could have ever been, capable of love. "I do not care if I had one Season or ten Seasons, I would not forsake my own self-worth for a gentleman who speaks ill of me, condescends me upon every turn, who . . ." She furrowed her brow. "How do you know I failed to make a match after a single Season?"

He blinked, and it occurred to her that the normally unflappable duke appeared startled by her question. *Hmm, well this was very interesting, indeed.* Not even her near drowning, his subsequent tenuous rescue, and the unchaperoned carriage ride had seemed to rattle him. And yet, this one question should silence him.

The duke smoothed his palms along the front of his coat sleeves. "It was merely a supposition on my part."

Katherine angled her head. "Yes, but you didn't say two or three or four Seasons. You said one." She smiled. "Never tell me you've been doing research on me, Your Grace?"

"Do not be preposterous," he snapped. "I do not conduct research on people." He raked a gaze over her person. "Particularly unwed young females."

He intended the words as an insult, that much was clear in his tone, and yet, his gaze lingered longer than was proper upon her plump breasts.

Katherine had always despaired over the unseemly mounds of flesh; her mother had even forced her to wear bindings, until one night Katherine had fainted from the tightness of the cloth wrapped about her person. Something in the duke's eyes; a hot, penetrating stare, however, made her feel, for the first time, the tiniest bit of female power.

Which was outright laughable. The Duke of Bainbridge had been abundantly clear that he no more desired her than she desired him.

And yet, she reveled in his focus. It made her feel the same heady power that Eve had surely felt after tempting Adam with that sinful piece of fruit in the Garden of Eden.

"Do you require any assistance, my lady?"

Katherine jumped at the unexpected appearance of the shopkeeper. He alternated his gaze between Katherine and the duke; a slight frown of disapproval on his small lips.

She smiled. "No, I am finding everything rather easily. Why, I found the sole remaining copy of *The Excursion*."

The duke's mouth flattened.

Katherine winked up at him as the shopkeeper returned to the front of the shop.

She made to step around the duke, but then, something gave her pause. It was the slightest something, reflected in the greens of his eyes, now deepened to the shade of emeralds, a glitter of emotion he likely didn't think himself capable of.

Pain.

The Mad Duke.

Her smile faded as she imagined him as an altogether different man; one who smiled, and teased, and loved. And who was also so very lonely at the Christmastide season. Katherine glanced down at the book, and then cleared her throat. "Here." She held the book out to him.

He stood stock-still, studying her with an inscrutable expression. Katherine pressed the volume into his hands. "I really wasn't all that interested in reading it," she lied. She'd been looking forward to reading Wordsworth's latest poem for an inordinate deal of time. There would be others.

She detected the white-knuckled grip he had upon the leather spine. "I don't need—"

"I'm sure you don't need anything, Your Grace. But sometimes, it is nice to simply have things one wants." Katherine dipped a curtsy, and continued on down the long row of shelving. All the while, she felt his gaze boring a hole into her back. She stole a sideways peek, and found him rooted to the same spot, studying her as if she were an oddity at the Egyptian Hall.

Katherine yanked her gaze back to the books in front of her. To give herself something to do, she tugged free the nearest book her fingers touched.

"I'd not accept pity from you," a low voice said close to her ear.

Katherine jumped. The book tumbled to the floor and landed upon the tips of her slipper. A gasp escaped her, as she shifted the injured toes.

The duke cursed. "Are you injured?"

She grimaced, shifting to alleviate the throbbing ache in her toes. "I survived a plunge into the Thames, I imagine I should be handling an injured foot a good deal better."

He grinned.

Katherine's heart rhythm increased several quick beats. Goodness, when he smiled, it transformed him into a really rather remarkable man. When she'd first made her Come Out, she'd visited the Royal Museum and observed the chiseled work of Michelangelo's *David*. With his smile, the duke could rival that great statue for a place of beauty.

Perhaps madness was contagious.

He bent down and retrieved the forgotten book. He turned it over in his hands, studying the title, his familiar frown back in place. Only . . . his lips twitched at the corner.

Katherine glanced at the title, and heat flooded her cheeks. "Er . . . uh . . . I . . ." *The Works of Leigh Hunt?!* Egad, the poet who'd been sentenced to prison by the Prince Regent for libel. Well, Katherine would certainly have a good deal of explaining to do if polite Society believed she read such scandalous works.

She accepted the book from him, and promptly stuffed it back on the crowded bookshelf. "I don't read Leigh Hunt's work," she said, detecting the defensive note in her words.

The duke inclined his head. "It would not matter if you did."

"Oh, it certainly would," she said. She could only imagine the furor if the *ton* believed the plain, bluestocking Adamson twin read the work of Leigh Hunt. "Not that I do. Because I don't," she said, hurriedly. Katherine bit the inside of her cheek to keep from rattling on. "Very well, then. I must be going."

Before the duke could utter another word, she spun on her heel and quickly exited the shop. A blanket of white covered the pavement, the snow that rained down from the sky, large, fluffy flakes. A sweet, uncharacteristic quiet filled the London air. Katherine searched around for her carriage.

From over her shoulder she detected the faint jingle of the bell from inside the bookshop, then the steady crunch of boots turning up the fresh snow.

Katherine's back straightened, and she resisted the urge to glance over her shoulder. She didn't need to look. She knew he was there, watching, walking over to her . . . and still, his commanding presence didn't fail to unnerve her.

Katherine gasped, as the duke stopped alongside her. She slapped a hand to her breast and spun to face him. "Must you always—"

"Here," he said, gruffly.

She blinked at the wrapped package in his hands.

"Take it," he ordered.

Katherine looked around, aware of the impropriety of accepting a gift from a gentleman, in a very public place, no less. Except the streets remained eerily empty, devoid of people passing by. She took the wrapped package from him, and proceeded to open it.

The Excursion.

Her heart did a quick pause, and then resumed its steady tempo. "No, you mustn't . . ."

She spun around in search of the duke, but his long-legged stride had put considerable distance between them; his black cloak stirred about his powerful legs, in a stark contrast to the white snow.

Her gaze fell to the book he'd given her. He was a perfectly odious bounder, and yet, twice now he'd shocked her with his generosity; one in risking his life to save her, and two in allowing her the sole copy of *The Excursion*. He struck her as a self-centered, unfeeling nobleman, and yet, with unexpected gestures, continued to defy the image of a boorish lout.

And Katherine hated that she did not know what to make of the gentleman. She preferred a world where black was black and white was white, and there were no colors in between. Her father's betrayal taught her that gentlemen were ultimately selfish creatures who put their own comforts and desires before all else.

In her clear world, with his harsh treatment and callous words, he was a reprehensible fiend.

But in a suddenly *unclear* world, the same duke who'd purchased the expensive volume for himself had now given it to her.

She dusted her gloved finger along the trace of snow that coated the leather cover. When she'd first learned of her family's financial situation, she'd lain awake in the middle of the night, a crushing fear upon her chest. In those scariest of times, she'd found solace in Wordsworth's poems. The sonnets had reminded her that for as tenuous as her circumstances were, and for all the fear she carried, there was always some far greater sadness.

Thinking of the Duke of Bainbridge, and all he'd lost, she rather believed he'd known that *greater sadness*. When she'd plucked the volume from the shelf, she'd hoped to aggravate the flinty-eyed duke. Now, staring down at it, considering what he'd done, and more importantly, what he'd known, Katherine knew very well it would be wrong for her to keep the book.

Just then, the footman rushed over to help relieve her of her package. She held a hand up. "Stephens, I need to return to the bookshop. I need to pen a note, and when I've finished, I'll require you to deliver this package to someone." Katherine handed it over to him, and turned back to the bookshop.

In that moment, Katherine realized the duke was not all he seemed.

And she didn't know why that thought should terrify her as it did.

Chapter 7

Jasper stomped his way through the snow, down the long stretch of pavement, onward toward his Mayfair Street townhouse, his hands empty from his visit at the bookshop.

He gritted his teeth so hard, pain shot from his jawline, and radiated up to his temple.

He'd recognized that look in her eyes; her eyes that put him of mind of warmed Belgian chocolate. The winter air swallowed the growl that climbed up his throat.

What in the name of St. Stanislaus was the matter with him?

He was the bloody Duke of Bainbridge. The Mad Duke, as Society referred to him. He did not wax poetic about the color of ladies' eyes. He had, once upon a lifetime ago, when he'd courted Lydia. But not any longer. He drew on her name, and closed his eyes momentarily. He froze.

Wind whipped around him, harsh and punishing, and he embraced the sting of the winter storm.

Jasper clenched his eyes tight, willing her precious face back into focus. Her eyes. They'd been blue. But the exact shade, he could no longer envision with his imagining.

As if in mockery of his efforts, Lady Katherine's brown eyes, filled with fire and passion, flitted through his mind.

Jasper shook his head and continued walking.

He could explain away his fascination with Lady Katherine. She, unlike the lords and ladies who'd had the misfortune of crossing his miserable path, appeared wholly uncowed by him. Rather, she seemed to find an unholy delight in tormenting him.

Since Lydia's death, nay, since he'd killed her, people had been wise to avoid him, and what was more, fear him. People didn't dare speak to him. And they certainly didn't tease him.

But Lady Katherine did.

Yes, he could explain away his fascination with the young lady. He could not, however, explain what had possessed him to purchase that damned volume of Wordsworth's and run after her like some callow youth.

Over the years, Jasper had embraced the stark coldness that filled him. For a man without a heart could never again know the mind-numbing pain of losing one's wife and child.

Then Lady Katherine had fallen into the Thames River and upended his icy world.

Seeming incapable of guile, she wore her every emotion upon her face like an artist's palate of colored paints. The lady's outrage, her fury, the amusement, hope, all of it, etched out upon the graceful lines of her heart-shaped face. She reminded him of the fresh innocence he'd possessed, of a simpler time, of the joy he'd known, before his world had fallen apart.

And it scared the bloody hell out of him.

At long last, Jasper arrived at his white stucco townhouse with the cold brick front that suited the bleakness of his life. He stomped up the steps.

As if on cue, the door opened, and Jasper sailed through the entrance. He shrugged out of his cloak, and tossed it to a waiting footman.

"Your Grace," the butler greeted with a deep bow.

Jasper gave a curt nod in greeting and continued onward down the long corridors, through the length of the house. He paused outside his office door a moment, and then entered.

Jasper kicked the door closed with the heel of his boot. A panicky sensation gripped his chest. He counted to ten, and when it didn't help, he counted again. Since Lydia's death, he'd found that focusing on those small, succinct numbers diverted his thoughts away from any unwelcome thoughts or emotions.

He crossed over to the rose-inlaid mahogany table and picked up a decanter of brandy. He poured the amber contents to the rim of a glass, and carried it over to the window. Jasper stared out into the intensifying storm, the flakes swirling outside the windowpane. He took a slow sip.

Coming to London had been the height of foolishness. He'd allowed Guilford to cajole him into paying a visit to his townhouse. As most members of the *ton* had left for their country-seats to celebrate the Christmastide season, Jasper would be spared the pointed glances and snide whispers as they gossiped about the Mad Duke. Ultimately, he'd been too much a coward to face the ugly remembrances that lived within the castle walls.

A knock sounded on his office door.

"Enter," he called, his gaze fixed in the streets below.

The door opened.

Then the soft shuffle of steps. "Your Grace, a package arrived for you."

Jasper stiffened.

A package?

"Your Grace?" the butler asked hesitantly.

"Leave it on my desk." *And get the hell out.* The words screamed inside his head, but he remained silent. He stared down into the contents of his brandy. He didn't want any blasted company this day. He blinked as the rich hue put him in mind of a fiery pair of brown eyes. "Christ," he hissed. Jasper downed his brandy in one long swallow, welcoming the trail it blazed down his throat.

He set the empty glass down upon a nearby table, and looked over to the package on his desk.

The fabric, dampened from fresh melted snow, was familiar.

Jasper hesitated, and then strode over to the desk. He picked up the package and undid the velvet ribbon that held the fabric together.

The Excursion

He fanned the pages of the book.

A note slipped out.

The Jasper Waincourt, 8th Duke of Bainbridge, cold, heartless bastard he'd become after Lydia's death wouldn't care about the blasted contents of the letter. That Jasper would have crossed to the hearth and hurled an unread note into the flames.

The Jasper Waincourt who'd attended the Frost Fair and rescued a young, unchaperoned lady bent down, and opened the scrap.

Your Grace,

I understand you find my company objectionable, which is all right, considering I'm not overly fond of your frowning countenance.

Jasper smiled, and continued reading.

I am, however, eternally grateful for your rescue. Even if you are not. Grateful to have rescued me, that is.

That gave Jasper pause.

The young lady couldn't be more wrong. It would have been a sad day if the light in Lady Katherine's eyes had been forever darkened by the icy river waters. The vellum crackled in his hands, and he forced himself to lighten his hold upon the page. He didn't care to consider just why it should matter so much to him. It just did.

> I greatly appreciate the kindness you showed this afternoon in offering me the sole copy of *The Excursion*. In spite of how it may have seemed, I was not merely baiting you. I am in fact, an ardent admirer of Wordsworth's work. Though in actuality, I did have a good deal of fun teasing you as well.
>
> I digress . . .
>
> I hope you enjoy the pages, as they should be enjoyed.
>
> Signed,
> Lady Katherine Adamson

Jasper examined the note, almost willing there to be more than—his finger tapped the parchment as he counted—ten . . . he blinked. She'd dashed ten sentences upon the page.

That diversionary number that had brought him temporary distractions over the years.

He strode over to the hearth, paper in hand, and extended it toward the flame. Black singed the thick ivory vellum, as the hint of a flame licked at the corners.

Jasper cursed and with his hand, killed the faint stirrings of a flame. The ink used by Lady Katherine smeared and smudged, but it remained readable.

Letter in hand, Jasper made his way over to his desk, pulled out the overstuffed leather chair, and sat.

It would be madness to send a note to the young lady. Jasper didn't give three goddamns on Sunday about propriety. Society could go hang.

It was this desire to write the note in the first place that should reserve him a spot at Bedlam.

But then, they did not call him the Mad Duke for little reason.

He tugged open the front drawer of his desk and pulled out a single sheet of parchment. Then, reaching for a pen, he dipped it in an inkwell, and proceeded to write a note to Lady Katherine.

The tip of his pen upon the paper tapped an annoyingly loud rhythm upon the hard surface of his desk. Jasper again dipped his pen in ink.

A knock sounded at the door.

"Enter," Jasper barked, not picking his head up.

What the hell did his butler want with him now? "Has the bloody Queen of England come to visit," he called, heavy sarcasm intended in that question.

"I do say I've never been confused for the Queen of England. That is certainly a first."

Jasper's head whipped up so quickly, he wrenched his neck. "Guilford," he said. He rubbed the aching muscles.

His friend strode over to the table with crystal decanters and poured himself a brandy. Glass in hand, he wandered over to claim the seat across from Jasper. His gaze paused a moment on the empty brandy glass. His eyes narrowed, and then his probing stare swung to the nearly completed letter. "What are you doing?" Guilford craned his neck in an apparent attempt to read Jasper's private correspondence.

Not that Lady Katherine was his business. She wasn't.

She was . . .

A winsome, fiery miss.

Where the hell did that thought come from?

One. Two. Three. Fou—

"Bainbridge, I say are you all right?"

"Fine," he snapped.

"Because you don't seem nearly as surly as your usual self. Oh, do not be mistaken, you're still quite foul, just not as foul as you usually are."

He'd had enough of his friend baiting him. Jasper tossed his pen down. "What do you want?" *He* personally wanted the other man gone so he could see to his letter for Lady Katherine.

Guilford hooked his ankle across his knee. "I wanted to issue an invitation to join my family for the Christmastide—"

"No," Jasper cut in. He did not celebrate the holiday season. The godforsaken time of year represented birth and life. His lips twisted at the bitter irony that it also coincided with the time Lydia and his child had been cruelly ripped from the living.

Guilford continued, either unaware or uncaring of Jasper's silent tumult. "I'd also wanted to inquire as to whether you'd returned the young lady's reticule?"

Lady Katherine as she'd been earlier that afternoon, with a mischievous smile and too-full laugh, flashed to mind. It would appear the ice princess had thawed, and in her place was a lively creature that continued to wreak havoc upon his life. He'd not encourage Guilford's questioning. "Which lady?" Jasper growled.

His friend grinned. "Never tell me you've heroically rescued another young lady besides Lady Katherine Adamson?"

"I didn't—"

"I merely noted that since you met your Lady Katherine you seem in a far less black mood than usual."

"She is not *my* Lady Katherine." He spoke through clenched teeth. "Do not make more of what took place at the Frost Fair than there was." Jasper picked up his pen and proceeded to compose his note to Lady Katherine. He'd not dare mention to Guilford that the high-spirted creature had occupied a corner of his mind since that chance meeting upon the Thames River. "The lady's affairs are her own."

"Oh?" Guilford took a sip. "I'd just imagined you'd be curious about the young lady."

Jasper began to count. He'd not indulge his friend. Jasper was not curious about anything, particularly marriageable misses with tart tongues. "Why should I care about matters involving the young lady?" The question was spoken for both Guilford's benefit, as much as for his own.

Guilford passed his glass back and forth between his hands. "Very well, then I shall not mention . . ." He took another slow, deliberate drink.

Jasper folded his hands on top of the desk. "What?" that one curt question cost him the hard-won effort to maintain a semblance of disinterest where the lady was concerned.

"Rumors would have it that her mother, the Countess of Wakefield, is eager to make a match between Lady Katherine and Mr. Bertrand Ekstrom." Jasper's brows dipped. What parent would dare wed their child to Bertrand Ekstrom? Jasper had known the loathsome bully in his Oxford days. It was no secret that the bastard had unnatural proclivities behind chamber doors. On the heel of that thought came the sickening image of Bertrand Ekstrom's stubby fingers binding Katherine's wrists to a bedpost and . . .

The pen snapped in his fingers.

Guilford frowned. "Are you all right?"

No, he was not all right, and he wished his friend would leave him to his own miseries. Jasper yanked his top desk drawer open and pulled out another pen.

Guilford carried on with a wave of his hand. "It would seem Ekstrom is next in line for the earldom behind Lady Katherine's young brother." His brow furrowed. "The boy's a mere thirteen or fourteen years, I believe."

Jasper would have bartered his own black soul to the devil for just one more breath from his son. Yet, Lady Katherine's mother would consign her to a life in which she'd be subjected to Ekstrom's perversions all on the possibility of a what-if? In that moment, he was struck by something he'd thought long dead and buried—sympathy for Lady Katherine. Such a spirited, bold woman deserved far more than an avaricious parent who'd sacrifice her happiness.

Guilford must have detected that he had an avid audience with Jasper, for he went on in a low, hushed tone. "I've heard Ekstrom has taken to using hot wax to scald . . ."

A film of red rage descended across his vision at the thought of Katherine's skin marred by the weasly bastard. He forced himself to take a steadying breath. "I know what you are attempting to do."

Because in the end, Lady Katherine and her future didn't matter to him. Jasper's future included no one and that was far safer than worrying after the fate of one young lady.

His friend sat forward in his seat. "Oh, and what is that?"

"The lady does not matter," he lied. She did. Whether Jasper wished it or not. Perhaps it was the bond of pulling her flailing body from the river and thumping water from her lungs until she breathed once more. Then his interest in her future could be explained. It should not matter the tinkling bell-like quality of her laughter, or the impish smile . . . his fascination with such attributes could be less easily explained.

Guilford finished his brandy, and set his empty glass down upon the edge of Jasper's desk. "You'd live your life where no one matters, Bainbridge. You'd go through life cold, unfeeling, untouched. That"—he shook his head—"well, that is a sad way to live."

Jasper surged to his feet. "What would you have me do?"

"I'd have you rejoin the living," Guilford replied automatically. He stood and met Jasper's stare. "I do not know if there is any real interest on your part in the Lady Katherine. I don't know if there is any young lady who could ever recapture your heart after Lydia's death. But I would that you try and at least find happiness where you can."

Jasper waited for the familiar sensation, that sensation of being kicked in the gut whenever he heard his wife's name mentioned.

It didn't come.

Which in itself sucked the breath from his lungs. He gripped the edge of his desk.

Guilford glanced down, and said nothing for a long while. They stood locked in a silent, unspoken battle. His friend broke the silence. He gestured to the surface of Jasper's desk. "I do know a gentleman does not pen notes to, how did you phrase it? Ladies that do not matter?"

Jasper opened his mouth to reply, but could not force words out.

Guilford bowed his head. "If you'll excuse me." He started for the door.

The hiss and pop of the blazing fire in the hearth filled the quiet. "I don't want your help, Guilford," Jasper barked after him.

His friend turned back to face him with a smile. "Fortunate for you, I don't care, Bainbridge." He closed the door behind him with a firm click.

Jasper stared at the door, long after Guilford had taken his leave. He reclaimed his seat, and stared blankly down at the note he'd penned. Guilford was his last remaining friend in the world, but oh, how he loathed the other man, just then. How dare Guilford force him to come London, and what's more, force him to confront what, until this very moment, he'd denied—he, Jasper Waincourt, 8th Duke of Bainbridge, was—lonely.

Jasper blinked down at the letter he'd written to Katherine. Guilford was correct. Gentlemen did not pen notes to ladies that did not matter.

He picked up the thick ivory vellum and crushed it in his hands.

Chapter 8

There was a time when meadow, grove, and stream,
The earth, and every common sight,
To me did seem
Apparell'd in celestial light,
The glory and the freshness of a dream.
It is not now as it hath been of yore;—
Turn wheresoe'er I may,
By night or day,
The things which I have seen I now can see no more.

—William Wordsworth, "Ode: Intimations
of Immortality from Recollections of Early
Childhood" in *Poems, in Two Volumes*

he words roused thoughts of the Duke of Bainbridge, as she considered the reality that they were
not so very different after all. Life had altered them both in
very profound ways.

A knock sounded at the door. She glanced up.

The butler cleared his throat. "You have a letter, my lady."

Her mother and sister's gazes swung to Katherine.

Anne set aside her embroidery frame and edged closer to
Ollie. She craned her neck in an apparent attempt to identify
the wax seal upon the missive.

With a frown, the servant pulled the silver tray bearing
the missive closer.

Katherine's heart warmed at his silent defense of her personal privacy.

Mother returned her attention to the embroidery frame stitched with a colorful peacock. "Who has written you, Katherine?"

Katherine bit the inside of her cheek to keep from pointing out that she surely could not yet know who'd written. "I'm not certain, Mother," she murmured, and accepted the thick, ivory vellum with a smile for Ollie. He gave an imperceptible nod, and ever so quickly winked at her.

She looked down at the letter with a familiar seal. A crest that bore a lion rearing up on its legs. Her heart paused.

"Who is it from, Katherine?" her sister asked with a dogged interest.

"Benedict," she replied instantly.

Anne frowned, and shot her a look that said she knew that Katherine lied.

Suddenly eager to escape her sister's probing fascination, lest her mother shift her attention away from the embroidery she presently worked on, Katherine stood. "If you'll excuse me. I find myself developing a megrim."

Her sister made no effort to conceal the unladylike snort that escaped her.

Katherine hurried out of the room, and wound her way through the house, abovestairs to her own chambers. She glanced over her shoulder to ascertain whether her sister had followed, and then slipped inside.

She closed the door, and turned the lock.

Katherine leaned against the door, and considered the letter in her hands. The Duke of Bainbridge did not strike her as the type of gentleman who penned words to young ladies. Her lips twitched with amusement. Quite the opposite.

She rather suspected he'd rather send all females, wed and unwed, to the devil quite happily.

Katherine slid her finger under the seal and unfolded the note.

My Lady,

I understand you are not overly fond of my, as you put it, frowning countenance, however, I would be remiss if I failed to write and inform you that I am grateful. Grateful to have rescued you, that is.

Katherine smiled, and continued reading.

Allow me to express my most humble appreciation to you for turning over the sole copy of Wordsworth's latest work to my ownership. In spite of my frowning countenance that day, I was not displeased with your generosity. I too am, in fact, an ardent admirer of Wordsworth's work.

I hope you will allow me to return the copy to your care upon my completion of the volume so that you might enjoy the pages, as they should be enjoyed.

Signed,
Bainbridge

Post Script

I understand by the words in your note that you did have a good deal of fun teasing me. You are forgiven.

A sharp bark of laughter burst from Katherine, and she stifled it with the tips of her fingers.

It would seem she'd learned something else about the Duke of Bainbridge—he did appear to have a sense of humor, after all.

Katherine folded up the note, and held it to her breast as she considered the implications of his words. If the duke were the cruel, heartless lout he'd presented since their first meeting, surely he'd be incapable of the words he'd written her. Nor, for that matter, would a callous figure of a man deign to read poetry, or send along a note of gratitude, or tease her for her own words.

Katherine walked over to her vanity and pulled open the front drawer. She placed the duke's note in the top and slid it closed. And then froze.

What foolishness was this? Keeping his note? It was not something a young lady kept, unless there was a reason in keeping it.

And there wasn't. A reason to keep it, that was.

Except . . .

Katherine sighed, and slid into the delicate mahogany rose-inlaid chair. She fetched a pen and parchment from her vanity drawer, and chewing her lip, studied the paper.

Your Grace,

I am so very honored . . .

An unladylike curse slipped past her lips. She wrinkled the parchment, and tossed it to the floor.

She dipped her pen into the ink, and made another attempt.

Your Grace,

I am eagerly awaiting the return of . . .

Katherine sat back with a huff, and tossed aside her next weakly started letter.

Why was she struggling so greatly to find the words to write to him?

Katherine began again.

Your Grace,

I thank you for your unexpectedly kind words. I'm glad that you're glad I did not perish in the Thames River.

She grimaced, but continued writing.

I must also thank you for the generous offer of Wordsworth's book. I would be most grateful if once completed, you did, indeed, share your volume with me.

> With Deepest Appreciation,
> Lady Katherine

Post Script

Though I do not care to hurry your efforts along, my family leaves in six days' time to celebrate the Christmastide holiday in the country, and it would be appreciated if I had Wordsworth's work for my long carriage ride.

Katherine read and reread the contents of the note several times, and then carefully folded it.

A knock sounded at the door.

Katherine jumped to her feet. She quickly stuffed the note into the top drawer of her vanity.

Another knock.

She hurried across the wood floor, the tread of her slippers nearly silent.

Katherine unlocked the door and pulled it open. She shrieked and slapped a hand to her racing heart. "Anne, you frightened me."

Her sister rushed inside. She closed the door behind them, and turned the lock.

"Mother wants you to make a match with cousin Bertrand," she said without preamble.

Katherine's heart froze, and then thudded painfully in her breast. She'd assumed Mother would allow the matter of Bertrand Ekstrom to rest for at least the Christmastide season. She'd hoped with the coming of a new Season, that Mother would set aside her rather low aspirations for Katherine, and allow her to make a match with . . . with . . . well, anyone other than cousin Bertrand.

"You can't wed him," Anne said flatly. She began to pace. "Neither of us can wed him."

"Mother wouldn't dare wed you to Mr. Ekstrom," Katherine said, unable to keep the bitter tinged resentment from her tone.

Her sister glanced at her. "Well, she daren't wed you to him, either. There is simply no need. Benedict is the current earl, and Aldora's husband has settled a grand sum upon us." She shook her head. "No, no. Marriage to him will simply not do." Anne stopped midstride, and pointed her finger at the air. "We shall simply have to find you a husband."

A laugh escaped Katherine. "You speak of it as though we're hunters in search of the local fowl." Her sister was fanciful and hopeful, but a hopelessly dangerous romantic.

Anne wrinkled her nose. "That is a rather horrid comparison." She shook her head. "It is settled. We will find you a husband."

Katherine scoffed. "Oh, and where do you propose to find this unwed gentleman before the start of the next Season?"

Unbidden the Duke of Bainbridge's harshly angular cheeks, his firm lips, and his tall, commanding form slipped into her mind. She gave her head a hard shake.

Anne's brows snapped together into a single line. "What is it?" she asked with all the intuitiveness of a twin sister who'd recognized more in Katherine's unspoken words.

I do not know what manner of games you play, madam. I do not appreciate your dogging my steps. I'll not be trapped into marriage.

Those were not the words of a man who'd gladly wed her, nor were they the words of a gentleman she should like to wed. No, Katherine didn't imagine she'd ever make a love match. She'd long ago accepted the cold practicality of an arrangement between her and a perfectly suitable, properly boring gentleman. That was the way of their world. But neither had she imagined herself wed to a coolly disdainful gentleman like the duke.

She shook her head. Mere desperation was what drove her fanciful musings.

"You have a gentleman who's captured your attention," Anne said on a gasp.

Katherine felt a rush of heat climb up her neck, and flood her cheeks. She shook her head adamantly. "No. No. Not at all. There is not anyone. There isn't," she insisted when her sister continued to study her with a probing stare.

Anne tapped the tip of her finger against her lower lip in a contemplative manner. "We must simply find that pendant. If we find it, then you won't have to bother with Mother's efforts between you and that loathsome Mr. Ekstrom."

A wave of guilt slammed into Katherine as she thought of the heart pendant contained within the reticule she'd lost at the Frost Fair. Even if she herself didn't believe in the powers of the pendant, it did not mean her sister did not. Aldora believed it had led her to her true love, Michael Knightly, and now Anne believed it would guide her to her future husband.

Anne's eyes lit with that mischievous glimmer Katherine had long ago learned promised trouble.

"No," Katherine said firmly.

"I didn't say anything," Anne groused.

"You were going to say—"

"That we should return to the Frost Fair," Anne finished for her.

Nausea churned in her belly at the mere thought of venturing out upon the Thames River. She fisted the fabric of her modest skirts and gave her head a firm shake.

Anne gesticulated wildly. "We never were able to search more than a handful of tents for the pendant that will lead us to the heart of a duke."

Katherine would require something a good deal more powerful than a silly talisman like the heart pendant to make a match. "No."

"But . . ."

"I said no, Anne."

"Hmph," Anne said with a flounce of her curls. "I'm merely trying to help you, Katherine."

Katherine felt immediately contrite. Society saw Anne as one of the Incomparables, but little else beyond that. Katherine knew, for the world's shallow perception of Anne, her sister was, in fact, good and loyal and would put her own siblings' happiness before even her own.

Katherine glanced down at the toes of her slippers. "It's unlikely I'll make a match in the next fortnight before Christmas," she murmured.

Again, the duke as he'd been yesterday morn, with his black cloak swirling about his long, well-muscled legs, came to mind.

Anne snorted. "You certainly won't if you remain in your chambers reading poetry."

Katherine managed a small smile for her sister. "Thank you, Anne."

Her sister's pretty blue eyes searched her face with an uncharacteristic seriousness. "I just want you to be happy."

"I am happy," Katherine said. She detected the defensive note that threaded those three words.

"Very well, I want you to believe in love."

Katherine fell silent, and averted her gaze. There had been a time when she'd believed in love. Now, she knew that love was just the silly dreams of naïve young ladies. The world they belonged to was one made of advantageous matches and familial connections. It was not a world that put any value on emotions such as love.

Mother had desperately loved their father. He'd repaid her love by abandoning her in the countryside and taking himself off to London to take part in the depravity of the gaming tables. In the end, he'd squandered nearly all their familial possessions, the unentailed landholdings, and risked their good names for his own shameful interests.

If that was love, then Katherine was quite content without it.

"Surely not all men are selfish beasts like Father," Anne murmured.

Katherine bit the inside of her cheek to keep from disabusing Anne of her childlike notions. Anne had seemed blissfully ignorant of the direness of their circumstances, and Katherine could not very well share with her now the terror that had gripped her during those uncertain years.

"Katherine?" Anne prodded.

Katherine shook her head. "Forgive me. I was wool-gathering."

Her sister sighed. "Very well. I'll not bother you further with the matter for now, but do not consider this conversation at an end."

Katherine smiled, recognizing the determined glint in her sister's eyes. If she knew her sister, she'd already composed a list of prospective bridegrooms for Katherine.

Why could Katherine only imagine one particular name upon that unwritten list?

Chapter 9

My Lady,

I've nearly completed my reading of Wordsworth's latest work. If you care to attain the copy prior to your departure for the Christmastide season, I shall have it during my daily walk in Hyde Park, alongside the Serpentine River Friday morn.

If you fail to make an appearance, I will consign the copy to a permanent place upon my bookshelf.

~B

*K*atherine stared down at the missive she'd received earlier that week, and then squinted off into the distance through the heavy snow falling from the white-gray morning sky. She trudged through the heavy snow. Though the London streets had been uncharacteristically empty, her carriage ride had been slowed by the violent storm. Now she quickened her step, wondering if the Duke of Bainbridge had tired of waiting for her to appear and had even now left, or . . .

"My lady, it is sheer madness to be out in this weather," her maid, Sara, said, a faintly pleading note in her words.

Katherine slowed her stride a moment, and glanced back. Sara huddled inside her brown cloak, her teeth chattered loudly in the quiet of the winter storm.

Katherine adjusted her own cloak, pulling it closer to herself. "I'll not be long. I merely am going to walk along the

Serpentine. You may remain here. The park is empty, no harm will befall me," she said when her maid opened her mouth to protest.

With that, Katherine turned on her heel, and trudged through the snow. Her serviceable black boots crunched noisily through the powdery softness that covered the ground. Sara was indeed correct—it was sheer madness to be out in such weather, and yet, Katherine desperately wanted the copy of Wordsworth's latest book. She stopped beside the Serpentine, iced over from the winter cold, and stared out across its surface.

It wasn't about her desire for the book.

Though she was looking forward to reading the volume.

For some inexplicable reason that defied logic and all good common sense she prided herself upon—Katherine wished to see the Duke of Bainbridge. She tucked her gloved palms into the muffler and rubbed the cold digits in an attempt to bring warmth back into them.

He wasn't here.

She snorted.

Whyever would he come out in such a storm?

She frowned. He could have had the decency to pen a note, informing her of his altered plans.

"Are you mad?"

Katherine shrieked and spun around so quickly her boots skidded along the snowy pavement, and she tumbled into the Duke of Bainbridge's arms.

His arms closed over her in a seemingly reflexive manner as he righted her.

Katherine swallowed, and glanced up, up, ever up his too-tall frame into his expressionless green eyes. Her breath caught. The green of his eyes put her in mind of the rolling hills and pastures in her family's countryseat of Leeds.

But he didn't release her. He continued to hold her in a most improper, but highly protective manner. In spite of the cold of the winter day, an unexplained warmth seeped into Katherine at the point where their bodies touched. It fanned out, thawing the chill, and replacing it with a most delicious heat.

Then he spoke. "What are you thinking coming out in this storm?" His words came cold and flat like the smooth icicles hanging from the wych elm tree.

Katherine blinked. "You said to meet you here so that I might attain your copy of—"

"Surely you have more sense than God gave a child, madam, not to brave a winter storm," he snapped. He released her suddenly and took a step away from her. His gaze raked the emptiness around them. "And unchaperoned, no less," he muttered that last part more to himself.

Katherine's brows dipped, and she counted to five in a bid to maintain her composure.

When her efforts proved unsuccessful, she proceeded to count to ten.

He lowered his midnight-black brows; giving him the look of a devil at play in the purity of the snow. "What are you doing?"

"I am counting," she snapped.

His eyes narrowed. "Counting."

"Yes. I find it calms me when I'm . . ." The duke's jaw went slack, his brows shot above to his noble brow. She angled her head. "Whatever is the matter with you?" she asked.

He closed his mouth so tightly; she detected the faint click of his teeth meeting teeth. That was going to give him a devilish headache. Which would only be fitting, the insufferable lout!

"Nothing," he growled. Except his tone implied it was not merely *nothing* that had earned his ducal disapproval.

Katherine took a step toward him. "You are also out in this storm," she said. He backed away from her.

She took another step toward him. This time, he remained fixed to the snow-laden pavement. The tips of her boots kissed the tips of his black Hessians. Katherine jabbed a finger at his chest. "Furthermore, *you* sent *me* a note, requesting my presence."

"I . . ."

She waved her finger up at him. "No, Your Grace." If he weren't so bloody tall, she suspected she could have done a more convincing job of conveying her disapproval with her finger. As it was, she settled for waving the digit somewhere in the vicinity of his neck. "You might have penned a second note to inform me that you wished to reschedule the meeting. It would have been the gentlemanly thing to do."

He lowered his head, so the tinge of mint, and something surprisingly sweet, the faintest hint of chocolate that clung to his breath, fanned her cheeks. Fire flashed in his endless green eyes, and God help her, with fury radiating from those moss-green irises, she thought he might kiss her. And what was more foolish was the desperate desire for him *to* kiss her.

"Did you hear me?" he snapped.

Katherine blinked up at him. Well, perhaps he didn't intend to kiss her. A gentleman would not speak in those cool, modulated tones if he had intentions of kissing—

"My lady?"

Katherine cleared her throat. "Er, what was that?"

"Do you have wool in your ears, my lady?" She suspected it was more likely she had wool in her brain. "I sent round a note."

He'd sent round a note? Impossible.

"I did not receive a note," she said a touch defensively, because if he had sent a note, and she'd been foolish enough to brave this frigid winter weather, well, it made her appear like nothing more than a silly ninnyhammer.

His head dipped lower and a black strand of hair fell across his brow. "Do you presume to call me a liar?" he hissed.

Odd, that single strand made him appear so much gentler, so much less reserved than the gentleman who'd plucked her from the Thames. Katherine's fingers fair itched to brush that lock back; so black it bore the faint trace of blue, like the midnight sky. She swallowed. Her eyes went to the faint indentation at the center of his hard, square jaw.

God help her, she wanted to lean up and explore the hard contours of his lips. The wicked thoughts trickled into her consciousness. She wanted to, though.

"I wouldn't dare," she whispered. Because it would be the height of impropriety and madness to kiss the stern, frowning gentleman. Ladies didn't kiss gentlemen.

He gave a curt nod. "Because I do not take charges against my honor lightly."

What in the devil was he talking about?

"You're out in the storm as well," she said.

He glowered at her. "I am not an unwed, unchaperoned—"

"I'm not unchaperoned."

"Young lady," he finished.

Her eyes went to his firm mouth. He most certainly was not a young lady. Katherine wet her lips. He'd been abundantly clear since he'd come upon her that her company was not desired here. She should turn around and flee.

What was it about him that held her fixed to the spot?

As he stood on the frozen path alongside the Serpentine, amidst the increasing snowfall, with the biting wind whipping about him, Jasper came to a most unwanted, unwelcome, and staggering realization.

He wanted to kiss Lady Katherine Adamson.

His gaze took in the delicate lines of her heart-shaped face; the almost cat-like quality of her brown eyes. And suddenly, eyes that were once merely brown put him in mind of the choicest brandy; warm and fathomless.

Jasper's body blazed to life with a heated awareness of her.

He told himself that his reaction was merely physical.

He told himself it was a betrayal of Lydia and her memory.

Bastard that he was, Jasper couldn't find the resolve to turn around and leave Lady Katherine's side.

"Your Grace?" she whispered.

"Jasper," he said, his voice harsh. God help him, he needed to hear his name upon her lips, to remind himself that, even in just that moment, he lived.

Her soulful brown eyes widened. "Your Grace?"

"My name is Jasper."

She tilted her head at an endearing little angle, and the tiniest fragment of his battered stone heart reassembled into the configuration of what it once had been. "Jasper," she whispered, as though tasting it upon her lips.

A primitive growl worked its way up from his chest, past his lips, and he took her mouth in a hard, unrelenting kiss.

Her body stiffened against his, and he thought she might pull away from the volatility of his embrace.

He should have expected more of the vixen who'd survived an icy plunge into the Thames.

Katherine leaned up on tiptoes and angled her head, allowing him a better vantage of her mouth. She moaned, and he slipped his tongue inside, exploring the hot cavern.

She tasted of tea and mint leaves, and he wanted to drown in the sweetness of her. She tangled her hands in the strands of his hair and gave a faint tug. He groaned, his shaft hardened. He'd been too long without a woman. His body merely sought the surcease to be found only in the honeyed depths of a woman's hot center.

He told himself that.

Over and over.

The words a chant. A litany.

Liar.

His hand worked its way inside the front of her emerald-green cloak, and he sought out the lush curve of her generous breast. Through the fabric of her wool gown, he teased the sensitive flesh of her nipple. His body ached to lay her down upon the blanket of snow, like the ice princess he'd once believed her to be, tug the cloak free, and expose the bountiful breasts to his worshipful gaze.

She moaned and leaned into his touch.

Encouraged, Jasper's mouth left hers. She cried out, in protest, her strong fingers made a desperate bid to guide him back to her.

But Jasper craved the satiny smoothness of her long neck. He placed his lips to the rapidly fluttering pulse there. She cried out, her legs buckled out from under her.

Jasper caught her to him, and continued his ministrations. "Jasper," she whimpered into his mouth.

Oh, God, the sound of his name, a breathy entreaty, threatened to drive him beyond the point of control.

His lips nipped at the sensitive flesh of her neck, and her whimper turned into a husky, primitive moan. He worked his hands down her back, to the gentle swell of her hips, and then tugged her against him. His shaft surged against the softness of her belly.

Her head fell back.

A blast of cool winter air whipped around them. It tugged several long strands of dark-brown locks free of the bonnet atop her head. The locks tumbled down past her shoulders. He took the lock and rolled it between his thumb and forefinger, inhaling the spring lavender scent of the strand, so at odds with the Christmastide season.

Passion blazed within her eyes . . . and jerked him from the moment.

Jasper released the strand of hair, and took a step backward. The horror of his actions, his absolute betrayal of Lydia's memory, stole through him; it sucked the breath from his lungs.

Katherine closed her eyes a moment, and snow swirled and danced about her flushed cheeks.

He spun away and battled the urge to pull her into his arms once again and continue exploring the warm, moist cavern of her mouth until she shook with desire.

Jasper raked his gloved hand through his hair. The abrupt movement sent snowflakes falling from his head. He stared out at the river. Since Lydia's death, he'd lived the past three years, three-hundred and . . . his mind spun . . .

Was it fifty-three days?

Or fifty-four?

Panic built in his chest; it pounded away at his insides as he confronted the nauseating truth—he'd lost count of the days since Lydia had been gone.

His gut clenched. How, in a matter of days, had this happened?

Gentle fingers touched his shoulder. "Jasper?"

He closed his eyes. What had possessed him to give her leave to use his name? Nay, not leave . . . he'd all but commanded it of her. Sheer madness. His lips twisted. Then, he was the Mad Duke.

The sound of his name on her lips spoken in her husky timbre served as a punishing lash upon his conscience.

Jasper opened his eyes, and stared blankly across the river. "My wife is dead."

Katherine moved ever closer. She stepped in front of him, silent. The fabric of her cloak brushed against his legs.

He stared past the top of her velvet-trimmed bonnet, which was still askew from their embrace.

"I'm so sorry," she said softly. A gust of wind caught those words and carried them to his ears.

"I do not want your pity." His words sounded hollow to his own ears. He no longer knew what he wanted.

"I don't pity you, Jasper."

He glanced down. A faint smile played about her lips.

"You are not the kind of man that one pities."

His jaw tightened, and he glanced away. No, he was a heartless, soulless bastard.

What was it about this small yet spirited woman that unearthed the parts of himself he'd tried desperately to bury?

"I hate water."

Jasper blinked. His gaze moved back to hers.

"I hate water," she said again. "As a child, we'd spend most of our days in my family's cottage in Leeds. When I was a girl of seven years, my sister and I would often go off on our own. We traipsed all over the countryside. It exasperated my mother to no end."

His lip tugged up at the corner as he considered his first meeting with Katherine. It would appear the young lady had not changed much since her earlier years.

She continued, and Jasper tried to follow the odd direction her thoughts had taken. "I am the younger twin." Yes, Guilford had mentioned as much. Her shoulders lifted in a little shrug. "I've always felt more like an older sister. Anne has always been the fanciful, whimsical sister. I've always sought to protect her."

He remembered the panicked, unholy light in her eyes as he'd pulled her from the river, considered her outing this day in Hyde Park in the midst of a winter storm. "And who protects you, Katherine?"

She opened her mouth. Then closed it. Her brow wrinkled. "Since my father died, my sister Aldora fashioned herself as something of a protector of my family." A sad little smile played about her lips. "Though, she wed three years ago, and now spends most of her time in the country." She shook her head. "That is neither here nor there."

He bit back a smile. "Your hatred of water," he guided her back to her earlier statement.

"Ah, yes. I hate water. One day, Anne and I were playing alongside a river that bordered my father's property. Anne's favorite bonnet, a pretty pink one with satin ivory ribbons, fell into the water. She was desperately crying, and so I climbed upon a long tree trunk that had fallen across the river."

The muscles in Jasper's stomach tightened. He knew intuitively where her story was going. He would rather not think about a small Katherine Adamson pulled beneath the surface of a river. Not when he'd rescued her from the Thames and knew the blood terror that had gripped her in that moment.

"I fell in," she said. "The current was fast-moving, and so very strong. It pulled at my skirts and dragged me under."

The image she painted roused the protective instincts he'd thought long dead inside him.

"I was certain I was going to die." Her words took on a faraway quality, as though she were speaking, but to no one in particular. "My sister managed to toss a long branch out, and I grasped onto it. She pulled me to safety."

How very strong she'd been, even then as a small child, to have battled past the terror to ultimately save herself.

Jasper would have been a boy of fifteen years or so; he wished he'd been there, just as he'd been those five days ago. He wished he'd been there to pluck her from the river so she could have turned her fear over to him.

"My point is this, Jasper," she went on. "I detest water. It's unpredictable and dangerous, and it terrifies me." She held her palms up. "But I cannot live the rest of my life avoiding water."

"You nearly drowned at the Frost Fair." He felt inclined to point out.

She took his hand in hers and turned it over. He stiffened.

"But I didn't, Jasper. Life is horrible and unfair and terrifying. But those are not reasons to stop living." Katherine touched her fingers to his gloved hand. "You didn't die, Jasper. You lived."

His hand tightened reflexively around hers. He'd lived when Lydia had perished. With his desire for his wife, and the need for an heir, Jasper had killed her with his selfish needs and ducal obligations. For more than three years, he'd punished himself for that great crime.

Only now, with Katherine's quietly spoken words did he confront the truth . . . Lydia was gone and no amount of self-flagellation would bring her back.

And he hated Katherine, in that moment, for opening his eyes to the reality of his miserable circumstances. "You need to leave," he ordered harshly.

She cocked her head.

"I said go," he forced out past tight lips. He needed her to leave. He wanted this woman who'd tossed his life into an upheaval to go, and let him go back to the emotionally deadened man he'd been these past three, nearly four years.

Katherine nodded. Twin splotches of color stained her cheeks. She dipped a curtsy. "Your Grace," she murmured.

He loathed the aching need to hear his name upon her lips yet again.

Katherine made to go.

"Your chaperone," he called out.

She frowned, her face calm and serene, brown eyes cool and removed—the ice princess returned. "You needn't worry about me, Your Grace."

No, he needn't.

And yet, he did.

Katherine dipped another curtsy, and then hurried off. He stared after her swiftly retreating figure, until she was nothing more than a small mark upon the snowy horizon.

He thought of the story she'd shared, of the small, unprotected girl fighting the fast-moving river waters. With a sigh, he set out to follow the now headstrong young lady still in desperate need of protection.

Chapter 10

*A*fter a long carriage ride through the snow-laden streets of London, Katherine at last arrived home. She climbed the steps with dreaded anticipation. Perhaps she'd not see her mother just yet . . . perhaps . . .

Ollie opened the door. She took a hopeful breath and stepped inside with a murmur of thanks for the old servant.

She freed the hook that held her cloak together and handed the sopping wet garment over. "Thank you," she said as he took her cloak. She shook out her snow-dampened skirts, the flakes dissolved into small droplets of water atop the marble floor. "I . . ." Her words faded, as she met her mother's scowling countenance.

Mother stood in the foyer, arms planted atop her hips. Anne hovered at a point beyond her shoulder. Her sister stood shaking her head in a commiserative way.

Katherine sighed. "Mother . . ."

"Where have you been?" Mother launched into a stinging tirade. "First you take yourself off to the Frost Fair, unchaperoned, and nearly find yourself drowned."

Sorry, Anne silently mouthed.

"Then you arrive with the Mad Duke . . ."

Katherine clenched her hands into tight fists. "He is not mad." He was hurting and scarred and forever changed by the loss of his wife. The pain he carried did not make him mad.

"Bah." Mother slashed the air with her hand. "You have run wild for the last time, Katherine." There was a hard edge, an unspoken order to those words.

Katherine's stomach tightened. "Mother . . ."

"I'm speaking to your uncle. You need a husband who will bring you in line."

Anne gasped. "Mother, no."

Mother carried on as though Anne hadn't interjected, as though Katherine's heart was not beating hard with panic. "Your actions will jeopardize your sister's ability to make a most advantageous match."

Her sister's ability.

Not Katherine's.

It was expected by all that beautiful, vibrant, accomplished Anne would secure a well-titled husband. The expectations, however, for Katherine were not so very great. They were rather bleak, in comparison to her sister's.

"Where were you off to in this storm?"

Katherine's mind went blank under the weight of the truth. She could not very well explain that she'd gone to meet the duke. Her gaze met Anne's, and the flash of something that looked very nearly like guilt, lit the blue irises of her sister's eyes.

So Anne was behind Jasper's missing second missive. Of course.

She offered her sister a gentle smile.

Anne had dragged Katherine along on any number of madcap schemes, the latest of which was their unchaperoned trip to the Frost Fair. The decision to brave the storm, and Mother's wrath, had been Katherine's alone.

"Get to your chambers," her mother snapped, jerking Katherine back to the moment. "I'll speak to you in private."

Katherine managed a tight nod, and with head held high marched past her mother, up the stairs, down the hall, to the security of her own rooms. Once inside, she closed the door, and leaned against the wood paneling, borrowing the support of the hard surface.

He kissed me.

Her eyes slid closed. And she'd kissed him with a desperate longing she'd never known existed within herself.

Katherine's childlike dreams of fanciful love had faded over the years, to be replaced with a woman's logic. The only dream she'd carried for so long was of a secure life, married to a gentleman who'd not squander their every last possession, but instead would care for her, give her children, and perhaps enjoy a quiet read beside a warm hearth.

Until his kiss.

Jasper Waincourt, 8th Duke of Bainbridge's one kiss and fevered caress had thrown into question everything she believed she'd wanted for herself. He'd awakened her to a burning passion that Katherine hadn't believed herself capable of. His heated touch had scorched her skin, and somehow, irrevocably altered her, in ways that terrified her—ways she could not consider.

Because she could not, would not ever wed a pitiless, cold man like the duke. His kiss might liquefy her, but he'd been clear, all gentleness within him had died with his wife.

Jasper could never be that gentleman to sit beside her, quietly reading, with a gaggle of children at their feet.

A knock sounded at the door.

Katherine jumped as the reverberations shook her back. She should have not spent her time ruminating about Jasper, but instead formulating a response for her mother's impending tirade. She took a deep breath, and turned around.

Her mother opened the door and sailed into the room. She ran a hard stare over Katherine's damp frame, a pinched set to her mouth.

But she said nothing.

Which was all the more terrifying for it. Mother was never short of words.

"Mother," Katherine began. "I'm sorry I was out in such weather. I desired a walk and fresh air is good for one's constitution."

Silence.

Katherine fisted the fabric of her skirts in her hands, and shifted on her feet. It would appear her situation was a good deal more dire than she'd even believed.

"You need to wed, Katherine."

A small pit formed in the bottom of Katherine's stomach. She trailed the tip of her tongue around the seam of her lips. Mother was tenacious, and when she'd settled her mind upon something, she could not be deterred from her course.

Mother would have her wed Bertrand Ekstrom.

It spoke to how little faith her mother had in Katherine's ability to make a match.

"I will," Katherine said softly.

"Wed Mr. Ekstrom," her mother finished for her.

Katherine shook her head, hard. "I've had but one Season." She bit the inside of her cheek to keep from pointing out that Anne would also have her second Season. She could never resent Anne for the special place she held in their mother's heart, even if it caused Katherine the greatest pain. "I'll not wed him."

"You're nineteen—"

"Nearly twenty," Katherine pointed out.

"And not free to make decisions until you reach your twenty-fifth year."

Katherine's jaw hardened. "He's an odious man, Mother." With a paunch waist and cruel set to his mouth, Bertrand Ekstrom, her distant cousin, possessed a cruel glint in his beady eyes.

Jasper slipped into her mind. Harsh and commanding, there was nothing soft about the young duke, and yet, she knew with a woman's intuition that he'd never be capable of harming her. Her body tingled in remembrance of his hot but gentle caress.

"He is next in line behind Benedict. Surely you learned with your father's unexpected death that life is tenuous for females. We have to do everything within our power to maintain our security. Your brother is only thirteen. He has a great many years before he can marry and what if he doesn't have a male child?"

Katherine bit her lip hard to keep from pointing out that it hardly mattered to her if Benedict someday produced one or none future heirs.

"I'll not wed him. These are not the Middle Ages, Mother."

"Your sister was prepared to sacrifice her happiness for the family."

In the end, however, Aldora hadn't. She'd found love with Mr. Michael Knightly, an obscenely wealthy gentleman and a second son. His funds had saved them from the dire financial straits they'd been in, and had smoothed over any disappointment Mother had harbored over Aldora's marriage to a second son.

Apparently Mother's now pressing concern was securing the familial line by wedding one of her marriageable daughters to the second cousin who stood to inherit if Benedict failed to do so.

"Mother, can we please discuss this after the holiday." If Katherine could not alter her Mother's intended course, then perhaps she could manage to convince her to cease the discussion of it until after the Christmastide season.

Her mother's mouth screwed up. Katherine thought she might press her argument, but then Mother nodded. "Very well." With a curt nod, she left Katherine with the misery of her own thoughts.

Katherine breathed a relieved sigh, her eyes sliding closed. Mother would not be deterred in her efforts; that much was clear. Nothing could alter her intentions for Katherine, except . . .

We shall simply have to find you a husband.

Anne had the right of it.

Only, where could Katherine find an unwed gentleman in such a short . . .

Short . . .

Her eyes flew open. No, her silent thoughts were utter madness.

He'd been abundantly clear that he had no interest in wedding Katherine or any other lady for that matter. He was cold. Cynical. Reserved.

Katherine began to pace.

With his title he was just a smidgeon shy of royalty and clearly unaccustomed to having his wishes thwarted. He was, if the reports were to be believed, as rich as Croesus.

Jasper Waincourt, the 8th Duke of Bainbridge, was also exceedingly logical, to the point of fault.

Surely if Katherine put her argument to him, he'd recognize that a union between them could be, nay, *would* be advantageous to the both of them. It would be nothing more than a strict business arrangement between a gentleman and a lady.

There would be no expectations of an emotional connection.

There would be no affection.

It would be a match based purely on a mutually beneficial contract.

They could carry on their own lives.

She'd provide him his necessary heirs, and she . . . her heart fluttered rapidly with fast-growing hope, well, she would be spared marriage to Bertrand Ekstrom and free of her mother's heavy hand.

Katherine could spend her days reading to her heart's content, taking unchaperoned walks if she so desired, all without the stern disapproval reigned down by Mother.

Filled with a sudden excitement, Katherine raced over to her small mahogany desk and pulled out a thick sheet of vellum. She reached for a pen and dipped it into the crystal inkwell.

Your Grace,

It occurs to me that I failed to obtain your copy of Wordsworth's latest volume. I would ask if when the winter storm abates, that you meet me in the same spot alongside the Serpentine River.

Ever Yours,
Katherine

Katherine read and reread the missive several times, and before she lost her nerve, folded it. She tapped her finger along the top of her desk. She did need to be certain he met with her, and if he'd mayhap decided to avoid meeting with her and instead keep his copy of Wordsworth's latest work, well then she wouldn't be able to propose her plan. She reached for another sheet of parchment.

When they met, she would put her plan before him. Misgivings stirred in her belly, but she tamped them down. He was a man of logic. Katherine would be able to reason with him.

The alternative was not to be countenanced.

Chapter 11

*S*eated at the breakfast table with a plate of bacon and eggs, Jasper sipped his coffee. He grimaced at the bitter taste of the vile brew, and reached for the morning copy of *The Times*.

"I can't imagine you drink that revolting stuff."

Jasper glanced to the door.

Guilford stood framed in the doorway. "I hope you don't mind. I took the liberty of showing myself in." He yanked his gloves off and beat them against each other.

Jasper glanced over the rim of his glass. He took another sip. "Guilford," he greeted.

Guilford's ginger brows shot to his hairline.

Jasper frowned. "What is it?"

His friend tossed his gloves upon the table, and wandered over to the sideboard. He proceeded to pile kippers and warm, flaky bread in a heaping pile upon his plate. He shook his head, and took a seat across from Jasper. "I can't fathom this remarkable transformation in you."

Jasper reached for his paper, and snapped it open to keep from encouraging Guilford's deliberate baiting.

Alas, Guilford was not to be deterred.

"You haven't greeted me with anything more than a growl, a go-to-hell, or a what-are-you-doing-here, in more than three years."

From across the table, Jasper detected the rhythmic tapping as Guilford drummed his fingertip along the arm of his chair. Jasper gritted his teeth, his eyes scouring the page for some bit of information that might distract him from Guilford. He rattled the paper.

"May I venture it is because of a particular young lady?" Guilford tilted his head.

"You may not," Jasper said, between clenched teeth.

He'd be damned if he'd mentioned the manner in which Katherine had slipped into his mind, or the feel of her lips, or the gentle curve of her hip, or . . .

"So it *is* about a particular lady."

Jasper lowered the paper and glared at Guilford. "I did not say it was about Katherine."

Guilford leaned back in the black Bergerè chair. He drummed his fingers on the arms of the seat. "Ahh, but I did not mention the *Lady* Katherine."

Christ.

Jasper raised the paper and scanned the page.

It would appear a Lord B and Lady M had been discovered in . . .

He tossed his copy of *The Times* aside.

He didn't give a bloody damn about the *ton*'s gossip. "What business do you have here?"

Guilford reached for his fork and knife and delicately sliced a piece of cold roast beef. He popped a small piece into his mouth and chewed with meticulous care. "I've learned additional information about the intended match between Bertrand Ekstrom and your Lady Katherine."

Jasper cursed. "She is not my . . . what did you learn?" he snapped. He told himself he inquired out of an apathetic interest in the woman he'd rescued. Except, as Guilford picked up his white napkin and dabbed carefully at his lips, he wanted to drag him across the blasted table and shake the words free from his mouth.

"It would seem," Guilford continued. "Lady Katherine's mother has spoken to the lady's guardian about arranging the match with Ekstrom after the Christmastide season."

Jasper wrinkled his brow and tossed aside his attempt at indifference. "Why would she not allow her to make a match during the Season?" Surely the young lady could do a deal better than Bertrand Ekstrom. He remembered the lush feel of her breast; the peak of that soft flesh puckered through the fabric, begging for his touch. His stomach tightened. She could do a good deal better. The muscles of his stomach convulsed. *Why did the idea of her with another ravage his insides?*

Guilford's shoulders lifted in a shrug. "I believe he's next in line for the earldom, behind the lady's brother, who's a mere boy."

So Katherine's happiness would be forfeited on a whole series of what-ifs. His fingers curled over the arms of the chair, hard enough for his nails to leave indents in the solid wood.

Jasper picked up his fork, and speared a piece of bacon. Ultimately, it didn't matter to him who the lady wed. "She is not my affair." *She is not my affair. She is not my affair.* It was a litany he didn't believe.

Guilford snorted. Neither apparently did Guilford. His friend opened his mouth to speak when a knock sounded at the door.

The footman approached with a silver tray bearing a letter atop it. Upon recognizing the familiar, elegant lines of the scrawl, Jasper's heart thumped an odd rhythm.

He accepted the note, and Guilford forgotten, unfolded it.

Your Grace,

It occurs to me that I failed to obtain your copy of Wordsworth's latest volume. I would ask if when the winter storm abates, that you meet me in the same spot alongside the Serpentine River.

Ever Yours,
Katherine

Disappointment stabbed at him. Her note was comprised of a mere two sentences. He frowned, and turned it over in his hands, and then studied the front of it yet again. Direct, and yet coolly polite, Katherine's letter was this time devoid of the characteristic teasing he'd come to expect from the young lady. He didn't know how to account for this . . .

Another servant entered, bearing another silver tray.

Jasper frowned, and reached for the missive.

Jasper,

If you would please deign to send round a note, this time regarding my request for a meeting along the Serpentine. I'm afraid I received quite the dressing down from my mother, at a time when I can ill afford to anger her.

The unwritten mention of Ekstrom. He clenched the parchment so tightly, he wrinkled the page. Jasper forced himself to keep reading.

If you are a man of integrity, then you'll honor your word and provide me with your copy of Wordsworth's work.

Jasper's frown deepened. The insolent bit of baggage. He'd been called mad, a coldhearted bastard, but no one had dared to question his honor.

I do not mean to impugn your honor. Though, I can certainly see how the above mentioned words might seem that way.

His lips twitched.

But it is with some urgency that I request to meet with you. And obtain that volume.

Ever Yours,
Katherine

Something in those final two sentences gave him pause. The last sentence seemed an afterthought hastily scratched upon the page.

It is with some urgency that I request to meet with you.

Those were not the words of a woman merely eager to obtain a book of poetry.

Guilford chuckled. "I would trade my countryseat in Sussex to know the contents of those missives."

Jasper folded the two notes, and stuffed them inside the front of his jacket. "Go to hell," he muttered, and picked up his coffee. He took a quick sip. The now cold brew slid down his throat, and he grimaced in distaste.

Guilford sighed, and tipped back on the legs of his chair. "Does your recent correspondence perhaps have to do with your Lady Katherine?"

"She is not my . . ." Jasper shook his head, and took another sip. He would not continue to be goaded by his friend.

Lady Katherine Adamson was not Guilford's business.

Jasper started as he realized that she was in fact, however, *his* business. His rescue, then their subsequent meeting at the bookshop, followed by their discourse on Wordsworth, and their assignation at Hyde Park made her more than a stranger.

His cup of coffee rattled in his hands, and liquid sloshed over the rim. A liveried footman rushed over to clean the liquid from the table.

Jasper ignored him, unable to form a coherent thought, and his mind raced.

Since Lydia's death, he'd gone to great lengths to shut himself off from the world. He had not wanted the emotional entanglements, the pitying stares, nor his name so much as breathed upon the lips of strangers who found a macabre fascination with his wife's death.

Yet, in the course of a week, Lady Katherine Adamson had slipped past his defenses so that he wondered after her well-being. It could not be more than that. He'd not allow for it. She meant nothing to him.

Nothing . . .

He'd resolved to never care again.

"There could be far worse things than finding yourself wed to Lady Katherine Adamson," Guilford interjected quietly.

Jasper started. His eyes narrowed. "Marriage?" he drawled. Perhaps it was Guilford who should earn the title of Mad Marquess. "I have no intentions of wedding again." He could not subject another woman to the hell that had claimed Lydia's life. His eyes closed and nausea churned in his stomach as he remembered the blood. There had been so much of it; a bright-crimson puddle upon the stark white sheets. Only this time, in his remembrance, Lydia's face shifted in and out of focus, alternating with a more recent visage; a minx with brown hair and brown eyes.

He clenched his eyes tighter, as bile burned its way up his throat, and he forced himself to swallow, lest he cast the contents of his stomach in the midst of the breakfast table. He counted to ten, and then opened his eyes. No, he'd not subject another woman to that, not even to preserve the title.

The legs of Guilford's chair rocked forward, and scraped along the wood floor. He propped his elbows upon the table and leaned over. "Surely you know you must honor your ducal responsibilities."

Jasper's jaw tightened. His ducal responsibilities could go hang. All they'd gotten him was a dead wife, and a dead babe.

"Is that why you've come by this morn, Guilford? To inquire as to my interest in Lady Katherine?"

"Well . . ."

"I helped pull the young lady from the river. Beyond that, I have little interest in Lady Katherine Adamson. My wife is dead. Dead." Her body was nothing more than cold bones that served as fodder for the worms in his family's cemetery.

"But Lady Katherine is very much alive," Guilford said quietly. He shoved his chair back, and waved off a servant who rushed forward to help. "I do not care if you court Lady Katherine or a courtesan or some other nameless creature. You need to accept that you lived, Jasper," his friend said, using his Christian name. "And no matter what self-imposed misery you create for yourself, it will never bring Lydia back."

Jasper stared down, unblinking at his plate in front of him, as he confronted the truth of Guilford's words. Nothing would ever bring Lydia back, and until he'd met Katherine, he'd thought his soul dead, as well.

He didn't think himself capable of lust or passion or desire again. Then he'd taken Katherine in his arms and been awakened to the reality that he was still very much a living, breathing man. He waited for the sting of guilt to slap him.

Only, it didn't come.

Guilford stood, and adjusted the lapels of his blue jacket. "Do you know what I think more than an odd coincidence?"

Jasper just stared at him.

"You haven't left that bloody castle in nearly four years. Aside from my fortunate self, you haven't spoken a word to nearly anyone. What is the likelihood you'd attend a public event such as the Frost Fair—?"

"You made me—"

"You are the Duke of Bainbridge. No one *makes* you do anything. You were supposed to meet Lady Katherine. I'm certain of it. If you'll excuse me, I've an appointment with Gentleman Jackson." With a short bow, Guilford exited the breakfast room.

Once alone, Jasper withdrew the two notes sent round by Katherine. The gentle scent of lavender that clung to her wafted from the thick sheets of vellum; heady like a potent aphrodisiac.

The lady posed a danger to the thick walls he'd constructed around his heart. He'd be wise to burn her letters, ignore her request, and take himself back to Castle Blackwood, forgetting there had ever been a spirited, winsome lady named Katherine.

Since he'd met Lady Katherine Adamson, however, Jasper had been anything but wise.

Chapter 12

*N*ausea churned in Katherine's belly, as she stared out over the frozen expanse of the Serpentine River. Jasper had agreed to meet her.

He'd promised to meet her at precisely five minutes past six in the morning, when the park was silent, and the night sky still clung to the horizon. Oh, his words had been anything but poetic.

My Lady,

You can expect my presence at the place we'd last met at precisely five past six. I value punctuality. The volume will be yours.

Bainbridge

Bainbridge. Not Jasper. Not the man who'd taken her in his arms, whose touch had melted her like the hot sun upon a blanket of snow. She didn't know what she'd expected of his missive. Mayhap, something . . . something . . .

Less *precise*.

She didn't know why she expected him to be different than the calculated, unbending man he'd shown himself to be.

Katherine touched the tip of her glove-encased finger to her lips.

It had been The Kiss, as she'd come to think of it, that accounted for this madcap scheme she was about to propose to him. That is, if he still intended to honor the words in his note.

"My lady."

Katherine gasped, and spun on her heel. Snow crunched under the heels of her boots.

Her gaze met Jasper's, and she swallowed hard. "You."

"Yes, me," he murmured, his emotionless tone gave little indication as to the nature of his thoughts.

"You came." Her cheeks blazed. "That is . . ." Her eyes fell to the book in his hands. "Oh, you have the book."

He handed it over, and Katherine accepted the volume. She studied the leather tome etched in gold lettering.

"I am a gentleman who honors my word, my lady."

Katherine glanced up at him, ever-serious, always frowning, and yet, somehow, his stoic reserve inspired a sense of confidence. This was not a man who'd squander his family's wealth, leaving them destitute at the mercy of the creditors and loathsome lords who'd called in their vowels.

It was also why he would make her an ideal match.

He sketched a bow, and spun on his heel.

Panic bubbled up her throat. "You are leaving?" Her voice emerged as a high squeak.

He turned back to face her, his black cloak gaped open to reveal his long, powerful legs. Her mouth went dry. Ladies were not supposed to notice things such as the breadth of a gentleman's thighs, or the ripple of muscle in his forearms, or . . . she gulped.

"My lady?"

She swallowed back her improper musings.

"Er . . . are you leaving already?"

Jasper arched a single, black icy brow. "I didn't believe there was another reason for me to stay."

That honest admission chafed, more than she wished. She didn't want to notice his uncharacteristic handsomeness or his honorable characteristics when he should disdain to notice her.

"Er . . ." She wet her lips, as the plan she'd concocted that had prompted her to send round the note requesting his presence seemed the height of foolishness. Had she imagined his kiss those two days ago?

Except . . . her body still burned in remembrance of his touch.

No, that had been no imagining.

"My lady?" he prompted again; a thread of impatience underlined that question.

Katherine jumped. "Katherine."

His brow wrinkled.

"That is to say, considering our initial meeting, and then our chance encounter in the bookshop, and then the time we met at Hyde Park, and you and I k . . ." He quirked that icy brow yet again. She waved her hand. "That is to say, *talked*. We spoke that day," she amended. If their kiss was wholly unmemorable to him, well, then she'd not do something so foolish as to mention that particular part of their meeting that day—even if it had been the single most passionate moment of her nineteen, nearly twenty years. "Well . . ."

"My lady?"

She stamped her boot in the snow. "I'm merely suggesting you call me Katherine because of, of . . . our friendship." She balled her hands in pained embarrassment.

His green eyes deepened to the shade of jade. He took a step toward her, and she took a hasty step back in retreat. He continued advancing, and Katherine scrambled backward until the heels of her boots reached the edge of the frozen river.

She glanced over, and her stomach lurched at how precariously close she'd come to the water. Her time at the Frost Fair had proven that even frozen water was not to be trusted.

When she turned back around, they were a mere hands width apart. Katherine gasped, and stumbled.

His arms shot out, and he gripped her by her forearms, steadying her.

"Thank you," she murmured, hating the breathless note to those two words.

He dipped his head. "Is that what we are, Katherine? Friends?"

Katherine would have to be a lack wit to not hear the mocking sneer to those two words. Suddenly too aware of his body's proximity to her own, she took a hesitant step around him, and placed several steps between them.

He advanced. A hunter stalking its prey.

Katherine picked her way carefully around the snow-covered trail, and tilted her chin up. "Yes. Why, I rather thought we were. You don't strike me as a gentleman with very many friends, therefore you should accept friendship where you can." His eyes narrowed further, to dark impenetrable slits. She wet her lips and backed up another step. She was rather certain he'd never harm her, but the dark look in his eyes would have made the most seasoned infantryman uneasy. "As your—"

"Friend?" he supplied, his voice dryer than a crisp autumn leaf.

She nodded emphatically. "Yes, as your friend, I thought I should provide a solution to your dilemma."

His firm lips twitched. She narrowed her eyes, and studied him more closely. Or she might have imagined the very slight movement. Or mayhap it was mere coincidence . . .

"I was unaware I had a dilemma."

Katherine jerked to the moment. She nodded, this time more slowly. "Oh, absolutely you do."

He folded his arms across the broad expanse of his chest.

Her eyes dipped lower, and she swallowed as her body recalled his hot, strong hands upon her person. Dukes were supposed to be hopelessly old, impossibly wrinkled, and sporting monocles. Yes, they most certainly possessed monocles. Dukes, most certainly, were *not* supposed to be great big, towering bears of men with their muscles straining the black expanse of their breeches.

"Are you warm, madam?"

Katherine blinked. "I beg your pardon?"

Jasper gestured to her. "You are fanning yourself, my lady."

Katherine stopped abruptly, and stared at her hand as though it belonged to another. "Katherine," she reminded him. She dropped her palm to her side. "After all we are . . ."

"Friends," he finished for her.

Something about the way he delivered that word; a silken caress, warmed in molten lava, cascaded over her; it unfurled in her belly, like a small flame that grew and spread like a great conflagration. Why, it would seem she was rather warm after all.

"Yes." Did that breathless response belong to her? It seemed more suited to scandalous ladies with rouged lips and daring décolletage.

His body stiffened, and she suspected he was of a like opinion. "Yes?" he whispered.

Oh goodness, this was not how she'd imagined this very direct, very matter-of-fact conversation to go. Katherine shook her head. "Yes, we are friends," she said.

His gaze remained fixed upon her, unblinking and unfathomable. "As my friend, perhaps you should enlighten me as to this pressing dilemma I'm unaware of," he said, wryly.

Katherine's mouth went dry. She took a deep breath, and pressed on before her courage deserted her. "Your Grace, will you do me the honor of marrying me?"

Jasper angled his head, and studied the lovely Lady Katherine, nay . . . just Katherine, as they were *friends*. He was just twenty-seven years of age so did not think it likely his hearing was failing him. It would appear he was madder than even Society believed him to be, because Jasper was ever so certain Lady Katherine Adamson had just proposed marriage to him.

He removed his black hat from atop his head, and beat it against his side.

Katherine cleared her throat. "I—er . . . will you? Marry me, that is, Your Grace?"

He ceased his distracted movement, and jammed his hat back on top his head. It would appear he'd heard her correctly, after all.

Still, it did beg for clarification.

"Did you just propose marriage, my lady?"

"Katherine," she corrected. She nodded; the abrupt movement dislodged the drab brown bonnet atop her head. Several strands of brown ringlets slipped down the side of her cheek.

Jasper's fingers twitched with the sudden desire to brush the silken tresses back, and tuck them behind her ears.

He shook his head. What in hell was wrong with him?

"And yes, I did." She took a step toward him, seeming unaware of his body's physical awareness of her lean, lithe frame. "Will you marry me?" she asked for a third time.

He opened his mouth to reply, but no words came out. He promptly closed it. Surely she jested?

And because he was at a loss of words, he said nothing.

Katherine caught her lower lip between her teeth, and worried that delectable flesh. She held her gloved palms up. "Of course, it would only be to solve your dilemma," she said.

Jasper folded his arms across his chest. "Ahh, yes, my dilemma. Do tell me about this dilemma."

Her eyes lit, and his response seemed to energize her for she began to pace a short path in front of him. Her boots left imprints upon the previously untouched snow. "Well, surely you know as a duke you have a certain ducal responsibility."

His body froze. Surely she did not imply what he thought she implied? Blood rushed to his shaft as he considered just then one very specific ducal responsibility. "Oh, and what is that?" he said hoarsely.

She glanced up at him. "Why, the matter of an heir, of course."

Jasper's eyes slid closed. Good Christ, she *had* referred to exactly what he'd believed she'd spoken of. What manner of innocent young lady proposed to a duke and spoke to him of his ducal responsibilities of acquiring an heir? Jasper waited for the familiar stirrings of agony and guilt at the mere mention of a babe. Instead, a forbidden image filled his mind. Katherine spread out upon satin sheets, her thick brown waves cascading about his naked skin, her generous breasts exposed for his worship. He counted to ten.

She ceased pacing. "Are you counting, Jasper?"

Not Your Grace.

Jasper.

He counted to ten, once again.

"I am."

"Oh," she said. She steepled her fingers and tapped the tips of them together. "Should I continue?"

"Please, do." he said.

She either failed to detect or care about the sarcasm in that two-word response.

Katherine resumed pacing. "Well, you do not care for life in London or the Seasons, which is very good because neither do I. You won't have to go to the trouble of leaving your estate and journeying to London and taking part in the marriage game. We can wed, and carry on quite amicably."

"Because we are friends?" His lips twitched again.

She frowned at him, no effort made at concealing the reproach in her pretty brown eyes. "Would you hear more?"

He waved his hand. "Oh, of course, my lady. Enlighten me."

"Katherine," she corrected. "After all, if we are wed, you should refer to me by my Christian name." She caught her lip between her teeth again. "Or at least I should hope we won't be the proper English couple who refers to one another by our titles or surnames. Mr. Waincourt," she said in a clear attempt at a proper, matronly, older woman. "Mrs. Waincourt," she said, dropping her voice several shades. In her attempt at a deep, masculine tone, her words emerged on a low, husky murmur better reserved for the bedroom.

He swallowed, his eyes unbidden went to her bow-shaped lips, and he tried to tamp down the desire to tug that silly brown bonnet with ivory lace trim from atop her head, toss it aside, and make love to her mouth.

She continued to trouble the plump flesh of that lower lip, the gesture more intoxicating than the most potent spirits. "Though, I suppose it would be Your Grace and Your Grace." She wrinkled her pert little nose. "That isn't at all endearing."

Jasper ran his gaze over her face as he realized for the first time that *she* was endearing; from her nervous little gestures, to the direct manner with which she spoke, to even that hideous brown bonnet she'd worn since he'd fished her from the Thames.

She blinked up at him. "Ahem." She coughed into her hand. "I said, 'ahem'."

"Do you have something in your throat, my lady?" he schooled his expression to hide all amusement.

Katherine frowned up at him. "It is Katherine. And no, I do not have something in my throat. I was trying to discreetly capture your attention."

"I should think if you have to explain as much, that your efforts appear unsuccessful."

"Decidedly so," she agreed with a nod. She tapped the tip of her boot on the pavement. "Well, what then? Will you wed me or not?"

"I would have to say . . . or not." Though Jasper was, for the first time in nearly four years, completely and utterly enchanted. And if he had been of the marrying kind, which he was decidedly not, then he would have very gladly accepted the lady's offer.

Katherine rocked back on her heels. Her expression so crestfallen that he nearly called the words back and accepted her hand.

"Oh." She blinked her wide brown eyes, giving her the look of an owl. "Well, this is certainly not how I imagined this would go."

A gust of cold wind whipped that brown ringlet across her cheek; it draped over her mouth. As if of their own volition, his fingers reached up to brush the strand back as he'd longed to do since he'd come upon her alongside the frozen river. "And how did you imagine this would go?" he asked gently.

Her soulful brown eyes met his, and he was struck by the great sadness he saw there. From the moment he'd come upon Katherine Adamson, she'd been fiery, and angry, teasing, and witty, but she'd never been sad. It shouldn't matter to him.

And yet, it did.

"Katherine?"

She looked out at the river. "Well, you would of course be condescending and mocking, which you of course were." He stiffened, not at all liking her unfavorable opinion of him. It mattered not that he'd spent four years purposefully crafting the image of an unfeeling bastard. He didn't like that Katherine saw him in that light. Katherine carried on. "You would have, of course, asked the benefits of a marriage to me."

Again, he imagined her sprawled out upon his bed. "Oh, and what would be the benefits of a marriage to you?" he asked, voice garbled.

Katherine's eyes lit, and the glimmer of sadness faded. She held a finger up, and then shifted the copy of Wordsworth's work. She reached inside her reticule and pulled out a note. She held it out.

His brow furrowed. "What is this?"

"A list with all the benefits in marrying me."

Jasper glanced down at it, staring blankly at the title.

All the Reasons to Wed Lady Katherine

"It isn't a very clever title," Katherine prattled on. "It isn't the title of the list that is important, of course, but rather the contents within the list."

The page shook in Jasper's hands.

Katherine's frown returned. "Are you all right?"

Jasper's shoulders quaked, and the oddest rumble built within his chest, steadily increasing, until something foreign, something exploded from his lips—laughter. Rusty and hoarse from ill use. It echoed in the quiet of Hyde Park.

She snatched the list out of his hands. "You needn't laugh at me."

Jasper continued to shake, as he laughed for the first time in three years. He laughed until tears seeped from the corners of his eyes, the feel and sound of it foreign, and yet, freeing. He'd never thought to laugh again.

As his laughter subsided to a small chuckle, he reached for the list. "If I may?" He took it from her hands.

She grabbed for it but he held the vellum beyond her reach. "Obviously you aren't aware that it is ungentlemanly to grab something from a lady's hands."

"Obviously," he muttered under his breath. He scanned the list.

I am well-versed in poetry. There was that.

I despise London. Well, they were of like opinions there.

I'll not require a large wardrobe or fine jewels. He had enough money to shower her daily with diamonds and sapphires if she so wished.

I can provide as many children as desired. His eyes fixed on that item. The images that crept into his mind of Katherine's satiny smooth skin bared to his gaze shifted, to an image of her abed, staring up with sightless eyes, the bed soaked in a pool of blood as she gave her life for one of those children. Nausea rolled in his gut. He crushed the page in his hands.

"You needn't wrinkle it," Katherine groused, pulling it out of his white-knuckled grip, seeming unaware of the hell that ravaged Jasper's mind. "I'm certain there are other reasons."

"And what of you, my lady? I don't imagine the contract be mutually beneficial for you. What desperation would drive a lady to ask a gentleman who is so, how did you phrase it? Condescending and mocking? To be her husband?"

Humiliated pain flashed in Katherine's eyes, and Jasper, who'd thought himself deadened on the inside, was knifed with guilt.

She stuffed the list angrily into her reticule. Her jerky movements sent Wordsworth's work tumbling to the ground. "It was silly of me to ask you." She spoke so quickly, her words spilled over one another, and blurred together. "I don't know what manner of madness would ever compel me to do something as foolhardy as to ask you for—"

Jasper kissed her.

He dimly registered the reticule slipping from between her fingers, and landing in the snow with a faint thump. He grasped her hips, and pulled her close, so that his shaft nestled in the soft flesh of her belly. His mouth slanted over hers angrily until her lips parted, and he slid his tongue inside to taste her; she tasted of cinnamon and mint leaves, and he wanted to lose himself forever in her.

Katherine reached up and wrapped her arms about his neck; her full breasts crushed against the expanse of his chest. She moaned, and he swallowed that sound. Jasper cupped her buttocks in his hands, and anchored her to him.

The distant echo of screeching kestrel split the silence; more powerful than the blare of a pistol. Jasper wrenched his mouth away. His breathing came in fast, deep pants, and it was all he could do to keep from pulling her into his arms again.

Her thick lashes fluttered open. "Well," she said, breathlessly. "I believe we might add that to my list, then."

Reality intruded, swiftly.

Ah yes, the list.

Katherine must have seen something in his expression for she cleared her throat. "I should be going then." She bent down and retrieved the leather volume and her reticule.

He should let her go. It would be wise to let her dip her curtsy, turn on her heel, leave, and forget they'd ever met at the Frost Fair. At the possibility of never again seeing her again, something wrenched inside him. She took a step to leave. "You did not ever explain what would be the benefit in marrying me, Katherine."

The tip of her boot hovered above the ground. She set it down, and eyed him warily, as though he'd set out some kind of trap that she were taking great pains to avoid.

"Well, I hate ringlets."

Jasper furrowed his brow. "I beg your pardon."

"And gowns made of too much ivory and lace." She waved her hand. "Mother insists I wear them because it is the ladylike thing to do. It would be such good fun to wear vibrant shades. I should like to wear a silken gown of the deepest sapphire hue. I imagine as your wife, I'd have a good deal of freedom in selecting my wardrobe."

"Undoubtedly," he said in serious tones. If Katherine were his wife, he would hire the finest modiste and let her select whatever fancy laces and satins she desired.

Her brows knitted into a single line. "Are you making light of me again?"

"I wouldn't dream of it," he said, dryly. "You'd wed me then to wear fine fabrics?"

She shook her head, dislodging one of those brown ringlets. "You misunderstand me, Your Grace. I don't give a fig about the type or quality of the fabrics. I merely want to make a selection of my own. It is rather tedious going through life having every decision made for you. It seems like such a very small thing, selecting one's fabric, and yet it is a luxury I'm not afforded. Instead, I must do as my mother sees fit, no matter how happy or unhappy those decisions make me."

Jasper didn't know if Katherine was aware of it, but somewhere along the way, she'd ceased to speak of fabrics and instead spoke of Bertrand Ekstrom.

It was also the moment he knew he would wed her.

"What else, Katherine?" he said, softly.

"I don't believe you'd squander your wealth." She glanced down at the snow. "I believe you to be a gentleman who'd not leave your family destitute, at the mercy of distant relatives."

"And is that what happened to you, Katherine? Your father left your family destitute?"

She snapped her mouth closed, and her lips flattened into a single, mutinous line.

A vise-like pressure tightened around the heart he'd thought deadened. Except, if it was dead, he should not feel this dull pain at the thought of a young Katherine destitute, desperate, at the mercy of others. If her father were not dead, he'd gladly grind the bastard's face beneath the weight of his fist.

Poor Katherine.

Katherine glared up at him, her eyes snapping fire. "I do not want your pity."

She possessed more strength and courage than most gentlemen he'd known in his life. "I wouldn't dare pity you," he murmured. Jasper didn't believe he could identify a single lady who'd be so bold as to propose marriage, all to save herself from her scheming mother's machinations.

Katherine's eyes ran a path over his face, as if trying to ascertain the sincerity of his words, and he hated that his vibrant, spirited Katherine should have such a guarded look to her. She nodded slowly. "Well, then. Thank you again for the volume."

She made to step around him, but he placed himself in front of her.

Her breath stirred little puffs of white winter air about her. She shifted the burdens of the book and reticule she carried. "What is it, then?" Heavy annoyance underlined her words.

There was something so very endearing about her unguarded reaction to him.

The volume in her hand fell again into the snow. Poor Wordsworth would be in quite the state if he could see the condition of his poor leather volume.

Jasper felt himself grinning in response.

"Yes," he said.

An unladylike curse escaped her as she bent down to retrieve her volume. "Yes, what, Your Grace?"

"Yes, Jasper," he corrected. "And yes, I'll marry you."

Chapter 13

After he'd made certain that Katherine had made her way safely home, the implications of their meeting hit Jasper with all the force of a heap of stone being placed upon his chest. With his mind spinning and gut clenching, Jasper, for the first time in many years, sought out someone else's counsel.

He clasped his hands behind his back and paced the Aubusson carpet in the Marquess of Guilford's office.

Now, it was one thing seeking out counsel; it was an altogether different thing in broaching such a delicate matter for discussion.

Guilford rested, hip propped at the edge of his wide mahogany desk. "I must say, this visit is rather something of a surprise."

Jasper glared over at him, and continued pacing.

What manner of madness had possessed him to accept Katherine's offer of marriage? He'd been so enchanted, so utterly beguiled by the sight of her with that silly bonnet and preposterous list, his acceptance had just tumbled from his lips.

He'd not considered the ramifications of marriage to . . . not just to Katherine, but to any woman.

He'd not risk an emotional connection, and he most certainly would not risk begetting another heir upon any wife. Nay, not just any wife.

He stopped abruptly in the middle of Guilford's floor.

Lady Katherine Adamson.

Jasper wiped the back of his hand across his eyes.

Christ.

"I venture something has happened to bring you out of your lair?"

Oh, something had certainly happened all right.

"I agreed to marry Lady Katherine Adamson."

His friend cocked his head. "What was that?"

Jasper resumed pacing. "Marriage. To Katherine . . . Lady Katherine," he amended. He slashed the air with his hand. "I know what you are thinking."

Guilford snorted. "Oh, I'd wager you most certainly do not."

Jasper gritted his teeth at the obvious humor in his friend's tone. He was glad one of them found the situation bloody amusing. The reality of it was that it was a blasted nightmare. He most certainly could not wed Katherine.

There was the matter of children.

And her damned smile. And her tight brown ringlets.

And . . .

Lydia.

He froze again, struck by the realization that he'd not thought of Lydia. What was happening to him?

"So you offered for the lady."

Jasper glanced up. "Not quite," he muttered under his breath.

Guilford scratched his brow. "What was that? I believe you said—"

"That I accepted the lady's offer."

A bark of laughter filled the room. Guilford shoved himself off his desk and strode over to the collection of crystal decanters on the table at the center of the room. "Am I to believe the lady offered for you? Lady Katherine offered for *you*?"

Jasper bristled at the insult. What was so bloody hilarious about Lady Katherine's interest in him?

Guilford must have followed the direction of his thoughts. "I must say I believe this is the first I know of a lady offering for a gentleman." He touched the decanter to an empty glass and splashed several fingerfuls into it. He held it out to Jasper.

Jasper waved it off. "I can't wed her."

The glass froze midway to Guilford's mouth. He lowered it to his side. "Never tell me you'd renege on your offer . . ."

"It was her offer," Jasper bit out. And then, "No, I wouldn't," he sighed. He might be a coldhearted bastard, dead on the inside, but he was still a gentleman. To not wed the lady now would be the height of dishonorable.

Guilford held his glass up in salute. "Well, then, congratulations are in order."

Jasper growled and resumed pacing. "I cannot wed her," he said more to himself.

"I believe you've already pointed out that you are a bit late in that regard," Guilford drawled.

Jasper strode over to the crystal decanters and reached for the nearest bottle. He poured a glass full to the rim.

"And spirits, too? Well, this is quite the day, indeed. What should I expect next? Horses to fly over the Serpentine?"

Jasper downed the contents in a single swallow. He grimaced at the fiery path it blazed down his throat. Whiskey. He'd picked bloody whiskey.

It seemed fitting, considering the day he was having.

Nor would it do to point out in the days since he'd met Katherine he'd consumed far more spirits than he had in the course of the four years. Guilford was already enjoying this a good deal too much.

"She had a list," Jasper said at last.

From over the rim of his glass, Guilford's grin widened. "A list?"

Jasper reached for another decanter, this time selecting a bottle of brandy. He sloshed a healthy amount of spirits into his glass and took a long swallow. "A list," he growled, waving his glass about. "You know, a list? Something one articulates . . ."

Guilford laughed. "I know what a list is. Don't be a bloody arse. What manner of list?"

All the Reasons to Wed Lady Katherine

The most recent events were disastrous in every way; Katherine's offer and his acceptance would only upset the carefully protected world Jasper had built for himself.

And yet . . .

He smiled in remembrance.

Guilford choked on a mouthful of brandy. "I say, are you smiling now?" He glanced over at the wide floor-length windows, and squinted. "Surely there are horses flying. There must be."

Jasper set his glass down hard enough to send droplets of moisture spraying over the rim of the glass and onto the rose-inlaid table. He'd had enough of Guilford having fun at his expense. He scowled until the grin fell from his friend's face.

"It was a bloody list of reasons to marry the lady."

Guilford's lips flattened into a tight line. The faint tremble however, indicated the concerted effort he made to tamp down his amusement. "That must have been quite an impressive list, then."

I can provide as many children as desired . . .

Jasper's eyes slid closed as he thought of the generous curve of her breast weighted in his hand; the peak of that mound of flesh . . . and not for the first time, he wondered as to the shade of that precious peak. He'd wager it was the faintest pink, like—

"By all the saints in heaven, you're smitten with the lady."

Jasper jerked to the moment. He felt a dull flush of heat creeping up his neck, and he yanked at his hastily tied cravat. By God, he was the Duke of Bainbridge. He did not turn red with embarrassment, and certainly not over a young lady in her first, going on second, Season.

"I am not smitten. I'm . . ." he searched for words. "Merely driven out of a sense of pity for her circumstances." Those words rang like a lie in his mind and in his heart.

"Pity?" Guilford pressed. He folded his arms across his chest. "Well, then, let us hear it? What would drive the miserable, recluse, all powerful Duke of Bainbridge to forsake his vow to remain unwed out of"—he arched a brow—"what did you say? Pity?"

"There's the matter of Ekstrom."

Guilford blinked. "You would marry her because of Bertrand Ekstrom?" Thick incredulity underlined his question.

The truth of it was, standing alongside the frozen river, with Katherine looking up at him with wide brown eyes, Bertrand Ekstrom had been the absolute furthest thing from his mind. Now, the thought of her with the loathsome, foul letch unleashed a primitive beast from deep inside him that wanted to tear from Guilford's office and hunt down Ekstrom.

"It was mutually beneficial for the both of us." Jasper settled for a safe answer.

His friend swirled the remaining amber contents of his glass. "How very practical of the both of you."

With her directness and bold spirit, Katherine Adamson seemed a good deal more practical than any other ladies he'd encountered in the past, including Lydia. His wife had dedicated her attention to her wardrobe and the running of his household staff. Furthermore, he could not imagine docile, gentle-spirited Lydia thwarting her parents' marital arrangements for her by boldly proposing to a gentleman.

Guilford set his glass down hard on the table with a loud *thunk*. "I would be remiss if I failed to inform you that Lady Katherine Adamson's intentions in wedding you are not strictly practical. A young lady would not brave your stern, miserable countenance if there were not feelings on her part."

Those words sunk into Jasper's brain. He blinked, and then gave his head a hard shake. "Bah, you're mad. Katherine is practical. She merely proposed a marriage of convenience."

His friend snorted. "Ballocks. I wager you are in for a good deal of trouble if you enter into this union believing that."

Jasper's jaw hardened. He'd not bother with Guilford's foolish suppositions. With the exception of two kisses, two passionate kisses that had set his body on fire with a potent lust and a desire to lay her down . . .

He shook his head so hard a strand of hair fell across his eye. Jasper brushed it back angrily. "I don't care to discuss the matter anymore."

Guilford's grin widened. "May I point out that you sought out my opinion?"

"No, I didn't," Jasper said, harshly.

"You didn't?"

"I didn't," Jasper confirmed.

"Then what—?"

"I merely came by to see if you'll be a witness to my nuptials." There would be no banns read in three successive Sundays. Jasper's next visit would be to put his formal offer to Lady Katherine's guardian. Then he'd wed the lady. He had little desire to be exposed to the *ton*'s scrutiny. They'd wed, retreat to Kent, and carry on their own separate, well-ordered lives.

Guilford's eyes moved over his face, and then a long beleaguered sigh escaped him. "I do not care for that look in your eyes. As your friend, I need to say that this is a horrendous idea. You don't allow a lady to offer marriage and wed her on a matter of convenience. Yes, a dreadful idea. Horrible. Bloody awful. All around madness."

Jasper gritted his teeth hard enough that they clicked together noisily. "Will you serve as a witness?"

"Of course I will." Guilford strode over, and slammed his hand against Jasper's back. "Congratulations, friend. And good luck."

As Jasper took his leave, he suspected he was going to need a good deal more than luck.

Chapter 14

Yes the realities of life so cold,
So cowardly, so ready to betray,
So stinted in the measure of their grace
As we pronounce them, doing them much wrong,
Have been to me more bountiful than hope,
Less timid than desire—but that is past . . .

—William Wordsworth, "Home at
Grasmere" in *The Recluse Part First*

$\mathcal{K}$atherine's gaze remained fixed on the words before her. She shifted the heavy leather volume given to her by Jasper; the words dark, the message bleak.

And she'd always before preferred the poems that recognized the flaws in love and the world around one, because she *knew* the flaws of love and the world around *her*.

So why was she ruminating over six lines, despairing over their bleakness? What great shift had occurred in the universe that she instead wanted to escape into the gentle joy and optimism to be found in Byron's sonnets?

"You have been staring at that same page for nearly an hour," Anne called from the seat she occupied at the pianoforte.

Katherine started, and the book slipped from her fingers onto her lap. "Surely it's not been an hour." She snapped it closed with a decided click.

Anne continued to play the haunting strains of Dibdin's famous "Tom Bowling." She waggled her brows. "Oh, it most certainly has been. Why, I've played pieces by Handel and Corelli and Gluck—"

Katherine set her book down beside her on the sofa. "Your point is quite clear, Anne."

Anne grinned and continued to play flawlessly. Her quick fingers moved expertly over the keys.

Katherine thought of the rather pathetic list she'd given to Jasper and winced. There'd been nary a ladylike quality to recommend her as a wife. Anne could fill several sheets of parchment with all her ladylike attributes. It had never mattered to Katherine the vast differences in them—until now. Now, she wished she didn't possess the tight brown ringlets and a remarkable lack of skills on the pianoforte, and embroidering, and watercolors, and . . .

"You've gone all serious again."

Katherine trailed the tip of her finger over the bruised leather spine of Wordsworth's volume. Several tumbles into the thick blanket of snow when she'd last met Jasper had resulted in a hopelessly ruined leather cover. "Have I?" she murmured, distractedly. It had been three days since they'd last met.

Three days since she'd given him that silly list.

Three days since he'd accepted her offer of marriage.

And since then, she'd not heard a word from him. Not a letter. Not a visit.

Katherine jumped to her feet and began to pace.

She'd surely shocked him with her request at Hyde Park. Perhaps he'd come to his senses and merely intended to carry on as though that particular exchange had never occurred. Katherine would then have to go on and marry that horrid

Mr. Ekstrom. Her stomach tightened into pained, twisted knots, and she wanted to blame them upon that horrid Mr. Ekstrom, but knew it was the thought of Jasper altering his decision that caused those pained, twisted knots.

"You seem rather upset."

Katherine glanced over at her sister. "I'm not upset." Only filled with panic at the prospect of wedding Mr. Ekstrom.

"It is that Mr. Ekstrom, isn't it?" Anne stopped playing. She shoved back the bench at her pianoforte and it scraped along the wood floor. "We merely have to find that pendant . . ."

"The pendant will do nothing, Anne. It is a foolish, child-like, wishful dream."

Anne's brow wrinkled. "But Aldora and Michael's . . ."

"Aldora and Michael's marriage had nothing to do with that silly trinket," her cry filled the cavernous space of the parlor. Her throat worked reflexively. Oh, how she envied Anne her innocence. Anne believed in dreams and wishes and magical pendants given to hopeful ladies by greedy gypsies.

A flash of hurt filled Anne's pale-blue eyes. She tipped her chin up a notch. "I know what you believe of me, Katherine. You and Aldora. You believe I'm fanciful and that I don't possess a brain in my head."

Katherine shook her head, besieged by sudden guilt. "Never, Anne." She'd seen her as the sister in need of protection from the woes thrust upon their family by a wastrel father, but never an empty-headed fool.

Her sister continued as though she hadn't spoken. "You both believed I wasn't aware of our financial circumstances. You believed I remained immune to the direness of our situation."

Shock slammed into Katherine, but Anne went on. "I am not silly or—"

"I don't believe you're silly—"

"Empty-headed," Anne said, her eyes blazed with more emotion than Katherine ever remembered in her gentle eyes. "I am, I *might* be, fanciful. And I might dream of love, and happily ever afters, but that does not make me silly." She angled her head. "Well, it might seem silly but I believe it is more hopeful. I'm hopeful that there are men who are good and don't squander their family's wealth, and leave them destitute, and force them to sell off all their possessions and release all their servants."

Katherine searched her sister's face, and the guilt inside spiraled and grew as she confronted the reality; she'd not protected Anne from their family's dire situation, no more than Aldora had protected Katherine. They'd all been touched by their father's selfishness.

Suddenly, she wished she had that heart pendant, wished she could turn it over to her sister who believed in love, and . . . Katherine blinked . . .

"What is it?" Anne asked.

. . . and realized she believed in love, too. She did not love Jasper Waincourt, 8th Duke of Bainbridge. She could not. She *would* not. Not when such a gentleman would never be able to love her in return.

"Katherine?" Anne asked again.

No. She appreciated his forthrightness, his regard for poetry, and his passionate embrace. There was nothing more.

There couldn't be.

"I'm so sorry, Anne." For not protecting you, for not sharing with you my fears, for losing the heart pendant worn by Aldora and her friends.

Anne captured her hands, and gave them a gentle squeeze. "There is no reason to be sorry. If you did want to perhaps join me again at the Frost Fair and search for—"

Katherine's laugh cut into her sister's words.

"What?" Anne said, defensively. "We simply will not find the heart pendant unless we search for it."

They would not find it, because Katherine had already lost it. What was worse was that Katherine was too much a coward to admit as much to Anne.

"Don't you dream of love, Katherine?"

"I'm too practical to dream of love, Anne," she said softly. She had. At one time. Back when she'd been a silly, naïve girl of fifteen years. Now, as a woman of nearly twenty years, a woman who had nary a suitor, or any offers for her hand, and who had to convince the Duke of Bainbridge to wed her, well, the dream of love didn't exist for ladies such as her.

"Well, that is very sad, then."

Katherine opened her mouth to respond when a high-pitched cry interrupted her response.

The door flew open.

Katherine and Anne's gaze swung as one toward the entrance of the room.

Mother stood at the center, her hand aloft, a scrap of thick vellum in her hand. "It is not to be countenanced," she cried.

Katherine and Anne exchanged looks. Mother's theatrics were often best reserved for the stage, but when she was in such a state, it was wise to avoid her.

She stormed into the room. Her deep-burgundy satin skirts slapped noisily against her legs. She stopped in front of them, and brandished the letter in her hand.

"A letter," she cried. "The . . . the . . . gall of the man. He dares to notify me in such a manner."

"Mother," Katherine began.

Her mother silenced her with a single, black glare. "Not a word, Katherine. This is entirely your fault. It matters not that he's a duke. He's a shameful, scandalous man. The Mad Duke," she muttered.

Katherine's heart sped up. He'd spoken to her guardian. He must have. There was no other accounting for Mother's fury.

Mother waved the paper about. "He's not been seen by Society in years, and all those hideous rumors about him murdering his wife." She shuddered.

Katherine stiffened. Fury lanced through her body. How dare her mother? Jasper was no more capable of murder than Katherine was capable of sprouting wings and taking flight. "That is unfair, Mother. He did not murder his wife."

"Do you even know what happened to her?" her mother shot back.

Katherine rocked back on her heels . . . because, no, she didn't. She did, however, know with great certainty that whatever had happened to Jasper's wife had been no fault of his. She was sure of it. "I do not. But neither does the *ton*."

"You defend him!" Mother wrang her hands together, crumpling the parchment in her fingers. "Oh, why, why, why did you go off to that fair? If you hadn't, then he wouldn't have offered for you, and your uncle wouldn't have said yes."

Anne gasped. Her eyes widened, and she looked to Katherine. There was a hint of shocked hurt there. Katherine's gaze slid away. As twin sisters they'd shared nearly everything. In this, Katherine had not deigned to mention her meetings with Jasper. It had just seemed too . . . too . . . intimate.

"The fiend won't even allow for the banns to properly wed. He insists on a wedding posthaste. Why, he won't even allow time for your sister and her husband to be summoned." She threw her hands into the air.

"Oh," Katherine said, flummoxed. She'd not given any thoughts to the details surrounding their nuptials. She'd imagined at least a private, intimate gathering with her family. The faintest little pang pierced her heart. What had she expected? Theirs was a match of convenience, nothing more. Yet . . . the tiniest, most infinitesimal smidgeon of her heart had dreamed of something very different than a hasty wedding without even her siblings present.

Mother sank down into the nearest sofa. Her skirts fluttered about her feet. She buried her head into her hands and shook it back and forth. "Now Anne's Season will be hopelessly ruined." Katherine balled her hands into tight little fists at her side. Yes, because that had always been Mother's primary concern: Anne securing the most advantageous match.

As if she detected the subtle hurt, Anne reached over and slipped her fingers into Katherine's. She gave them a slight squeeze, and a smile of support for Katherine.

"Oh, I'm certain the connection to any duke will not hurt our place amongst the haute *ton*, Mother," Anne said. She released Katherine's hand and tugged free the paper in their mother's hands. She skimmed the sheet. Her eyes widened. "What?" Katherine reached for it, but Anne shifted it away from her grasp, and continued to read.

Mother ignored Anne. "Your uncle considered nothing more than the duke's title. I'm certain of it."

"I'd venture he also considered the very, very generous terms of the contract," Anne muttered.

Katherine grabbed for the parchment, her heart thudding hard in her breast. This time, Anne turned it over.

Katherine began to read, and promptly choked.

He'd settled £1200 upon her annually as pin money? By all the saints in heaven.

"That is a small fortune," Anne murmured, eyes wide and unblinking.

She was to have a country cottage in Kent.

Anne scratched at her brow. "All money brought by your dowry is to revert over to you if anything should happen to him." She shook her head. "I dare say this is very generous, Mother."

Generous? Katherine's throat worked reflexively. Generous? Through his magnanimous gesture, Jasper had ensured she'd never be dependent upon him as Mother had been dependent on their wastrel father.

"I do not care if the duke gave her the Queen's crown," Mother cried. "The man killed his wife. Surely that matters to one of you?"

A knock sounded at the door.

Three pairs of eyes swiveled to the entrance of the room.

Katherine's stomach lurched. *Oh, goodness.* Her toes curled inside her ivory satin slippers.

The butler cleared his throat, his small blue eyes wide in his pale face. "Er, the Duke of Bainbridge to see Lady Katherine."

Jasper's imposing figure filled the doorway. An enormous specimen of a man, the smallish butler seemed a mere flicker in his shadow. Jasper glanced at her momentarily; his expression the hard, inscrutable one she'd come to expect.

Humiliation over her mother's outburst melded with pain for the ugly insults Mother and all of Society leveled at this generous, if cold, gentleman. Society didn't know him to be a man who'd risked death to rescue her from the frozen depths of the Thames. They didn't know the man who appreciated the tortured words of Wordsworth. And they most certainly didn't know he'd sacrificed himself to wed plain, bluestocking Katherine Adamson, saving her from Mr. Ekstrom.

His gaze slid away from Katherine, and then he pinned Mother to the spot with his flinty, emerald-green eyes.

She paled and then scrambled to her feet. Her eyes darted nervously about the room. For the first time in Katherine's lifetime, she found her mother an unsettled, stammering, bundle of awkwardness. "Uh, w-welcome, Y-Your Grace. Tea?" she squeaked.

Jasper arched a midnight-black brow.

"Uh, th-that is," Mother crushed the fabric of her skirts in her hand. "That is t-to say . . ."

"I believe my mother is offering you tea, Your Grace," Anne said. She dropped an elegant curtsy and smiled. God love Anne; she epitomized ladylike elegance and grace.

Alas, it appeared this husband-to-be of hers was wholly unaffected by her sister's gentle charm. Jasper peered down the length of his slightly crooked Roman nose at her, and remained silent.

Nor did it fail to escape Katherine's notice that he'd failed to bow.

Anne's smile dipped.

Katherine's gaze moved between Jasper, and her sister, as she considered for the first time how very important it was for Jasper and her sister Anne to like one another.

She hurried across the room. "Your Grace," she said.

He froze her with a look . . . and the words died on her lips.

This was clearly not a man eager to make her his wife. This was the coldhearted beast who'd harshly reprimanded her after he'd pulled her from the Thames.

She staggered to a stop several feet from him, hating the unease that coursed through her. The Jasper she'd come to know did not elicit this uncertainty. He laughed; albeit rusty and harsh, but he laughed. And he spoke in gentle tones.

Mother seemed to compose herself. She tilted her chin up a notch, and cleared her throat. "Your Grace, may I offer you—"

"A moment alone with Lady Katherine," he interrupted in a low, dark tone.

Mother paled, and managed a jerky nod. "V-very w-well. Come along, Anne," she said, and snatched Anne by the forearm and steered her from the room as though she were an archangel saving her daughter from a dark demon.

The door closed behind them, and Katherine stood stock still in the middle of the room with that dark demon. She folded her hands in front of her. "Jasper," she said quietly.

He said nothing.

Katherine caught her lower lip between her teeth and troubled the flesh. His eyes narrowed as he followed that distracted movement.

She stopped. "You know, there really is no reason for you to be so surly."

His nostrils flared, but other than that, he gave no outward reaction to her statement.

"Anne was perfectly polite—"

"And your mother?" he interjected, his voice as cold as the hard edge of a knife.

Katherine took another step toward him until they were a mere hand's-breadth apart. "I'd not find fault with you for the crimes of your father or mother."

His body went ramrod straight; his broad shoulders stiffened within the fabric of his black coat.

Some volatile emotion flared in his eyes, and Katherine took a hasty step backward. All of a sudden, her mother's outrageous charge about Jasper surfaced. Katherine knew with certainty the words to be false; Jasper could never commit an act of violence, most especially against a woman . . . yet, his hardened eyes and the rigid set to his square jaw would be enough to give the most courageous gentleman pause.

It struck Katherine that she knew nothing of Jasper's parents, and that she'd quite callously insulted them. "Is your mother—?"

"Dead," he said flatly.

Her heart twisted with pain for him. "I'm sorry," she said.

He flexed his jaw. "Don't be."

Just that. Two words. A chill ran along her spine. What manner of man was he that he could be so emotionless when speaking of his parents?

He brushed his fingertips along the edge of her cheek, and she flinched.

A wintry smile formed on his lips. "What, are you regretting your offer, my lady?"

Katherine hesitated. "Of course not." However, even he seemed to detect the uncertainty in her reply.

He cupped his hand around the nape of her neck, and warmth fanned out from the point where his fingers touched her skin, and raced through her. Her heartbeat fluttered wildly in her breast with a heady awareness of him.

Jasper dipped his head, so close their lips nearly met. "Not even with your mother's charges against me?"

Her heart paused a beat. Something in his question begged her to ask him more, and God help her for being a coward, even as she longed to know the details surrounding his wife's death, she couldn't bring herself to ask the words.

He touched his finger to the tip of her nose. "Come, Katherine. I'd imagine you're very curious to know the details? What? Silence?" He made a tsking sound. "How very disappointing when I've come to expect boldness from you."

Katherine took a step backward, placing distance between them. She yearned for the gentleman who'd given her the last copy of Wordsworth's volume. Not this . . . not this . . . coolly mocking stranger.

Ultimately, her desire to know the secrets of his past won out. She took a deep breath. "What happened to your wife?"

Chapter 15

*A*hh, so there was the bold-spirited, inquisitive woman he'd come to anticipate since their meeting at the Frost Fair.

Since he'd entered the parlor, she'd eyed him with that wariness he'd come to expect from members of Society. Not her. Not Katherine.

Jasper stalked over to the corner of the room and pulled back the curtains to peer down into the bustling London streets. Something about that hesitancy in her brown eyes, the shade of disapproval in her tone, did something to him. He gripped the edge of the window sill. Goddamn him for caring.

"I must say, I'm still disappointed, Katherine."

From the glass windowpane he detected the nervous manner in which she shifted upon her feet. "Your Grace?"

With her telltale reactions, Katherine conveyed her every unspoken word and emotion; she'd be wise to avoid any gaming table.

He turned around slowly to face her. "Surely you intend to ask the question?"

Her chest rose and fell in a rhythmic slowness. She met his gaze squarely. "And what question is that, Jasper?"

A mirthless laugh burst from his chest, bitter and angry to his own ears. "Come now, Katherine. Surely you're curious enough to ask the question of the man you'll wed. Do you wonder as to the truth of the rumors? Did the Mad Duke truly kill his wife?"

Katherine shook her head quickly. "I don't listen to gossip, Jasper." She folded her hands in front of her. "I know you aren't capable of hurting anyone."

He'd killed Lydia as if he'd plunged a dagger through her heart.

Bitter pain dug at his heart like a thousand rusty, jagged knives being applied to the deadened organ. Katherine's tone and the directness of her gaze spoke to her conviction. Oh, how misguided she was in her faith. Guilford's words trickled into his consciousness. *A young lady would not brave your stern, miserable countenance if there were not feelings on her part.*

The sooner he disabused his wife-to-be of any grand illusions of him, the better off they'd be.

"I fear you are wrong on that score, my lady."

Katherine's small, lithe frame stilled. Then, her arms fell to her sides and hung there, awkwardly. "I don't . . ." He took a step toward her. She wet her lips and went on. "I don't . . ."

"You don't what?" he said on a silken whisper. "Believe it?"

She glanced over her shoulder toward the closed door, and Jasper suspected she considered her escape. Good, Katherine, that is wise. *You should turn on your heel and run as far and fast as your slippers will carry you from my miserable self. You'd have been fortunate to have any other gentleman rescue you that day at the Frost Fair.*

Katherine looked back at him. "No, Jasper," she said at last, with that same misplaced faith in him. "I don't believe you killed your wife."

"Oh, you would be wrong, my lady." He reached a hand up, and captured one of those tight brown ringlets between his thumb and forefinger.

Katherine winced, as if his nearness caused her physical distress.

"Should I tell you of the blood and the screams?" he hissed.

Katherine swatted his hand away. "Stop it," she commanded. She clamped her hands over her ears. "I do not believe you. If you do not want to wed me, then you should say as much. You shouldn't tell these . . . these . . . great, horrific lies." Her voice shook under the weight of her fear. It lit her eyes, and caused her lean limbs to tremble.

He circled her wrists with his hands and gently removed them from her ears. "They aren't lies," Jasper went on. If she wanted to wed him, then she should know what kind of monster she'd take for a husband.

Katherine's breath came fast and heavy, as though she'd just run a good a distance. If she were wise, she would run a good distance away from this room, away from him.

She yanked her hands back, and for a brief moment he thought she might flee. He should have known better of his bold-spirited, indomitable Katherine.

She folded her arms across her chest, and tapped her foot in a fast, staccato rhythm upon the wood floor. "Well, then. Tell me the details, Jasper. I want to know. I deserve to know."

Yes, she did. All of it.

"I loved my wife," he said without preamble.

Katherine's lips parted ever so slightly, and then she seemed to remember herself, and snapped them closed.

"Would you care to hear the details, Katherine?" he taunted.

Katherine's heart froze. She reminded herself to breathe.

I loved my wife.

Of course he had. Jasper's retreat from Society and the private manner in which he lived his life alluded to a love for the woman who'd been his wife. But there had been no details, nothing more than suppositions—until now. The knowing somehow made the agony of his indifference all the more painful.

Did she care for the details? Why she'd rather have the lashes upon her lids plucked one at a time than hear of his love for the paragon of a woman who'd been his wife. It was selfish and wrong . . . but she could no more stop the ugly sentiments than she could stop from breathing.

Instead she said, "Yes, Jasper. Tell me the details." *Because I'm a glutton for pain and suffering.*

"Her name was Lydia, and she was the most beautiful woman I'd ever seen; her hair was the color of spun gold, and her eyes like the deepest, clearest blue seas." He wandered back to the window, his carriage proudly erect and unmoving.

As he stared down into the streets below, silent and unspeaking, her heart spasmed. The image he so poetically painted of his wife—nay, *Lydia*—was one of a woman who'd inspired romantic words from this now cold, unfeeling Jasper. Lydia, the grand beauty, and surely a diamond of the first water. Not like Katherine with her silly brown ringlets and dull brown eyes, who would never inspire any grand sentiments in a gentleman.

She sank into the nearest seat, an overstuffed King Louis chair.

Jasper glanced over his shoulder and ran a disinterested stare over her still form. "I courted her. I fell in love with her. The kind of love those foolish poets write of."

Oh, God, why did her heart crack in the manner it did? She swallowed past a swell of emotion in her throat.

He carried on. There was no need for questions or prodding on her part. Jasper had retreated to that place inside himself he'd dwelt in since she'd first met him at the Frost Fair.

"She loved London, and I, once upon a lifetime ago, also loved London. I was so very comfortable there."

Something else she'd not known of him. She'd believed his absence from London these years had been because he'd detested the overcrowded, dirty, gossip-driven glittery world. No, his self-imposed exile had been motivated by his love for Lydia.

Katherine gripped the corners of her seat. It would appear they had even less in common than she'd ever believed.

Jasper gave his head the slightest shake. "The day I learned Lydia was with child, I insisted we retreat to my holdings in the country. And those eight months were the happiest of my life."

Oh, God, surely he could detect the loud cracking of her heart. Why? Why would the blasted organ splinter apart if she weren't in love with him? She could not love him. Not this . . . stranger who still mourned his dead paragon of a wife.

Jasper went on. "It was a Sunday when she felt a tightening pain. I insisted she rest. I sent round for a doctor but continued to carry on with the estate's business while she suffered in the solitary confines of her own chambers." His face contorted in such unguarded grief, Katherine dropped her gaze. "That is the kind of man you'd wed."

"What happened?" Did that whisper belong to her?

His fiery gaze flew to hers. "Would you care for the details, Katherine?"

She shook her head quickly. "N . . ."

"The doctor summoned me."

His eyes took on a faraway look of a man who'd come close to the fiery pits of hell and had been forever scorched by its flames. "Would you hear how she screamed for three long days, until her voice went hoarse and then silent from the bloody shouts of terror and agony that ravaged her throat?"

Katherine again shook her head. "No . . ." She cried, and surged to her feet, filled with an image of him beside his wife as she fought to birth their child.

"Or would you have me tell you of how with her last gasping breath she gave life to a small blue babe?"

A muscle ticked in the corner of his eye, and his hard visage blurred before her. She dashed a hand across her eyes, realizing she cried for the agony he'd known, for the loss of his love, and for the tiny babe. Katherine angrily swiped at the mementos of despair; Jasper would not welcome her pity.

As she expected, his gaze momentarily fell to her tear-stained cheeks, and when he looked back at her, a stiff, macabre grin turned his lips.

"Or would you rather I tell you of how I held that babe, who struggled to breath for two days, sucking in raspy gasps for air?"

She closed her eyes at the heartrending image he painted.

"Would you hear of how he turned into me, and then drew his last breath?"

Katherine struggled to swallow around the enormous lump of pain that clogged her throat. She forced her gaze to Jasper's. He stood stock-still, the harsh angles of his face etched in grief, as though the moments of years past were as fresh as if they'd just transpired.

In that moment, confronting the depth of her feelings for this man, Katherine realized if she could bring back Lydia and that small, nameless babe, she'd relinquish him . . . even if that meant he'd have never been there to save her at the Frost Fair. "I am so sorry, Jasper." She willed him to hear the depth of sincerity in those five words.

His square jaw flexed. "You and Society wonder if I killed my wife." His long-legged stride closed the distance between them. He stopped at the foot of her chair, so she was forced to crane her head back to look at him. "And the truth is, I did, Katherine. I killed her as surely as if I'd put a pistol to her."

Katherine surged to her feet. "You didn't," her voice shook with emotion. She reached a hand up and touched his cheek. As though the pain of his loss had not been great enough, he'd had to contend with Society's jeering whispers and horrid accusations. The Mad Duke, they called him. His only madness had been in loving so very much.

He flinched at her touch, and she dropped it back to her side with humiliated rejection.

"Would you still wed me, Katherine? Would you wed me, knowing I'm a monster?"

She studied him, her heart squeezing. *Oh, Jasper.* He'd loved so very much, it had turned him into this black, empty shell of a man. She could no sooner turn and walk away from him than she could cut her hand from her own person. "I would," she said softly.

Jasper's eyes locked with hers; the dark black of his green irises moved over her face. Then, he dropped his brow to hers. "Then you are a fool," he said on a harsh whisper.

Perhaps she was. But the moment his hand had closed around her wrist, and he'd pulled her gasping and desperate from the frozen waters of the Thames, their lives had become irrevocably connected, and she'd become his, as he was hers.

She wrapped her arms around his massive frame and turned her cheek into his chest. Katherine detected the hard, rapid beat of his heart. It thumped hard against the wall of his chest, the muted beat muffled by her ear. His arms hung by his side, and then he raised them ever so slightly, as if to enfold her in his embrace. But then he let them fall back down.

Katherine edged away from him; she leaned up on tiptoe and pressed her lips to his.

Jasper's muscles strained the fabric of his midnight-black garments, and then he took her in his arms. His mouth slanted over hers again and again; fast, hard, and furious as he tasted her lips. Theirs was not a gentle exchange but a volatile explosion of passion to rival the most violent of summer thunderstorms.

She opened her mouth and allowed him entry. His tongue slid inside, possessive and searching, and she met the bold thrust and parry of his kiss.

He folded his hand around her neck and angled her head, so he could better plunge his expert tongue into the cavern of her mouth.

Katherine moaned and the life seeped down her legs, and down her feet, until she was reduced to nothingness in his arms. He caught her to him, and anchored her against his chest.

His kiss was what drove poets to memorialize their words upon a written page and drove women to sin, and young ladies to toss aside their good name and respectability. And she took his kiss. All of it.

A gasping cry escaped her as his hand cupped her breast, the breathless sound swallowed by his mouth. His mouth left hers, and she tangled her fingers into the thick strands of his black hair and tugged, in a desperate attempt to bring his lips back to hers.

Her efforts proved ineffectual and he continued his quest. He kissed a path down her temple, and to the sensitive flesh where her neck met her ear.

A breathless giggle escaped her.

Jasper pulled back and glanced up at her, questioningly.

"It tickled," she said weakly, wanting to toss her head back and shout with frustration, desperate for him to continue.

Jasper touched the tip of his finger to that sensitive patch of flesh, and then lowered his lips again to the skin there.

"Oh, Jasper," she whispered on a breathy laugh.

"You are certain you still wish to wed me?" he asked again. The faintest hint of uncertainty underlined that question and her heart flipped at the crack in the cold veneer he'd perfected these many years.

Was he mad? His hot touch fueled the dreams of him, and their future, a future where those kisses were not mere kisses, where he showed her the truth behind every last secret she'd wondered of between a man and woman.

She cupped his cheek, and leaned up. "There isn't another man I'd rather wed."

His gaze seared her, bore through hers with a staggering intensity, and with a foolishness more reserved for a naïve debutante, Katherine waited with suspended breath for him to utter like words.

The words however, did not come.

Instead . . .

He nodded curtly. "Very well. We shall wed within the week."

Jasper stepped away from her, sketched a hasty bow, and stormed from the door as though a fire had been set to the parlor.

Katherine stared at the empty doorway long after he'd left. She folded her arms across her chest and hugged herself tight. Jasper could not be clearer than if he'd committed the words to paper, that his interest in her was of a practical nature. There were no intoxicating feelings and desperate longings where he was concerned—not for her. Perhaps all those volatile emotions had been buried with his Lydia.

Her nails dug into the exposed skin of her forearms.

Only . . . his kiss, his touch made her dare to dream, dare to believe that he would eventually come to care for her, as she cared for him.

A knock sounded at the door, and Katherine looked blankly at the entrance as her sister peeked her head in. A wide smile wreathed Anne's porcelain-fine cheeks. "Hullo." She peered around the room as if to ascertain Katherine was alone. "May I come in?"

Katherine nodded, grateful for her twin's presence.

Anne entered, and closed the door behind her. "Mother is livid."

Katherine considered Mother's vile charges when Jasper had arrived earlier. Mother should be ashamed, more than anything else.

Anne tugged Katherine over to the plush, powder-blue velvet-upholstered sofa. "Sit," she commanded as if speaking to a small child.

Katherine smiled weakly up at her sister. Though a handful of minutes older, Anne had never really *seemed* the older of the two. Always ready with a smile, Anne always landed them in any number of troublesome situations. In this moment, however, with her serious expression and calm demeanor, she was very certainly the elder sister. "Well, when I proposed we find you a husband to save you from that horrid

Mr. Ekstrom, I never once imagined you'd find someone who could be far worse."

Katherine shook her head. "No, Anne. He's . . . he's . . ."

Anne's brow wrinkled. "He's what?"

Brave. Hurting. Strong. "He's a good man," she finished lamely.

Anne sat back in the folds of the sofa. "He's a very severe gentleman. I should like my gentleman to smile a good deal and not be so serious like the duke." A long sigh slipped past Anne's bow-shaped lips. "I could never despise anyone who would save you in such a heroic manner as the duke did. But beyond that, there seems little to recommend him." She wrinkled her nose. "Though that *is* a very high recommendation."

One time when Katherine and Anne had been girls of just seven or eight years, they'd been traipsing through the woods of their father's estate. They'd come upon a red fox; its front leg had been caught in a snare, and hopelessly broken and bloodied. The creature's lip had pulled back as it snapped and snarled.

Katherine bit the inside of her cheek to keep from explaining that Jasper was that scared, hurt fox. She loved her sister and trusted her implicitly but still could not betray Jasper's privacy in telling of his past.

"You mustn't wed him unless you wish to," Anne continued. "It shan't be easy with the holiday nearly upon us, but we must find someone to rescue you from both Mr. Ekstrom and the Duke of—"

"I asked him to marry me, Anne."

Her quietly spoken words brought her sister up short. Anne's eyes widened in her face, giving her the look of a night owl. She opened her mouth, but Katherine interrupted her.

"I could not wed Mr. Ekstrom, and the duke, he will be good to me. He will allow me my freedoms and . . ." Her words trailed off, because beyond that, she wasn't altogether certain what type of marriage they would have. There certainly would be none of the grand love he'd known with his last wife.

Anne drummed her finger over the arm of the sofa. "I must say when I dreamed of the heart of a duke for the both of us, I had a far different vision than you married to that beas . . . er, gentleman," she amended when Katherine shot her a reproachful look.

And, sitting there, if Katherine were being entirely truthful, even with just herself, she could admit that she too had longed for something more than a marriage of convenience.

Chapter 16

When Katherine's father, the Earl of Wakefield, had died, a heavy pall hung like the thickest rain cloud upon their household. Shortly after she'd learned of his sudden death, she'd been seated in his office, perched on the edge of a leather winged-back chair, with the ormolu clock atop the fireplace mantle tick-tocking a steady beat. She still remembered the emptiness of that dark day.

Standing at the center of that same room, Katherine considered how very similar that day was to this, her wedding day. She stole a sideways peek up at Jasper. Attired in his customary black jacket, black breeches, stark white waistcoat, and gleaming black Hessians, with his too-long black strands of hair shoved back behind his ears, he put Katherine in mind of that fallen angel Lucifer, cast from the gates of Heaven.

His shoulders stiffened, as if he felt her stare upon his person, but his gaze remained trained on the small vicar officiating the services.

Her gaze slid away, over to the spot her mother and Anne occupied upon the brown Italian-leather sofa. They sat, with like expressions of pained regret carved upon their faces.

"Madam," Jasper bit out.

Katherine jumped, and heat flooded her cheeks as she realized the time had come to recite vows that would forever bind her to this dark near stranger. Her mouth grew dry as the implications of this vow registered. In wedding Jasper, she'd forever be tied to him. The buried hopes she'd only just now acknowledged surfaced, with images of a gentleman who loved her and read poetry to her while their children played at their feet.

She sprung forward on her feet, feeling much like a bird poised for flight.

The gentleman alongside Jasper coughed into his hand.

Katherine looked at the Marquess of Guilford. He met her gaze and gave a gentle smile. Something in his eyes, a silent encouragement, the promise that she was not wrong in her decision this day, strengthened her resolve.

"I, Katherine Adamson . . ." She proceeded to recite the remainder of her vows.

Jasper frowned, and she wondered if he'd expected her to cry off. He clearly didn't know she was a woman with too much honor to ever jilt her respective bridegroom.

Then, in the presence of her mother, sister, and the Marquess of Guilford, and in the absence of her brother, Benedict, sister Aldora, and her husband, Michael, Lady Katherine Adamson became the Duchess of Bainbridge. She expected she should feel . . . something; a new bride's excitement or jittery nervousness . . . not this . . . this . . . emptiness.

There was a flurry of signing required of her and Jasper, completed in silence. The only occasional utterances were spoken by the Marquess of Guilford to the vicar.

She studied her husband as he bent over a sheet of parchment and scribbled his name in the requisite places. He tossed the pen down atop the desk. "It is done," he said quietly.

It is done.

No, that wasn't quite right—it was merely the beginning of the rest of her life.

He held his arm out to Katherine. She studied it, unblinking, and then placed her fingers atop his coat sleeves.

Mother scurried to her feet, a brittle smile on her lips. "Cook has prepared a splendid wedding feast—"

"No," Jasper said his tone harsh.

Mother blinked. "Your Grace."

"There will be no breakfast. The air is thick with snow, and if we are to reach my estate, we'll need to leave posthaste."

Katherine's hand fell back to her side. She angled her head and tried to make sense of Jasper's words. When she'd thought of marriage to him, she'd known they would live together, most assuredly in the country, considering his recent revelation about London. "But it is very nearly Christmas," she blurted. Five pairs of eyes swiveled in Katherine's direction, and panic began to build within her chest. "I imagined we would spend the holiday with my family," she said on a rush. "Aldora and . . ."

Jasper narrowed his eyes. "Aldora?"

Oh, God, he is still a stranger to me, as I am to him. He's not even met my sister. "And Michael. And then there is Benedict, who will be coming soon."

The Marquess of Guilford looked at her with such a pitying expression in his warm blue eyes, but the kind gesture only fueled her panic.

"Isn't that right, Mother?" Katherine swung to face her mother and sister. "Surely Benedict should have arrived already, but he will be so disappointed if we do not remain for Christmas."

"No," Jasper snapped. "My driver has been instructed to wait. We leave immediately."

Anne seemed to sense the desperation that bubbled to the surface, and nearly consumed Katherine. She clapped her hands and beamed at Jasper. "I have a splendid idea. What if we join you for the Christmas season and then . . ."

"No," Jasper cut in. The vein that ran the length of his neck throbbed. "There will be no company."

"I don't understand," Katherine whispered. She winced as the words tumbled into the quiet of the room, and the interlopers of her private despair stared on.

Jasper dusted his immaculate white gloves together. "We leave now."

That was it. No gentle answer. No patient explanation.

Her eyes slid closed. *Good God, what have I done?*

When she opened them, Jasper studied her. For the briefest, slightest moment, she detected a warmth in the fathomless green depths of his eyes. Only, it must have been a flicker of the fire within the hearth responsible for the slight glimmer, for she blinked, and firmly back in place was that coolly mocking expression she'd come to expect.

Katherine searched the room, but there was no one to make him see reason. He was the all-powerful, truculent Duke of Bainbridge, so very clearly accustomed to having his every wish and desire met.

She grunted as Anne hurled herself into Katherine's arms. She clasped Katherine tight, and stroked a soothing, reassuring circle over her back. "I've known since the moment he sent round a note to cancel your meeting in the park that he was for you, Katherine. I just wasn't certain *you* knew it."

Katherine drew back, startled. "I thought you didn't approve."

Her sister's eyes sparkled. "I didn't approve when I thought you might not care for him." Anne must have seen the shock written on Katherine's face, for she squeezed her shoulders. "Remember, he saved you. There is surely good inside him," she whispered against her ear.

Yes, Katherine knew that, and yet, the idea of going off with him to his country estate, alone, shut away from her family, filled her with a stony resentment. She hugged her sister back, hard, and then made her good-byes to Mother.

They made their way through the house, to the foyer, and out the front doors held open by Ollie. The butler inclined his head and opened his mouth . . . perhaps to offer congratulatory words to the newly wedded couple? Only Jasper settled his heavy palm along the base of her back and steered her forward. She frowned up at him, but he appeared wholly unaffected by her displeasure.

They trudged through the snow-filled ground, over to the carriage. Jasper waved off the servant and handed her inside. He leapt up behind her.

The driver closed the door behind them. As the carriage lurched forward carrying Katherine off to her new home, she felt much the way Andromeda had surely felt chained to that rock in hope of salvation from a powerful avenger.

She sat pressed against the corner, and stared at Jasper. His gaze remained fixed at a point above her shoulder, his square jaw firm and unmoving. He might as well have been carved of stone for all the emotion expressed.

Husband. He is my husband.

Resolve strengthened Katherine's spine. If he thought to intimidate her with his harsh coldness, he was to be sorely disappointed in her as a wife. She glared at him.

"You are being an absolute brute," she snapped.

At last, he looked at her.

Jasper stared at this slip of a woman forever bound to him. *His wife.*

Oh, good Christ in heaven. He'd pledged to never again wed, promised to never turn himself over to the hands of another who could inflict the mind-numbing pain he'd known upon Lydia's death.

For the better part of the day, throughout the brief ceremony he'd detected the faint tremor in Katherine's hands, the panicked glitter in her brown eyes, and it had struck him that this woman would belong to him.

Until death they do part.

And then as he'd stood there, with those ominous five words flitting through his mind, he'd imagined a hellish existence in which it was no longer Lydia's lifeless body he held, but Katherine's. Ice climbed up his spine, and chilled him inside and out. She would not die. He'd not allow it.

"Did you hear me?" she snapped. "I said, you're an absolute brute."

She was perfectly correct; he was an absolute brute, a horrid beast, but he'd forgotten long ago how to interact among the living.

"My apologies," he said, startling himself as much as her by the concession.

Her mouth fell agape.

Jasper leaned across the carriage and gently touched his fingers to her chin.

Katherine snapped her lips closed. "Well," she said, and shifted on the bench. "Er, well, then. Thank you."

Jasper settled back in his seat . . .

"But that still does not pardon you."

His lips tugged at the corner. "Pardon me?" Katherine possessed more steely strength and courage than the most hardened battlefield warrior.

She nodded. "It is nearly Christmas."

He knew that. For three years and three-hundred and sixty-four days, he'd well-known the significance of that date. Only, for him it no longer signified birth and a season of hope, but rather the bleak, emptiness of death. "I know that, Katherine. I do not celebrate Christmas."

"That is silly." She pointed her eyes to the ceiling of the coach.

The wind howled as if saddened by the reminder of Lydia. Silence echoed his dark musings, punctuated by the rapid churn of the carriage wheels as it turned up snow and gravel in its wake.

The irony did not escape him either; tomorrow would be the anniversary of Lydia's death, and he should celebrate it married to his new bride.

Katherine continued, seeming unaware of his dark musings. "Christmas is meant to be a time of joy and peace. You've been shut away for so very long. Let us return to London, see my family, and celebrate with them."

A harsh, ugly laugh burst from his chest. "Is this what this is about, Katherine? Is this truly about me? Or is it about you having what you desire? Are you merely trying to twist me about your clever finger in order to have your way?"

She slapped him. His head whipped back under the ferocity of her blow.

He flexed his jaw. Christ, she could lay out most gentlemen he'd known in his miserable life.

The color drained from her cheeks. Her skin went a pale shade of white to match the fresh fallen snow of the passing scene. "F-forgive m-me," she stammered.

He blinked under a staggering realization . . .

She fears me.

Which infuriated him far more than a deserved blow to his person.

His callous words were inexcusable.

He waved off her apology. "I deserved that."

She wet her lips. "You did deserve it."

"I know," he said. "I stated as much."

"Right." Katherine fell silent. She shifted her attention to the window. The wind whipped against the carriage. It battered the black lacquer doors. Her long, delicate fingers pulled back the red velvet curtain and she glanced out the window.

Jasper studied her within the reflection of that ice-frosted glass panel.

"Aldora," she whispered.

He angled his head. "I beg your pardon."

She fixed her gaze out the window. "It occurred to me how very little we know of one another, Jasper. Aldora. She is my sister."

He knew that. Guilford spoke of the eldest sister and the woman's husband. Jasper would not humble himself by acknowledging he'd discussed her life and family quite freely with his close friend and confidante. "And Michael?" he said, knowing very well the wealthy young lord with a scandal attached to his name.

"Is Aldora's husband. She intended to wed his brother, the Marquess of St. James, because our family . . ." Her words trailed off.

Jasper told himself not to pry; his marriage to Katherine had been a matter of convenience, nothing more. The details surrounding her life and that of her family's should not matter. In delving into those details, her life only became that much more entwined with his. "Because your family . . . ?"

Katherine gripped the fabric of her emerald-green muslin cloak. "My father was a wastrel. He spent his days and nights at the gaming tables, and indulging in spirits, and he squandered everything not entailed."

Ahh, she'd alluded to as much in her proposal to Jasper. He was filled with the same icy rage as when she'd humbled herself by offering herself to him, a heartless bastard, all to thwart her grasping mother's intentions for her.

"Nearly four years ago, he died suddenly of an apoplexy." When his world was coming apart at the proverbial seams, so too had Katherine's. Jasper tried to imagine her then, a mere girl on the cusp of womanhood watching her every last earthly possession removed and sold to pay for her father's sins.

Katherine glanced at him. "Then the creditors began coming round."

His gut churned. He wished he'd known her then; wished he could have silently paid off those creditors and spared her the terror of being turned out, with no monetary security.

"They took Anne's pianoforte, even her ribbons. They took all the unentailed property. My b . . . they took everything," she amended, as though shamed in acknowledging her own material losses.

I will shower you with anything and everything your heart should desire.

"Aldora, she is the eldest and therefore needed to make a match and save us all from ruin." She troubled the flesh of her lower lip as she was wont to do when agitated. For everything he did not know of her life, he knew the very subtle nuances of her body's every movement.

"Aldora had been given a pendant by her friends; a simple gold heart given them by an old gypsy, purported to lead them to the heart of a d . . ." Her blush deepened. "Er, a dear man who would love her."

Her telling reaction indicated there was more to her sudden discomfort. "Aldora thought with our family's scandalous circumstances and dire financial straits that a powerful, wealthy, titled lord represented our hope for security." She untied the strings of her bonnet, and removed the hideous thing. She tossed it across the carriage where it landed with a solid thump at his feet. "I detest that bonnet," she muttered.

And bonnets. He would commission the finest milliner to design a limitless number of bonnets for her to choose of. One for every day of the year.

"I take it she did not marry the marquess?"

Katherine grinned. "She married his brother." She waved her hand. "There was some scandal that clung to her husband, Michael, but it mattered not. Aldora loved him."

The red in her cheeks deepened to the hue of summer berries, and suddenly Jasper had a desire for the sweet fruit.

He shifted on the seat "And what of you, Katherine? Surely you must have dreamed of love for yourself?" *Or at least more than this cold, practical contract you've entered into with me.*

She lifted one shoulder in a slight shrug. "When I was younger, perhaps. I'm nearly twenty years, and far more logical."

Jasper had known love and great loss, but the thought of his brave, bold, spirited Katherine never knowing love herself scraped at his insides like the edge of a blade being applied to his flesh.

Except . . . on the heel of that, was the thought of her with some nameless, carefree gentleman capable of laughter and love, and with every fiber of his selfish being, Jasper gave thanks that she belonged to him.

"You've not spoken of your family, either, Jasper." Her quiet murmur interrupted his musings. "Do you have any brothers or sisters?"

Jasper bent down and retrieved her bonnet. He studied the ivory-lace trim. "I have no brothers or sisters." His had been a lonely childhood. There had been no laughter or merriment within the walls of Castle Blackwood.

"What of your mother and father?"

"They are d . . ."

"Dead. I know." She leaned over and took her bonnet back. "I imagine there is certainly more you can say of the people who gave you life."

Oh, he could say any manner of things about them, none of which would be appropriate for a lady's ears. "My parents were cold, selfish individuals. It was a match based on their mutually distinguished positions in Society." His parents' had been a scandalous union; both his mother and father carrying on with very public affairs.

Katherine set her bonnet upon her lap and toyed with the strings that dangled from the ivory creation. "Surely there was some affection there," she protested. "Even as my parents' marriage was carefully arranged by their fathers, my mother very much loved my father."

A harsh chuckle escaped him. "My parents detested one another. My father had a string of mistresses, my mother a string of lovers. I assure you, Katherine, there was little affection between them."

Her eyes widened. "Oh," she said faintly, the color deepening on her cheeks.

Sweet Katherine. She spoke of logic and practicality and the benefits of a marriage based on convenience, but for all of it, she was still hopelessly innocent, and the thought of that raised an unholy terror inside of him.

Suddenly uncomfortable with the intimate direction their conversation had taken, Jasper cleared his throat. "You should rest, Katherine. The snow will slow our travel to Castle Blackwood."

She peeked out the window. "Will you tell me of it?"

Jasper sighed. He should have expected with her stubborn streak that his words should have the opposite request. "It is cold. Dark. Expansive." Devoid of cheer. For a too-brief time, however, there had been laughter within those castle walls. Now all that remained were the echoes of Lydia's agony and his own despair.

Katherine wrinkled her nose. "That hardly sounds like a warm place to call home."

"I never suggested that it was."

She pursed her lips. "Well, you have me there."

And this time, it seemed his laconic responses halted her steady stream of questions.

He desired silence. So why did he feel a pang of regret when she folded her arms, closed her eyes, and shifted away from him—the loss both physical and not.

He pulled out his watch fob and consulted the time. With their travel slowed by the conditions, they should have to stop at an inn along the way. Meanwhile, he would be shut away in this suddenly too-small carriage with his new wife's lean, lithe frame and breasts made for sin.

A small sputtering snore slipped past her lips. Jasper tucked his timepiece away.

He sought the steady, slow rise and fall of her breaths. Except . . . he squinted in the dark . . . and grinned. "Are you feigning sleep, Katherine?"

She shook her head. "Er . . . No. That is." Her lips settled into a mutinous line. She burrowed deeper into her corner.

He reached across the carriage and pulled Katherine onto his lap.

She squeaked. "Wh-what are you doing?" She wiggled back and forth.

Jasper groaned as his shaft leapt in response. "Be still." Hoarse desire laced his command.

She stopped abruptly. "I'm sorry. I didn't mean to hurt you."

Oh, by all the saints, she truly was this innocent. He counted to ten.

Katherine shoved an elbow into his stomach, and he grunted. "Did you hear me, Jasper? I said I was sorry for hurting you."

He closed his eyes, and again counted to ten. What manner of madness had possessed him to drag her delectably lush body atop his? Where nothing more than the thin threads of their garments separated his flesh from hers?

"Jasper . . . ?"

"Bloody hell, I heard you." Jasper took a deep breath, and gentled his tone. He opened his eyes, braced for the shocked hurt in her brown eyes. "Oomph." All the air left him on a hiss, as she planted her fist into his stomach.

In the short span of time they'd been married, she'd delivered an impressive slap to his cheek, elbowed him in the side, and now planted him a jab Gentleman Jackson himself would have been proud of. He'd married quite the bloodthirsty wench.

Katherine squirmed in an apparent attempt to free herself. But her delicious movements only brought the sweet curve of her buttocks closer into contact with his rock-hard shaft. Had it been any other, more mature, more experienced woman, he'd believed her undulating movements intentional.

However, not even the Mad Duke of Bainbridge could mistake the fury flashing in his wife's eyes as passion. In the event there was even the slightest bit of doubt, her next words killed all wonderings.

She jabbed a finger into his chest. "Let us be clear, Your Grace," *Ahh, so it was, Your Grace, now.* "You are the one who denied us the generous wedding breakfast arranged by my mother. It is you who is determined to run off to your"—she held her hands up mockingly and deepened her voice—*"cold, dark, expansive* castle." Katherine pointed her eyes to the ceiling of the conveyance. "Cold, dark, and expansive," she muttered, as if more to herself. "Who describes one's home in those terms?" She jabbed her finger again at his chest. "Furthermore, who would care to live in a home that is cold, dark, and expansive?"

Jasper opened his mouth but was silenced by her black glare. Goodness, with that reproachful stare, his wife could rival the sternest matron at Almack's.

"And lest you forget, Your Grace, it is you who scooped me up and placed me on your lap." She wiggled her rounded buttocks upon his center, and his head fell back as he sent a silent prayer for patience skyward.

Alas, life should have well taught him that there was no God, not even one to oversee such small favors. Katherine continued to squirm on his lap, and with a startled screech, toppled backward.

The muslin fabric of her cape and her satin skirts flew over her head.

"Bloody hell," she cursed, and struggled on the floor of the carriage.

Jasper swallowed, knowing it was the height of ungentlemanly behavior to not immediately help her up, but he remained frozen at the sight of her flesh exposed to his hungry stare; the trim ankles, the lean, legs, and lush thighs that were meant to wrap around a man's waist, urging him on . . .

He groaned.

Katherine batted at her fabric, and shoved it down into place, favoring Jasper with another scowl. "You're groaning, Your Grace? It is I who is seated here upon the floor of the carriage."

He leaned over her. "Need I point out, Your Grace," Katherine's brows dipped. "That you are the one who squirmed yourself free."

"Well," she said on a huff.

Jasper reached down, and gently pulled her back up, and settled her on the cushions of the seat opposite him, a safe distance . . .

His eyes dipped lower as he considered her now concealed, willowy limbs. Or, a safer distance, anyway.

Jasper rested his neck along the back of his seat and stared up at the ceiling of the carriage. It was going to prove a very long journey with his wife.

Chapter 17

$\mathcal{K}$atherine yawned, and placed her hands along the base of her back. She arched the cramped muscles, knowing Mother would be scandalized should she see her bold display of discomfort, and stared at the sign dusted in snow that hung alongside the inn's door.

Fire and Brimstone

She scrunched up her nose. Well, really, what a rather horrid name for an establishment, and not at all the place a young lady envisioned spending her first day as a married woman.

Jasper touched a hand to her lower back and she jumped.

"Are you all right, wife?"

Wife.

That one word, spoken in a silky, mellifluous baritone warmed her more than a blazing fire on a winter's day.

Katherine reminded herself that her husband was surely accustomed to more sophisticated, less moon-eyed young ladies, and tossed her curls. "Quite fine."

He started forward, and Katherine stared after him.

It appeared to take him a moment to register that she did not follow, and he glanced back, a question in those green eyes that made her yearn for the spring.

"I lied," she confessed. She pointed at the sign. "Fire and Brimstone, Jasper? It is a horrendous name for an inn. Why, why . . . one might as well call it Hell and Damnation."

Did his lips twitch? With amusement? *Oh the lout.* "As a learned woman, I would gather you do not judge a volume by its title alone."

Hmph. Very well. So he was correct, in this regard. She quickened her step, and then looped her arm through his.

The tightly coiled muscles cased within his coat bunched under her touch. A smile played about her lips. Her stoic husband might maintain a cool disinterest where she was concerned, but every so often his body would betray him and reveal that he was not as indifferent as he appeared.

They entered the inn. Katherine shook out her skirts and, all at once, registered the absolute stillness of the dimly lit establishment.

She froze and glanced up to find a quite full inn . . . and all sets of eyes were trained upon her and Jasper.

A smallish, older gentleman with a bald pate rushed over. "May I help you . . . ?"

"The Duke and Duchess of Bainbridge. We require rooms."

Those quietly spoken words still managed to thunder through the still room.

The innkeeper's eyes widened, and he bowed low at the waist. "Your Grace, it is an honor. How many rooms may I—"

"Two," Jasper interrupted.

The innkeeper nodded. "I have two rooms available, a fare of roasted beef and potatoes. And a tankard of ale." He motioned to the lone empty table in the corner of the inn.

Two rooms?

Two.

As in, more than one.

She shook her head. Her husband was merely doing the polite gentlemanly thing in procuring two rooms, so that she might prepare . . . prepare . . .

Katherine fanned her cheeks and looked around the crowded taproom floor. Her eyes collided with a buxom serving girl with a pitcher of ale and an empty tankard in her hand. The lush creature trained her eyes on Jasper.

Katherine fisted her hands at her side.

Jasper looked at Katherine. "Are you all right, Katherine?"

Her mouth tightened.

With the exception of the fiery jealousy that ripped through her usually calm sensibilities, she was perfectly fine.

She nodded, and followed Jasper and the innkeeper abovestairs. He led them down a narrow hall and stopped beside one door. "Your Grace," he murmured to Katherine, and held the door open.

Katherine peeked inside.

Yes, she'd well learned that one should not formulate an opinion of a book on the mere title alone . . . and yet, in this regard, it would appear Fire and Brimstone was in fact an apt moniker.

A colorful, albeit tattered coverlet was turned down at the corner of the wide-bed at the center of the room. The nightstand with a broken leg and small, deeply scratched vanity were, otherwise, the only pieces of furniture.

She became aware of Jasper and the innkeeper studying her with intent expressions. "It is lovely," she said to the proprietor who beamed with her praise.

"Please have a bath readied for Her Grace, and a meal."

Katherine warmed at the gentle consideration her husband was showing her, and watched as the innkeeper hurried off.

Alone in the confines of the too-small room, she suddenly became aware that this wintry cold, starless night was, in fact, her wedding night. Her mouth went dry, and she peered up at her husband.

"Is there anything else you require, Katherine?"

She shook her head. At least she didn't *think* she required anything. With the exception of a hurried, heavily veiled conversation with her mother about instruments and matters of wifely duty, Katherine had little idea what to expect in terms of the marriage bed.

Oh, Aldora, whyever did you not come to London earlier? Katherine sighed. Of course her sister and brother-in-law had wee Lizzie, their now two-year-old daughter to consider. Still, it would have been quite helpful if Aldora had been around to have a . . . a . . . talk with Katherine about what would unfold this night.

"Katherine?" Jasper said softly.

She jumped. "No. Nothing. I require nothing. At all. Other than the bath, of course, and the meal you arranged, Jasper." Katherine bit the inside of her cheek and willed herself to silence.

His eyes moved over her face a moment, and then with a clipped bow, he took his leave.

Katherine stared at the closed door behind him. She shrugged out of her cloak and, wandering over toward the bed, tossed the garment at the mattress. The emerald-green muslin landed in a noisy, fluttering heap upon the heavily nicked wood floor.

She smoothed her palms over the front of the gown she'd worn during her wedding.

Lady Katherine, the Duchess of Bainbridge.

The title of duchess might mean a good deal to so many, but Katherine remained wholly unimpressed by her new title. She was no different than the woman she'd been prior to speaking those vows in the office of her home. Nay, her former home.

Only, she caught her lower lip between her teeth, perhaps she might feel differently when her husband returned and made their marriage official.

Katherine sank into the mattress, and the old bed creaked in protest.

Jasper had insisted they leave her maid behind, and now Katherine was left to wonder if her husband intended to see to her disrobing himself.

Oh, dear. Katherine fanned herself, as she was filled with a sudden nervous anticipation.

She sat. And waited for her husband to return.

Jasper had spent the better part of two hours drinking the fine ale and eating the roasted beef at the Fire and Brimstone Inn.

The serving wench stopped beside his table. "Would you care for more, Your Grace?" she murmured in a husky whisper that promised lusty delights. She held up the tankard between the very generous mounds of her enormous breasts that spilled over the blousy white shirt she wore.

Jasper shook his head, and returned his stare to the tabletop.

He'd not had a woman since Lydia, and the overblown fleshiness of the obvious servant did not inspire any grand desire as he expected it should.

Instead, his mind drifted to the lean, spirited vixen who now occupied a room abovestairs.

Jasper waved the serving girl back over, and motioned for her to refill his glass.

She leaned forward. "Is there anything else I can get you, Your Grace?" she whispered.

He considered her a moment. Most men, especially men who'd been without a woman for almost four years, would have been seduced by her plump form and breathy words.

But some matter of madness had taken him over, where all he wanted, all he desired, was his new wife. Jasper shook his head and took a long swallow. She shuffled off.

What had Lady Katherine Adamson done to him? No, not Lady Katherine Adamson. Her Grace, the Duchess of Bainbridge.

He tossed back the remainder of ale, and sat long after the last patron had stumbled out the front door or abovestairs to seek out their rooms. Until only the innkeeper's heavy footsteps as he shuffled about the space wiping down the tables filled the quiet.

Jasper pulled out his timepiece.

The two hands fixed pointedly upon the twelve. Midnight.

A new day. Another year. Four years, to be precise.

It had been four years since Lydia had left him. Each day that marked the passing of another year had been a dark one; darker than even the private bowels of hell he'd dwelt in since he'd buried her and his son beneath the cold winter ground.

As he sat there staring into his empty tankard, he tried with a desperate urgency to bring her visage to the forefront of his mind. Only, it was now as though he were staring at her beloved face down a long road, thick with fog. He could no longer close his eyes and inhale the scent that had been solely her own; the shade of her golden tresses pale to the now vibrant deep-brown ringlets that haunted his thoughts.

And he felt the very worst kind of bastard for taking her life and not having the decency to at least hold her memory forever close.

Jasper shoved the glass aside. It scraped along the worn surface of the table. He buried his head in his hands.

Goddamn you, Katherine, what have you done to me?

He stood, unsteady from too much drink, and made his way abovestairs to his rooms. As he walked, his booted feet carried him closer and closer to one specific door.

Jasper paused beside it. He reached for the handle and then froze. He let his arm fall back to his side.

With a silent curse he reached for it again. He pressed the handle, and then closed his eyes.

He could not.

His past selfishness had taken the life of his wife. As much as his body throbbed with an unholy desire to turn the handle, storm across the room, and strip Katherine free of the delicate cloth that clung to her slim, full-breasted figure—he could not break that silent pledge he'd taken.

His ducal responsibilities of producing an heir and carrying on the familial title could go hang.

Only, an image danced through his darkly desperate musings, of Katherine heavy with his child, a smile on her lips. He lowered his forehead to the thick wood panel and banged it back and forth. Jasper would not be seduced by the desire for that dream of a life.

He turned on his heel and continued on to the empty, lonely room next door. He opened the door, and entered his rooms, closing the door behind him.

His eyes quickly surveyed the drab place. Jasper sought out the stiffly uncomfortable mattress and, in the same attire he'd worn for his wedding, lay down upon it. He stared blankly up at the paint that chipped away at the ceiling, acknowledging the truth—he cared for Katherine.

And it raised holy terror inside him.

Chapter 18

$\mathcal{K}$atherine mumbled under her breath as she sifted through the trunk brought up last evening. She tugged out a rumpled ivory gown and proceeded to dress. Her mouth settled into a firm line as she reached her arms behind her back in an attempt to button the silly ivory garment. Her muscles ached at the awkwardness of her body's movement.

Buttons.

She'd be glad if she never saw another blasted tiny button again. Or any button, for that matter. After this she hated them all with like intensity.

It felt like a very little victory when she managed to slip the top buttons into their respective loops. Abandoning her efforts, Katherine began to pace.

He'd not come. She'd sat perched at the edge of the bed, staring expectantly at the door, waiting for the moment he would knock, enter, and . . . and . . . do whatever it was bridegrooms did with their new wives on their wedding night. When a sharp rap had sounded at the door, she'd leapt to her feet, and breathlessly pulled open the wood panel, only to admit that same voluptuous tavern wench who'd eyed Jasper as if she were thirsty and he was the last drop of water on earth.

As she'd filled the small wooden tub, the woman had peered at Katherine with a mocking gleam in her cerulean-blue eyes.

Only after she'd left, and Katherine had struggled out of her garments, popping free three, mayhap four, pearl buttons did the ugly, niggling suspicion wrap its tentacle-like fingers about her brain—an image of Jasper and that woman took hold and refused to let go.

He wouldn't betray her. He might have married her on a matter of convenience, but he'd not carry on with another woman; especially not on their wedding night.

Then she'd thought of his memory of his own parents, and Katherine had been struck by the ugly truth—he'd never spoken to her on the matter of being faithful.

She shook her head, and her pacing increased in rhythm. Her slippers tapped a steady drum beat as she marched back and forth across the cramped chambers.

Surely there was some explanation as to why he'd not come. Why he'd forced her to await him with a virginal trepidation, until her eyes had grown heavy.

A firm, single rap sounded at the door.

She ignored it.

Another knock.

Katherine froze midstride and glared at the door.

The handle turned and Jasper entered. His massive frame filled the small doorway, giving him the look of a giant in a fey creature's house. "I knocked," he said, his tone surly and unforgiving.

Her eyes narrowed and she counted to ten to keep from hurling every last unladylike word in her vocabulary at his head.

She propped her hands upon her hips. "I know."

He entered, and his stern ducal stare surveyed the room. With the heel of his boot, Jasper kicked the door closed behind him. "Is there something you wish to say to me, wife?"

Katherine planted her hands upon her hips, and before she lost her resolve, said, "Is that what I am?"

His nostrils flared. "I beg your pardon?"

"Your wife. Is that what I am? I imagine, considering last evening, I'm still merely just a bride." Her whole body warmed with embarrassment.

Jasper took a step toward her.

She remained rooted to the spot. If he thought to intimidate her, he could go to the devil. In just two strides, his long, muscular legs ate up the distance between them. She forced her chin back and glared at him.

He took her by the forearm and she gasped. "What are you . . . ?"

Jasper methodically buttoned the back of her gown. She suspected she should feel some degree of appreciation, and yet, his intimate knowledge of a lady's apparel only further infuriated her.

"We should arrive by midafternoon," he said.

Jasper strode to the door. Katherine gathered her cloak and hurried after him; filled with an irrational fear that he intended to leave her at the inn.

Suddenly, he stopped at the door. Katherine collided with his back; the effect the same as if she'd walked into a mountain. All the air left her, and she stumbled.

Jasper turned with a surprising alacrity for one so broad, and righted her. His face remained that unreadable mask she'd come to expect from this man who was now her husband. She swallowed, hating the manner in which her skin burned from the feel of his fingers touch on her forearm, not when he should appear so callously indifferent to her own presence.

A brown lock tumbled over her eye. She blew it back. "Thank you."

He nodded curtly, and then pulled the door open. He stepped aside and allowed two waiting servants entrance. The young men scurried in and saw to the trunks.

And through this, Jasper waited for Katherine. He held his arm out. The newly wedded couple moved with a stilted awkwardness through the quiet inn. At this early hour, most of the guests were surely abed.

Not Katherine. She'd been up counting the minutes tick by as she awaited her husband to make his appearance.

They reached the taproom. The plump tavern wench who'd so covetously eyed Jasper swept up the floor. She glanced up, and her eyes locked on Jasper with a heated intensity.

Katherine's fingers tightened reflexively about her husband's coat sleeves as she was filled with ugly, all-consuming jealousy. She released Jasper's arm. Not for the first time since she'd been counting those minutes ticking by, she wondered if her husband had sought out the model of lush femininity. She stole a sideways glance at Jasper, but his gaze searched the taproom, not so much as pausing to note the woman's presence.

Relief flooded Katherine.

The innkeeper rushed over. "Thank you, Your Grace. I hope everything met with your approval?"

Jasper reached into his coat and withdrew a small sack of coins. He tossed it to the proprietor.

The man's eyes widened like he'd been handed the King's Crown. "Th-thank you, Your Grace!"

Jasper turned to Katherine, "We must not tarry. Come along."

He didn't wait to see if she followed, but strode toward the door. The innkeeper raced over to the entrance of the establishment. He pulled open the door.

Katherine's back straightened as she became aware of a pair of eyes trained upon her. She looked to the woman who'd eyed Jasper with interest. An almost gloating expression lit the servant's eyes, as though she'd clearly identified Jasper's total lack of interest in Katherine.

With hurt pride, Katherine pulled her cloak close and marched outside through the snow, with her head held high, toward the waiting carriage.

Jasper stood conversing with the driver. Jasper paused as Katherine reached the side of the coach, and then wordlessly handed her up into the carriage.

A startled squeak escaped her, and she scrambled over to the corner of the wide black lacquer conveyance. She strained to hear the muffled discourse between Jasper and the driver, but the quiet words were lost.

With a sigh, she sat back in her seat, and pulled the curtain back. Thick frost covered the windowpane flecked with frozen snowflakes. She ran a finger over one star-shaped flake.

The carriage dipped ever so slightly as her husband's broad, thickly muscled frame filled the inside of the conveyance.

He claimed the seat across from her, and then the door closed behind them.

A few moments later, the carriage lurched forward and they were off to the cold, dark, expansive castle her husband had dwelt in for the better part of his life.

A blanket of quiet enveloped them in an uncomfortable fold. She bit the inside of her cheek. In the frosted windowpane she detected the immovable lines of Jasper's face.

She'd never seen him express any grand emotion. Oh, she knew he surely had—at one time. For his Lydia. Her heart twisted, and it was like a vise was squeezing the blasted organ. Jasper had surely not abandoned his first wife on their wedding night. And he'd certainly allowed the woman a maid to help with her daily and nightly ablutions.

Yes, Katherine would venture that his first wedding had been met with great celebration and laughter and a wondrous feast.

Unlike his wedding to Katherine, which had been a hurried affair, not even worthy of the meal arranged by Cook.

Tears blurred her vision, and she blinked back the tokens of embarrassed hurt. When she'd asked Jasper to wed her, she'd not really considered anything beyond being free of Mr. Ekstrom and Mother's horrid plans for her future. And so, she'd not really considered the possibility that she'd be met with such an icy disinterest from Jasper.

Her hair was the color of spun gold.

Katherine angrily shoved a now-limp brown ringlet back behind her ear. The mocking strand fell right back into place. She hated ringlets as much as she detested ivory and white ruffles. She didn't expect Jasper should love her. She had expected that he might feel . . . *something*, because he, even with his wintry treatment of her, had come to mean something to *her*.

His disinterest last evening bespoke a different tale.

Fool.

A single tear streaked a path down her cheek, and she discreetly swatted at it. She'd not further humiliate herself by turning into a watering pot in front of him.

Another blasted drop squeezed past her eyelid.

She folded her trembling hands into the fabric of her cloak, in a desperate attempt to conceal any weakness. Jasper was not a man who'd respect weakness, and surely not in the woman who was now his wife.

Or bride. She was still embarrassingly, and most assuredly, a virgin.

Oh, bloody hell. The tears fell in earnest.

For the first time, Katherine appreciated that Jasper's total disinterest spared what was left of her tattered pride.

Christ.

She was crying.

Jasper's heart squeezed in a clear reminder that the organ still beat.

Something about her, tucked forlorn in the corner, making a desperate attempt at concealing the crystal drops that fell down her cheeks, ravaged him.

He would trade his bloody landholdings if it would spare her pain . . . and yet, he didn't know how to call forth the words to halt her grief.

Did she regret her decision to wed him?

His gut twisted in a tightly coiled knot at the thought of it. Jasper could not blame her for any regrets she carried over their marriage. He was a coldhearted, unfeeling bastard of a man. If he wasn't, he'd know just what words to utter to ease her pain, he would take her in his arms and rub soothing circles over her back, and he would drive back her quiet tears, replacing them with joyous laughter.

Instead, he reached into his jacket, and fished out the white monogramed kerchief. He handed it over to her. "Here," he said, his tone gruff.

Katherine didn't take her gaze from the window, but her fingers grasped the small square, and she blew her nose noisily into it. All the while her shoulders trembled.

The sight of it threatened to turn him into the Mad Duke Society proclaimed him to be.

"What is it, Katherine?" *I should have done so much differently. I should have allowed your maid to come and attend you so you had at least that comfort. I should have allowed you to break your fast, and done so with you. I should have . . .*

Never wed you.

Because the man Jasper now was, the man he'd become four years ago to this day, would never be worthy of her.

Katherine shook her head. His usual loquacious, bright-eyed sprite uncharacteristically silent.

He should cease his line of questioning. Katherine did not want to speak to him. She wanted to carry on with her own private misery, but he could no sooner stop the questions than he could stop his heart from beating.

Jasper leaned over and touched his fingers to her chin. She resisted, but he gently turned her to face him.

Oh, God. Her eyes were twin pools of despair.

I did this to you. Just as he'd known any woman to enter his life would know hurt, he'd gone ahead and wed her anyway.

"You didn't come," she whispered.

He stared at her and trailed unblinking eyes over her precious face.

"Last evening," she continued. Her fingers plucked at the corners of the soiled kerchief in her hands. Any other young lady, he expected, would drop her gaze demurely to the floor. Even through her tear-filled eyes, Katherine looked at him with a bold, piercing directness. "I thought mayhap you spent the evening with that . . . that woman."

It took a minute for those last words to sink into his mind. He furrowed his brow. "What woman?"

Katherine swiped the back of her hand over her eyes. "At the inn. I saw the manner in which she studied you, and thought perhaps you accepted the invitation I saw there."

Jasper sat back in his seat flummoxed. His brows snapped into a flat, angry line. "You believed I would be unfaithful to you on our wedding night?"

Her shoulders lifted in a little shrug. "I . . . I didn't know how to otherwise explain your absence."

He struggled to tamp down the disappointed rage, that she should believe he would be unfaithful to her . . . on their wedding night no less. His innocent wife was the only woman he longed to see bared before his hungry gaze as he worshipped her with his body.

The thought should terrify him more than it did. Instead, he was filled with sudden images of her creamy white thighs spread as she held her arms up to tug him down closer so he could plunge into her center.

He longed to forget the vow he'd taken and explore the wonders of her body.

As the silence stretched on, Katherine glanced back out the window.

Jasper lowered his hand onto hers and stilled the distracted movements of her fingers as she toyed with his kerchief. "You waited for me?"

Katherine nodded.

His breath left him on a hiss as the implications of her hurt registered. She didn't realize the terms of the contract they'd entered into.

"Katherine," he began slowly. "When I agreed to wed you, I thought it was clear ours would be a marriage of convenience." His mind turned over that not too long ago day. Surely he'd used those words. Only . . . he'd not been specific. How could he have stated those bold terms for an innocent young lady? And in not speaking those words, Katherine clearly failed to understand that he could not make her his wife in the way she expected.

Five little lines wrinkled her brow. "I don't understand." Hesitancy slowed those words.

"Ours will be a marriage in name only."

She angled her head, as though trying to make sense of his words. Katherine shook her head, but remained silent.

Compelled to fill that silence, Jasper continued. "I thought I'd been clear, Katherine. I would wed you to spare you from a marriage to Bertrand Ekstrom. I cannot, will not, ever take a wife to the marriage bed. Not again."

Her warm brown eyes were a mirror into her soul; and he detected every last emotion, from the shocked hurt, to the humiliated pain, to the biting resentment, in their depths.

"I . . ." she shook her head. She tried again. "I . . ." She closed her mouth and shook her head once more. Her gaze fell to her lap. "Oh, my . . . I didn't understand. I didn't . . ." Katherine held her palms up, and his kerchief fluttered to the floor. "I promised to give you children."

He'd not disabused her of that notion, in large part because he'd believed his intentions of a marriage in name only had been clear to her. Only, at her words, Jasper imagined a sweet, plump baby girl with thick brown ringlets and Katherine's winsome smile.

Katherine pressed her fingers to her temples, and rubbed them in little circles.

"Katherine . . ." Jasper reached for her.

Katherine recoiled from him as though she found his touch repulsive. She shook her head. "Don't. Just—don't." His jaw hardened, and he made another attempt to take her into his arms, but she looked at him with pleading eyes. "Please."

He did not recognize this battered and broken woman before him. In that moment he'd challenge the devil himself to a duel if it would bring back her smile. But he *was* the devil. He nodded curtly, and sat back.

The carriage ground up snow beneath its powerful wheels and he looked outside.

Four years ago he'd imagined he could never know a greater pain than the loss of Lydia. Looking at Katherine, withdrawn from him and anguished, he realized with a staggering shock, he'd been wrong—it would seem he was still capable of not only inflicting but also feeling great pain.

Chapter 19

*J*asper drummed his fingertips on his hard-muscled thigh. "We've arrived," he said, his tone brusque.

Katherine shifted and peered out the carriage window into the dark. She squinted, attempting a glimpse of her new home. Regret twisted in her heart. *Home.*

In order to have a home, one required a family, and the Duke of Bainbridge had been quite clear—he had little intention of ever considering her a wife. In the true sense of the word, that was. She'd never have children. She sucked in a breath at the heartbreak of such a grim truth. She considered Aldora and Michael's precious little Lizzie. There would be no Lizzie with bright eyes, or a husband to carry that nameless babe upon his shoulders, as they went on pretend journeys to make-believe places.

Pain licked at her insides.

A servant pulled the door open. Jasper leapt down in one fluid movement, his legs remarkably steady for one who'd spent nearly ten hours in the cramped confines of a carriage.

Katherine took a moment to compose herself, and then stepped down. Jasper extended a hand. She studied it, filled with a childlike urge to swat at it. But she'd not been a child for a very long time. Katherine accepted his offer of help and exited the conveyance.

She looked up at the imposing facade of Castle Blackwood. She shivered. Cold. Dark. Expansive. With its medieval turrets, it most certainly was all those things, and it perfectly suited her dismal mood.

Katherine stiffened as Jasper touched his hand to the small of her back. He adjusted his long-legged stride to match her smaller strides as they walked closer and closer to this new place in which she would spend the remainder of her days. Alone.

Odd, she'd been so concerned with thwarting her mother's efforts between her and Mr. Ekstrom, she'd not considered the possibility that she could then enter into a loveless contract with a man who saw her as nothing more than a stranger to share his keep with.

The snow crunched under the heels of her slippers; the thin satin fabric hopelessly ruined from her walk into the Fire and Brimstone Inn last evening. Had it really been less than a day since her world had become unraveled like the stitches upon an embroidery frame?

From the corner of her eyes, she noted Jasper studying her feet with a black scowl.

"You should be wearing boots, Katherine."

Her mouth flattened. "I would have, if I'd had the time to properly prepare for our travels, Your Grace."

His jaw flexed, but he refused to rise to her baiting. Just then she hated him for such indifference.

They climbed the long stone steps, dusted in snow.

A waiting butler pulled the front doors open. The ancient servant with heavily wrinkled hands and shocking white hair greeted them. He bowed deeply when they entered. "Your Grace." His gaze slid momentarily in Katherine's direction, and then she might as well have been invisible for all the notice he paid her.

While Jasper spoke to the butler, Katherine rubbed her arms through the fabric of her cloak, and glanced up, up, up the towering stone walls to the ceilings above. She imagined the ladies of the past who'd been dragged to this remote, lonely castle by the lord of the manor and forced to spend the rest of their days. Unlike Katherine, who'd come here of her own volition, with the dream of . . .

Something so vastly different than the contract Jasper spoke of.

"Katherine, this is Wrinkleton. Wrinkleton, the new Duchess of Bainbridge."

Wrinkleton. Well, that was a rather apt sobriquet.

"Your Grace," he murmured.

She inclined her head in greeting. "A pleasure, Mr. Wrinkleton."

He bowed, and dropped his eyes deferentially to the floor. "Congratulations upon your recent nuptials. If there is anything you desire, I'm at your service."

Oh, if you could manage a smiling husband, and a gaggle of sweet babes, that would be just splendid. Oh, and a cup of warmed chocolate, for good measure.

She managed to muster a halfhearted smile and settled for, "Thank you." She peered around at the tapestries that hung upon the stone walls, covered with crisp white linen. Katherine resisted the urge to wander over and tug those linens free. What did they conceal?

"Allow me to show you to your room, Katherine."

Jasper's quiet words spun her back around. He didn't wait to see if she followed, but started up the long, winding staircase that led to the rooms that would belong to her. Forever. And ever. And ever.

Katherine issued a final thank you for the butler, and then scrambled to keep up with her husband. The great, big dunderhead.

He'd not kept the same rooms with her last evening.

She stomped up the steps.

He'd not even had the decency to secure a lady's maid for her.

She marched onward, content to trail after his broad-backed frame.

Why, she hadn't had a . . . a . . .

"Wedding night," she muttered.

Jasper spun so quickly she stumbled into him.

Katherine would have surely tumbled down the stairs, but he caught her by the arms. "Have a care, Your Grace," he commanded in the same way a governess might scold a recalcitrant child.

She pressed her lips together, and jerked free of his hold. She proceeded to march ahead until she reached the main level of the keep. It mattered not that she didn't know down which long hall her chambers happened to be. She'd rather knock on every other blasted door than bear the bluntness of his angry gaze.

"Right, madam," he drawled from behind her with the faintest trace of amusement lacing his directions.

Oh, the dunderhead was enjoying this.

Katherine tossed open the first door. Again, those crisp white linens covered the furniture and portraits that adorned the spacious parlor. She closed it and moved to the next. A drawing room.

Next. Her fingers grasped the handle.

"Do not."

She spun around.

Fury snapped in his eyes. "Do not."

Katherine turned and glanced back at the door, filled with a sudden urge to press her fingers to the handle and see what dark secrets were hidden beyond the thin wood panel.

Instead, she pulled her hand back, and then followed him in mutinous silence, wondering that he could be so entirely different people; the man who'd given her the last edition of Wordsworth, and now this threatening duke.

He stopped at the end of the hall, and flung open a door. "Your chambers, Katherine."

Your chambers.

Not *our* chambers.

Of course they would keep separate rooms.

Especially when he had no intention of consummating their marriage.

With a tentative step, she walked inside, and did a turn around the space. The residences Katherine had considered home through the years had never been modest, smallish places, and yet, she could fit several of her bedchambers into this one. Resplendent in dark Chippendale furniture, from the four-poster bed to the armoire, a king or queen could comfortably sleep here. Yet, with the brocade wallpaper in deep-green shades and matching curtains, the room was devoid of cheer.

Jasper pulled off his gloves and dusted them together. "I hope the room meets with your satisfaction."

"Undoubtedly so, Your Grace."

How very stiffly polite they were.

He gave a satisfied nod, and started for the door.

The reality that when he stepped out of the room, she would be completely and utterly alone in this dark, foreboding house filled her with a sudden trepidation. "You are going?"

Jasper swung back around.

She curled her toes inside the soles of her slippers. Who knew embarrassment could sting worse than the bite of a vicious hornet? "That is to say . . ."

I don't want to be alone.

I want a real marriage with you.

I care for you. Her eyes slid closed. *Oh, God, I am a complete and utter fool.*

"Katherine?"

Her eyes snapped open. "Well, that is to say I thought we might sup together or that mayhap you'd show me around the manor, or even stay to discuss . . ." She wracked her mind.

He folded his arms across his broad chest. "To discuss, what, Katherine?"

"The weather," she blurted. "Or perhaps the Christmas-tide festivities."

"There will be no celebrations for the Christmas season." The harsh pronouncement bounced off the otherwise still room, echoing around them in cruel mockery.

She settled her lips into a mutinous line, and took several steps toward him. "You've taken me from my family, at the holiday season no less." She jabbed her finger at the air as she advanced. "You forced me to leave my home at the Christmastide season, my sisters and brother. You provided no maid." She jabbed her finger again, and stopped in front of him, so close she had to tilt her head back and strain to see him, so close their feet brushed. Katherine stuck her finger into his bearish chest. "You will *not* take away my holiday season. Is that clear, Your Grace?"

Oh, what she wouldn't trade to have just another several of inches or so with which to boldly face down his impossibly tall frame. She jabbed at him again.

"And what was that for, Your Grace?"

"For being so blasted tall," she muttered.

He blinked. "I beg your pardon."

"For being so bloody foul," she amended, for that might make more sense to her surly ogre of a husband.

He captured his chin between a thumb and forefinger and rubbed it contemplatively. "I'd rather thought you said—"

"You're wrong," she cut in. Her eyes narrowed. "And you've deviated beyond the point, Jasper. We will celebrate Christmas."

"I do not—"

"You do now, husband. So accustom yourself to the very thought of it. Now," she marched over to the door and pulled it open. "If you will? I have matters to attend."

With his unreadable gaze, he did a cursory search of the barren room.

If he so much as mentioned the absence of any trunks or material possessions that constituted things she could attend to, by God, she'd plant him a facer.

Jasper stood there, a firm set to his intractable lips, and then took those remaining paces out into the hall, pausing a moment to turn back.

He opened his mouth, and Katherine closed the door. She turned the lock with a satisfying click.

Through the years, as the Duke of Bainbridge, Jasper had come to expect certain deferential treatment where he was concerned. Hardly obsequious on his part, but rather demonstrated through the actions and words of those who'd crossed his path since he'd been a surly babe in the nursery.

He knew he stared, and had lost track of how many minutes he'd now stood rooted to this particular spot staring at the door his new wife had closed in his face.

And locked, the devilish imp had locked it as well.

Because he'd become so accustomed to those certain deferential treatments afforded his status, he found himself quite flummoxed by being shut out of a room in his own manor.

He supposed many of the previous Dukes of Bainbridge who'd lived within these dank walls, many, many years ago, would have taken the door down with their hands.

The other Dukes of Bainbridge surely would have been too occupied by their mistresses to either know or care that said door had been locked.

Lest he be discovered by his rather limited household staff gaping at a door like a nannypanny, Jasper spun on his heel and strode with determined steps through the house, until he at last reached the library.

People didn't defy him, and yet, this small slip of a lady had not only defied him but commanded him, insisting he celebrate the Christmastide season.

Jasper shoved the heel of his Hessian boot against the door. He relished the reverberations as it shook in its frame.

Lock the door on him, had she.

Jasper stormed over to the floor-to-ceiling-length shelving of books, and tugged free a white sheet draped across the leather volumes. It danced to the ground in a noisy, wrinkly heap. He stepped over it, and furiously scanned the titles of books he'd not touched in years.

He pulled out a collection of Coleridge's poems and tossed it to the floor. The disregarded sheet dulled the solid thump of the book hitting floor.

What had she expected of him?

Jasper pulled out one of Byron's works. His eyes skimmed the title, and then he dropped it atop the forgotten Coleridge works. Considering the fury thrumming through his energized frame, Jasper would sooner burn the romantic work of Byron than read it.

She'd been clear that theirs would be a marriage of convenience and that she carried no real affection for him. His brow wrinkled. Or, he'd not believed she'd mentioned any-thing where emotion was concerned.

His Katherine was practical and logical and not like the heady, flighty creatures flitting around London.

Only in the two days and a handful of hours since they'd been wed, she'd shown herself to be a highly emotional crea-ture, and he didn't know how to handle such feelings. Espe-cially not with the years he'd been shut away from Society. And especially not with Katherine, the one person who'd managed to infiltrate the fortress he'd constructed around his heart.

He preferred the cool indifference he'd carried toward not only life but anyone who crossed his path.

Jasper didn't want to worry about another being hurt, or injured, or even happy, for that matter; because all of those sen-timents required something of him, and he didn't want to give anything, because frankly—he didn't have anything left to give.

Or he'd thought he had nothing left to give, no warmth or joy or interest—until Katherine.

He reached slowly, absently for another book and stared unblinking at the title.

She'd forced him to accept the disquieting, uncomfortable truth.

He cared.

Somehow, she'd shattered the lie he'd made of his life since Lydia's death.

Wordsworth.

Jasper reared his arm back to toss the volume atop the copy of forgotten books, but froze. He lowered it, and stud-ied the title a minute. An hour?

He walked over to the leather sofa, creased and weathered from age and wear, and sat with Wordsworth's book on his lap.

Before Lydia, he'd considered himself a sensible gentleman. He'd possessed a reputation amongst the *ton* as a ruthless, emotionless man. Then Lydia had shown him happiness could exist.

With her death, he'd realized happiness was nothing more than an illusion and so he'd retreated from Society and buried himself in the solitude of his castle to lick the wounds left by his misery.

Now, with Katherine, she'd opened his eyes to the staggering truth—he lived; he lived, and still felt desire and all other sentiments he'd hoped to keep buried.

Jasper shoved the book atop the pile of misbegotten books where it fell open upon its spine.

He rested his elbows onto his knees and stared down at the floor, as he acknowledged the truth: he did not, *could not,* resent Katherine. Rather—he hated himself. For seated there, he couldn't dredge forth Lydia's face. Not the color of her hair, or the sound of her laughter. Nothing.

In his mind's eye, she'd been replaced by a woman with tight brown ringlets, a tart tongue, and a husky alto laugh. A woman unimpressed by his title who challenged him on every score.

His gaze landed on that open page.

On that best portion of a good man's life,
His little, nameless, unremembered, acts
Of kindness and of love.

She wanted him to again celebrate Christmas, and though it seemed the ultimate betrayal of Lydia and his unborn babe, Jasper was fast finding it nigh impossible to deny Katherine anything.

Chapter 20

$\mathcal{K}$atherine walked a circle around the massive stone foyer, hands propped upon her hips. She angled her head and studied the white sheets draped over the tapestries hung on the stone walls. She'd expected the servants would have removed the coverings, and yet, in the light of a new day, the draperies remained.

Katherine nibbled at her lower lip and wandered closer to the nearest sheet. She really couldn't see to the proper Christmastide trimmings with the castle in its present state. Arching on tiptoe, she made a grab for the corner of the covering.

"Might I be of assistance, Your Grace?"

Katherine screeched and spun around to greet the butler. She pressed a hand to her racing heart. "No. I was just . . ."

He angled his head.

Katherine's lips flattened. "Actually, yes, Wrinkleton, you can be of assistance. I'd like to take this down." She pointed up at the sheet. "And that one." She waved her finger over to the next covering. "And all of them. If you would be so good as to send several footmen."

The servant blinked like a night owl. "Remove them?"

Ahh, it would appear they were up at the duke's urging, and not merely because Jasper had been in London. "Remove them," she said with a nod.

The older servant shuffled back and forth upon his feet. He held his hands folded in front of him, wringing them in an agitated manner. "His Grace would—"

"Want me to do as I see appropriate with the household furnishings." She crossed her fingers and hid them in the folds of her skirt.

A bead of sweat dotted Wrinkleton's brow. He removed a kerchief from within his jacket and dabbed at his head.

"If you'd speak first to the duke, and ascertain if that is to his pleasure, I'd most surely assist, Your Grace. It is just . . ." his words trailed off. "What are you doing, Your Grace?" he blurted, in his seeming nervousness forgetting his status. Or mayhap it was merely that he feared his employer that much.

She'd forgotten that whole Mad Duke nonsense.

"I'm taking them down myself, then," she murmured, and made a swiping grab for the nearest sheet.

The momentary thrill of satisfaction surged through her, as her fingers made purchase with the fabric.

She tugged it back and forth, and then in a fluttering cloud of white, it tumbled to the floor.

Katherine stared at it with satisfaction, ignoring the manner in which the butler closed his eyes and shook his head back and forth.

"I assure you, my husband will voice no complaint." After all, this seemed a rather small indulgence in the scheme of the cold, practical union Jasper insisted upon.

She would have wagered the nails upon one of her hands that he muttered, "We shall certainly see."

Katherine mustered her most winning smile and returned her attention to her task. "Will you send round the servants? Or shall I . . ." Her words ended on a breathless whisper. "Oh, my goodness."

The meticulously stitched fabrics could rival any embroidery in all the kingdom. She tiptoed closer to the work of art.

She angled her head and studied the piece. Adorned in a cascade of red, fuchsia, and violet rose bushes with a powder-blue sky filled with white clouds, the image drove back the cold of winter, and called forth thoughts of spring.

"Her Grace completed them."

It took a moment for the servant's words to penetrate her awe. Katherine blinked.

The butler coughed discreetly. "Forgive me, Your Grace."

Katherine glanced over her shoulder. She spoke with gentle tones. "You've nothing to apologize for, Wrinkleton." The stunning craftsmanship called her notice once more.

The former duchess had managed this? A pang pulled at her heart, as she imagined a happy woman married to an equally happy man, sitting together. In that vision Jasper sat reading poems to his perfect duchess, who completed the embroidery.

Her throat moved up and down in a reflexive manner, and she loathed herself for begrudging them the happiness of even an imagined bucolic moment together.

"Your Grace?" Wrinkleton spoke again, interrupting her melancholy musings.

"Then they need to come down, Wrinkleton. It is unfair to the duchess's memory." And if he'd not help her, well, then she'd tear down every last one of the sheets herself.

With an unladylike leap that would have earned her quite the setting down from Mother, Katherine reached for another sheet. From beyond her shoulder, she registered someone moving close and then stopping beside her.

She peered over at Wrinkleton.

He cleared his throat. "Then, please allow me to offer my assistance."

A polite rejection hovered at her lips, at the prospect of burdening the older servant, but instead she nodded. They set to work, and a short while later, the tall, imposing foyer had been transformed into a kind of floral heaven forever memorialized upon the fabric by the former duchess. "I've not much time," she went on, and moved over to the next sheet, "before the eve of Christmas."

Katherine stepped back and considered the work she and Wrinkleton had done here. A kind of bittersweet wistfulness filled her heart. How very odd to consider that these masterpieces were done by the woman who'd earned Jasper's love, and that they should hang here forgotten and forlorn for none to see.

She meandered over to the corner of the explosion of roses and studied the fabric. A chill stole through her as she considered that the other woman's fingers had handled the piece. It served as a stark reminder that Katherine was nothing more than an interloper on what had been a true marriage between Jasper and Lydia, his true duchess.

Her gaze climbed up the product and settled on the vicious thorns upon the fuchsia rose bush. She angled her head. How very out of place those vicious points were. Mayhap sewn there by the other woman to remind whichever woman who entered these halls of the danger in expecting affection from the duke.

The greenish-black thorn blurred before her eyes, and with a frustrated sense of shock, Katherine realized that tears threatened to spill. She blinked them back. She'd not shed a tear since her father had died and left their lives in utter shambles. Now, since she'd met Jasper Waincourt, the 8th Duke of Bainbridge, he'd turned her into a veritable watering pot.

A white kerchief dangled before her, and she stiffened, accepting the silent offering from Wrinkleton. She discreetly dabbed at her eyes. Taking a steady, controlled breath, she looked to the butler.

"Now, is there perchance a footman who might assist me?"

Jasper tapped the tip of his pen in a distracted rhythm atop the surface of his mahogany desk. The click-click-click-click of the pen meeting wood uncharacteristically loud in the quiet of his office.

His steward had left him several hours ago.

He paused, midmovement, the pen suspended above the surface of the desk.

Jasper suspected he'd offended his wife's sensibilities with his clear articulation of the expectations for their union. She'd not joined him to break her fast, and had remained conspicuously absent.

He tossed his pen down and leaned back in his chair. The leather creaked in protest.

Jasper did not care for what change his actions had wrought upon his wife. The Katherine he knew since he'd first pulled her free from the Thames had a vibrant spirit that could not be quashed, and yet in the matter of her forty-eight hours and handful of minutes since she'd become his duchess, she'd closeted herself away in her chambers and not come out.

And he didn't like her absence from his life.

Rather, he *detested* it.

His gaze strayed over to the wide floor-length windows along the back wall of his office. The grayish-white sky perfectly suited his mood.

He swiped a hand across his face.

He might not want a marriage in the true sense with his spirited wife, but neither did she deserve his recent callous treatment. With her absence, she made him feel . . . feel . . . guilty. And he didn't like to be made to feel guilty. Or feel *anything*, for that matter. With a growl, Jasper surged to his feet. He'd done a formidable job of separating himself from the thoughts and feelings of those around him.

Then Katherine stumbled into his life, literally stumbled, if one considered their meeting at the Frost Fair, and in one fateful meeting, she'd thrown his world into upheaval.

Jasper wrenched the door open and stormed through the entrance. He marched with deliberate steps toward her chambers.

Well, he'd not allow her to play wounded soul any further. She'd suggested a marriage of convenience. In her discussion, she'd been practical in all matters pertaining to a possible match between them. Now she'd act the injured party for an agreement she'd willingly entered into.

His bootsteps marked a staccato path upon the floor.

Jasper took the stairs to her rooms two at a time. His long stride made short work of the space between them. He reached for the handle of her door, and then paused, remembering himself.

In spite of her bold spirit and fiery eyes, Katherine was still an innocent, proper, young lady. If he were to simply storm her chambers like the lords of old, then she'd only further retreat into this protective indignant state she'd created for herself.

So he knocked.

And knocked again.

And . . .

"Bloody hell," he muttered.

Jasper jerked at the lapels of his double-breasted jacket. He was the bloody Duke of Bainbridge. He made for the handle yet again, but stopped and forced himself to draw in an even breath.

"Katherine?"

Silence.

Jasper turned the handle and entered.

His gaze scoured the room. The immaculately folded bed indicated she'd risen some time ago.

With a scowl, Jasper turned back around.

He cursed.

"Christ, Wrinkleton, don't you know one mustn't sneak up on a man? What is it?"

Wrinkleton inclined his head. "My apologies, Your Grace." Though in Jasper's estimation, the butler hardly sounded apologetic. "But Her Grace is not here."

"Not here?" Jasper repeated, knowing he must sound like a perfect lack-wit.

"She has gone out, Your Grace."

Gone out.

Gone out?

Surely he'd heard the man wrong. Jasper glanced over to the windows and scowled. The snow continued to fall in earnest. What madness possessed his young wife to go out in such weather?

Then he thought of their first fateful encounter. Should he expect any different in the woman who'd forsaken a chaperone and braved Society's censure to take part in the festivities of the Frost Fair?

"Yes, that is correct, Your Grace. She's gone out," Wrinkleton said in slow, exaggerated tones.

Jasper narrowed his eyes upon the old, family servant. The man had known Jasper since Jasper had been tormenting his tutors, and running the servants ragged with his antics throughout the castle. Otherwise, he'd hardly tolerate such insolence, in anyone . . . except Wrinkleton.

The sparkle in the other man's gaze said he knew as much, too.

"When?" Jasper said in crisp tones.

Wrinkleton scratched at his brow. "I believe an hour or so, Your Grace."

"An hour?"

Jasper turned on his heel and strode with furious speed through the halls, down the stairs, and . . . staggered to a halt within the foyer. His gaze collided with the tapestries upon the walls—the exposed embroideries. A flash of blinding fury clouded his vision. He searched around for his butler. "Wrinkleton, what the bloody hell is the meaning of this?"

Jasper's booming question resounded off the stone walls, and echoed throughout the house.

Wrinkleton continued his slow, very slow, descent down the stairs. A footman hurried forward, his gaze directed at the floor. He held out Jasper's cloak and hat.

Jasper grabbed the items and the young man hurried off. He jammed his hat on his head.

The butler scratched his brow. "What is the meaning of what, Your Grace?"

Jasper closed his eyes and counted to ten, praying to a God he'd ceased to believe in, for a modicum of patience for his servant. He opened his eyes. "The. Tapestries. That. Hang. From. The. Wall."

"Ahh, those," Wrinkleton said, and there was that little glimmer of merriment firmly back in his cloudy blue eyes.

"Yes, those," Jasper snapped, and then remembered himself. He was being a churlish bastard. It was hardly the other man's fault that . . .

"Her Grace and I thought to remove them earlier this morn."

So it would appear it had been the old servant's fault.

And what was more . . .

Katherine's.

"Where is she?" Jasper snarled, feeling like some kind of untamed beast. He tossed his cloak over his shoulders.

"She is nearby, Your Grace."

Jasper blinked. "Nearby." Oh, how he wished he was a bigger bastard for he'd gladly sack Wrinkleton in that moment . . . if he didn't feel this blasted sense of devotion to the old servant.

"Nearby," Wrinkleton repeated with an annoying amount of humor in that word. He walked over to the door and pulled it open. A faint gust of wind caught the snow and sent flakes blowing inside, where they landed in small piles upon the floor. "I venture you should find her somewhere near the end of the drive, atop the hilly knoll with the cluster of evergreens."

What in hell was she doing out in this godforsaken day? A blast of cold air blew snow into his eyes. He brushed the bothersome flakes back, and set out in search of his wife.

His footsteps ground the untouched blanket of snow into large booted imprints. Here, he'd imagined Katherine with a quivering lip and hopelessly sad eyes as she cowered away in her chambers like a wounded doe.

Jasper snorted. He should have known better. Katherine might have been shocked, even hurt by the great misunderstanding of the terms of their marital arrangement, but not even those momentary injuries would blight her spirit.

His black cloak whipped about his legs.

And she'd taken down the blasted sheets he'd ordered up upon the death of his son. In the span of not even a day as lady of the keep, she'd toppled his carefully ordered world, and somehow managed to sway Wrinkleton's loyalty toward her plans for Castle Blackwood.

He'd expected the sight of Lydia's work, boldly exposed in the foyer should have ravaged his heart, and yet, instead he'd eyed it with a fond remembrance. None of the gripping pain or bitter resentment for his loss had filled him.

In that moment, standing in the foyer, he'd not thought more beyond the tapestries than that. Instead, he'd thought of Katherine, defying his orders, wreaking havoc upon his household, and more, setting out in such foul weather.

Jasper froze and squinted off into the distance. He made out the ever so faint slightness of a figure; the splash of her green-emerald cloak a beacon amidst the pure white snow.

His heart kicked up a funny beat within his chest, and he set out after her. As his legs ate up the distance to the rise, the quiet winter air caught the husky purity of her tinkling laugh and carried it to his ears.

When last he'd left Katherine, she'd alternated between hurt indignation and wounded sadness, of the like that had robbed him of sleep. It had taken all of his self-control to keep from tearing down the door between their chambers, and taking her into his bloody arms, sending his plans of a marriage of convenience to the devil.

Jasper quickened his step, filled with a sudden desire to know just what had accounted for her joy.

He marched up the rise, and froze, midstep.

A young footman, a bloody handsome footman grinned down at Katherine.

Jasper narrowed his eyes into impenetrable slits as the servant said something to her, and a red blush stained her cheeks.

By Christ, he'd kill him. Enlivened by an unholy rage at the sight of the appreciative glimmer in the man's expression, Jasper tramped the remaining way.

The servant looked up and caught sight of Jasper. The color leeched from his olive-hue cheeks, leaving him the color of the snow. He shifted the burden of evergreen branches in his hands, and sketched an awkward bow. "Your Grace."

Jasper's scowl darkened.

The young man gulped.

Good. He should be afraid. Very afraid.

Katherine belonged to him.

Katherine stiffened and slowly turned to face him. "You." So much bored resignation filled that single utterance that Jasper had to resist the urge to gnash his teeth like the foul beast that reigned within him: the beast who wanted to gnash his teeth and toss down the knoll the handsome servant who'd dared to look at Katherine.

Jasper shook his head. What manner of madness was this? He was not one given to fits of jealousy. He never had been. Until Katherine. What was she doing to him?

Without removing his gaze from Katherine's, Jasper said to the young man, "You may return to the castle."

The servant bowed, and at Jasper's low, commanding tone, hurried off with the load in his arms. Jasper looked at him from the corner of his eye until he'd disappeared from his periphery.

And, unlike the pale blush and smile she'd worn for the servant, she had nothing but a frown for Jasper. "What is that about, Jasper?" As though she intended to start off after too-handsome-footman, she took a step around him.

Jasper stepped into her path.

She took a step in the other direction.

Jasper matched her movement.

Katherine tipped her head back and glared up at him. "Hmph."

All the rage he'd carried at the sight of her alone with too-handsome-footman faded, replaced with a sudden, over-whelming urge to take her in his arms and reacquaint himself with the moist heat of her mint-scented breath.

She bent down and retrieved a large evergreen branch, which only served to remind him that it was late in the after-noon and they were out in a storm, doing . . . doing . . .

Whatever it is she was doing.

"What are those?" he asked, as she bent down to pick up another.

"They are branches."

Jasper began to count . . . only she continued to fill her arms with the greenery. With a curse, Jasper bent and res-cued the burden from her arms. "I see that they are branches, Katherine. What exactly are your intentions for them?"

She pointed her eyes toward the snowy sky. "Why, I intend to arrange them into a festive coverlet for my chambers."

He furrowed his brow. "What . . . ?"

"I am being facetious, Your Grace," she said on a belea-guered sigh. Then, "Hold those. Carlisle was so good as to leave a small pile over by the base of the tree."

Jasper studied the delicious sway of her hips as she hurried off to a nearby tree. He reminded himself to follow after her. "Who the hell is Carlisle?"

"The footman." She didn't break her stride, but continued moving forward. Katherine stooped down and shoved another handful of branches into his arms.

That increasingly familiar haze of red clouded his vision, at his wife's casualness over the too-handsome footman. Jasper had learned the perils of employing young footmen early on. His mother had quite scandalously, unashamedly taken any number of them as lovers.

"I'll not be made a cuckold."

Katherine stumbled to a halt, to peer up at him. She cocked her head at an appealing little angle. "I beg your pardon? Did you just say . . . ?" She shook her head. "I'm not even going to deign to reply to that," she muttered from beneath her breath.

Something about her casual dismissal of his words eased the tension in his chest.

She stopped suddenly and turned around. "Here."

"Oomph."

She slammed another branch into his chest. "You carry these, and I shall collect this pile here," she said, stooping down to pick up the last shorn pile of evergreen branches.

Jasper stared after his wife's retreating frame, as she picked her way gingerly down the snowy rise. "Where are you going now?"

Katherine didn't even break her stride as she continued down the hill. "I'm returning to the castle. I've much to do to prepare for the eve of Christmas."

He sucked in a deep breath, and counted to ten.

If anyone had told him even a fortnight ago that he'd be wed to a saucy minx with a stubborn spirit, he would have laughed in their outrageous face. He had been so very determined to maintain the isolated existence he'd dwelt within for the past four years. More than that, he'd embraced the life he'd made for himself. If he didn't accept people into his life, he could not risk being hurt as he had upon Lydia's death.

Only now, with these stirrings of vexing annoyance and wry amusement, he'd come to realize he missed feeling . . . alive.

Jasper set out down the hill. His long-legged stride quickly ate up the slight progress Katherine's much smaller legs had made.

"I told you I do not celebrate Christmas."

"And I told you I intend to celebrate anyway, Jasper. So it would seem we are at an impasse," she said, her gaze trained in the distance.

Her tone suggested she had little inclination of abandoning her efforts.

"My wife died three days before Christmas."

Chapter 21

*K*atherine drew to a slow halt as Jasper's words saturated the air around them.

My wife died three days before Christmas.

Which made so very little sense, because she was Jasper's wife. His words slammed into her with all the force of the blustery winter wind.

He spoke not of Katherine but of another; a woman who held his heart and consumed his thoughts and for whom his memories were still so strong, he left white sheets draped upon the furnishings to blot out reminders of the real duchess.

Suddenly his avowal to not celebrate Christmas made sense. Katherine's arms fell by her side, and branches tumbled with a soft thump into the thick blanket of snow. And because she really knew not what to say to fill this strange disquiet, she said, "Oh."

Just that . . . oh. Not for the first time in her life, Katherine wished she possessed Anne's effortless ability to fill awkward voids of silence. Then, Katherine would know just what to say to ease her husband's jagged hurt.

Instead, she forced herself to look up at him.

Jasper's curiously empty stare remained fixed at a point beyond her shoulder. Her chest tightened at his suffering, more tangible than a physical wound.

Katherine might represent a formal contract, based on not even the slightest hint of affection on his part, but in the days she'd come to know Jasper, she cared about him, and could not bear the sight of his suffering.

"I am so sorry," she said quietly.

His shoulders lifted in a slight shrug. She thought he might speak, but words did not come.

Then it registered . . . three days before Christmas.

Her mind turned quickly.

Oh, God. The day they'd left the inn had marked the anniversary of his wife's passing. The day Katherine had lamented over her still virginal state, Jasper had been mourning the wife of his heart. She gave her head a slight, sad little shake, as so much of Jasper's surly coldness became clearer.

"I swore to never again celebrate, not just the Christmastide season, Katherine, but anything. It seemed an insignificant sacrifice to make in terms of what I'd done."

Katherine suspected she might look upon the holiday season with such seething resentment if she were to experience the kind of loss known by Jasper. If she were to lose her own husband . . . her throat worked reflexively at the tortured imaginings of a world without Jasper. In a short span of time, he'd come to mean so very much to her. Her eyes worked a path across his face. She detected the faint muscle that twitched at the corner of his eye. "You didn't do anything, Jasper. Lydia's death, it was not your fault."

He dropped the branches. They fell with a soft thump into the snow. His mouth twisted in an empty smile. "I killed her because of my desires to continue the Bainbridge line."

Katherine moved close and took his hands in hers. His body stiffened, and even through the fabric of their gloves, her skin warmed at the contact of his touch. She squeezed his hands. "It is illogical for you to blame yourself. Of course you would have had a family with Lydia." A pained ache tugged at Katherine's heart as the momentary dream of a babe flitted across her consciousness. She looked at their connected fingers. "You blame yourself because you love her." *Even now.* "And would do anything to bring her back, but living a life devoid of all happiness will not do that, Jasper. It will only remind you of that horrid day of her death, and the dark days to follow. It doesn't allow you to celebrate the years of joy you knew as her husband, and the love you carry in your heart, for her."

Jasper pulled his hand free and flexed his fingers as though he'd been repulsed by her touch. "If I hadn't gotten my child upon her, then . . ." His words ended on a harsh whisper.

Katherine tilted her head back and studied the thick grayish-white winter sky. Snowflakes danced and fluttered down, and she raised a finger to capture one of those elusive flakes. A fat snowflake landed upon her glove and quickly dissolved into a small bead of water. Here a moment, gone the next. So very delicate and fragile.

Katherine folded her arms and burrowed into the folds of her cloak. "You mustn't blame yourself, Jasper."

For years, Jasper had been besieged by nothing but despair at this time of year as it marked another passage in time of Lydia's absence from this earth. Now, guilt of an altogether different kind filled him. At some point since he'd pulled Katherine from the Thames, the ache in his heart for the loss of Lydia had dulled, and lifted.

Katherine spoke and her words pulled him from the thick, quagmire of guilt he slogged through. "Do you know, I hate London," she said.

Jasper hated London, but it hadn't always been that way. There'd been a time when he'd been more comfortable in London at the height of a Season than anywhere else.

"My family had a property in Hertfordshire. Mother found it too provincial and quite detested our visits there. Father enjoyed the hunting. And I," she glanced over at him, "I enjoyed every aspect of it. Lush green, rolling hills. Magnificently tall trees made for great big swings. I would sit upon this wide, wooden swing and read Byron's poems. They were so very romantic and beautiful and I loved them with an innocent heart." She painted such a beautiful, bucolic image, Jasper wanted to join in her memory of simpler times.

He said nothing in response, instead trying to follow along with her disjointed thoughts.

"As I told you before, Father gambled away everything."

The muscles in Jasper's stomach tightened at the reminder of her wastrel father's ill regard for a young Katherine and her family.

"He lost the cottage in Hertfordshire," she said quietly. "The last night we lived in that cottage, I took one of Cook's knives and etched my initials into the wood frame of my bedroom door." A woeful smile curved her lips. "I wept from the moment I learned we would be forced to surrender the property in Hertfordshire until the day we departed, never to return."

Jasper imagined his strong, beautiful Katherine with a knife, carving away at her bedroom door as her shoulders shook from the force of her sobbing. His eyes slid closed. There was a special place in hell reserved for cowardly bastards who left their families destitute. And when Jasper joined Katherine's father in the bowels of hell, he'd punish him for having ever reduced her to tears.

Jasper reached out and brushed the back of his knuckles across the satiny smoothness of her cheek.

His touch seemed to draw her from the pained remembrance of that moment. "Then the creditors collected my books."

His hand paused midstroke. Oh, God, he didn't want to hear another blasted bit of this bloody story.

"They took every single volume, and I swore I'd never, ever again pick up another book of Byron's sonnets," she said. "With the loss of nearly all our personal belongings and estates, the silly sonnets of love and purity and innocence all seemed so very puerile."

Katherine leaned into his touch the way a kitten stole warmth from its master. "I swore I'd never read another book of poetry again," she said.

Jasper understood that, all too well.

"But then, I began to miss the words. Those sonnets had carried me away to beautiful places of love and even loss. No matter how much I pledged to never touch a volume, my heart craved it as much as my mind." Katherine stepped away from him, and wandered ahead several steps, until he was filled with a sudden fear that she intended to leave and he'd never know the remainder of her story.

Except, she only paused at the peak of the hill, and stared out at the smallish-looking landscape below. "I felt that in picking up another book, it made me weak, and it reminded me of all my hurt and anger and resentment. But the heart knows what it needs, Jasper. I could no sooner refrain from opening the pages of another book than I could give up food. I allowed myself just one poet." Katherine reached for another flake. She caught one effortlessly between her gloved fingers.

Wordsworth.

"Wordsworth," she said.

"Byron and all those other romantic poets seemed so very silly, but Wordsworth, he seemed real. His words are not always joyous and hopeful."

He understood, because it had been what had drawn Jasper to the poet's works.

With that one story, Jasper now understood her desire for the lone copy of Wordsworth's volume at the bookshop. His heart thumped hard in his chest, as he silently acknowledged her great sacrifice—she'd given the lone book to him.

Jasper stood there, appreciating her delicate profile.

As though she felt his gaze upon her, Katherine turned around to face him. "I hated my father for losing everything that I'd at one time valued. I resented the loss of all those material possessions, but you see, Jasper, if none of those great sadnesses had befallen me, I would have never discovered Wordsworth." She lifted her shoulders in a slight shrug. "Perhaps it seems a very small consolation. After all, Wordsworth can never rival Byron in terms of greatness but happiness can still be found—just on a different page."

Somewhere along the way, they'd ceased to speak of poets. Rather, a more significant meaning was buried within his wife's words.

Jasper trailed his eyes over her pert nose, her full lips, and the cat-like slant to her brown eyes. *Oh, Katherine, is that what you believe you are? A mere consolation? A lesser work?*

Nothing could be further than the truth.

Katherine cleared her throat, and walked back over to the forgotten pile of branches. She bent down and proceeded to collect the thick, evergreen branches. Unbidden, Jasper strode over to her. He hesitated.

She paused in her efforts and, from where she knelt in the thick blanket of snow, glanced up.

Jasper lowered himself to a knee. "Here," he murmured. He relieved Katherine of her burden and then made short order of picking up the other displaced branches. He stood.

Katherine caught his gaze with hers, and then smiled up at him. "I imagined you would leave them here, considering my intended use for them."

He frowned and glowered at her from the corner of his eye. "I'm not an ogre, Katherine." Is that what his new wife believed? That he'd show his displeasure by abandoning her to her own efforts.

"Well, sometimes you are." A mischievous glimmer sparkled in her eyes.

Jasper's lips twitched in response. "Yes, yes I am," he concurred.

It struck him then, how very much he'd like to remain here atop this snowy knoll, just the two of them and the quiet peace of the winter sky. The snow continued to fall down at an increasingly heavy rate, and it wouldn't do for them to remain in the cold this far from the castle. "We should return," he said, the words dragged reluctantly from him.

Katherine placed her fingertips along his forearm. His body went taut at her delicate touch. She seemed unaware of his body's physical reaction to her nearness; the mad rush of desire that coursed through him, his racing heart, the quick rise and fall of his chest. He wanted her. He wanted her with an aching desperation that dared him to spit in the face of the pledge he'd taken, all to claim her as his own.

"You do realize I intend to use these to decorate for Christmas?"

"I do," he drawled. He'd come to know Katherine enough to know nothing would deter her from whatever she endeavored to do.

"And you'll not issue any further complaint on the matter?" She eyed him with the skepticism of one who expected she was being tricked in some way or another.

"Katherine, would any complaints on my part yield a different outcome?"

She chewed at her lower lip. The wind caught a brown ringlet. It fell across her eye. She blew it back. "No."

He gave a curt nod, and shifted his bundle.

"I should also inform you now, husband," he'd noted she seemed to use the term husband when she was upset with him. "I intend to celebrate with a great Yule log and a magnificent feast," she said as they stomped through the snow.

The British would be wise to turn his relentless wife upon the French to halt Boney's mad efforts of domination. The bloody French would be powerless when faced with Katherine's steely resolve.

Lost to his own ponderings, it took a moment for Jasper to realize Katherine no longer walked beside him. He paused, and turned back around.

Katherine stood frozen in the winter landscape.

"What is it?" The quiet of the winter storm carried his words with a false loudness.

"I don't even know what you eat." Her warm breath blended with the cold, and sent little puffs of white air past those plump lips.

"What I eat?" A branch fell from his arm, and Jasper cursed. He bent down to pick it up. With her abrupt shifts in conversation, Katherine would drive him madder than a Bedlamite.

She gestured with her hands. "Well, that is to say, I do not know what your favorite meals are. It just seems like the thing a woman should know about her husband." Red color slapped her cheeks. Katherine glanced down at the snow, and scuffed the tip of her black boot along an undisturbed patch of earth. "Not that we have a true marriage, of course."

An overwhelming desire to take her in his arms and explore each corner of her body filled him. With her clever and courageous spirit, Katherine was so vastly different than any young lady he'd ever known.

A snowflake landed on the tip of her nose. She stared at it until her eyes crossed in the middle.

He shifted his branches and brushed away the moisture.

Katherine widened her eyes, seeming as startled as he himself was by his touch.

Jasper turned around and resumed walking.

He knew the moment she'd reached his side, not simply because of the crunch of snow under the heels of her serviceable boots, but because his body seemed to have developed an innate sense of awareness. Perhaps it came of a bond shared from saving a person from certain death, or perhaps it was something more, something he could not allow himself to think of.

"I prefer roast chicken," she continued, "and croquettes of sweetbread. I adore them served hot with a slice of lemon." She wrinkled her nose. "Mother detests lemons and is always insisting Cook finish the sweetbread with parsley, but sometimes Cook will set aside a dish served with lemon just for me, and I'll sneak down to the kitchens late at night. Of course, the sweetbread is no longer hot at that point, but the gesture is a lovely one, don't you think?"

He believed his wife talked—a lot.

"If you've not given a consideration for the Christmas meal," she went on.

"I have not," he said curtly.

"Then, perhaps you'll allow me to see to the preparations with Cook," she said, as though he'd not even spoken.

They reached the base of the hill, and started down the path Jasper had followed when he'd first set out in search of Katherine. Only now, a fresh cover of snow had covered all trace of his boot steps.

"And of course, no feast would be complete without a splendid dessert."

"Of course."

At his dry response, Katherine shot him a sideways glance. She pressed her lips tight together, and jerked her chin up a notch in clear displeasure.

The swirling wind, and the freshly fallen snow turned up by their steps the only sounds in the silence, it struck him then, how just the sound of her voice filled him with a lighthearted enjoyment he'd thought forever lost. He mourned the absence of her words, spoken with such enthusiasm.

They continued on. By the stiff set to his wife's shoulders and the swiftness of her step, he deduced he'd earned his wife's displeasure. And why shouldn't she be annoyed? Always smiling and merry, she'd bound herself to him, a miserable, cold, unfeeling blighter.

The long drive came into focus. Jasper paused at the edge, even as Katherine marched ahead. "Turtle soup." His voice echoed around them.

Katherine's steps slowed, but she remained with her eyes fixed ahead, toward the castle.

"And roast quail. I detest orange pudding, but love Shrewsbury cakes," Jasper said. He adjusted the pile of branches in his arms so they were more precisely arranged, and tucked them under his arm. He resumed walking.

Katherine once again fell into step beside him. From the corner of his eye, he detected her stare directed upward at him. He expected her to fill the silence.

The time he'd come to know Katherine, however, should have taught him Katherine wasn't one to do the expected.

She remained silent.

They reached the middle of the drive and Katherine placed her fingertips upon his arm.

Chapter 22

He'd not pulled away. That should mean something. Of course, it could also very well mean nothing, which was entirely more likely, but still, Katherine had placed her hand on Jasper's arm, and though he'd stiffened, he'd not shaken free of her touch.

"Your Grace, will this do?"

The butler, Wrinkleton, pulled her from her silly musings.

Katherine gave her head a clearing shake, and returned her attention to the efforts in the hall. She followed the direction of the butler's slightly bent finger up toward the collection of ivy woven along the tops of the floral embroideries. Katherine smiled. "I would say so, Wrinkleton, and you?"

He angled his head and studied them a moment and then nodded slowly.

Katherine reached for an apple and carefully secured it to the evergreen. And she wanted to consider which should be added next to the bough—the paper flowers she'd made last evening or the tiny child's doll—but could not for all the Wordsworth sonnets, roast chicken, and croquettes of sweetbread combined, cease thinking of her husband.

She'd entered into their marriage under the illusion that it was a matter of convenience for the both of them; she would escape Mother's plans to wed her off to horrid Mr. Ekstrom, and Jasper would find in her his duchess and she'd do . . . she furrowed her brow, whatever it was that duchesses did.

Katherine supposed she should have considered that part beyond the whole heir and a spare bit. Because when he'd informed her that he had no intentions of consummating their union, well then she would have had some idea of what that meant for her future.

She picked up the small baby doll and turned it over in her hands. A pang jabbed at her heart like a tiny needle prick being touched to the hopeless organ. As it was, all she now knew was that it was not for her future. No sweet-faced ringlet-less daughters or troublesome little boys.

With a sigh, Katherine set aside the child's toy and reached for the paper rose. She secured it to the evergreen.

But now she knew he enjoyed turtle soup and detested orange pudding but loved Shrewsbury cakes . . . and he hadn't withdrawn his hand. He'd held hers back, which had only forced Katherine to confront the truth.

She'd not merely wed Jasper Waincourt, the 8th Duke of Bainbridge, as a matter of convenience.

She'd wed him because somewhere between the Frost Fair, the Wordsworth volume, and the talk of dinners and desserts, she'd come to care for him. With his gruff directness and the unexpected kindnesses he'd shown her at every score, his happiness had come to mean a very good deal to her. Her eyes closed a moment as she thought of the suffering she'd seen in his usually hard eyes, and she realized his happiness had come to mean more to her than her own.

Katherine would not allow herself to consider the whys of that. Her mind screeched at the edge of anything more than that.

"Your Grace?"

She looked up again from her work, as Wrinkleton gestured to the boughs of evergreen along the staircase rail.

"It looks splendid," she assured them.

The footman hanging the evergreen paused to smile at her, and then moved on to hang the next.

Katherine fixed another smallish red apple to the thick green branch and forced herself to confront the truth of her situation. She cared for a gentleman whose heart had been buried four years ago upon the death of his true wife. It mattered not that he'd gripped her fingers in his, because the moment they'd arrived at the castle, he'd stormed off as though she'd bore the plague, and she'd not seen him in the days since.

Which only indicated their intertwined hands had been altogether insignificant, merely an attempt to warm his frozen fingers, surely.

A small sigh escaped her, and she lifted the kissing bough. She turned and handed it off to Wrinkleton, who waited just at her shoulder.

He handled it with a manner of reverence reserved for his employer's family jewels, turning it cautiously over to another footman who rushed over.

"If you could just place it there," she murmured, gesturing to the corridor that spilled from the foyer to the main living quarters.

As the young servant climbed the tall ladder to position the arrangement in its respective place, Katherine studied it with her head tilted.

The only kissing to be done under the kissing bough would be servants stealing secret moments; there'd be no kisses for the lady of the manor.

She shoved aside her melancholy, and reached for a cluster of hollies.

A loud knock sounded on the front door, and the red berries slipped from her fingers onto the green bough she'd moved to.

Katherine furrowed her brow and looked to the front entrance, and then over to Wrinkleton.

The old butler scratched his thinning white hair, head cocked at an odd angle, clearly accustomed to a shocking lack of visitors through the years.

The pounding ceased so that Katherine suspected she might have imagined it, but then that could not account for Wrinkleton hearing the very same . . .

Another knock.

That sprung Wrinkleton from his shock, and the butler hurried with a step better suited to a man many years his junior. He pulled the door open. The tall, commanding figure in the entranceway froze, hand midknock. The gentleman shifted the bundle in his arms.

Katherine stared at the entranceway. Her eyes widened, her heart suspended in a breath at the precious trim frame in the doorway.

She cried out and sprinted across the stone floor. "Aldora!" Her sister just made her way into the foyer when Katherine flung her arms around her sister.

Aldora wrapped her arms around Katherine, and because she was so very lonely, and in need of a lovingly familiar face, she promptly burst into tears. "Wh-what are you d-doing here?" She blubbered like a babe who'd taken its first fall.

Aldora leaned away from her. Through the thick frames of her spectacles, she peered at Katherine, a dark frown on her lips. "How could we not come? We arrived in London only to discover you wed and were whisked off for the holiday." She pursed her lips, and glanced around with guarded caution in her eyes.

Katherine stepped away from her sister's comforting embrace, and turned to greet her brother-in-law, Michael.

He stood, with a resolute set to his jaw, and a hard glint in his eyes. He perused the room, and then focused on Katherine. "Congratulations are in order. I'd like to meet your husband," the clipped words more a command than a congratulations.

Katherine shivered, imagining the steely edge in her brother-in-law's words would drive most men to terror.

"Papa, snow, more snow. I see, Papa. I see more."

Then the veneer of ice melted as Michael's attention shifted to his and Aldora's just two-year-old daughter.

He dropped a kiss atop her crown of brown curls. "It's too cold, Lizzie. We'll rest, and eat, and then I'm sure your Aunt Katherine would dearly love to play with you."

Katherine's heart flipped within her breast as a yearning unfolded in her belly with a lifelike force as Lizzie looked to her with impossibly wide brown eyes.

A big smile filled the babe's chubby, dimpled cheeks, and Katherine's throat worked up and down.

As if of their own volition, her arms opened. Lizzie struggled against her father's embrace a moment, until Michael turned her over into Katherine's arms.

Katherine held her cradled to her heart. She pressed her cheek along the top of Lizzie's brown curls, and inhaled the unmistakable scent of the child's innocence. "Oh, sweet Lizzie, how I've missed you. Have you come to visit me for Christmas?"

Lizzie nodded against her. "Papa say cakes and tarts."

Katherine leaned back and nodded solemnly. "Oh, absolutely, cakes and tarts for the Christmas feast. There could be no more perfect treat."

Lizzie's grin widened.

From over the top of the girl's head, Katherine noted Wrinkleton. The servant shifted back and forth, with tentative glances stolen about the wide foyer, as though he feared the castle were on the cusp of being stormed.

"Wrinkleton, will you inform the housekeeper to have the finest guest chambers prepared. My family will be spending Christmas with us."

Jasper stared down at the neat columns upon the opened ledger. He inked the far right column, and tossed his pen down onto the otherwise immaculate surface of his desk.

Embers from the blazing fire within the hearth cracked and popped in the quiet. Jasper leaned back in the folds of his wingback chair, and stared into the dancing reddish-orange flames.

He was a bloody coward.

Since the moment he and Katherine had returned from their outing in the snow, and she'd slipped her small, fragile hand into his larger one, she'd unleashed an inexplicable panic within him. Jasper had fled her side that day, and avoided his wife.

He took his meals within the confines of his own rooms, he tended to the affairs of his estate, and he tried with a desperateness to put thoughts of Katherine and her delicate hands and winsome smile from his mind.

Jasper swiped the back of his hand over his face. To no avail.

In the privacy of his own thoughts, he could at least be honest with himself—he'd come to care for Katherine.

He who'd resolved to never again care for another, and open himself to the pain and suffering that inevitably came from caring too deeply.

Somewhere along the way, since their fateful meeting at the Frost Fair, Katherine's warmth had slipped inside his cold and empty being, and gradually spread throughout him. She'd taught him how to once again smile, and tease, and be teased, and it terrified the bloody hell out of him.

Jasper shoved back his seat, and he stood. Clasping his hands behind his back, he wandered over to the edge of the hearth and stared contemplatively down into the roaring blaze.

He could not account for the manner of madness that had allowed him to accept the offer she'd proposed—an offer of marriage, a marriage of convenience. At the time he'd thought himself driven by an almost sense of pity, an altruism to help the forlorn young woman avoid a match with that bastard Bertrand Ekstrom. He would give Katherine his name, his protection, and that would be the extent of their union.

He'd not let himself imagine sharing the same home as man and wife, he'd not thought of the one wall separating his bed from hers, or the unholy desire to tear down the door and at last lay claim to her heart, body, and soul.

So now he cravenly stood, closeted away from the lure of Katherine's charm.

A pounding echoed around his mind.

Jasper blinked, and with a frown, glanced around his office.

No, no, that was not in his mind.

Then it stopped, and his attentions returned to the warm fire.

The pounding resumed.

Followed by a muffled cry that carried through the stone walls of the castle. *Katherine!* Jasper's heart stopped.

With a speed born of terror, Jasper sprinted across the room. He pulled the old door open hard enough to nearly tear it from its hinges. He raced down the long hall, toward the foyer toward his wife's sharp cry. Jasper didn't pause to consider what manner of harm could have befallen her. What . . .

Jasper staggered to a halt, and the air left him as though Gentleman Jackson had dealt a swift punch to his solar plexus.

He stood, and with a horrified fascination stared at Katherine cradling a child close to her heart.

Jasper's eyes slid closed as the terror of his past, of a breathless, lifeless babe merged with a dream of this pink-cheeked, grinning babe held against her breast.

For a brief, infinitesimal moment Jasper allowed himself to cling to that wispy dream for more with Katherine. He clung to the image of Katherine heavy with their child, and a smile on her cheeks as they discussed names for a precious girl who would have Katherine's shining brown eyes.

A crimson stain splashed over the alluring image, and swallowed Katherine. A hideous grimace contorted the generous smile, and Jasper's body jerked.

His eyes flew open, and he stared at the strangers in his foyer.

"What is the meaning of this?" Jasper barked.

Wrinkleton and several footmen scurried off, as the unfamiliar young woman and tall gentleman looked to him with like disapproving expressions.

"Jasper," Katherine greeted with a smile. She turned the babe over to the tall, glowering gentleman, and hurried over to Jasper's side. "I have the most wonderful news." She gestured to the small trio. "My sister Aldora has come to spend the holiday."

A muscle ticked at the corner of his mouth.

The bespectacled Aldora smiled and dipped a curtsy. "Your Grace, it is a pleasure to meet you."

"And this is her husband, Lord Michael Knightly, and their lovely daughter, Lizzie," Katherine went on. "They will stay through—"

"No."

Katherine blinked. She scratched at her forehead. "Through Epiphany," she went on. "I've instructed Mrs. Marshall to have the finest chambers readied, and—"

He cleared his throat. "May I speak to you, Katherine? In private." He could not have this cold castle filled with people and merriment. He'd been alone too long. Katherine's presence here alone terrified him.

Katherine touched her fingers to his sleeve, and her soulful brown eyes beseeched him. *Ah, God, I cannot deny you anything.*

He turned to Knightly and held out his hand.

The other man eyed him a moment. He shifted the baby in his arms and then, with his free hand, accepted the other man's offering. "Bainbridge."

Jasper clenched and unclenched his jaw, wanting nothing more than to toss Katherine's family from the castle. He didn't need the tableau of the bucolic family they represented.

Only . . .

Katherine's smile glowed brighter than a blue moon in a summer's night, and damn if his chest didn't tighten in the oddest way for it. She clapped her hands together. "This is just splendid," she said, her eyes meeting Jasper's.

Mrs. Marshall, the housekeeper, appeared. The older, plump woman with gray hair and wrinkled cheeks curtsied. "Your Grace, rooms have been readied for your guests. Their trunks have been brought to their chambers. If I may show them abovestairs?"

Katherine removed her hand from Jasper's arm, and his skin immediately cooled from the loss of her touch. She rushed over to her sister Aldora and hugged her arm. "Mrs. Marshall shall have the servants ready a steaming bath for you, and you can rest. I'll have a dinner prepared, and—"

Aldora laughed. "Thank you, Kat. It is ever so good to see you."

Katherine bussed her on the cheek.

Mrs. Marshall led the trio abovestairs. They'd reached the top of the landing when the brown-haired angel peeked out from behind her father's shoulder and smiled at Jasper.

Jasper recoiled as though he'd been gutted with the edge of a dull blade. His vision turned to black, and his breath came fast. He'd not allowed himself to think of any child since the death of his son. Closeted away as he'd been at Castle Blackwood, he'd not confronted the reality of smiling, innocent babes with full, dimpled cheeks and glimmering wide-eyes. And he'd not allowed himself to imagine his son beyond that blue, lifeless creature he'd held as he'd drawn his last pained breath.

Until now.

His son would have been four.

Oh, God. The echo of a child's laughter ricocheted around his mind. He gripped the fabric of his jacket to keep from

clamping his hands over his ears and drowning out the tor-
turous sound.

Now he saw that lifeless babe as a boy of four years, atop
a pony, waving at a proud Jasper, who stood off to the side,
coaching his son, guiding him.

He nearly doubled over from the pain of his imagining.

He dimly registered Katherine's long fingers closing about
his hand. "Jasper?"

Jasper jerked. One wrong move would shatter him into a
million shards of nothingness.

He counted to ten. Once his breathing resumed its normal
cadence, Jasper pulled back. He swiped his palms along the
front of his jacket.

"Jasper . . . ?"

"In my office, madam," Jasper bit out.

He spun on his heel, and stormed toward the corridor,
when it registered that his wife remained rooted to her spot
in the foyer. With a growl, Jasper looked to his wife.

Katherine seemed unaware of the very thin thread of control he clung to. She stood, hands planted upon her sweetly
curved hips. "I'll not be ordered about like a child, Jasper. I
am not 'madam.' My name is Katherine. If you wish to speak
to me, then . . ." Her words ended on a squeak and she staggered back a step as he strode back toward her.

His rage deepened. "Do you believe I'd hurt you?" he asked,
his tone harsh. He might be a miserable, foul-mouthed,
uncouth bastard, but surely she knew he'd sooner chop off
his own arm than allow harm to befall her?

She shook her head once.

He leaned down so close their breaths mingled as one.
"Are you afraid of me?"

Those familiar lines appeared in her brow. "Afraid?" she repeated. Her lips twitched. "Of you?"

"You took a step backward."

"Because you startled me."

Some of the tightness in his chest eased at her plainspoken admission. He forced himself to take another breath. "Will you follow me to my office, Katherine?"

She nodded, and slipped her arm through his.

He made to pull away, but she placed her other hand upon the one looped under his arm, and locked him into place.

As he guided her to his office, his skin burned through the fabric of his jacket at the absolute rightness of her fingers on his person.

What have you done to me, Katherine?

Chapter 23

$\mathcal{A}$s Katherine entered her husband's office, she peered at the purely masculine, massive space resplendent in deep sapphire and black colorings and Chippendale furnishings. She stared about bemused at the size of the one room that could have housed the entire first floor of her family's former Hertfordshire cottage.

Katherine took in the elaborate Renaissance works of art upon the walls, the long-case clock, and gold trim throughout the border of the room. She'd lain awake more times than she could remember, from fear as her worldly possessions were stripped away from her family, fearing they'd be destitute, hating Father as each property was taken, until barely anything remained. They could have paid all of father's debts surely with the wealth to be found in this one room. And yet, when everything had been taken from her family, she'd refused to surrender to the despair.

How could she show Jasper that his past needn't define his future? Show him there were new days and different smiles and unfamiliar laughter. He could love the time he'd known with Lydia and yet appreciate that he lived.

She turned to look at him.

Jasper met her gaze square on and then he stalked over to the sideboard and picked up a decanter.

He sloshed several fingerfuls of brandy into the glass, and her stomach tightened. She'd never before seen him drink.

Then again, when would she have?

She hadn't even considered the fact that he might partake in spirits. Or that he might do it frequently or infrequently.

As if he noted her stare, Jasper's broad, muscle-hewn frame stiffened. "What?" he growled. He took a long swallow of his drink.

"You w-wanted to see me." She detested the faint tremor in her words, and prayed her husband did not note the quiver there.

Katherine should have well-learned by now that her husband possessed a heightened sense of awareness.

His frown deepened. He set his drink down, and folded his arms across his chest. "Katherine, I would speak to you of your—"

"I don't want you to drink," she blurted. An immediate rush of heat filled her cheeks. His brows dipped. She hurried on. "I know it is not my affair whether you drink or not, particularly as ours is a marriage of convenience, but drink makes one unpredictable and unreliable, and," *stop talking, Katherine. Stop talking,* "and I would feel vastly better," *not that you'll necessarily care if I feel vastly better if you don't drink spirits,* "and if it is just the same to you, I'd rather you abstain from drink."

He said nothing for so very long, Katherine thought mayhap he'd not heard her spoken words.

Jasper walked over to her, and stopped. He reached up and brushed the back of his knuckles along her jaw. "Is that what your father did, Katherine? Did he indulge in spirits?"

Her skin burned from the butterfly soft caress. She swallowed, and managed a jerky nod.

"And then he lost your family's wealth and property," he said with a gentleness she'd not come to expect from him.

Katherine wet her lips. Jasper's gaze dropped to her mouth, and fixed there. "He drank heavily and gambled even more heavily. Mother did not voice any disapproval. She said it was not the place of a wife, but when they took my last book of poetry, I lay abed wondering if her words might have made some difference in our circumstances."

His eyes moved somberly over her face. "And you'd ask that I not indulge in spirits?"

The heat in her cheeks spread, and spilled down her neck, and coursed lower. She had no right putting requests to a man who'd wed her on a matter of convenience. Yet . . . Katherine nodded. "I would."

He said nothing. The steady beat of the long-case clock marked the stretch of silence.

Her gaze slid away, and then Jasper dropped his brow to hers. "Very well, Katherine."

She tilted her neck back to look at him. "Very well?"

"Very well," he repeated.

She gave him a tremulous smile. "Thank you, Jasper." She leaned up on tiptoe and kissed his cheek. She spun on her heel to leave him to his work.

Strangers had stormed his castle. Boughs of holly and ivy now hung throughout his home. A babe occupied his guest chambers.

With all that, it appeared his wife intended to walk out of his office.

Katherine grasped the door handle.

Yes, yes, she *did* intend to walk away from him.

"Katherine," Jasper's voice boomed off the walls.

She turned back to face him. "Yes, Jasper?"

"I brought you here to speak to you."

Katherine held up a finger. "*Asked* me here."

He lowered his brows.

"You asked me here," she clarified. "Remember, I'll not be ordered about."

"I wouldn't imagine it," he drawled. King George himself couldn't order this one about.

Her full, kissable lips pursed in a way that made him want to cross over to her and lay claim to the sweet nectar of her mouth.

His gaze moved beyond the lush pout of her red lips, lower to the graceful curve of her neck, downward, and pausing upon breasts sized perfectly for the palms of his hands.

Katherine cleared her throat. "Are you all right, Jasper?"

No, you've driven me to distraction with unquenched desire, you spirited minx.

Jasper folded his arms across his chest. "I wanted to speak to you of your family."

Katherine opened and closed her mouth several times. "My family?"

He nodded once.

Her fingers smoothed over the sides of her floral-patterned day gown, the only tell-tale gesture of her nervousness at their current exchange. "Oh." Katherine glanced momentarily over at the door, as though considering escape, and then returned her attention to Jasper. "It is ever so wonderful they have come, isn't it?"

At his silence, she trailed the tip of her tongue over the seam of her lips. He'd trade all the money in his coffers to lay her down here in his office and worship her mouth with his own, to learn the secrets of her body that made her cry and moan with breathless desire.

"Jasper?"

Jasper started, and tugged at his immaculately folded cravat. "I do not have company at Castle Blackwood."

She nodded in a way that suggested she understood as much. Then, "Is that all, Jasper?"

He angled his head, flummoxed by Katherine's agreeability. He'd expected there to be all manner of foot stamping and fiery shouts from his spirited wife's delectable lips. "It is clear then?" Because in the time he'd come to know Katherine, he'd come to realize that nothing was ever truly clear.

Katherine nodded, this time more emphatically. The sudden gesture sent a brown curl falling across her brow. "You are perfectly clear, Jasper. There are to be no guests." She brushed the strand back. "If you'll excuse me." She started for the door.

A mere ten more steps and she'd be out the door, away from his office, and he'd be alone with his dark musings and deepest yearnings. An odd panic filled his chest. "You will speak to them, then?" he called out, as her fingers pressed the handle.

Katherine spun back around, her lips screwed up. "Speak to whom?"

Jasper closed his eyes and counted to ten, and because counting to ten didn't seem to have any calming effect on him where his wife was concerned, he instead sent a prayer skyward for patience. "Your sister and her family," he said, when he opened his eyes.

Katherine raised a hand to the panel of the door, and drummed her fingertips in a distracted, staccato rhythm. "Whatever for?"

Oh, Christ. "About leaving," he snapped. Enough with this blasted discussion, already.

Katherine's hand froze midbeat and then fell by her side. She took a step toward him. Then another. And another. Until the tips of their feet met. She looked at him through eyes of impenetrable slits that would have raised holy terror in any other man. "You'd have me send my sister out for the holiday?"

Jasper frowned, and glanced over at the heavily curtained windows. "It is not snow . . . Oomph." His words ended as Katherine jabbed him hard in the chest.

"You would have me send her and sweet Lizzie—"

"Lizzie?"

"Her and Michael's babe," she didn't so much as pause. "You would send them away in this cold, forsaken weather for the holiday?"

"Not now," he amended. "But after they've rested a day or so." He lowered his voice. "I believed I was clear when I said there are to be no guests."

Katherine's brows shot to her hairline.

Jasper tugged at his collar. He'd imagined himself incapable of being shamed.

Katherine proved that thought wrong with the next jab of her finger. "And they are not guests, Your Grace." They appeared to be back to the whole 'Your Grace' business. "They. Are. Family." She jabbed him again. "And they are staying. All of them. Are there any other matters you cared to discuss?"

Jasper shook his head.

She gave a flounce of her curls. "Very well. Then if you'll excuse me." And with all the grace and aplomb of Helen of Troy, Katherine strode from the room with a determined step. She slammed the door in her wake.

The abrupt movement displaced a log within the hearth, and the fire snapped and hissed with a fury to match Katherine's rage.

Jasper shook his head. "Well, then, I am very glad we had this discussion, Your Grace," he murmured into the quiet.

He grinned.

Chapter 24

*K*atherine stomped through the castle, wishing she hadn't donned her ivory satin slippers, instead wishing she'd opted for the thick, black serviceable boots she wore in her jaunts through the snow. Because the soft pad of her slippered feet served as no suitable match for the outrage thrumming through her.

"Guests," she mumbled beneath her breath.

Yes, the solid click of her boot-heels upon the hard stone floor would be vastly preferable.

A maid peeked out from one of the doors, and then must have seen something dark in Katherine's expression, for she ducked back into whatever room she'd been tending. Katherine didn't even know how many rooms or what manner of rooms existed within these cheerless, dank walls.

She increased her pace. And this is what he'd turned her into? A frowning, scowling, boot-wearing, fast-moving duchess, who inspired fear in her staff.

With a quiet curse, Katherine spun back around, and walked several paces. She paused inside the doorway.

A parlor.

She wrinkled her nose. A rather garishly gold parlor.

Her gaze landed upon the maid who polished a small porcelain figurine. The maid gulped and fell into a deep curtsy. "Your Grace," she said softly.

"I'm sorry," Katherine blurted.

The young maid cocked her head, frozen in the dip of her curtsy. "Your Grace?"

Katherine waved her hand. "For . . . for . . . being unpleasant. It was not my intention." The girl angled her head further. "To be unpleasant, that is."

The maid's mouth fell open wide, like the trout she and Aldora used to fish from father's well-stocked lakes. Well, his one-time well-stocked lakes. The fish were one of the first items to go upon Father's gambling debts.

"Have a good day . . . ?"

"Mary," the young woman blurted. "My name is Mary."

A perfectly suitable Christmastide name. An unspoken reminder that this was a joyous time of year; a time of beginnings and hope and birth. "It is a lovely name," she said with a smile.

The maid beamed. "Why, thank you, Your Grace."

"Lady Katherine," she corrected. If she wasn't to receive guests and her family was not welcomed, then the friendship of a maid would be welcome.

"Oh, I couldn't," the maid held her hands up in shocked protest.

"Of course you can. It's merely a name," *and I'm hardly a wife, in the true sense*. Why with just a slip of paper, an unconsummated marriage could be annulled. Not so very easily, but still, it could be severed, and . . . "Of course you can," Katherine said again.

Mary smiled, and curtsied again.

"Good day, Mary."

"Good day, Your . . . Lady Katherine." Katherine turned and took her leave, and continued to make her quiet path through the house, this time with less fury to her footsteps.

She ran her fingers over the wallpaper, done in dressed stone, a somber, dark remodeling done at some point to match the foreboding darkness of Castle Blackwood. Katherine paused in the corridor and traced the fabric made to look like stone. How very real it seemed, how very much like the thick blocks that were used to construct this castle many, many years past. And yet . . . she layered her palm to the wall, aware the texture of the smooth fabric was at odds with the image presented to those who walked by these walls.

From the corner of her eye, she detected the white sheet draped across a door.

Then, no one passed through these halls.

There are to be no guests.

Katherine removed her hand from the fabric and hugged her arms to her chest. No one had visited this castle since her husband shut himself away from the world and ordered draperies hung upon doors and over objects reminding him of all he'd lost.

Suddenly, a vicious, potent loathing of that wholly pure white sheet filled her. She'd be glad to never see a reminder of the color white.

Her feet carried her onward, toward the drapery. Katherine tilted her neck back and stared up at the covering. She grasped it between her fingers and tugged it free. It danced down in heavy, noisy flutters, unleashing a soft breeze.

Katherine glanced around, but the corridor remained eerily silent. Who would be here after all? Certainly not Jasper, who'd not come after her. And why should he? Katherine was nothing to him.

Nothing at all.

With a stony set to her lips, she pressed the handle, half expecting it to be locked. The door opened and she stepped inside.

An ivory silk wallpaper striped in thick gold bands lined the portrait room. Katherine hesitated, but an enigmatic pull lured her deeper into the generous space.

With a slowness of step, Katherine moved down the row of lords and ladies and children forever memorialized within these hallowed walls. Paintings of long ago, of ladies in modest, somber tunics, and gentleman with thick, well-trimmed beards and serious frowns.

Katherine paused beside a portrait of a stunning couple with a small boy at their feet. The brittle set to the woman's red lips bespoke of anything but happiness. One of her hands rested upon the sleeve of a familiar-looking, great big bear of a man with a broad nose and blackness in his emerald-green eyes. The gentleman's hand lay possessively upon the shoulder of a somber, angry-looking boy. Katherine stepped closer. Oh, God. Her heart tugged, and she focused on the boy's young, but harshly noble, features.

Jasper and his parents.

My parents were cold, selfish individuals. It was a match based on their mutually distinguished positions in Society.

She shivered, and the cold inside had little to do with the chill of the dark, closed-off room and everything to do with Jasper's miserable childhood.

Katherine's father had left her family in financial ruin. He'd left them desolate and seen them stripped of all their worldly possessions. As a young girl, she'd known the cloying fear of their desperate circumstances. But never once had there been a shortage of love in their oftentimes noisy, usually chaotic, household. Katherine shared a bond with her twin sister, Anne, and a deep love for Aldora and her young brother, Benedict. Even Mother with her social aspirations for her children had shown affection toward her daughters and son through the years.

So very different than the world forever captured upon canvas by a too-knowing, intuitive painter. An artist who'd accurately immortalized the resentment, the loneliness, the hurt of a boy who could be no more than nine or ten years of age.

She closed her eyes.

Oh, Jasper. Is it a wonder you've this rigid shell about you?

Unable to bear looking on the remembrance of his past, Katherine turned to go, when her eyes snagged upon another of those single white sheets.

She wet her lips, but could no sooner leave without ripping that covering down than she could turn Aldora out for the holiday.

Directly opposite the unhappy rendering of Jasper's family hung the covered portrait. Katherine made the very long walk to that sheet, and in a single pull, delicately tugged it from the top of the mahogany frame, inlaid with narrow gold bandings.

Her heart thudded hard against the wall of her chest, and her breath caught on a shuddery gasp.

For all the misery and vitriol captured in Jasper's parents' renderings, this painting depicted the very opposite—joy, unfettered love, tranquility.

The golden beauty stood with the tips of her long, elegant fingers resting upon Jasper's sapphire-blue coat sleeves. Only this Jasper was nothing like the cynical boy of nine or ten years. His gentle, loving stare forever fixed upon his wife's perfect, heart-shaped face. The woman—no, Lydia—gazed up at Jasper with such unadulterated love, Katherine felt like the worst sort of interloper. It was as though the artist sneaked upon an intimate exchange and forever committed it to the canvas. Their locked gazes depicted two who shared a secret that none of the mere mortals looking on were privy to.

Katherine rubbed her chest in an attempt to dislodge the odd knot formed there. Her efforts proved futile.

This moment, this was why Jasper stared at Katherine and the rest of the world with icy disdain. This was why he frowned and snarled and snapped like an injured animal. Because how could one know this . . . this . . . splendor, and ever survive after having it so cruelly plucked from their grasp?

Katherine bent down and picked up the thick, shockingly heavy white sheet filled with a wholly selfish, and horrible urge to toss the covering back upon the mahogany frame.

Because then she wouldn't have to see it, and know just why Jasper could and would never love her.

Tears filled her eyes and Katherine blinked back the salty drops of despair, humbled by the depth of her vileness. Knowing it was horrible and wrong, as she gazed up at Lydia, the true Duchess of Bainbridge, bitter jealousy flared inside Katherine for this dead woman who'd taken Jasper's heart.

The rapid beating of her heart slowed. Katherine blinked and took a staggering step backward. "No," she whispered into the quiet. Her heart resumed its cadence, and then steadily increased in an ever pounding rhythm until she slapped her hands over her ears to dull the loud *thump-thumpthumpthump* that echoed even within her head. "No," she whispered again, shaking her head.

It could not be. Because if it were true, it would destroy her in ways the frozen River Thames never could have . . .

Her eyes slid closed. A fat, single teardrop squeezed past her clenched lids.

I love him.

The tear blazed a warm path down her cheek. She brushed the drop back, but another only took its place, and another, and another.

She'd gone and fallen in love with a man whose heart forever belonged to another—to a woman without silly brown ringlets and dull brown eyes. To a woman whose beauty inspired the great poets like Wordsworth and Byron to forever honor them within the verses of their sonnets.

And Katherine? Well, she would never be anything more than . . . more than . . . whatever she was. Her breath grew ragged.

I cannot bear this. With a great, gasping sob she spun on her heel and fled through the door.

All the air left her on a *whoosh* as she collided with a wall.

She bounced backward and landed on her buttocks. Pain radiated up along the point of contact, and shot up her spine.

The blasted tears continued to fall as she gazed through blurry vision up at Jasper's frowning countenance.

He loomed over her, a great big, unbendable oak of a man. "Katherine?" He held his hand out. "What is . . . ?" She reached for him, just as his hand fell back to his side, and his words died.

Katherine gulped, and shoved herself awkwardly to her feet. She followed Jasper's gaze across the portrait room. With the intensity of his stare, he threatened to bore a hole through that fragile canvas. Then his eyes drifted lower—to that blasted white covering. Her stomach flipped over itself.

"Jasper, I . . ."

His gaze swung angrily back toward hers. "What are you doing in here? I ordered this room closed off."

The image of the smiling, loving-eyed Jasper flitted across her mind. She didn't even need to glance back at the portrait; it would be forever etched in her mind. How very different than the vitriol that fairly dripped from the blacks of his eyes as he studied her.

Katherine ticked her chin up a notch. "I know, Jasper. I took the coverings down."

"Why?"

Why, indeed?

She didn't really have a suitable answer for him . . . or herself. Jasper preferred his life cloaked quite literally and figuratively in the shroud of the past. He'd wed her but remained committed to their maintaining a coolly polite union. Unbidden, her gaze drifted to the point beyond her shoulder, to the 8th Duke of Bainbridge with his sneering lips and flinty eyes, and wondered if this was to be her future.

Only . . .

Her eyes drifted downward to the somber, young Jasper, remembering there would be no young boys or girls, somber or smiling.

"I'd not live in a museum, Jasper," she said at last. Katherine gestured to the portraits carefully hung throughout the room. "You order the servants to cover tapestries and paintings. You lock off doors and have sheets draped across the entrance." She shook her head, willing him to see. "This is no way to live, Jasper. You lived, whether you would have traded places with Lydia. You lived, and she . . ."

"Don't," he barked.

"Died," she forced herself to continue.

An icy cool to rival the brewing snowstorm outside the thick windowpanes emanated from her husband's stiffly held frame.

Realizing the aching directness of that one word, she held a hand out to him. "You lived," she said again. *And I, too, am alive.* "So live, Jasper." Katherine finished lamely. She wished she possessed the words of the great poets because then mayhap she could drag her husband back from the shadow of despair.

Jasper lowered his brow. "Tell me, what would you have me live for, Katherine?" She would have to be as deaf as an ancient dowager not to detect the slight mocking edge to that question.

"I'd have you live for you," she replied, angling her head back ever so slightly to directly meet his gaze. Jasper's happiness could never be inextricably intertwined with her own, the way it had been with his first wife.

The Jasper memorialized in the painting beckoned and she turned to face him. "I want you to be like that, Jasper." Her softly spoken words filled the portrait room.

His entire body jerked as if he'd been struck. He shook his head. Once. Twice, and then again. "I can never again be that man, Katherine. The sooner you realize as much, the sooner we can carry on living our own lives."

Part of her heart chipped off and dissolved within her chest. That was all he imagined for them—an existence where they carried on their separate existences.

Katherine gave a jerky nod. "If you'll excuse me? I'll leave you to your own affairs." Before she did something utterly foolish, such as throw herself into his arms and humble herself with the words of love that hovered on her lips, she dipped a curtsy, and walked out with her head held high.

Chapter 25

Katherine sat at the window-seat that overlooked the back expanse of Castle Blackwood. The rolling hills, covered in a thick, undisturbed blanket of snow reminded her of the days she'd been a girl racing and rolling down the snow-covered hills of Hertfordshire in those very rare times when they were graced with snow.

"You squeezing me, Kat."

Katherine loosened her hold upon Lizzie and placed a kiss upon her cheek. "I'm so sorry, dear Lizzie." She rustled her chin atop her crown of soft curls. "You're just so impossibly sweet, I'd gobble you up like Cook's plum pudding at Christmas." She smothered the small girl's cheeks with kisses until the little girl gasped for breath.

Katherine relented, and with a smile, shifted her attention back to the outside grounds.

"May I join you?"

She glanced back and smiled. "Of course, Aldora."

Her sister walked over. She hovered at the edge of the window seat. From above her wire-rimmed spectacles, Aldora arched an inquisitive brow. "Do you intend to stare out the window all day? Or will you at last speak to me of what happened?"

Truth be told, Katherine would vastly prefer the whole staring out of the window business to the inevitable discussion her sister wished to have. With Lizzie in her arms, Katherine turned and set the small girl on her feet.

Lizzie toddled over and settled at her mother's feet. Aldora leaned down and handed a small doll with golden curls and a long, flowing floral-patterned gown to Lizzie. The little girl proceeded to dance the doll about the floor.

Only the perfect golden ringlets upon the doll put Katherine in remembrance of Lydia's glorious flaxen curls captured within her painting alongside Jasper.

"Kat," Aldora prodded.

Katherine sighed and glanced down at her toes. "I don't know what you'd have me say, Aldora?"

Did her sister want her to speak of her and Jasper's chance meeting at the Frost Fair? Her marriage of convenience? Her husband's impossible lack of regard for her?

"I'd have you start from the beginning," Aldora said gently.

Katherine swallowed, and raised her gaze to Aldora's. And as there could be no more better place to begin, Katherine said, "He saved me." The seconds fell away to minutes, which might as well have given way to hours. Katherine lost track of the passage of time as she spoke of everything from that lone volume of Wordsworth to Katherine's outrageous proposal of marriage.

At some point, Aldora scooped up her daughter and rocked her to sleep.

Katherine studied the slumbering babe. A ball of emotion lodged in her throat. "I've a marriage of convenience, Aldora." She waved her hand. "It is what I proposed—"

"But it is not what you desire," Aldora interjected quietly. With her free hand, she pushed her spectacles farther back on the bridge of her nose.

Katherine shook her head back and forth. "No. It is not what I want."

I want baby girls who play with dolls and sleep in my arms. I want a smiling portrait with a man who gazes at me like there is no other more beautiful than me. Not just any gentleman. Jasper. I want Jasper.

Aldora caught her lower lip between her teeth and worried the flesh. "I wanted you to wed for love, Katherine."

She *had*, however inadvertent it may have been.

"A man who loved you in return," Aldora continued.

Katherine surged to her feet and began to pace. "I did not have the luxury of patience in the matter of marriage. Mother—"

"Would not have spoken to Uncle about plans for a union without Michael's knowledge," Aldora said. She rose and carried Lizzie over to a plush, gold-upholstered sofa. She lay the small girl down, and placed a calming hand along her back when she stirred.

Katherine shifted under the weight of that truth. Somewhere inside, she recognized the truth in her sister's words. Mother would've wed Katherine off to Mr. Bertrand Ekstrom, but not without Michael's agreement on such a union. After all, Michael saved them from certain ruin, and with his connection as the Marquess of St. James's brother, Mother deferred to Aldora's husband.

When Lizzie's breath settled back into that smooth, steady cadence of sleep, Aldora turned back to Katherine. She crossed over, and rested a staying hand on Katherine's shoulders, steadying her frenetic movements. "I believe your decision to wed the duke stemmed from more than your fear of wedding Mr. Ekstrom." She wrinkled her nose. "Not that the thought of marriage to horrid Mr. Ekstrom wouldn't be cause enough. But you could have wed anyone, Kat."

An inelegant snort escaped Katherine. "I know what I am, Aldora. I'm no grand beauty." It was a fact in which she'd been comfortable since she'd been a small girl not much older than Lizzie. There were diamonds of the first water . . .

And everyone else.

Katherine embraced the category of *everyone else*.

Aldora's mouth set in a mutinous line. "Don't be a ninnyhammer, you are perfectly lovely."

As an adoring older sister, she'd seemed to only see beauty in Katherine—even when the world had not.

Katherine directed her eyes to the ceiling. "I've brown hair."

Her sister folded her arms across her chest and arched a *brown* eyebrow.

"Set in hopelessly tight ringlets," Katherine went on. She waved a hand over Aldora. "You've not had tight brown ringlets in a very long while."

"That's one of the many benefits of marriage," Aldora muttered from under her breath. "Being free of Mother's rather er . . . *questionable* fashion dictates." She gave her head a shake and returned the conversation to the heart of the matter. "I'd have you be happy, Katherine."

"I am happy."

Aldora gave her a skeptical look through the thick frames of her lenses.

"Well, mayhap not altogether happy. Not in the same way you and Michael are. Rather in a . . . a . . ." Less loving, less bucolic way. "Less predictable way," she settled for.

"Do you believe he'd ever harm you?"

"No," the response burst from Katherine's lips. She shook her head. "He would never hurt me." She touched a hand to where her heart beat. Then, some pain was far greater than the physical kind.

"You love him," Aldora said softly.

Katherine's hand fell to her side. She swallowed hard, and looked away from the pity teeming in the brown irises of her sister's kindhearted eyes. "I . . . I . . ." Katherine buried her head in her hands and shook it back and forth. "I love him," she breathed the word into existence. "It is the height of foolishness, and he is oftentimes boorish and rude." But then there were the Shrewsbury cake and Wordsworth book moments when he showed himself to be so very much more than the unyielding figure he presented to her and the world.

"But you love him regardless," Aldora intoned, as only one who also loves truly can understand.

Katherine managed a jerky nod. She hugged her arms tight to her waist. "He can never love me, though," she whispered.

"Of course he can," Aldora said, with all the cocksure arrogance of an eldest sister.

Lydia's smiling visage danced to the fore, yet again. Sadness filled Katherine's being. She could not share the darkest, most pained secrets her husband harbored. "He can't." There would always be Lydia and the small babe he'd lost.

Aldora must have heard the truth in Katherine's two-word utterance, for she passed a slow, searching gaze over Katherine's face. Then, she crossed over and folded Katherine in her arms much the way she'd done when Katherine was a small girl who'd scraped her knee running through the hills of Hertfordshire.

Katherine accepted the warmth and support she'd so desperately missed since the day she'd wed and made the journey to Castle Blackwood.

Her sister raised her hand and stroked the back of her head. "Come, now. It is the eve of Christmas. There is no time for sadness on such a day."

Katherine mustered her best attempt at a smile. "I should speak to Cook and see how the evening's dinner plans are progressing."

Aldora bussed her on the cheek and returned to the sofa on which Lizzie still slumbered peacefully.

As Katherine made her way from the room, she wondered if she'd ever been so blissfully innocent and untouched by the world's hurts. She wound her way down the long stone corridors. The thin red rug lining the hall muted the tread of her footsteps. She continued walking until she reached the recently decorated foyer.

Katherine paused to assess the completed work done by her, Wrinkleton, and the footmen. Lush green boughs adorned with clusters of red holly berries and ivy sprigs brightened the cheerless space. Her gaze climbed up the high ceiling to the kissing bough she'd arranged with apples, papered flowers, and the small doll.

Before Aldora and her family left and returned to London, Katherine would instruct one of the servants to take down the arraignment and retrieve the small doll. Lizzie would love the tiny, little babe.

"Katherine," a deep baritone drawled from beyond her shoulder.

She shrieked and spun around. An increasingly familiar heat flooded her cheeks. Her husband stood at the entrance of another corridor. "Forgive me, I didn't hear you," she murmured.

Jasper's gloriously long legs closed the distance between them. He touched her chin. But otherwise remained as silent as the grave.

Her eyes slid closed. What game did he play with her? Could he not see his mere presence alone was destroying her? "What do you want, Jasper?" she asked, wearily. She did not want to carry on as they were, with his harsh outbursts and her fleeing like a naughty pup sent from the kitchens.

Jasper's hand stilled, but he did not drop his arm back to his side. "It looks beautiful, Katherine."

"What does?" she blurted.

With a sweeping gesture, he motioned to the holiday decor.

"Oh." She fiddled with the fabric of her gown. "I didn't believe you'd noticed, Jasper."

I notice anything and everything where you're concerned, Katherine.

Since that not too distant day ago when her high-pitched desperate cry reached his ears across the Thames River, he'd developed a keen sense of awareness of his wife.

Just as he'd known the harshly spoken words he'd hurled at her in the portrait room had wounded her.

Now, as she stood before him, with an uncharacteristic wariness in her usually cheer-filled eyes, he confronted the change their short marriage wrought upon his wife. He'd thought himself content to live a solitary life, buried away in his castle. Until Katherine, he'd not realized the truth; he'd not been content, but rather he'd been hiding, embracing his sorrow as a kind of penance.

In just a few days, she'd torn down those protective white coverings throughout the castle and restored a sense of joyfulness to the cold, dank walls of the castle.

Katherine made to step around him. "If you'll excuse me," she murmured. "I should speak to Cook regarding dinner for the evening."

Jasper matched her movement, effectively barring her escape.

She wrinkled her brow, and took an opposite step left. Jasper matched her movement, again.

Katherine looked up at him, imploringly. "Jasper, what do you want of me? You were so very clear in the portrait room. You desire nothing from me."

Oh, how wrong his hopelessly alluring wife was. He desired too much from her. More than he deserved. More than he'd ever believed himself capable of.

"You're under the bough," he murmured in a gruff, husky whisper.

Katherine tipped her head.

Jasper raised his hand and curved it around the nape of her neck. Ever so gently, he tipped her head back so she might view the kissing bough above them. "We're under the kissing bough," he amended.

Her gaze locked on the piece. Then, her throat worked. She closed her eyes. "I don't understand," she whispered.

Jasper leaned down and placed his lips to her fast-beating pulse there.

Her eyes slid closed. Jasper moved his search upward to the corner of her lip. He placed a kiss upon her siren's mouth, and continued on, kissing her cheek, the tip of her pert nose, her gloriously long, thick brown lashes.

"What are you doing?" Her voice broke on a breathy moan.

"Tell me to stop, Katherine. Tell me, and I will stop now, and leave." *It will kill me, but I shall do it because* I'm *helpless to deny you anything.*

Katherine raised her fingers to his jaw. She stroked her knuckles across his skin. A muscle twitched at the corner of his eye. She met his gaze with a boldness better suited to a woman many years her senior. "I do not want you to stop, Jasper."

I am lost.

Jasper swept her into his arms and strode up the long, sweeping staircase, down the long corridor, hating the massiveness of the castle. Her quick breaths, blended with his harshly drawn ones, punctuated his steps. He pressed the handle of her bedchamber doors and kicked it closed behind them hard enough to shake the wood panel in its frame.

Jasper strode over to her wide four-poster bed and lowered her onto the green woven coverlet. Katherine edged backward, into the center of the mattress. Her skirts climbed up around her ankles, ever higher, exposing the muscles of her calf that spoke of a woman who excelled at horseback riding. His body turned to stone as he imagined those legs wrapped about his waist, urging him on.

She angled her head, and a brown ringlet fell over her cheek. "Jasper?" Just that. His name, a breathless moan that bespoke of innocent desire.

A groan rumbled from deep within his chest. He shrugged out of his jacket and then tugged his shirt free. He tossed them both aside.

Katherine's eyes, the color of the finest French brandy, widened. God help him, he should go slower. She was an innocent, unschooled in the ways of lovemaking.

And he'd never been consumed by this uncontrollable, burning desire to lay claim to a woman.

From the moment he'd held her to him in the confines of his carriage that fated day he'd saved her, he'd battled his hungering, convinced himself his desire stemmed from the many years he'd gone without a woman.

Now, studying her delicate frame upon her bed, elbows propped behind her, and her lips swollen, Jasper could no longer deny the truth—he wanted Katherine. Only her. Just her. Forever.

And he'd allow the terror of that reality to seep into his mind after he made her his.

Jasper tugged off his boots, one at a time, all the while his gaze remained fixed on Katherine.

She followed his every movement; a becoming pink blush bathed her cheeks. He threw the gleaming black Hessians atop his now rumpled jacket upon the floor, and hovered at the edge of the bed.

Don't do this.

Yours is a marriage of convenience.

Your heart is dead.

This is a betrayal of Lydia.

. . . Only.

. . . It felt like none of those things.

As he lowered himself beside Katherine's still form, a sense of absolute rightness besieged his senses.

Katherine scrambled up right, and pushed herself to her knees. "Jasper," she whispered.

He came up beside her. "Yes, Katherine?"

She blinked. Her gaze fell to his chest. The pink hue of her cheeks flamed red. "I d-don't know," she stammered. "I don't know what I'd intended to say. I just—"

Jasper kissed her to silence.

Her body went taut in his arms, and then her slim arms climbed up his neck. Katherine angled her head, allowing him better access to her mouth. He slipped his tongue inside. All the while, he worked the long row of buttons down the back of her gown. One popped off. He cursed and wrenched his mouth from hers.

Katherine moaned in protest.

He turned her and kissed the exposed flesh of her neck and continued his efforts with the impossibly small buttons. He cursed when another popped free.

"I never want to see you in another gown of buttons," he rasped, and then he gave a gentle tug. Tiny, pearl buttons showered the bed and rolled to the floor with a tiny thud. He gently divested her of her gown, baring her chemise-clad frame.

Jasper groaned. He closed his eyes and counted to ten, praying to a God he'd ceased to believe in for patience from ripping that flimsy garment apart and mounting her like a wild beast until he found surcease in her tight, moist heat.

"Are you all right, Jasper?" Tentative fingers brushed the muscles of his forearm. They leapt under Katherine's gentle touch.

Jasper opened his eyes, and with a desperate groan, pulled her to him. He lowered Katherine to the mattress, pulling the chemise over her head. He tossed it to the floor where it joined his garments.

Pink.

The tips of her perfectly shaped breasts were a delicate shade of pink. Jasper closed his mouth around one of the buds.

Katherine gasped. He expected she'd pull back in maidenly modesty. Not his Katherine. He should know how very unlike anyone else his Katherine was. She tangled her fingers in his hair and held him close. "Oh, Jasper. That feels delicious," she moaned.

Her words fueled his ardor. He pulled back and removed his breeches, kicking them to the floor, and then moved his ministrations to the peak of her other breast. Jasper captured the bud between his fingers, and he gently rolled the tender flesh until Katherine's eyes widened, and she arched and twisted wildly underneath him.

A primitive growl climbed up his throat, and he worked a hand between her legs. His fingers delved into the thatch of brown curls. He parted her folds and explored her center. A groan rumbled up from his chest. She dripped honeyed heat, coating his fingers with her desire.

He slid a finger inside her, and she gasped. "Jasper." He responded by sliding another deep inside.

His wife clenched her legs about his hand and arched into his caress.

The thin thread he desperately clung to slipped. Moisture beaded at his brow, as he battled four years' worth of self-control.

He moved over Katherine's writhing form and inserted his knee between her thighs. He pressed his hardened shaft against her center, and propped on his elbows, frozen above her.

Oh, God. I'm going to lose control. I've wanted you for so long, Katherine.

"Jasper," she moaned, arching against him.

"Forgive me," he whispered.

He plunged into her hot heat. Wet warmth closed around him, drawing him in until he wanted to forever lose himself inside her.

Katherine cried out, and a spasm of pain contorted her face.

He froze, forcing himself to stop, when all he wanted with every fiber of his worthless being was to plunge deeper inside her, over and over again until he spilled his seed at long last . . .

A pained groan ripped from inside him.

"Jasper, are y-you all right?"

He chuckled at Katherine's breathless concern. His large shaft had her stretched to full, and she should worry after him?

Jasper placed a kiss at her temple. And began to move.

Her eyes widened, and she caught her lower lip between her teeth. He fixed his gaze to the sight of it, anything but the alluring draw of her wet core as he moved in and out. In and out.

It'd been too long.

Jasper increased his rhythm. Katherine matched his rapid thrusts, arching up. Her nails scraped along his back, as she encouraged him on.

"I cannot wait, Katherine," he moaned. "I . . ." Oh, God. He needed to wait . . . just . . .

Katherine's eyes widened, and her whole body stiffened in his hold. "Oh, God," she cried, and then her wet sheath throbbed and pulsed under the force of her release. Her body trembled as she came, sucking him deeper.

He didn't want to . . .

He couldn't spill his seed . . .

Not. Again.

Jasper flexed his hips and poured himself in long, rippling waves inside her. His hot seed flooded her, filled her, and he tossed his head back with a primitive roar.

Jasper collapsed atop Katherine's still form, bracing himself upon his elbows to avoid crushing her.

As the mindless sated state of desire began to recede and his breathing resumed a normal rhythm, he rolled off of

Katherine. The enormity of what he'd done, the mistake he'd made, began to seep into the blissful moment, until horror melded with terror replaced the sweet release he'd experienced in Katherine's tight, virginal heat.

Even now, his seed could be taking root and ultimately destroying her.

Nausea roiled in his belly.

Katherine curled up next to him, and he recoiled as she brushed a kiss alongside his bicep. "I love you, Jasper," she whispered.

His heart slowed, slowed, and then thudded to a stop as her words crept around the hopes he'd not known he carried.

No, he couldn't . . . she couldn't . . .

Love destroyed.

As much as he longed to be selfish and reach out and grasp with his greedy hands all that she offered, he could not be responsible for extinguishing Katherine's effervescent glow. It would destroy him in ways that even Lydia's death hadn't managed to do.

Oh, God, what have I done?

Chapter 26

*K*atherine dipped her spoon into the small dish of plum pudding and polished off the holiday dessert. She sat back in her seat, deliciously warmed by the roaring fire that blazed within the hearth.

She studied her sister and Michael a long moment. The two of them eyed one another as though there was not another soul present, the way Jasper gazed upon his wife in their blissful portrait. Odd, how such a thought brought her pain just that morning, and now, after Jasper's loving a short while ago, she should feel nothing but this . . . this . . . sense of fulfillment.

She loved him.

And it mattered not that he'd not spoken the words in return. For he'd tossed aside his vow of a marriage of convenience, and made her his wife in all sense of the words.

Heat raced up her neck and flooded her cheeks. She stole a sideways peek at her husband.

Seated at the head of the table in his midnight-black evening jacket and expertly folded white cravat, one would never gather from the hard glint in his inscrutable expression that a short while ago he'd been . . . been . . .

She fanned her cheeks. Making love to her.

I'm no longer a virgin.

She smiled. With the exception of a slight soreness betwixt her thighs, there remained little evidence of Jasper's passionate loving.

"I must say I'm surprised at the evening's course," Aldora called from the opposite end of the table, jerking Katherine uncomfortably back to the moment.

Katherine frowned. "You did not care for the meal?" She spent the previous morning with Cook discussing and planning all the details for the Christmas Eve feast.

Aldora waved her hand. "I just know you've never cared for roast quail."

She detected the slight stiffening of Jasper's broad shoulders, the one telltale indication he'd been following any of the discourse that evening. Until the near imperceptible stiffening he'd appeared wholly unaffected by her family, and the Christmas Eve dinner, and . . . Katherine, herself.

"Everything has been splendid," Michael intoned.

Aldora frowned. "Of course, dinner could not have been more wonderful. Your Cook did a magnificent job with the fare. I merely meant I always believed you'd detested roa . . ."

Katherine shook her head, with her eyes imploring her sister to silence.

Aldora's eyes widened a bit, and then she snapped her lips closed. She picked up her spoon and dipped it into her cup of plum pudding.

Lizzie slid out of her seat.

"Lizzie," Michael called.

The little girl ignored him, and wandered down the edge of the table.

Katherine held her breath as she paused at the arm of Jasper's chair.

He picked up his glass of red wine and took a sip. His jaw taut.

"Bear," Lizzie whispered.

His seat slid backward along the wood floor, as though he were a moment away from leaping from his seat, and fleeing the room like the hounds of hell were after him. The muscle in the corner of Jasper's eye ticked.

Lizzie reached for his free hand and tugged. "Bear," she said, a bit louder this time.

"Lizzie, come here," Aldora called, shooting an apologetic glance at Jasper, who remained stoically silent through the exchange.

He finally dropped his gaze to Lizzie.

She jabbed a finger at his plate. "I have your cake."

Jasper's frown deepened, and Katherine made to rise and go to the girl. But Jasper reached for his Shrewsbury cake and handed it over.

Lizzie accepted the sugary dessert with a wide-toothed smile. "Thank you," she said, and proceeded to scramble onto Jasper's lap.

Aldora gasped. "I am so sorry, Your Grace." She rose, and hurried to retrieve her daughter but Lizzie burrowed against Jasper's chest. She smattered flaky white bits of crumb onto his immaculate black jacket. Aldora shot a questioning glance between Michael and Katherine, and then back to Jasper. "Lizzie, come here."

The little girl took another bite of Shrewsbury cake. She shook her head, and a brown curl fell over her eye. "No. Bear," she insisted.

Jasper sat immobile, as though he'd been turned to granite. His hand came up, hovered about Lizzie, and Katherine thought he intended to turn the girl over to Aldora's care.

Then, he rested his fingers atop Lizzie's crown of brown curls, and gave an awkward pat.

The last tiny sliver of her unguarded heart gave way, and fell into Jasper's hands.

Lizzie grinned around a mouthful of cake. "Bear," she said again.

Jasper reminded himself to breathe. He counted to ten. When that proved ineffectual, he counted another ten. And another.

He dug his toes into the soles of his boots to keep from upending the girl and tearing from the dining room like a madman escaped from Bedlam. Then, isn't that what he was? The Mad Duke.

How else could he account for the alarm roused by this small slip of a child?

The girl, Lizzie, reminded him of his loss. He closed his eyes a moment and willed Lydia's face to the surface.

But it would not come.

He clenched and unclenched his jaw and accepted the staggering truth—Katherine had weaved her way into his every thought, and had dispelled the memories he'd held most dear.

In the course of a fortnight, he'd thrown aside his vow to remain unwed and celibate. And now, a short while after spilling his seed inside Katherine, he partook in a Christmas Eve sup.

Katherine caught his gaze and smiled. She raised a spoonful of plum pudding to her lips. Her mouth closed over the small bite. A faint remnant clung to her full lower lip. He wanted to go over and kiss the mark away. Then the tip of her tongue darted out and captured the small dab of pudding.

Small fingers still caked with Shrewsbury cake tugged at Jasper's jacket, recalling his attention.

"Bear?"

He swallowed and looked down at Lizzie. "Yes?"

The small child possessed the courage and boldness of her aunt, for she grinned up at him. "Sing."

He'd rather lob off his right arm than sing before this table of strangers and his delectable wife.

Jasper shook his head. "No."

Her lower lip quivered. "S-sing."

Jasper glowered. "No," he said this time with more firmness.

Tears welled in her very familiar warm brown eyes. A sudden image filled his mind. Katherine as a small girl with the same brown curl hung over her innocent wide-eyed stare. His mind went numb with a longing for the dream Lizzie represented.

"P-please, Bear," she said on a trembling whisper.

Oh, for the love of Christ in heaven and all his blasted saints.

"Lord Redford loved his cards,
He played them all the time,
Wagered land and all his wealth,
And lost them to Lord Grimes."

As his slightly discordantly sung ditty ended, an uncomfortable pall fell across the table. The little girl clapped at his feeble attempt at song. In the thick blanket of discomfort, it occurred to Jasper the enormity of the *song* he'd just sung to little Lizzie.

Jasper's eyes found Katherine, who sat, shoulders squared, head at an awkward angle.

My father was a wastrel. He spent his days and nights at the gaming tables, and indulging in spirits, and he squandered everything not entailed.

Bloody hell, he could not even do this right.

He shifted the bundle in his arms and made to set Lizzie down, but she tugged at his arm.

"Again. Again," she urged.

Aldora rushed over, and Jasper was never more grateful to see another person in his life. He handed off the two-foot burden to her waiting arms. "Your Grace," she murmured, her gaze averted.

Jasper surged to his feet. He sketched a deep bow. "Good evening," he mumbled. Taking care to avoid Katherine's eyes, Jasper turned on his heel and left.

He only managed to make it to the end of the corridor.

Katherine's slippered feet tapped a swift beat along the floor in her haste to reach him.

Jasper cursed and increased his pace.

"Jasper?" His name emerged slightly breathless from the quick pace she'd set for herself.

Her faint mutter carried down the long corridor and echoed off the stone walls. He forced himself to stop.

Katherine came to stop alongside him. Her eyes moved over his face. "Are you all right, Jasper?"

You've thrown my entire world upside down, Katherine. No, I'm not all right.

"Fine," he said quietly. He made to leave, but she touched her fingers to his sleeve.

The delicateness of her touch reminded him of all manner of wicked things they'd done together just that morning. Once hadn't been enough.

He swallowed hard.

It would have to be.

"Because you don't seem all right," she blurted. Katherine caught her lower lip between her teeth as she so often did, and again, his mind and body stirred with the memory of her mouth upon his, the satiny softness of her breasts, the delicate pink tip engorged from his ministrations.

He groaned. She would be the death of him.

"Jasper . . ."

"No, I'm not all right," the words burst from his chest. Servants could be nearby, her family still took their dessert at the end of the corridor in the dining room. Those realities should have been enough.

Instead, he began to pace there along the thin strip of red carpet. He dragged his hand through his hair. "You instructed Cook to prepare roast quail."

She blinked. "I believed you liked roast quail."

Jasper paused. "But you do not." He didn't know that much about her. But she'd cared enough to ask him about his favorite meals, and then had Cook prepare it for the eve of Christmas dinner, in spite of the fact she abhorred it.

Katherine touched a tentative hand to his shoulder, and jerked him back into his frenetic pacing. "What is this about, Jasper?" she prodded, with such gentleness his gut clenched.

"I sang that bloody ditty," he spat.

A gentle understanding lit her eye. He did not deserve her pardon. "It is f . . ."

He glared her into silence. "Do not say it is fine," he bit out. "It is not fine. Your father gambled your family's wealth and security away and I sang a bloody ditty about it."

Katherine held a palm up in attempt to stay his movements.

He ignored her.

"Jasper, it was merely a song." The corners of Katherine's lips tugged ever so faintly; he suspected she might smile. "A rather poor choice of song for a child, perhaps."

Any other woman would be spitting fury with their vitriolic words and burning eyes. She should be livid, and he
would be deserving of any indignation.

Except Katherine's lips at last gave in to a full smile,
revealing a faint dimple in her right cheek. Jasper jerked to
a sudden stop. And that was another blasted thing. He'd not
even noted the dimple before this moment. How could he
have failed to note the precious little indentation in her right
cheek?

Jasper resumed pacing. "I didn't even consider the child,"
he groused under his breath.

Katherine blinked. "I beg your pardon."

His hand slashed the air. "The child. Lizzie. I didn't know
another blasted thing to sing to the child. It hadn't even
occurred to me, until just this moment, the absolute unsuit-
ability of such a piece."

If his son hadn't died, Jasper would be well-versed in the
care of young children. He would certainly know the interests of a child two or three years of age, and which songs to
soothe their troubled thoughts, and coax a smile. "I sang a
bloody tavern ditty to a child," he repeated with a shake of
his head.

Katherine stepped in front of his path, so that Jasper was
forced to either bowl her down, walk around her, or stop.

He stopped.

Katherine placed her palms upon his chest. His heart
stirred. "She loved your song."

"It was inappropriate."

She nodded, and touched the tip of a well-manicured nail
to his lips, silencing him. "She enjoyed it, Jasper. You made
her smile. Does it matter how or why? It just matters that
you did." She opened her palm and cupped his cheek. He

caught her wrist and dragged it to his mouth, placing his lips where her pulse fluttered wildly.

"Jasper?"

"Yes, Katherine?" he whispered against her wrist.

She giggled. "That tickles."

He responded with another kiss to the sensitive intersecting of her palm. She swatted at him. "S-stop," she commanded. "Jasper?"

He sighed, and pulled away. "Yes, Katherine."

"Can we go abovestairs?"

Jasper narrowed his eyes. "Abovestairs?"

Katherine wet her lips. "Er, yes." She scuffed the tip of her ivory slipper along the floor. Did his wife have slippers of any other color? He imagined her in a scandalous red slipper. Imagined himself tugging it loose, tossing it aside, and then lowering her stockings inch by agonizing . . . "I was hoping, that is to say, imagining," She furrowed her brow. "Well, imagining might not be the right word."

"Katherine?"

"Yes?"

"Out with it."

Her eyes widened. "Oh, er, yes, of course. I want to spend the night with you." Her cheeks flamed a red to match the carpet, only heightened by the pale white of her satin evening gown with those ridiculous lace ruffles along her décolletage.

Did she just say . . . ?

"I know it is not at all the thing. Wives and husbands sharing the same chambers. Mother and Father never shared a chamber." She grimaced. "Not that I care to think of Mother and Father sharing a chamber. It is just . . ." Her words ended on a high-pitched squeak as he swept her into his arms.

"What are you . . . ?"

"Katherine?"

"Yes?"

Jasper shifted her in his arms, angling her in a way that her breasts were crushed against his chest. "Will you cease talking?"

"Er, right, yes, of course." She peeked around his shoulder. "Jasper?"

He sighed. In addition to spirited, he would add loquacious to his wife's sometimes endearing, and in this instance exasperating, attributes. "Yes, Katherine?" He pressed his lips to the place where her neck met her ear.

She giggled and swatted at his chest. "That t-tickles," she managed to pant out between gasping laughs.

And ticklish. He could add ticklish to the growing list of his understanding of Katherine Waincourt, the Duchess of Bainbridge.

"You were saying?" he whispered against her neck.

She erupted into another fit of laughter. "Someone w-will undoubtedly hear us or see us."

"Undoubtedly," he said with a sardonic smile.

Katherine slapped her hand to his chest again. He grunted. She was rather strong for one so diminutive. "It wouldn't do to create a scandal here."

Jasper shook his head, bemused. "Katherine, you are my wife. There will be no scandal." And if a servant was unwise enough to step into their path, then he'd sack the damned fool.

Katherine frowned. "I do not like that dark glower, Jasper."

It appeared she'd also come to know him. Jasper ignored her and carried her up the long, sweeping staircase, down the hall.

He paused a moment outside his chambers. No one had entered these rooms in a very long time. Not even Lydia had frequented his rooms. Instead, Jasper would pay visits to her, and then she'd insist for propriety's sake he return to sleep in his own chambers.

Jasper pressed the handle and carried Katherine inside.

Chapter 27

$\mathscr{K}$atherine imagined this is how mere mortals felt upon entering the dragon's lair. She shoved aside such silly musings as Jasper carried her over to his wide four-poster bed, and deposited her amidst the center of the soft feather mattress.

A little grunt escaped her at the unexpectedness of the movement.

She shoved herself up on her elbows and eyed her husband.

Jasper shrugged free of his jacket and tossed it to the ground. His black waistcoat and shirt followed. Her mouth went dry as his hands went to the fastenings of his form-fitting breeches.

Then he turned his attention to her.

Oh, God, I will never have enough of him.

Then, with the infinite gentleness she'd come to expect from him, Jasper sat at the edge of the bed. He held his arms out and Katherine scrambled onto his lap.

She captured his face in her hands. "I love you, Jasper." Katherine willed him to hear the strength of her profession. "I . . ."

He kissed her until all rational thought fled with the magic of his kiss. His hands worked her gown up over her ankles, calves, ever higher, and then around her waist. The cool night air slapped her skin belied by the warmth of his kiss. Then his expert hands moved to the back of her gown.

Jasper paused. "I. Thought. I said. No buttons." He punctuated the hoarse command between deliberately placed kisses to her eyelids, earlobe, the corners of her mouth.

Katherine moaned, and arched her neck back. "I don't have any other gowns," she managed to rasp.

He helped turn her around and devoted his attention to sliding each one of her pearl buttons free of the tiny grommets along the back of her gown.

Oh, God, she'd never before realized how very much she detested buttons.

"There," he whispered, and slid the silly ivory ruffled satin gown down her frame. It fell past her hips, and Katherine kicked it off.

Next, Jasper moved to her chemise and stays, removing them in short order so he'd bared her body to his hot gaze.

Katherine expected she should feel some maidenly embarrassment for the heated manner in which he studied her. But all she felt was a hunger for more. For him.

"What have you done to me, Katherine?" he groaned.

Their bodies met; hers soft and curved, his hard, and muscle-hewn.

Jasper worked his hand down between their bodies and stroked her damp core. "You are beautiful, Katherine. You've made me forget all the vows, all the pledges I've taken. I'm powerless against you."

His tantalizing words wrapped headily about her. She clamped her legs tight around his hand, a ragged moan slipped past her lips as Jasper's thumb pressed into her nub. As if of their own volition, her thighs fell open. Her head fell back. "I love you," she said again.

Her words seemed to drive him to a frenzy. His lips slanted over hers, his tongue forced its way inside, and she met his in a bold, nearly violent parry, even as his hand continued to deliberately torment her womanhood.

Jasper's fingers caressed her moist center and she arched her hips, struggling to open her eyes.

He broke their kiss, and she moaned in protest, mourning the loss of him.

"You are so beautiful," Jasper rasped out. He inserted a finger in her center.

Her eyes slid closed at his words, and he continued to caress her. Those words, when uttered as they were, hoarse with passion, Katherine found she believed him.

"Do you like that, Katherine? If you tell me you do, I shall give you more than you'd ever imagined."

More than this volatile storm raging through her?

"I do," she cried. "That is, I do," he teased her nub, and she caught her lower lip between her teeth. "Oh, goodness. I do like it, Jasper. Please," she implored. She could not survive this passionate torture, no matter how much she reveled in his ministrations.

Jasper lowered her to the mattress and followed her with his body.

He inserted his shaft inch by agonizing inch. Beads of sweat dripped from his brow.

Heat filled her at the hungry desire reflected in the near black of his emerald stare.

Jasper's breath grew labored, and then he plunged deep inside her.

Katherine cried out, and then he began to move. Her hips rose and fell to match his steady, rhythmic thrusts.

I love you. I love you. I love you.

Katherine didn't know if the litany filled the air around them or merely rang inside her head.

But she loved him.

He thrust again.

With a savage intensity that terrified her.

He withdrew.

And her heart would belong to him.

He plunged deep.

Forever.

Katherine's body stiffened, and then she exploded in a burst of flashing colors of the Vauxhall Gardens fireworks she'd once viewed.

Jasper's muscles went taut beneath her fingers. His face contorted in a paroxysm of rhapsody and agony, and then he spilled his seed inside her body as she convulsed around him. He collapsed, and braced himself above her until he could once again breath, and then rolled away from her.

A sated smile tugged at her lips and she curled against her husband's side.

Jasper's arm hovered a moment about her, and then he pulled her close.

With the fire's embers popping in the hearth, and the cool winter air howling against the windowpane, Katherine drifted off to sleep.

A deep rumble pierced the edge of Katherine's consciousness. Her lashes fluttered open. She yawned and blinked back the thick fog of sleep.

She struggled to adjust to the dimly lit room as she tried to sort out her whereabouts.

Another bear-like rumble caught her notice, and she looked around.

Her gaze alighted upon her husband sprawled on his back, a broad arm draped over his brow, his lips slightly slack in his slumber.

She flipped onto her side and studied him. How very unguarded, how very uncomplicated he appeared with the hard edge of wakefulness stripped free.

He shifted, drawing her attention to his broad, muscular chest covered in a spriggy mat of dark curls. She hesitated, and then caressed the delicate wisps of hair. She jumped as he broke into a sputtering snore.

Katherine lay back down, knowing she must have the world's silliest smile upon her lips, but she'd not been able to stop grinning since that morning, when Jasper made her his wife in every sense of the word.

And he'd made love to her, again.

In all her nineteen years, she'd not known joy such as this. *I love him.*

Her smile fell. Jasper hadn't returned those very important words. There would always be Lydia. His heart would forever belong to his first, beautiful paragon of a wife who'd masterfully completed tapestries that still adorned the walls of the castle.

But perhaps—she rolled back to her side, and examined him—perhaps just a small sliver of his heart remained alive, and that tiny sliver could one day belong to her.

Jasper shifted on the pillow. His smooth, even breaths indicated he still slept.

Her gaze snagged upon the faintest scrap of fabric concealed beneath his pillow. Pale green like mint leaves, the cloth had a familiar look to it. Katherine hesitated. Her gaze moved between Jasper's closed lids and the hint of green.

Mother had despaired of Katherine's unrelenting inquisitiveness. The whole "curiosity killed a cat, thou hast mettle enough to kill curiosity," business.

Katherine inched closer to the head of Jasper's enormous four-poster bed. Breath held to make sure he still slept, she lifted the edge of his pillow.

And froze.

Her heart pounded loud in her own ears. She shoved the corner of the pillow up and reached for the familiar, long-forgotten reticule she'd thought to never again see. Katherine held it in tremulous fingers, as her heart beat with a greater sense of urgency within her breast, the steady *thumpthumpthumpthump* filled her ears, confused her thoughts.

Why . . . ?

What . . . ?

How could this be?

She opened the small reticule and her breath caught.

The heart pendant glimmered back up at her.

The heart of a duke.

He'd rescued her reticule.

Katherine angled her head, wrinkling her brow.

. . . And he'd kept the small article.

Why would he—?

"What are you doing?"

The bag slipped from her fingers at the harsh growl.

Her head snapped up and she met her husband's furious gaze.

Katherine swallowed hard at the burning hot fury detected in the blacks of his eyes.

"J-Jasper," she stammered.

Jasper stared with something akin to horror at the blasted green reticule given to him by Guilford a lifetime ago.

Heat climbed up his neck.

"J-Jasper, you have my reticule."

Yes, he'd kept her bloody reticule. He despised the weakness within him that made him hold onto the frippery, and he cringed . . . sleep with it beneath his pillow.

"Why do you have my reticule?" Katherine angled her head, moving her gaze from Jasper to the rumpled green fabric.

He swung his legs over the bed, feeling like an untamed beast.

"Jasper, I asked—"

Jasper whipped back. "I heard you," he barked and bent down to retrieve his breeches. He should have never taken her to his chambers. He should have never made love to her. Or poured his seed into her. Or . . .

With another growl, he jammed his leg into one of the holes of his breeches and yanked it up.

He no longer recognized this . . . this . . . weak creature Katherine had turned him into.

Jasper stuffed his other leg in, and pulled his breeches up.

His life had been fine until her. He'd been content to wallow in the misery of his own creation. He'd been safe and protected, and then with one crack of a thin sheet of ice, she'd tumbled into the surface and toppled his world.

"Are you going somewhere, Jasper?" A quizzical note threaded her question.

Jasper stooped to rescue his white cambric shirt. He pulled it overhead.

In that moment, he hated Katherine for forcing him to live again and opening him up to the perils of caring. Not when living was so bloody hard and uncertain.

He reached for his jacket.

Katherine scrambled over the edge of the bed, glorious in all her naked splendor. "I don't understand why you'll not speak to me." Brown curls hung over her cream-white shoulders and draped across her breasts. The pink tip of one perfect mound of flesh peeked from between the strands, the tempting image she presented mocked his steely resolve.

Jasper spun toward the door, but Katherine rushed around to plant herself in front of him. She planted her hands upon her delicately flared hips. She narrowed her eyes. "Is this about the reticule?"

This was about everything.

"Because I don't know why you held onto it, Jasper." Her soft, gentled words washed over him until his fingers itched to reach the short distance between them, take her into his arms again, and make love to her. "But I have to believe it means something, Jasper."

Her supposition killed his desire swifter than a plunge in an icy lake.

He shook his head. "You incorrectly assume, madam. It means nothing." Jasper made to step around her.

She matched his movement. "Then why did you keep it?" she challenged. "Why if . . . ?" Her question ended on a gasp as he pulled her close.

Jasper lowered his head, so their noses brushed. "It means nothing. Do you hear me, Katherine? Nothing."

Most ladies would have recoiled at his icy fury. Katherine tossed her head back like a Spartan princess. "If it meant nothing, you'd have returned it to me, Jasper. Or you would have left it that day at the—"

"I didn't find your bloody reticule. Guilford did," he cursed, and released her with such alacrity she stumbled back a step.

Katherine righted herself. Red color slapped her cheeks. "Oh." Her gaze slid away for a moment.

And Jasper despised himself for the uncertainty he detected in her usually spirited, warm brown eyes. Because the truth of it was Guilford had rescued the item, but Jasper had retained it for reasons he didn't, couldn't force himself to consider.

Her eyes, they returned to his. "You needn't push me away, Jasper," she said softly. "I love you."

Jasper's body jerked. Oh, God.

This he couldn't stand. He could not crave her love. Could not want it. She would destroy him in ways Lydia hadn't managed to.

Taking a steadying breath, Jasper squared his shoulders. "Katherine, ours is a marriage of convenience. I've told you before. I loved my wife and she is dead. I've nothing left to offer you, and I certainly don't want your love."

Katherine blanched and her whole body jerked as if he'd struck her a physical blow. The sight of her suffering struck him worse than a lash across the back.

Wind beat hard and cruel against the glass window panes, the spirits railing at him.

Katherine gave a jerky nod. "You needn't leave your chambers, Jasper," she said with a shocking strength to her words. She fetched a sheet and draped it about her slender frame. "I'll l-leave." This time her words broke, and his gut clenched.

Katherine marched back toward the door, more regal than any queen.

He wanted to reach for her. Halt her forward movement. Beg her forgiveness.

Katherine opened the door. It closed behind her with a soft, decisive click.

And he did none of those things.

He was a bloody bastard.

Chapter 28

*K*atherine studied the familiar copy of Wordsworth's latest works she and Jasper had sparred over. She fanned the now well-read pages, swallowing past the silly lump in her throat.

She didn't have another drop to shed for Jasper. A knock sounded at the door, jerking Katherine from her reverie. "Enter," she called quietly.

The door opened. Aldora hovered at the entrance. Her gaze went from Katherine, and then over to the small valise at the foot of Katherine's bed.

Katherine handed the book over to the maid Mary, who'd been so good as to serve as her de facto lady's maid.

Mary placed it in the valise and looked around. "Is that all, Your . . . Lady Katherine?"

The unspoken question pertained to the mound of ivory and white satin gowns heaped upon the center of her bed. Katherine never wanted to see another white gown for the remainder of her days. "I do not require anything else, Mary. Please, do with them as you would."

Mary nodded, and bobbed a curtsy.

Aldora advanced deeper into the room.

"That will be all, Mary," Katherine said, dismissing the young servant.

The maid dropped her gaze to the wood floor and sketched another curtsy. She hurried from the room.

"Are you certain you want to leave?" Aldora asked when the door clicked shut. "He is your *husband*, Katherine."

The gentle reminder brought tears to Katherine's eyes. She swatted at them. "Bah, silly tears," she muttered.

Aldora handed over a handkerchief.

Katherine accepted it and blew her nose noisily into the white fabric etched in Michael's initials. She remembered the cruel words Jasper had hurled at her last evening, made all the more cruel for the truth to them. "Ours is a marriage of convenience, Aldora. I wed him to be free of Mr. Ekstrom and he wed me for . . ." For reasons she still didn't fully understand. "I'm a bother to him. He'll be grateful for my departure." Her heart wrenched. She loved him. Would always love him.

Aldora took her hands. "I believe he must care for you in some way." She gave her fingers a gentle squeeze. "The duke does not strike me as a gentleman to do something because he doesn't want to. He wed you for a reason."

Katherine shifted the conversation to a far safer topic. "If you're too tired from your journeys and you'd rather wait until tomorrow to leave . . ."

Aldora sighed. "Michael has seen the carriage readied. Though I'd not imagined we'd spend Christmas traveling back to London."

Nor had Katherine.

Tears blurred her vision yet again. She blew her nose noisily into the soiled linen.

"Does he know?" Aldora asked gently.

Katherine shook her head. "I will speak to him. He'll be relieved, I'm sure of it."

"No gentleman cares to be abandoned by his wife," Aldora said with a wry twist to her words.

A frisson of guilt spiraled through Katherine, but she brushed it aside. Jasper couldn't have been clearer in his feelings regarding their marriage.

And Katherine? Well, she found herself a bigger coward than she'd ever believed, because she could no longer share the same walls with Jasper and the ghost who would forever hold his heart. The pain of unrequited love would slowly destroy Katherine until she became the same empty shell of a person Jasper had become after his wife's death.

Her eyes shifted to the reticule atop the pile of white and ivory gowns. She reached for the delicate purse, and made to place it inside the valise. Something gave her pause. She set it back down on the mountain of white.

"Michael said if you're determined to journey with us to London, then we'd be wise to leave within the hour."

Katherine nodded.

Her sister opened her mouth, as though prepared to say more, but then gave her head a sad little shake, and took her leave.

Katherine stared at the closed door a long moment.

She would leave within the hour. She'd resided within the walls of the castle not even a full week, and yet it felt as much a home as her childhood cottage in Hertfordshire.

Within the hour, she'd leave and Jasper would remain, and continue on the solitary existence he'd dwelt within for the past four years since Lydia's death.

She rubbed a hand over her chest to ease the dull ache where her heart beat.

With a sigh, Katherine started toward the door.

The sooner she made her good-byes, the sooner she could attempt to put back the small pieces of her broken heart and resume living.

A knock sounded on Jasper's office door.

He frowned, and picked his head up from the ledgers. "Enter," he barked. Jasper returned his focus to the neat column of numbers. "What is it, Wrinkleton?" he snapped. His servant knew not to enter the private sanctuary of Jasper's office without good cause.

And Jasper had made it abundantly clear through the years—there were no good causes.

The delicate clearing of a throat, jerked his head up. Katherine stood with her arms folded behind her. She leaned against the door. "Jasper," she said quietly.

Ink spilled from his pen, and he glanced down distractedly at the now mussed row of numbers, then back to his wife. Jasper dropped the pen down and rose. "Katherine."

His stomach twisted. He'd not seen her since last evening when she'd marched from his chambers draped in nothing but a white sheet. He'd tortured himself by sitting with his back against the walls separating them, the bitter sound of her tears reached to him through the plaster walls until they'd faded from great, gasping sobs to small, shuddery gasps, and then nothing, indicating she'd at last slept.

Not Jasper.

In the end, though, his own fear of loving her had frozen him to the spot outside her chamber doors.

Rooted as he'd been to the door, he'd focused on the ormolu clock atop his fireplace as it had ticked away the minutes of the late morning hours, ushering in a new day.

Katherine caught her lower lip between her teeth as she was wont to do. She shifted on her heels but remained fixed at the entrance of the door, as though one wrong word from him and she'd take flight.

"What is—?"

"I'm leaving," she blurted.

He blinked, certain he'd heard her wrong.

"I'm leaving," she said again, this time stronger. Her gaze slid to a point past his shoulder. "Michael has seen the carriage readied. I . . . we, leave within the hour."

Jasper's whole body froze. He feared if he moved in the slightest, he'd splinter into a million tiny pieces of fragmented nothingness. "Leaving," he repeated, the one word utterance hollow to his own ears.

Katherine stepped away from the door and glided toward him. "I am so very grateful to you for everything, Jasper," she said softly. "You wed me when you didn't need to, or want to."

Oh, God, I did. I did want to wed you, Katherine. It is everything that came after the marriage I feared.

He struggled for the words that at one time in his youth he would have been able to call up. He would have known the pretty, flowery compliments, the gentle praise to keep her at his side. Only the four years he'd spent in hell had robbed him of his ability to do so.

Jasper sat back in his seat.

Katherine carried on in a rush. "I can never repay you for what you've done." A wistful smile played about her lips, so he was forced to wonder at the secrets contained within the fragile expression of mirth. "Thank you."

She would thank him? Thank him as though he'd helped her across a puddle, or held a parasol above her head, shielding her from the sun?

Pain twisted and turned inside him. "What if I say I do not want you to leave?"

Katherine flinched at the harshly spoken question, and he knew in that moment she would turn, walk out the door, and out of his life. *Oh, God, if my heart is dead, what is this sharp, jagged ache tearing at the organ?*

"Come, Jasper. This is your home, and I'm merely an interloper here."

You are no interloper. You are my wife.

Tell her, you bloody fool. Tell her before she leaves.

He opened his mouth.

She angled her head, as if awaiting the unspoken words he could not dredge forth. Katherine gave her head a sad little shake.

Jasper surged to his feet so quickly, his winged back chair tipped backward. "Where will you go?"

Katherine glanced momentarily at the fallen chair. Then back to him. Her shoulders lifted in a slight shrug. "I imagined I might make my home in your townhouse in London." A pretty pink color filled her cheeks. "That is, if you'd permit me to make my home there. I'd rather not return to my mother's . . ."

"It is yours," he said hoarsely, coming out from behind his desk. *It is all yours, Katherine.*

"Thank you."

He stopped in front of her. So formal. So very polite. How could they be so stoically calm with talk of her walking from the room, and out of his life?

"Is there anything else you require?" Jasper's distant question may as well have belonged to a stranger.

She shook her head. "No, Jasper." Katherine studied her hands a moment, and then crossed the small distance between them. She leaned up on tiptoe and pressed her lips to his.

He closed his eyes in an attempt to forever hold onto the scent of honeysuckle and lemon that clung to her. "I . . . I . . ." *Love you. Tell me you love me, Katherine, even as undeserving as I am.* "Be happy, Jasper," she whispered, and then stepped away from him.

She dropped a curtsy and walked out of his office. Out of his life.

Jasper's gaze fixed on the door. His throat moved up and down.

How could he ever be happy again when with her, she'd taken his every last remaining reason for dwelling on this earth?

He wandered over to the front of his office and pulled back the thick brocade curtains covering the windowpanes. He peered down at the snow-covered drive as footmen hurried back and forth with trunks and valises belonging to Katherine's family.

He stood there, fixed to the spot, waiting for the moment Katherine stepped into that carriage.

He waited so long he convinced himself that he'd imagined the whole hellish exchange.

Then she appeared. The green muslin cloak a bright flash of color in a stark, white horizon. He'd come to know her so well, he could detect her body's every nuance. She stiffened, as though she knew he studied her. Her chin ticked up a notch, and then she drew her hood up, and stole from him the vision of her lush brown ringlets and warm brown eyes.

Jasper rested his forehead alongside the wall and shook it slowly back and forth.

Do not leave.

Please do not leave.

The quiet of the cool winter's day magnified all sound and he detected the moment the carriage door opened and closed.

Jasper's eyes snapped open and he scrambled back to the edge of the window in time to see the footman hand her up into the carriage.

He devoured the delicate span of her back, the bold tilt of her neck, and cherished his every last glimpse of her until the door closed, and Michael Knightly's black lacquer carriage rocked forward.

Jasper pressed his brow against the glass panes and peered after the slow-moving conveyance until it dissolved into nothing more than a faint mark in the horizon.

Once again, left—alone.

The walls he'd constructed around his heart, the ones Katherine had rattled from the moment he'd pulled her from the Thames, fell firmly back into place, surrounding the wounded organ that beat within his chest. He embraced the hurt, fueled the bitter resentment tearing through him.

With a steely set to his jaw, he dropped the curtains back into place.

He'd stood mooning like a lovesick swain over his wife long enough.

Katherine had left.

And it was now time to move forward.

Part II

Spring 1815

How does the Meadow-flower its bloom unfold?
Because the lovely little flower is free
Down to its root, and in that freedom, bold.

—William Wordsworth, *A Poet!*
He Hath Put His Heart to School

Chapter 29

Where Fear sate thus, a cherished visitant,
Was wanting yet the pure delight of love
By sound diffused, or by the breathing air,
Or by the silent looks of happy things,
Or flowing from the universal face
Of earth and sky . . .

—William Wordsworth,
"The Wanderer" in *The Recluse One Winter*
With a Baron To Enchant a Wicked Duke

Katherine glanced up from the pages of her book and tried to blink back a sneeze. The fragrant cuckoo flowers and bluebells in full bloom of this floral sanctuary of Kensington gardens tickled her nose.

"Achoo!"

A white kerchief appeared over the page of her book.

She accepted the white scrap of linen "Achoo!" and sneezed into the previously unsullied fabric. "Thank . . ." Katherine blinked, as the sudden, unexpected appearance of a mysterious kerchief registered.

Katherine spun about the wrought-iron bench.

"Your Grace," an increasingly familiar Earl of Stanhope drawled.

She pointed her eyes skyward and snapped her volume closed. "Lord Stanhope."

The tall, impossibly handsome rogue claimed the seat next to her. "Henry," he corrected.

Katherine grunted and shifted in her seat. "This seat is not designed for two people, Harry." Katherine handed back the soiled linen.

Harry heedlessly stuffed it back into the front of his jacket. His lips curved up in a partial grin. "You know I detest when you call me Harry."

She did, which was why she'd taken to calling him Harry.

His smile said he knew as much. "Why do you insist on coming here? You can't even tolerate the collection of scents in this godforsaken landscape."

Katherine swatted his arm. "I adore this place." This floral haven had become a kind of sanctuary in Society's glittering world of falsity and unkindness.

The other, the reason she could not speak of, even to this man who'd become her only friend, was because it reminded her of those splendorous tapestries hung throughout Castle Blackwood. Even if the poignant beauty served to remind Katherine of Jasper and his love, Lydia, then Katherine would welcome even that fragile remembrance of her time there.

Harry flicked her nose. "Why so melancholy, Kat?"

She shook her head. "It is nothing," she assured him.

They sat in companionable silence and stared out at the crimson orb as it rose above the horizon, bathing the gardens around them in a soft orange-and-red glow. Purple-and-pink clouds floated along the sky, better suited for floating cherubs than the dirty London town.

It was her birthday. She felt vastly older than her mere twenty years. Then, having one's heart so hopelessly and helplessly broken tended to age a lady. Tears blurred her vision.

The kerchief reappeared. "Consider it a birthday gift," he murmured.

She accepted it with a wan smile and discreetly dabbed at her eyes. The pain of missing Jasper had not lessened in the months since she'd come to London.

He'd not come for her. A small sliver of her had thought perhaps she'd come to mean something to him and he'd not allow her to leave.

How hopelessly naïve she'd been. A person had but one heart to give. Jasper's belonged to Lydia. And Katherine? Well, hers belonged to Jasper, now and forever.

"How do we intend to celebrate?" Harry murmured. He draped his broad, muscled arm along the back of her seat.

"We don't," she muttered.

"Egad, you're in quite a foul mood today, aren't you?"

She nodded. "I am."

From the corner of her eye, she detected the grin on his lips. "Your duke?"

In the months since she'd first met Harry Falston, the 6th Earl of Stanhope, he'd come to know her well enough that they often knew what the other was thinking.

He drummed his fingertips along the back of her seat.

Katherine drew in a deep breath, inhaling the sweet scent of roses in bloom. "Achoo!"

Harry sighed and extracted another, clean, linen. He handed the monogrammed fabric over to Katherine. "Keep it," he said. "As long as you insist on coming here, I shall have to continue to carry an endless supply of kerchiefs. My valet is growing quite irate at their mysterious disappearance."

She managed a smile. "You are too good to me, Harry."

He snorted, and stretched his long legs out in front of him. "Just have a care not to say as much in front of Society, or you'll surely shatter my well-earned reputation."

Katherine leaned back in her seat. Her fingers plucked at the corners of Harry's kerchief. They struck quite the pair. Her, the Duchess of Bainbridge, whose marriage remained shrouded in mystery to the *ton*, and Harry the unrepentant rogue who'd earned the censure of every polite Society matron.

Theirs had been a rather ignominious beginning. While attending a soiree, Katherine had stolen a moment outside for air. Harry had followed her and made her a rather indecent proposal. She'd punched him in the nose.

After that, he'd set himself up as a kind of protector from the steady barrage of gentleman who'd incorrectly assumed her absentee husband made Katherine fair game for an illicit affair.

She imagined if Society stumbled upon them at this unfashionable hour, they would have raised more than a few brows.

Harry shattered the quiet. "I suppose if I were truly a good friend I would suggest you return to Bainbridge's cold, dark castle and make amends with the undeserving bounder."

Katherine folded her hands on her lap and studied the interlocked digits, silently.

"But I'm not a good friend. I'm a rogue and still hold onto hope that you'll forget your miserable husband and—"

"Harry," she said firmly, interrupting him with a scowl. It mattered not that he jested, any and all mention of Jasper still rubbed as raw as vinegar being poured upon an open wound.

Harry shoved himself to his feet and stood over her. "You believe I jest, Kat."

She shook her head, wanting him to stop, needing him to stop. With the exception of her sister, Harry had become the one friend whose company she enjoyed. Never one to take himself or anything at all seriously, he provided the perfect foil to Jasper's dark forebodingness and, what's more, helped her forget, even for just those slips of moments in time, how close she'd been to having everything she'd never known she needed in life.

He reached his hand out. "Kat—"

The whinny of a horse cut across whatever Harry's intended words were.

Katherine glanced down the gravel riding path, and her heart thudded wildly in her chest at the approaching rider.

She rose. Her rose-colored skirts fluttered about her feet as the Marquess of Guilford drew his mare to a stop a short distance away. He dismounted.

Harry frowned at the sudden intrusion. "Guilford," Harry drawled. He sketched a short bow.

Jasper's friend, the lone witness to their nuptials, ignored the other man. He directed a serious stare at Katherine.

Her heart wrenched, feeling ever closer to Jasper just by the appearance of his friend. A question as to her husband's well-being sprung to her lips but Guilford spoke before she could formulate words.

"Your Grace," he said, in short, clipped tones suggesting his disapproval of Katherine's companion.

"My lord." Even as she curtsied, a frown turned her lips. She'd not be made to feel guilty for keeping company with Harry. Nothing untoward had or would happen with the roguish earl. Katherine might be lonely and broken-hearted, but only one man could fill the empty hole left by Jasper's disinterest—and that man happened to be her stubborn, aloof husband.

Harry looked between them. The uncharacteristic hardness in his eyes indicated he'd detected the undercurrents of tension between Katherine and the marquess.

"I hope you are finding your time in London pleasant, Lady Katherine," Guilford said dismissing Harry outright.

"Most pleasant," she lied through her white teeth.

Harry snorted, and then covered a hand to his mouth, feigning a cough. She shot him a sideways look, knowing he detected the untruth in her words.

Guilford's gaze slid back over toward the other man. His lip pulled at the corner in a disapproving sneer. When he returned his hard stare to Katherine, he gave a curt nod. "I bid thee good day, Lady Katherine." He turned on his heel and strode back toward his horse.

A frenzied sense of panic filled her breast. Lord Guilford represented the last fragile connection to Jasper.

Katherine hurried after him. Harry's kerchief fluttered to the ground, forgotten.

"My lord," she called, just as he grasped the reins of his mount.

He stiffened and turned back to face her. "Your Grace?"

Katherine stumbled to a halt in front of him. She wet her lips and glanced around at the empty park. "My husband," she whispered.

He furrowed his brow. "Lady Katherine?"

"How is he?" she implored him with her eyes. Jasper occupied every last corner of her thoughts. She yearned for just some word on the man who would forever hold her heart.

Guilford's frown deepened, and his gaze skittered to a point beyond her shoulder. By the icy disdain in his usually affable stare, she suspected Harry hovered in the distance.

"He is . . . much the same," Guilford finally said, when he'd looked back at Katherine.

A woeful smile tugged at her lips. "That is saying nearly nothing, my lord."

Guilford folded his arms over his chest. "And what would you have me say, Your Grace? What words do you seek?"

His furious disapproval could not be clearer if he mounted his horse and rode through Hyde Park shouting disparaging words of her.

"I . . ." she faltered. All of Society erroneously assumed the Mad Duchess had taken Harry as her lover. The gossip columns bandied that tidbit about as though it were more delectable than a Gunter's ice. After all, with his reputation as unrepentant rogue, how could Society think anything else of Lord Stanhope? "I . . ." She could not discuss such an intimate matter with Lord Guilford. "If you see him, will you let him know I've asked after him?"

Guilford searched her face with his eyes, and then gave a curt nod. "As you wish. Is there anything else you require, Lady Katherine?"

Tell him I love him. I've never stopped nor will I ever. My heart is and will always belong to him. Tell him to come to me. Tell him my life is empty without him.

Instead, she said, "No, that will be all, my lord. Thank you."

Guilford nodded again. He swung his leg over the chestnut mare, and panic built in her breast. She took another step toward him. "My lord, is he . . . well?"

The marquess shifted the reins to his other hand, and his knees tightened about the flanks, in a clear attempt to soothe the eager-to-gallop horse. His mount sidled backward. Lord Guilford lowered his voice. "It is my belief, Your Grace, that Bainbridge has not fared well in your absence."

Her heart thudded hard. She held up a beseeching hand, though Lord Guilford could not give her that which she needed. Only again seeing Jasper would be the balm upon her aching soul.

Guilford continued, seeming to understand her unspoken question. "He's been rather . . ." He paused, as if searching for the appropriate words. "Surly. Angry. Angrier than usual," he clarified with the pointed look she gave him. A ghost of a smile played about his lips.

Her eyes slid closed a moment. She forced them open. "Thank you."

He bowed his head and kicked his mount forward.

Katherine dimly registered Harry's approach.

"What was that about?" Harry murmured, staring off in the distance at the marquess's swift retreating form.

She shook her head. "It is nothing," she said, unable to speak of Jasper's friendship with the marquess, and the marquess's opinions of Jasper.

Harry held out his arm. "Will you join me for a stroll, Your Grace?"

"Er, I think I care to just sit here, Harry."

His gaze searched hers. "You're certain?"

She nodded.

With a sigh, he extracted a third kerchief. "Then, as you were, madam."

Katherine caught it in her fingers. "Thank you, Harry," she said softly, for so much more than just this scrap of fabric.

Harry beat his hand against his side. "You're desiring your own company, aren't you, Kat?"

He'd come to know her very well in these past months. Rather, they'd come to know one another. They could finish one another's sentences. They were of like opinions on matters pertaining to the *ton*—they both abhorred London's gossipy Society members.

And they'd come to know and respect one another enough to not delve too deeply into the secret demons that tormented them.

She smiled wanly up at him.

"You know he's not deser—"

"Hush," she chided him. No one, not her twin sister, Aldora, or Michael, and not Harry knew the kind of man her husband was. Jasper possessed the valor to jeopardize his own life to pluck a stranger from the water. He gave the sole volume of poetry to a teasing young lady even as it happened to be the only enjoyment he took from life. He sang taproom ditties to babies. It was Jasper who'd deserved more—Jasper who'd *had* more, in his wife, Lydia.

Katherine would never be anything but a pale shadow in the other woman's otherworldly glow of perfection.

Harry captured her hand and raised it to his mouth. He brushed his lips along the tops of her knuckles.

After he'd taken his leave, Katherine returned to what had become an all-too-familiar wrought-iron bench within the garden, considering Guilford's appearance. And more, his revelation of Jasper.

In the time she'd known Jasper, she'd found him to be a surly, obstinate bear of a man. Surely Guilford's claims that Jasper had become even more so had nothing to do with her departure from his life. Why, he'd surely resumed the normal cadence of the comfortable, solitary existence he'd carried on since Lydia's death, four . . . now four years and four months ago.

But what if he does miss you? A voice whispered at the edge of her mind. *What if he harbors the same regret in your going, as you do in leaving?*

Katherine picked up Wordsworth's volume, and fanned the now all-too-familiar pages. She paused upon a familiar verse.

Full often wished he that the winds might rage . . . She continued reading.

> *When they were silent: far more fondly now*
> *Than in his earlier season did he love*
> *Tempestuous nights—the conflict and the sounds*
> *That live in darkness. From his intellect*
> *And from the stillness of abstracted thought*
> *He asked repose; and, failing oft to win*
> *The peace required, he scanned the laws of light*
> *Amid the roar of torrents, where they send*
> *From hollow clefts up to the clearer air*
> *A cloud of mist that, smitten by the sun,*
> *Varies its rainbow hues. But vainly thus,*
> *And vainly by all other means, he strove*
> *To mitigate the fever of his heart.*

She'd been a coward of the worst kind to leave him as she had. It had seemed, at the time, her self-preservation was dependent upon distance between her and Jasper's apathy.

Katherine had learned all too quickly, no matter the distance, no matter the time separating them, self-preservation would be futile. Whether Jasper wished it or not . . . she belonged to him.

Chapter 30

*J*asper stared unblinking at an all-too-familiar white sheet draped across the door. He folded his hands behind his back and continued to study the thick, crisp white linen, obscuring the wood panel and delicate handle.

Every day he rose and passed this bloody door and tortured himself with the evenly hung, thick white sheet.

With a curse, he ripped it viciously from the wall and it toppled to the floor in a noisy puddle of pooling fabric. He pressed the handle and tossed the door open hard enough it bounced back against the plaster of the walls.

An eerie quiet filled the chambers.

Jasper hesitated a moment, and then after the four months, five days, and a handful of hours since Katherine had climbed into Michael Knightly's carriage, he entered his wife's chambers.

I love you, Jasper. The ghost of her whisper lingered in the walls of this room, so very real, he glanced around expecting to see her smiling visage and warm brown eyes.

Empty silence mocked his foolish yearnings.

With a curse he pivoted on his heel and took a step toward the door, but then the faintest hint of honeysuckle wafted in this dark space and filled his senses with a heady remembrance of how very close to perfect his life had been.

Jasper clenched his eyes tight and willed memories of her aside. Katherine with terror in her eyes as he'd plucked her from the river. Katherine's cheeky smile as she'd taken the last copy of Wordsworth's book. *Katherine as she'd cradled the girl Lizzie close to her chest.*

Oh, God, I cannot bear this. Jasper forced his eyes open, rubbing the spot in his chest where his heart had rested.

After he'd lost Lydia and his son, Jasper had imagined he would never recover from the abyss of despair. He'd thought his heart dead within his chest.

A hollow, mirthless laugh burst from his chest and bounced off the walls. How fitting he should discover himself capable of loving only after Katherine's departure. Nay, not merely loving anyone . . . but his impossibly headstrong, passionate wife.

Jasper wandered deeper into the room. He'd ordered it closed off by the servants, barring all from entry. Beckoned by the wide, canopied bed where they'd first made love, he sank onto the edge of the mattress, his gaze fixed on the mound of ivory and white ruffled skirts.

Well, I hate ringlets. And gowns made of too much ivory and lace. Mother insists I wear them because it is the ladylike thing to do. It would be such good fun to wear vibrant shades . . .

Jasper reached for one of the gowns and drew it to his chest. And closing his eyes, he buried his face into the satiny smoothness of the modest lace creation. The sweet, delicate scent of her he'd so craved these months filled his senses more heady than the most potent aphrodisiac. It drugged him like an opiate, filling him with an insatiable need for her.

Jasper released the gown so quickly it slid from his fingers and fell to the floor.

What in hell was wrong with him? Mooning over her like a lovesick swain. She'd left him. She had made the decision that a life without him was preferable to a life with him.

With a curse, Jasper surged to his feet. The abruptness of the movement toppled her mountain of white and ivory garments.

A lone green piece, like the hint of earth poking out from a blanket of snow. Jasper swiped at the reticule. He passed it back and forth between his hands, and with a snarl, brought his arm back to hurl the item across the room.

Then froze.

He closed his eyes again and sucked in a breath. Not even his potent fury had shielded him from the depth of love he carried for Katherine. He exhaled on a broken, shuddery hiss.

Jasper wandered over to the corner of the room, and peered out into the sun-kissed grounds below. The lush green of the rolling hillsides and noisy chatter of birds so vastly different than the frozen world he and Katherine had dwelt within during their short time together.

He tugged at the drawstring of her reticule, and glanced distractedly down into the small purse. His heart paused a beat.

She'd taken the small heart pendant he'd slept with since Guilford had brought the items to him a lifetime ago. Pained regret tugged at him. He reached inside and pulled out a lone scrap of paper.

He knew the contents of her small reticule enough to recognize the folded note a more recent addition.

With trembling fingers, Jasper unfolded the sheet.

Dearest Jasper,

By this point, you have learned the worst kinds of truth of me. I am a coward. You wed a coward. I convinced myself the offer I'd put to you that snowy day in Hyde Park was driven of desperation, an attempt to avoid marriage to Mr. Ekstrom. Now I can be true enough to myself, and now to you, at least on the pages of this sheet, to at last admit, my offer had nothing to do with horrid Mr. Ekstrom, and everything to do with you.

I love you. Rather desperately, I'm afraid. And I now know you can never love me, which is through no fault of your own. Your Lydia will forever hold your heart, and if I were to remain at Castle Blackwood, I would be forced to face the truth of that love, and the depth of my own despair when you could never return the sentiments I carried in my heart. And that I could not bear.

I wish you happiness.

I love you.

Forever Yours,
Katherine

Jasper's throat worked spasmodically. His fingers curled over the lone page until it crumpled noisily in his hands. Panicked, he lightened his hold, and awkwardly smoothed the precious sheet of vellum.

With his body and mind numb, Jasper wandered from the chambers, through the long corridors, down the stairs, and into the once closed off room.

He stepped into the portrait room, striding past the bitter visages of his parents and younger self, and made his way very deliberately over to one particular canvas.

Jasper paused and stared up at the smiling couple, not recognizing the youthful gentleman with a carefree glimmer in his eyes.

"I . . ." Jasper paused, and looked around, ascertaining he was in fact alone. He returned his attention to Lydia's golden countenance. "I didn't mean to forget you, Lydia," he said at last, into the quiet.

The couple continued to smile almost benevolently down at him.

"I thought to honor your memory and the love I carried for you by shutting myself away from the world." He drew in a shuddery breath. "I didn't think I could ever love again." Jasper held his palms out, Katherine's letter and reticule an unwitting explanation. "I met a woman. I didn't intend for it to happen." And yet, if it hadn't happened, then Katherine's lifeless body would forever dwell under the surface of the Thames River. A chill stole through him and iced him over at the sheer horror of the imagined tragedy. "And I love her, Lydia." Tears blurred his vision. "I cannot carry on without her." Tears trailed down his cheeks and he let them fall unashamed and unchecked. "I need to say good-bye, Lydia. Because if I do not say good-bye, I can never be free. And I need to be free." He tucked Katherine's belongings inside his jacket, close to his heart. "So be at peace, Lydia."

Jasper didn't know what he expected. Just then, a ray of sunlight slashed through the clear glass windowpanes, and cast Lydia's smile in a sea of shimmering light, a kind of benediction. An absolution of the guilt he carried. In that smile dwelled a woman who'd not have ever wanted him to punish himself for the loss of her life.

Then the sunlight faded, dimmed by a cloud.

Jasper blinked, and wiped his tear-dampened cheeks.

"Your Grace?"

He froze, his body going taut at the unexpected appearance of Wrinkleton.

"Yes, Wrinkleton," he said with his back to the man, unwilling to turn and display his earlier expression of emotion for the servant.

Wrinkleton cleared his throat. "The Marquess of Guilford arrived a short while ago. I took the liberty of showing him to your office. He said he was here on a matter of import."

Jasper frowned, turning quickly on his heel. He nodded and gave a murmured thanks.

Jasper couldn't imagine what matter of import should take Guilford away from London during the height of the Season—with the exception of one person.

Heart racing, Jasper all but sprinted through the castle toward his office.

Knowing his panicked thoughts surely foolish, Jasper paused outside his office doors and smoothed his palms over the front of his jacket.

He entered the office.

Guilford stood over by the sideboard, pouring a glass of brandy. He glanced up, with a half-smile for Jasper. "So good to see you, Bainbridge," he said over the rim of his glass. "I hope you don't mind, I availed myself to your spirits." Pause. "You look like hell."

Jasper grinned, and Guilford choked on his brandy. "By God, did you just smile?"

Jasper's smile widened, and he crossed over to his desk. He sat, hip propped on the edge, arms folded over his chest. "I did."

Guilford shook his head and took another sip. He gestured to Jasper's decanters. "A drink, friend?"

Jasper chuckled at his friend's comfortable show as host in Jasper's own home. He waved off the offer. *My father was a wastrel. He spent his days and nights at the gaming tables, and indulging in spirits, and he squandered everything not entailed.*

Even in the darkest days since Katherine had left when he'd craved the mindlessness of drink, he'd not indulged in spirits—not when he'd be forever tormented with thoughts of all she'd suffered because of her father's drinking and gambling.

Jasper motioned for Guilford to sit. "What takes you away from London?" *Do you have word of my wife?*

Something in the hesitant way Guilford's gaze slid from his made Jasper wish he'd not sworn off drink. Jasper straightened and claimed the seat behind his massive desk.

"I've seen your wife," Guilford said after he'd taken his seat, volunteering information that saved Jasper from asking the question that would expose the depth of his feelings for Katherine.

Jasper steepled his hands in front of him, atop his chest to still their tremble. "Oh?" His heart raced with a desperate urgency to demand his friend spill every last word he had of Katherine.

Guilford lifted one shoulder in a far-too-nonchalant shrug. "She's become the toast of the *ton*."

Jasper's gut clenched. She'd always possessed a beauty that defied the mere physical type, the kind worn deep on the inside, and that emanated out like an ethereal glow that belonged to angels and the like.

Guilford fished into the front of his jacket and withdrew a neatly folded newspaper. He set it down on the mahogany desktop and took a seat.

Jasper's eyes fell to the copy of *The Times*.

"They say she's taken a lover."

Jasper's body jerked at the unexpectedness of Guilford's statement. The air left him on a swift, noisy exhale. Oh, God, Guilford may as well have taken the medieval broadsword from the wall and hacked at Jasper's heart. Jasper shook his head.

Lies. All lies. It couldn't be true. Katherine was not the kind of creature capable of deceit and treachery. She'd not betray him. She loved him.

But then, you never reciprocated those feelings of love. She humbled herself before you, and you scoffed and jeered at every turn, until you drove her away.

Why should she have remained faithful?

"And what do you say?" His question emerged angry with all the same harsh bitterness he'd harbored deep inside since Lydia's death. His breath froze as he waited with a kind of dreaded anticipation of Guilford's response.

Guilford frowned. "I say if you truly care, you'd get yourself to London."

Jasper growled. "Who is he?" He punished himself with the abhorrent images of Katherine's splendidly naked body stretched out for some nameless, faceless bastard's worship.

His gut roiled, until he thought he might cast up the contents of his stomach.

Guilford shifted in his seat. "The Earl of Stanhope." He took a sip of his brandy. "You've been away from Society for some time." He waved his hand. "There's a scandal in the man's past. He's something of a rogue. Frowned on by Society's most polite hostesses, sought after by Society's most notorious widows."

And Stanhope had set his lascivious sights upon Katherine.

Jasper picked up the pen on his desk, and to give his fingers something to do, he passed it back and forth between hands. That, or mount his horse, ride to London, and use these same hands to bloody the faceless bastard senseless.

No, you gave her up. You let her go, a jeering voice taunted from deep within.

She'd given him her love, trusted him with her heart, and he couldn't have been brave enough to give her the words she deserved, the words that lived inside him.

"Do you believe she's taken him as a lover?" He grimaced. Even as he said the words, he dismissed them. Katherine possessed an honor and integrity not found in most gentlemen. She would not be capable of the deceit demonstrated by his parents.

Guilford lifted one shoulder in a casual shrug. "I believe Stanhope's determined. And she's lonely."

How could his friend be so nonchalant when Jasper hung on the edge of true madness?

That response did little to ease the tumultuous storm raging through Jasper. He wanted to flip his desk, storm from the room, and hunt down the Earl of Stanhope for daring to encroach on that which was Jasper's.

"Have you," he paused, "seen them together?"

Guilford looked away a moment. "I have," he said at last.

The pen in Jasper's hand snapped in two.

"I came upon them at Hyde Park," Guilford went on.

Hyde Park belonged to Jasper and Katherine. It had been the place they'd gone in the quiet of the snow to share the Wordsworth volume. It had been the place Katherine had asked him to marry her and spoke of them having babes together with a shocking candidness.

And now, it was the place she visited with the Earl of Stanhope.

Guilford leaned back in his chair and hooked one ankle over the other. "What do you intend to do?"

Jasper's jaw hardened. "I'm going to London."

Stanhope and Katherine should be prepared . . .

The Mad Duke intended to fight for his wife.

Chapter 31

*K*atherine stood with a glass of champagne between her fingers, enjoying one of the very small luxuries of being a married woman. She'd detested ratafia as much as she detested ivory and white satin.

"You do know you've scandalized Mother with your gown this evening," a voice whispered close to her ear.

Katherine spun to greet her sister Anne. A smile wreathed Anne's cheeks; the faintest dimple indicated her pleasure. "Anne."

Anne eyed her glass of champagne longingly. "I'd trade one of my hands to be rid of ratafia and free to indulge in champagne."

Katherine snorted and deposited her champagne glass onto the tray of a servant. "Just be sure you don't go and trade the hand you use for holding glasses, or it would certainly dull your pleasure."

Anne sighed and took a final sip of her drink. She deposited the empty glass upon the same servant's tray. "You do know Mother has been eyeing you with that stern frown upon her lips?"

Yes, Katherine had detected the signature frown worn by her mother since she'd entered Lord and Lady Harrison's ball a short while ago.

Anne glanced around and then leaned close. "I think you look splendid, Kat."

Katherine smiled. "As my twin sister, you have to say that."

Her sister pointed her eyes to the ceiling. "Hardly. Haven't you learned I don't do anything I'm supposed to do?" Yes, the years had certainly taught Katherine that very fact about her headstrong, if whimsical, sister.

Anne glanced down forlornly at her ivory satin skirts with a lace, ruffled trim. "I'm entirely too old to be as ruffled as I am."

Katherine studied her sister a moment. Whereas ivory and white fabrics had dulled Katherine's drab brown locks, the colors only served to heighten Anne's golden beauty. Anne epitomized the perfect English lady. "You're beautiful," she said with all sincerity and no trace of resentment. As twins, they shared a unique, unbreakable bond. She could not envy Anne her beauty. Never Anne.

Anne tugged at her skirts and feigned a short curtsy. "Perfect, proper English miss, no?" She sighed. "I'd trade even the forbidden champagne for your sapphire skirts."

She glanced down momentarily at the gown designed by Madame LeBlanc, the most sought after French modiste in London and smoothed her palms over the front of her sapphire-blue satin gown with its crisp plaiting.

When she had taken her leave of Castle Blackwood, Katherine had arrived at a staggering, if saddening, realization. She would not have her children. And she would not have the husband to sit reading poetry with around the hearthside. But she would have her sapphire-blue gown.

In the end, she'd lost Jasper, but she had her dress.

And that would have to be enough.

Anne looped her arm through Katherine's. "How very fortunate you are," she said on a sigh. She gave Katherine's arm a faint squeeze.

A tightness settled in Katherine's chest. She had a husband in love with a ghost. She would never have children of her own. Her heart would forever belong to Jasper, whether she wished it or not. Her lips twisted wryly. Fortunate, indeed.

She reached up and fiddled with the heart pendant looped around her neck. The latch clicked and the chain slipped into her hand.

"What are you—?"

She held out the necklace. "Here, Anne," she said softly. Katherine no longer needed the insignificant bauble that forever reminded her of the heart she'd never possess. But, her innocent, whimsical sister still believed, and for that, Anne should be the sole owner of the pendant.

Anne stared down at it a moment. She wet her lips and then reached tentative fingers toward it. She pulled her hand back. "You still need your duke's heart, Katherine. I can w—"

"Take it," she insisted. Anne could free her of at least the small reminder of all she'd never have.

Her sister's fingers closed around the precious memento. She looked down silently at the bauble, a wishful smile playing upon her lips. She glanced up . . . and her smile promptly withered upon her lips to be replaced with a scowl.

Katherine followed her disapproving stare over toward Harry, the Earl of Stanhope.

Anne mumbled under her breath. "I do not know why you associate with that man. Mother is right where he's concerned." She grimaced. "And you know I do detest admitting Mother is ever right about anything."

From a short distance away, Harry caught Katherine's gaze, and gave a devilish wink.

Katherine shook her head. What an insufferable rake he was.

"Winking at you in the midst of a ball," Anne muttered. "Why, you're a married woman."

"He's been a friend to me," Katherine gently chided.

"That man can have no intentions that are honorable, Kat," she said in a hushed whisper. "He's vile, and rude, and completely condescending, and boorish, and . . ."

"Who is this paragon of a person you and your sister discuss, Your Grace?"

Anne screeched and yanked her arm free of Katherine's. High color flooded her cheeks as she glared at Harry. She gave a flounce of her curls, otherwise ignoring him. *And cunning*, she mouthed back at Katherine as she took her leave with one last black look for Harry.

"Lovely creature," Harry said, a wry twist of humor to his words. He took Katherine's hand and bowed over it.

She discreetly pinched the soft flesh of his palm. "Do be kind, Harry. She's my sister. And she loves me," she said, pulling her hand back.

Harry motioned to a passing servant and retrieved a glass of champagne. He took a long swallow and peered out at the dancers, who performed the lively steps of a country reel. "It would seem we've earned Society's censure again, this evening." His tone hardly sounded repentant.

Katherine followed his gaze to the stern matrons who peered down their noses at her and Harry.

"Should we wave and smile?" Harry proposed.

She swatted at his arm. "You'll do no such thing."

He sighed. "You are a spoiler of good fun, Kat."

She hardly cared for her name being dragged through the gossip columns as had happened since she'd made her entrance into Society as a married woman. The gossips had speculated as to her swift and secretive marriage to the Duke of Bainbridge. Then there had been the gossip as to her appearance in light of her husband's absence. Then the rogues and their vile intentions had descended.

Harry had kept ranks with them for a very brief moment, before becoming her confidante and, ultimately, her protector from the lascivious gentlemen desiring a place in her bed.

Katherine searched the crowd, beset by an odd disquiet.

"Are you looking for someone in particular, sweet Kat?"

"Do hush," she scolded from the side of her mouth. "Don't be gauche."

He staggered back a step, a hand to his breast. "You insult me, Your Grace. Next, you'll be leveling the same harsh insults as your sister."

Her lips twitched with a distracted sense of mirth.

The orchestra concluded the country reel to a smattering of polite applause from the dancers who'd just concluded the set. They began to pluck the strands of the forbidden waltz.

Harry held his arm out. "A waltz, Kat?"

An odd hum filled the already noisy crowd of guests. She glanced around disinterestedly at the nobles staring toward the center of the room. Katherine placed her fingers along Harry's coat sleeve. The hum increased in volume like a million honeybees swarming upon the lavish ballroom.

The crowd parted for her and Harry as he escorted her onto the rapidly filling dance floor. All the while, the lords and ladies looked at her, tittering behind their hands, and then off to the entrance of the room.

A sense of disquiet filled her, and she glanced around, but with her height, remained unable to see that which had attracted the *ton*'s notice.

Katherine positioned her hand upon Harry's shoulder, even as he placed his upon her waist.

Harry grinned down at her. "It seems we've attracted even more than usual interest from the . . ." His words died, his smile slipping to a single, indecipherable line.

She wrinkled her brow. "What is it, Harry?"

His hard, hazel stare remained frozen on the entrance of the room.

"Harry?" Katherine shifted in his arms, as she attempted to see what had garnered his attention. "What do you . . . ?" She blinked. Her hands fell uselessly to her side, as she took a staggering step away from Harry.

Her heart threatened to beat a painful path right out of her chest.

Jasper.

She'd dreamed of him for so long. Conjured him at those loneliest nights in her dreams, only to wake and find her bed frigidly cold. And now, with all her most desperate yearnings, had imagined him here.

The crowds hushed whispers faintly registered.

Mad Duke.

. . . His wife.

Earl of Stanhope.

Except, if the stoic, fierce-looking midnight devil with a day's growth upon his strong cheeks were merely an object of her imagining, how did those around her also note his appearance?

Katherine swayed. She would have knocked into a waltzing couple, but Harry reached out to steady her.

Shocked gasps, delighting in his bold handling of her, filled the room.

Katherine ignored them. She walked from the dance floor, Harry forgotten, and froze beside Lady Harrison's enormous Doric column, attempting to steady her too-fast breaths. She folded her hands behind her back and borrowed support from the pillar.

His harsh, angry emerald gaze searched the crowd, and then because for all that had come to pass between them, there would always be that inextricable pull that had drawn them together since the fateful day of the Frost Fair, he found her.

Their eyes locked. The graying, plump hostess appeared at Jasper's side. She opened her mouth to speak, and Jasper started forward, leaving the older woman gaping like a fish tossed ashore.

Oh, God, he is here.

Why is he here?

It could not be for her.

A hand fluttered about her breast, as she tried to still her fast-beating heart.

The crowd parted for Jasper. Lords and ladies melted away to clear his path across the marble ballroom floor, over to Katherine's pillar. He cut an impressive figure. Several inches past six feet, and all great big muscles, his frame better suited a man who worked the land with his broad hands and not a duke just a smidgeon shy of royalty.

At last he reached her.

Katherine swallowed hard, and tipped her head back. Her eyes searched the hard, angular planes of his face. Since Michael's carriage had taken her away from Castle Blackwood, she'd tormented herself with a slip of a dream in which Jasper came for her. In all her grandest dreams, he would come, take her from London, and profess his love. In the cold light of day's reality, however, she knew it unlikely she'd ever again see her husband—not with his love for Lydia.

And because she'd never dared to believe he *would* come to London, she had no words for him, this man whose life meant more to her than even her own.

Her throat moved up and down as his hard, fiery stare slipped over her face, down lower. He paused at her daring décolletage, and then returned his gaze to hers. "Katherine," he said, in the same, harsh tones he'd used when rescuing her from the Thames.

His words transported her back to that hellish day, a day that had brought him into her life, and for which she would have suffered that icy plunge again.

"Jasper," she whispered.

Jasper's neck burned from the bold stares directed upon him and Katherine. He ignored their whisperings of the Mad Duke. All the *ton* could go hang. They mattered not at all.

None of them did.

No one . . .

But her.

He reacquainted himself with each precious line of her heart-shaped face. He took in her rich brown hair, artfully arranged atop her head, with diamond teardrop-shaped combs holding back deliberately placed strands. Two loose tresses hung over her right shoulder, drawing his attention momentarily to the swell of her bosom. A vise-like pressure tightened about his heart as he mourned the loss of those tight brown ringlets. Gone was the young lady in ivory skirts with too many ruffles. In her place stood this boldly clad siren with her generously curved body and slim waist.

Jasper's skin tingled at the sudden awareness of eyes upon his person. He stiffened, and glanced at a point beyond Katherine's shoulder. His gaze locked on a tall, unfamiliar gentleman. And Jasper knew.

Knew with all the intuitiveness of a man hopelessly in love with his wife that the golden-haired Michelangelo hovering nearby, with a flinty expression in his eyes, was none other than Lord Stanhope.

Jasper's fists curled into tight balls at his side. With a growl, he grasped Katherine by the hand, and tugged her forward. His bold actions were met with horrified gasps and increased whispers.

Katherine gasped and nearly stumbled. He righted her, and proceeded to guide her forward.

"Jasper, what are you doing?" she whispered at his side.

He gritted his teeth, unwilling to have this exchange. Not here. Not in front of the *ton*.

Not in front of Stanhope.

"Will you slow down," she implored.

Jasper cursed, earning another flurry of whispers and ever-widening stares. But he slowed his stride. They made their way up the long staircase, through the corridor, out to the foyer.

When they became free of Society's impolite stares, Katherine dug her heels in. Her brows stitched into a single line. "Jasper, what are you about?"

Jasper took a deep breath. "Come with me, Katherine." He really was creating quite a scene and she really did require her cloak . . . but he needed to be free of this crowded hell. His throat closed up, choking off breath, and he feared he'd suffocate from the attention fixed on him.

Her lips dipped in a frown. She folded her arms across her chest.

He closed his eyes a moment, and then opened them to find her standing there, an insolent brow arched. Jasper tried again. "Katherine, will you please come with me?" *Come away with me.*

She hesitated a moment. And for that seemingly infinitesimal moment, he suspected she intended to deny his request. His breath came faster. Then, she nodded slowly, and marched toward Lord and Lady Harrison's front doors.

This time, Jasper hurried to catch his wife. She started for his black lacquer carriage, and accepted the hand of a nearby servant, who reached out to hand her up.

Jasper glared at the young man who dared touch her hand.

The servant paled to the color of his white, powdered wig, and then scurried off.

Jasper leapt into the carriage. His eyes struggled to adjust to the dimness of the space. When they did, they alighted upon Katherine seated in the far corner of his carriage. An unreadable expression on the face that had haunted his dreams.

The carriage rocked forward. And still they sat there in silence.

He'd thought of no one but her since she'd walked out of his life. After Guilford's visit to Castle Blackwood, Jasper had ordered his horse saddled, and he'd ridden like the devil himself had been at his heels. He'd raced his poor mount, working him into a fine lather.

In his mad race to London, he'd considered what words he would say to Katherine. He would profess his love, and beg her to return with him. He imagined he'd have pretty compliments and recite sweet verse to convince her that she desired a life with him.

Instead, he'd arrived at his townhouse to find her gone. And the horror of imagining her with Stanhope had become all the more real for Jasper's sudden arrival in London.

A vitriolic, violent jealousy had filled him until he'd wanted to stalk through the London streets like an untamed beast and pull open doors until he found Stanhope and destroyed the fiend.

Jasper gnashed his teeth. "Have you taken a lover, Katherine?" He winced. The steely, angry accusation would hardly convince Katherine to set aside her feelings for Stanhope and return to Castle Blackwood.

Katherine's brows dipped. She leaned across the carriage, and the honeysuckle scent, so boldly hers, wafted about them, and filled his senses. "I. Beg. Your. Pardon?" Cool rage underlined those clipped words.

Jasper fished into the front of his jacket and withdrew a sheet he'd neatly torn from *The Times*. He handed it over to her.

Katherine hesitated a long while, and then accepted the paper. She skimmed it. Her gaze narrowed. And then she wrinkled the item into a ball and threw it at his chest. She touched her hands to her chest. "Do you believe this of me?"

Jasper glanced down momentarily at the rumpled words that had turned him into the kind of Mad Duke who stormed, uninvited, into a ball and dragged his wife from the ballroom, amidst a sea of curious stares. "I . . . oomph," he grunted as she stuck a finger in his chest.

"I am not your mother, Jasper," she said, her words, flat and emotionless.

"Stanhope?" Jasper forced the bastard's name past his suddenly dry mouth.

Katherine must have seen something in his eyes, for her mouth softened, and she shook her head back and forth slowly, sadly. "Oh, Jasper," she said. "Harry is a friend. Nothing more."

Harry.

She referred to Stanhope by his Christian name.

"Gentlemen do not become friends with young ladies, Katherine," he bit out.

"This one did," she replied. "When I desperately needed one, Jasper." She folded her arms to her chest, as though warming herself. "Is that why you've come? To determine if I've been unfaithful to you, Jasper? I have not." Her gaze slid to the window, and she tugged back the velvet curtains to peer into the passing streets. "If that is why you've come, then be assured I've not taken a lover. Nor do I intend to. So you can return me to the townhouse and return to Castle Blackwood."

His stomach flipped into itself. "Is that what you want, Katherine? For me to leave?"

If she said yes, it would shatter him.

Katherine dropped the curtain and it fluttered back into place. She turned a sad smile back at him. "Do you know what is so very odd, Jasper?" She didn't wait for him to answer, but continued. "Since the Frost Fair, since we first met, I came to know you, better than even myself, I sometimes believe. I know the manner in which you grit your teeth and square your jaw when you're irate. I know you despise any showing of emotion." She shook her head, unhappily. "Yet, you should know me so little. You read words in the gossip column and believe me no better than your parents."

"No," the denial burst from him. Katherine couldn't be further from the mark. He well knew she was nothing like his viperous mother and dastardly father.

Katherine held her palms up, almost beseechingly, and it threatened to rend him in two, this his proud Katherine humbled herself before him. "Then, why did you come, Jasper?"

"Because I'm a bloody fool."

Chapter 32

*H*er heart cracked at Jasper's words. Her husband considered himself a bloody fool for coming to her.

The carriage rocked to a slow stop, and she started, realizing the carriage had arrived at her . . . his . . . *their* townhouse.

A servant rapped on the door, and she reached for the handle.

Jasper's large, gloveless hand settled over hers.

A thrill coursed through her in remembrance of his touch, and she closed her eyes as a wave of longing filled her.

"Katherine," he said hoarsely. He yanked his fingers back and her skin cooled from the loss of his skin upon hers. Jasper raked his hand through his hair. "I'm blundering this quite badly. Which can of course be explained by the fact that I'm a great, big bastard. I let you go," he said arresting her gaze with his. "I let you go because I did not allow myself to accept the truth."

Katherine angled her head. Her heart slowed and then picked up a too-quick rhythm in her chest. "What is that, Jasper?" she whispered.

The servant knocked. "Not now." Jasper's booming command bounced off the walls of the carriage. He returned his attention to Katherine. "You terrified me, Katherine. From the moment your hand touched mine as I pulled you from the Thames, our lives became inextricably intertwined in ways I fought." Jasper sucked in a deep breath, as though he'd run a great distance. "I could not allow myself to believe I cared for you, because I could not bear the thought of losing you."

As he'd lost Lydia.

And then Katherine had gone and left Jasper, too. Oh, God, how had she left him? Even as it had been an attempt to protect herself, she'd wrought this great hurt upon him.

"Jasper," she said brokenly. "I should have never left you." She should have stayed and fought for him, even if it had been a ghost she'd been left to battle for Jasper's heart.

He must have seen something in her eyes for he reached across the carriage and cupped her cheek in his hand, angling her face toward his. "You thought me incapable of loving you because of Lydia, but . . ." He closed his eyes a moment. When he opened them, her heart twisted at the raw emotion there. "But the truth is, Katherine, you had my heart since the moment your water-drenched ringlets broke the surface of the Thames." He leaned across the seat and rested his brow against hers. "I saved you that day, Katherine. But the truth," he shook his head gently back and forth, "the truth is you saved me." His words washed over her, and emotion clogged her throat. "You made me to feel and dream and love again."

Tears filled her eyes, until his dear face blurred before her. She blinked back the blasted droplets.

Then his words registered.

Love.

Another knock sounded on the carriage door.

"For the love of God, I said not now, man," Jasper barked. He looked back at Katherine. "With my unwillingness to let you into my life and love you as you deserve to be loved, I drove you away. I'm asking you to forget Stanhope. Forget the gowns of vibrant shades. Forget this. Forget all of this, and come back to me. Please. I love you, Katherine."

The faint muscle at the corner of his eye twitched, the one indication of how very much that speech had cost Jasper.

Love for him coursed through her, potent and powerful.

"Katherine . . ."

She leaned across the carriage seat and kissed him. Her lips found his in an achingly sweet meeting of two lovers who'd at last found each other. Katherine pulled away. She placed a kiss at the corner of his eye, where that muscle throbbed.

"Without you, none of this means anything, Jasper. Not the gowns. The mindless amusements."

"And Stanhope?" he asked, his voice gruff.

She shook her head. "Has always been, and will only ever be, a friend, Jasper." She touched two fingers to his mouth. "You are all I want. All I need. I will give up everything I have, all I am for you. I love you."

His throat bobbed up and down. "And you'll never again leave me."

Katherine knew he spoke of more than the mere parting of the now. She ran her finger over his lip. "And I will never again leave you," she pledged.

"Oh, Katherine," he whispered and gently pulled her onto his lap, folding his arms about her.

And there, in the confines of the carriage, as Jasper took her in his arms, Katherine realized how very wrong her sister Aldora and her friends had been.

Katherine didn't need the heart of a duke.

She only needed the heart of *this* duke.

Epilogue

Hertfordshire
Nine months later

*A*n endless scream ripped through the walls of the modest farmhouse.

Jasper sat perched at the edge of his seat, head buried in his hands. They should have remained in London. Instead, Katherine had insisted she see out the remainder of her confinement in Hertfordshire.

Jasper cursed, wishing he'd never purchased the country cottage her father had gambled away, because then they'd be in London where there were surely better midwives than . . .

"Ahh, God!"

He pressed the backs of his hands against his eye and fought the overwhelming urge to cast up the nonexistent accounts of his stomach.

A hand settled on his arm. "She'll do fine, Bainbridge."

Jasper's bleary gaze shot up angrily at his brother-in-law, Lord Michael Knightly, and he prepared to tell the other man just what he thought of his empty words.

Knightly opened his mouth to speak when Katherine's guttural moan reached through the door.

Jasper leapt to his feet and began to pace across the thin runner that ran along the hardwood floor.

For seven long hours, Katherine had labored to bring their child into this world. All the darkest nightmares that had haunted him, tortured him, tormented him played out with her every moan, her every cry, her every groan, until he feared he'd go mad.

He should have never touched her. His seed was poison.

If she died, he could not carry on. It would destroy him.

Knightly reached over and placed a staying hand on his arm. "She is a strong woman. I promise you, she will be all right."

Knightly spoke as a man whose wife had delivered first Lizzie, and more recently their second babe, a full-cheeked boy with thick black curls. He didn't know the agony of holding one's wife as she . . .

"For Christ's sake," Jasper hissed and strode to the chamber doors.

Another cry split the quiet of the cottage, just as he pressed the handle of the door.

The thick, graying doctor stood alongside Katherine's mother and Aldora. The trio stared slack-jawed with shock at his appearance.

It was the doctor who spoke. "Your Grace, you should not . . ."

Jasper glared the older man into silence. He would have to drag his dead, lifeless fingers from this room before he again left Katherine's bedside. "Get out," he ordered everyone present. They exchanged a look.

"It is fine," a far too-weak voice called from the bed.

His gaze sought Katherine's, and his heart plummeted to his stomach. He dimly registered the bloody sawbones and the countess taking their leave. Then the door closed.

Katherine's hair hung in damp, strands about her waist and shoulders while her cheeks remained flushed red from her exertions.

"What are you doing here?" she said with far more stoic calm than he'd have imagined possible considering the pain he'd heard in her earlier screams.

Then her face contorted, and she sucked in a long, slow breath, letting it out slowly.

Jasper strode over to her bedside. He pointed a finger at her. "I forbid you to die, Katherine. Do you hear me? I absolutely forbid it. You promised to never leave me."

She bit her lower lip as another shudder of agony wracked her frame. With a slow, steady breath, she regained her composure. "I'm not going to leave you, Jasper. I'm too stubborn to die."

He thought of her flailing, fighting figure as he'd pulled her out of the Thames River over a year ago. No, there was no stronger woman than his Katherine.

Jasper sank down to his knees beside her bed and captured her hand. "Promise me, Katherine. I . . . I need you to promise me."

She touched her free hand to his head. "I will not die," she said with such conviction, he dared to believe her. Katherine closed her eyes, and her fingers tightened hard about his hand.

Jasper winced from the strength of her grip.

"Jasper?"

"Yes, Katherine?"

"Will you please send for my mother and Aldora? I believe the babe is coming."

His gut clenched, and he surged to his feet so quickly he nearly toppled backward. He steadied himself, and raced to the door, knocking into a rose-inlaid side table.

Jasper wrenched the door open.

The doctor rushed inside, having clearly, and accurately, anticipated he would be needed.

"It should not be much longer, Your Grace," the doctor assured him, even as Katherine's mother and Aldora secured their spots alongside the bed. "If you'll wait—"

"No," Jasper bit out. "I'm not going anywhere."

And he didn't. He remained for the next thirty minutes as Katherine labored to bring their child into the world. He remained when her voice turned hoarse from the strength of her cries.

And he remained when his son came squalling and angry into the world, as fat as a cherub with a shock of brown curls atop his head.

And later, when no one remained but Katherine, Jasper, and their babe, Jasper lay curled up at his wife's side and studied the glassy-eyed boy with big cheeks, who clutched at his finger.

Katherine leaned into Jasper, and angled her head up, looking at him through tired but contented eyes.

"Are you happy?" she whispered.

Jasper smiled. For the first time, in forever . . . "I am."

The End

Turn the page for an excerpt of *More Than a Duke*!

Chapter 1

London, England
1815

*I*n a Society that placed such value upon honor, respectability, and virtue, Lady Anne Arlette Adamson came to a very interesting revelation. A young lady would discard her self-worth and sense of decency . . . all for a glass of champagne.

Or more precisely, *two* glasses of champagne.

The full moon shone through the Marquess of Essex's conservatory windows and splashed light on the two sparkling crystal flutes. Drawn to them, Anne wet her lips and did a quick survey of her host's famed gardens, searching for any interlopers. Lured by the forbidden liquor, she wandered over to the table strewn with vibrant pink peonies and blush roses and picked up a flute. She angled her head. Eying the pale, bubbling liquid contained within, a sudden desire filled her, to taste the fine French brew.

Of course, young, unwed ladies did not drink champagne. At least that was what Mother was forever saying. A mischievous smile tugged at the corners of her lips. Then, she'd never been lauded as the obedient, mild-mannered daughter. Anne raised the glass to her mouth . . . and froze.

An *honorable* young lady however didn't drink champagne belonging to two other people.

She sighed and set the glass down.

With a frown, she began to pace the stone floor. Where was he?

She'd heard rumors of his notorious assignations, knew he planned to meet . . . she wrinkled her nose, *some* widow or another, in the marquess's conservatory.

Perhaps the rumors were just that, mere rumors. Perhaps . . .

The click of the door opening sounded off the glass walls of her floral haven. Anne jumped. Her heart pounded hard and she raised a hand to her chest to still the sudden increased rhythm.

For the first time since she'd orchestrated this madcap scheme involving Harry Falston, the 6th Earl of Stanhope, she questioned the wisdom of such a plan. Enlisting the aid of one of Society's most scandalous rogues would hardly be considered one of her better ideas. The ladies adored him, the gentlemen wanted to be him, the leading hostesses frowned at him from one side of their fans and tittered behind the other.

He also happened to be the gentleman who'd tried—and failed—to seduce Anne's twin sister, Katherine.

For all Anne's twenty years, she'd forever been considered the more spirited, imprudent twin sister. Of course, being the more sensible of the twins, Katherine had not fallen prey to his devilish charms. However, in a wholly *insensible* thing to do, her sister had befriended him, a rogue of the worst sort who didn't even have the decency to respect Katherine's marriage . . . or *any* marriage, for that matter.

The door closed. With breath suspended, she slipped behind one of her host's towering hibiscus trees.

Good, respectable young ladies, marriageable young ladies at that, should have a care to avoid Society's most notorious rogue.

Her nose twitched and she widened her eyes in attempt to hold in a sneeze. Then, she'd not paid too close attention to the *ton*'s rigid expectations for a young lady.

The tread of a gentleman's footsteps echoed off the glass windows. "Hullo, sweet."

Oh, by Joan of Arc and all her army. *Hullo, sweet?* That was the kind of claptrap this rogue was known for? His husky baritone however, well, that was better suited for the Gothic novels she'd taken pleasure in reading before her mother had gone and stolen her spectacles. But "Hullo, sweet"? She shook her head. It would take a good deal more than an unclever endearment to earn her favor.

The bootsteps paused. She peeked out from behind the tree.

Her breath caught. The moon bathed the lean, towering gentleman in soft light. The earl's gold locks, loose and unaffected, gave him the carefree look of one who flouted Society's rules. But then, isn't that what the Earl of Stanhope had earned a reputation for? Which made him perfect. Perfect for what she intended, anyway.

The sweet fragrance of the hibiscus tickled her nose yet again. She scrubbed a hand over her face hard and drove back a sneeze.

The earl cocked his head, as if he knew she stood there secretly studying him, quietly admiring him. It really was impossible not to. His black-tailed evening coat clung to sculpted arms. Anne continued to scrutinize him with objective eyes. Gentlemen really shouldn't have sculpted, well-muscled arms. Not like this. Why, they were better suited to a pugilist than a nobleman.

A grin tugged the corner of his lips up in a hopelessly seductive smile. She fanned herself. Well goodness . . . mayhap it wasn't the champagne flutes after all but the pirate's grin that made foolish young ladies toss their good names away.

She stopped midfan. Not that she would be swayed by such a smile. No, the gentleman she would wed was serious and respectable and obscenely wealthy and unfailingly polite and just enough handsome. Not too handsome. Not unhandsome. Just handsome enough.

The earl shrugged out of his coat. He flipped it over his shoulder in one smooth, graceful motion. The effortless gesture jerked her from her musings.

Anne swallowed hard. Yes, he was entirely more handsome than any one man had a right to be. She supposed she really should announce herself. Especially considering his . . . er . . . arrangements for the evening.

"You do know, sweet, if you're content to stand and watch me remove my garments, I'd be glad to provide you such a show. I would, however, vastly prefer you allow me to slip the gown from your frame and . . ."

She pressed herself tight against the tree. Her arm knocked the branch of the hibiscus and wafted the cloying, floral scent about the air. "Achoo!" Blast and bloody blast.

The earl's grin widened as he yanked a stark white kerchief from his jacket and wandered closer. He extended the cloth. "Here, sweet—"

Anne stepped out from behind the tree. The earl froze, the stark white linen dangled between them. His hazel eyes widened. She plucked the kerchief from his fingers and blew her nose noisily. "Thank you," she said around the fabric.

"Bloody hell, Lady Anne," he hissed. "What in hell are you doing here?" He shrugged into his jacket with the speed surely borne of a man who'd clearly had to make too many hasty flights from disapproving husbands.

She frowned. "You really needn't sound so . . . so . . ." Disappointed. "Angry, my lord."

He took her gently by the forearm. "What are you thinking?"

She tugged her arm free. "I require a favor—"

"No." He proceeded to pull her toward the front of the conservatory.

She frowned up at him. "You didn't allow me to ask—"

"No." He shook his head. "Mad," he muttered to himself. "You're completely and utterly mad. And maddening."

"I am not mad," she bit out. She really wished she was as clever as her eldest sister, Aldora. Aldora would have a far more clever rebuttal than "I am not mad" for the scoundrel.

His mouth tightened. And she swore he muttered something along the lines of her being the less intelligent of her sisters.

Anne dug her heels in until he either had to drag her or stop. She glowered up at him, this rogue who'd tried to earn a spot in Katherine's bed. Alas, Katherine loved her husband, the Duke of Bainbridge, with such desperation the earl hadn't had a hope or prayer.

He folded his arms across his chest. "What do you want then, hellion?"

She gritted her teeth, detesting his familiarity that painted her as the bothersome sister. Still, she required something of him and as Mother used to say, one can catch more bees with honey than . . . she wrinkled her nose. That didn't quite make sense. Why would anyone want to catch a bee? Unless—

The earl took her, this time by the wrist, and began tugging her to the door.

"I need help," she said and pulled back.

To no avail. He held firm. The man was as powerful as an ox. "No."

Most gentlemen would have inquired if for no other reason than it was the polite, gentlemanly thing to do.

Anne at last managed to wrest free of his grip. "Please, hear me out, my lord."

He took a step toward her. "By God, I'll carry you from the room this time." The determined glint in his eyes lent credence to his threat.

She danced backward. "Oh, I imagine that would be a good deal worse." He narrowed his eyes. "Your carrying me," she clarified. "Imagine the scandal if—"

Lord Stanhope cursed and advanced. "You risk ruin in being here, my lady," he said, his voice a satiny whisper that sent warmth spiraling through her body.

She shook her head. People might believe her an empty-headed ninnyhammer, but she was not so foolish to be swayed by a crooked grin and a mellifluous whisper. She took another step away from him. Her back thumped against their host's table. It rattled and one of the champagne flutes tipped over. She gasped as the pale liquid spilled across the wood table and threatened her skirts.

Lord Stanhope yanked her away from the dripping champagne and tugged her close. "Tsk, tsk, my lady." He lowered his lips to her ear. "However would you explain returning to the ballroom with your skirts drenched in champagne?"

Anne glanced up. And wished she hadn't. *Really* wished she hadn't.

The earl's impossibly long, thick golden lashes were enough to tempt a saint, and after more than twenty years of troublesome scrapes, Anne had earned a reputation amidst her family as anything but a saint.

A lock toppled free from the collection of ringlets artfully arranged by her maid. She brushed the strand back. It fell promptly back over her brow.

The earl collected that single curl between his fingers and studied the strand bemusedly. "A ringlet," he murmured. His lips twitched as though he found something of the utmost hilarity in her gold ringlet, immediately snapping her from whatever momentary spell he'd cast.

She swatted at his fingers. "What is wrong with my ringlets?" She knew there was a more pressing matter to attend. But really, what was wrong with her ringlets?

He tweaked her nose. "There is *everything* wrong with them."

Well! Anne gave a flounce of those ringlets he seemed so condescending of. "I've not come to speak to you about my hair."

The earl narrowed his gaze as he seemed to remember that one, they were shut away in their host's conservatory one step from ruin and two, she was the sister of the twin he'd once tried to seduce. And more specifically, the sister of the twin who'd looked down a pointed nose at him whenever he was near.

With trembling fingers, she righted the upended flute. "I require but a moment of your time."

"You've already had at least five moments."

Distractedly, she picked up the crystal flute still filled to the brim and eyed the nearly clear contents of the glass. It really did look quite delicious. "Do you mean five minutes?" Because there really wasn't such a thing as five moments. Or was there? She raised the glass to her lips.

With a growl, he snatched it from her fingers with such ferocity the exquisite liquor splashed her lips.

"What are you doing, Lady Adamson?" he asked, his voice garbled.

She sighed. She really should have tried the bubbly drink before he'd arrived and gone all serious, disapproving-lord on her. "If you must know, I'd intended to sample—"

"You are not *sampling* anything, my lady." He set the flute down so hard liquid droplets sprayed the table.

Yes, it seemed the roguish earl had gone all stodgy. She released a pent-up sigh of regret. What a waste of perfectly forbidden champagne.

Footsteps sounded outside the door and her head snapped up as suddenly, the ramifications of being discovered here with the earl slammed into her. She felt the color drain from her cheeks and frantically searched around.

The earl cursed and taking her by the hand, tugged her to the back of the conservatory. His hasty, yet sure movements bore evidence of a man who'd made many a number of quick escapes. He opened the door and shoved her outside into the marquess's walled garden.

"You really needn't—"

"Hush," he whispered and propelled her further into the gardens. From behind the marquess's prize-winning gardens, the moon's glow shone through the clear crystal panes and briefly cast the earl's partner in a soft light. The tall, voluptuous lady walked about the conservatory.

"The Viscountess of Kendricks?" Shock underscored her question. "But she is recently widowed." Granted she'd come out of mourning, but that was neither here nor there. Oh, he had no shame.

Lord Stanhope clamped his hand over her mouth. He glowered her into silence and pulled her back, before the viscountess caught sight of them.

Oh, the highhandedness! She'd never been handled thusly in her entire life. She glared up at him.

At long last he drew his fingers back. She continued to study the lush creature, a recent widow with a hopelessly curvaceous figure.

Anne frowned. Mother said gentlemen didn't desire ladies with well-rounded figures but Anne quite disagreed. All the well-rounded ladies seemed to, for some unknown reason, earn the favor of all manner of gentlemen. The respectable ones. The less respectable ones. Even the old ones with monocles.

A sly smile played about the viscountess's lips as she paused beside the table. Even with the space between them, Anne detected the viscountess's lazy yet graceful movements as she picked up the still full glass and took a slow taste of the bubbling champagne.

Envy tugged at Anne. He really should have allowed her just a small sip. Surely there was no harm in a mere taste of the French liquor. And now this blousy creature with her . . . She wrinkled her brow. "Has she dampened her gown?"

The widow froze midsip and glanced around.

Lord Stanhope cursed softly, clapped his hand across Anne's mouth yet again, and whispered harshly against her ear. "Hush, you silly brat, or you'll see the both of us ruined."

Anne pointed her gaze to the moon above. As if a rogue, especially this particular rogue, could be ruined. She, on the other hand . . . She swallowed hard. She danced with disaster. With good reason, of course. But still, disaster nonetheless.

"Hullo, my lord," the woman called into the quiet. A smile played on her too-full lips. "Are you teasing me, Lord Stanhope? I'm eager to see you. Will you not come and see how eager I am?"

Anne glanced up the more than a foot distance between her and the earl to gauge the gentleman's, er . . . eagerness. He appeared wholly unmoved by the woman's none-too-subtle attempt at seduction. His narrow-eyed gaze remained fixed on Anne. Annoyance glinted within the hazel-green irises of his eyes.

"Lord Stanhope?" the woman called again.

Oh, really. She tapped a foot and wished the bothersome baggage would be on her way already. As charming as the Earl of Stanhope seemed to most ladies, she was quite confident that no gentleman could manage to lure her away from polite Society—for any reason.

Lord Stanhope reached down between them and through the ivory fabric of her satin skirts, wrapped his hard hand about the upper portion of her leg, effectively stilling her moments.

Anne's breath froze and she looked at him.

Be still, he mouthed.

Her throat convulsed. Odd, they were just fingers on just a hand, so very uninteresting, something possessed by everyone. And yet, her skin thrummed with awareness of his touch. She swallowed again. There was nothing *uninteresting* about his fingers upon her person.

"Stop tapping your foot," he whispered against her temple. His words had the same effect as a bucket of water being tossed over her foolish head.

"She's not going to hear my foot," she shot back. "It is more likely she'll hear your constant haranguing."

He closed his eyes and his lips moved as if he were utter-
ing a silent prayer. Which was peculiar, because she'd not
ever taken him as the religious sort.

"Lord Stanhope?" the woman called again, impatience
coating her words.

Anne sighed. She'd had this all planned out. She'd speak to
the earl. Enlist his help and be gone before his trysting partner had arrived. That had been the plan. Then again, a lifetime of scrapes that had gone awry should have prepared her
for how this evening would likely turn out. "Oh, for goodness sake, will she not go already?" she muttered. "Whyever
is she so insistent on seeing y—"

The earl cursed under his breath. "For the love of all that
is holy." And then, he kissed her. Hard.

Anne stiffened and leaned back a moment, eyes opened,
studying his impossibly long golden lashes. She trembled
under the heated intensity of his kiss, a kiss that drove back
all logic. He slanted his lips over hers again and again and
she moaned, but he only swallowed the desperate sound. He
slipped his tongue between her lips and boldly explored the
contours of her mouth.

The tension she carried inside slid down her body and
seeped from the soles of her passion-weakened feet as she
went limp. He caught her to him and cupped her buttocks in
his hands, anchoring her body to his.

Then he stopped.

She blinked up, dazed, waiting for the world to right itself.
Goodness . . .

She tugged her hand free and fanned herself.
Goodness . . .

So *this* is what young ladies threw away their reputations
for. It would appear it had nothing at all to do with the wicked

smiles. Or even the forbidden champagne. She'd venture the champagne was merely a little extra sin for a lady's troubles.

Anne stole a glance up at Lord Stanhope and her eyebrows knitted into a single line. The bounder had his gaze trained on the conservatory windows, looking . . . looking . . . wholly unaffected. Impossibly composed. And horribly disinterested. He released her so quickly, she stumbled backward, catching herself before she made a cake of herself and fell at his feet.

She frowned as he turned abruptly and walked away. "That really wasn't well done of you, my lord."

He swung back around and took a step toward her. "Do you know what was not well done, my lady?"

"Uh, well . . ." She retreated and then remembered herself, angling her chin up. After all, there could very well be any other number of offenses she might hold him responsible for. She ticked off on her fingers. "There was the hand over my mouth." She shook her head. "Not at all well done of you. Then there was the kiss." Her cheeks burned with embarrassment. "Certainly not well done of you." Definitely pleasurable, however. "Or you setting me aside so—"

By the saints, he mouthed, appearing more and more religious. "I referred to *your* actions, my lady. It wasn't well done of you to drive away my company for the evening, Lady Adamson."

Humph. "Oh." She wrinkled her nose. That wasn't at all gallant.

His golden lashes swooped downward as he peered at her through a narrow-eyed gaze. "Now, say whatever it is you've come to say so I might be rid of you." He folded his arms across his chest.

Why, with his clear desire to be free of her, she may as well have been the gorgon Medusa with her head of serpents. She bristled, all foolish desire replaced by annoyance. How dare he? How dare he kiss her and remain wholly unaffected by that soul-searing moment? She shook her head once. No, that was not quite right.

"Lady Anne," he said again, this time with even more annoyance.

How dare he kiss her, *period*. No further outrage needed. How dare he kiss her? Rather, that is what she'd meant. "I need help."

He scoffed. "Yes. So you've said. Four times now."

"Oh." Had she? She really didn't remember . . .

He gave her a pointed look and she jumped. "As I was saying, before I was interrupted." She gave him a pointed frown. "I require a bit of help."

"Five times," he muttered under his breath. He really was quite infuriating.

"I am—"

He drummed his fingertips upon his coat sleeves. "If you say you're in need of help, I'm leaving without a backward glance, Lady Anne," he said drolly. He rocked on his heels and she suspected his words were no mere idle threat.

Anne smoothed her palms over her skirt and drew in a steadying breath. With the time and care she'd put into her plan, she had imagined this conversation would go a good deal more smoothly than this botched attempt on her part.

The earl cursed and spun on his heel.

"Wait!"

He continued walking toward the glass door back into the marquess's conservatory.

Her foot snagged a particularly nasty root in the ground and she cursed. She pitched forward. Lord Stanhope swung back around and closed the distance between them in three long strides, catching her before she hit the ground. The breath left her on a swift exhale. "Oh." The touch of his hand burned through the modest fabric of her satin gown. "Thank you," she said breathlessly.

He grunted and set her on her feet. Humph. Who knew the Earl of Stanhope did something as barbaric as grunt? He resumed his hasty exit, wholly unaffected. *Well!*

"Stop," she cried softly into the quiet. Her voice echoed off the brick walls.

His broad shoulders tightened under the folds of his black evening coat. He changed direction yet again and advanced on her. Fire snapped in his eyes.

Anne stumbled backward. A friend of Katherine, Anne knew little of the Earl of Stanhope beyond the roguish reputation he'd earned amongst the *ton*. She couldn't be altogether certain he'd not hurt her. She swallowed hard and continued to retreat. And her slipper caught that blasted root again.

This time she landed with a solid thump on her buttocks. "Ouch." She touched a hand to her bruised derriere and then remembered herself.

He froze above her with a glower on the chiseled planes of his face. "Are you trying to compromise your reputation, my lady?"

"No." *Not per se.*

He stretched out a hand. "Because I'll not be caught in a compromising position and forced into a wedded state with one such as you."

She ignored his offering and shoved herself to her feet. "With one such as me?"

"An impertinent, empty-headed young lady without a serious thought in—"

She jabbed a finger into his chest. He winced and she delighted in that slight twinge of discomfort from him. *The cad.* "I've had quite enough of your insults. I don't like you any more than you like me, my lord." She'd long tired of Society, her family, everyone's rather low opinion of her. But she required his assistance and when one required help, it behooved them to set aside their pride.

"You have two minutes, my lady," he bit out.

Her mind raced. How did a lady ask such a question as the one she'd put to him. There was no polite way to make a request as the one she intended to make—

"Your first minute is up, my lady," he said, his voice heavy with annoyance.

Anne took a steadying breath and opted for direct honesty. "I'd like you to teach me how to seduce a man."

Other Books by Christi Caldwell

Historical Romances

Lords of Honor Series
Seduced by a Lady's Heart
Captivated by a Lady's Charm
Rescued by a Lady's Love
Tempted by a Lady's Smile

Scandalous Seasons Series
Forever Betrothed, Never the Bride
Never Courted, Suddenly Wed
Always Proper, Suddenly Scandalous
Always a Rogue, Forever Her Love
A Marquess for Christmas
Once a Wallflower, at Last His Love

Sinful Brides Series
The Rogue's Wager
The Scoundrel's Honor

Standalones
'Twas the Night Before Scandal
The Theodosia Sword

Contemporary Romances

Danby Novellas
A Season of Hope
Winning a Lady's Heart

Author's Note

*I*n the years between 1309 and 1814, the Thames River froze twenty-three times, in a period noted as a Little Ice Age. The Frost Fairs, a kind of Christmas market and circus, took place during this Little Ice Age. One could purchase food and drink, such as tea and coffee, but alcohol tended to be the main beverage purchased at the Frost Fairs. In addition, bowling, bull-baiting, sledging, and various other activities took place upon the ice.

The Frost Fair also served as an economic benefit to English merchants and vendors who relied upon the Thames River to transport goods and supplies. Unable to ship goods due to the severe ice, the English merchants were able to rent space and sell goods upon the Thames.

In February 1814, *The Times* reported that no lives were lost on the parts of weak ice on the Thames River at this particular Frost Fair, but that several individuals were immersed when the ice gave way.

Lady Katherine Adamson, though fictional, was intended to be one of those retrieved with some difficulty from the frozen waters.

Acknowledgments

To Ms. Julia Quinn

Thank you for an advance copy all those years ago that got me through at least one long day of bedrest. And thank you for the support you've shown to me as a writer.

About the Author

USA TODAY bestselling author Christi Caldwell blames Judith McNaught for luring her into the world of historical romance. While sitting in her graduate school apartment at the University of Connecticut, Christi decided to set aside her notes and pick up her laptop to try her hand at romance. She believes the most perfect heroes and heroines have imperfections, and she rather enjoys torturing them before crafting them a well-deserved happily ever after!

Christi makes her home in southern Connecticut, where she spends her time writing her own enchanting historical romances, chasing around her spirited son, and caring for her twin princesses in training!

Connect With Christi!

Christi's Website christicaldwell.com

Christi's Facebook Page https://www.facebook
.com/Christi-Caldwell-215250258658392/

Christi's Twitter Page
https://twitter.com/christicaldwell
@ChristiCaldwell

Christi's Amazon Profile https://www.amazon.com/
Christi-Caldwell/e/B0061UVSPO/
ref=sr_tc_2_0?qid=1483995621&sr=1-2-ent

Christi's Goodreads Profile
https://www.goodreads.com/author/show/
5297089.Christi_Caldwell

Subscribe to Christi's Newsletter
http://christicaldwellauthor
.authornewsletters.com/?p=subscribe&id=1

Contact Christi http://christicaldwell.com/contact